Addy Starr

Addy Starr

Ruth Ryan Langan

5 Addy Starr

This title first published in Great Britain in 1992 by
Severn House Publishers Ltd.
This edition licensed by Severn House Publishers Ltd,
produced by Magpie Books Ltd, and published by Parragon
Book Service Ltd in 1995.

A copy of the British Library CIP data is available from the British Library.

ISBN: 0 75251 264 1

Printed and Bound in Great Britain

To Tom
The Key.

To Tommy, Carol, Mary Margaret, Pat, Mike
The treasure.

To Aubrey, Haley, Tommy, Caitlin Bea and Bret
Charles
The future.

Chapter One

"All the king's horses and all the king's men couldn't put Humpty . . ."

The words of her sister's nursery rhyme played through Addy O'Brien's mind as the bus passed through mile after mile of rockstrewn Nevada desert.

Nothing would ever be put back together. Not her life. Not her family. Certainly not her lost childhood.

Every so often she'd spot a ramshackle ranch in the distance. The house looked dusty and isolated. Even the livestock in the fields looked tired. Cows dozed in the unrelenting sun. Horses stuck their heads through split-rail fences, tugging at tufts of brown grass.

Beside her a drunken passenger snored and shifted until his head bobbed on her shoulder. She pushed him away and he sat up, blinking furiously, until, minutes later, he was snoring again.

Addy tried not to think about where she was heading. Instead, she closed her eyes and thought about her goodbye. It had been oddly unemotional, considering the fact that it was a final break with all that she had ever known.

"I cannot recommend this job," Rose Carpenter had said in that matter-of-fact tone. "The work will be much harder than anything you've ever done before. And you will have no one there to turn to if it doesn't work out."

"It's a job." Addy had refused to meet her eyes. "I'll be caring for someone who needs me."

"You'll have no one. No one in Reno will know you."

That was just fine with Addy. She didn't want anyone to know Adelia O'Brien. Not her past. Not her pain.

1

She smiled, thinking about Savannah's words of advice. "If I don't like something about my life, I invent something better. Hell, even my name isn't the one my parents gave me. I'd rather be Savannah any day than Shirley."

Just thinking about Savannah made Addy grin. She wondered what the outrageous child-woman was doing now. Ida said she was probably hooking in Vegas. Addy was half inclined to agree with her. But she hoped, with all her might, that Savannah had found someone who would be willing to look beyond the gaudy makeup to the tender heart Savannah kept hidden deep inside.

Addy intended to take Savannah's advice. The old Addy had died. Like Humpty Dumpty, she'd been shattered beyond repair. But she had constructed a new Addy. Today was her twenty-first birthday. On this day she would be reborn. Or reinvented. Her smile grew.

"Reno," the driver shouted as he brought the bus to a hiccupping stop.

Minutes later, belching exhaust fumes and dust, the bus pulled away from the curb. When the dust settled, Addy picked up the battered suitcase she'd bought at a garage sale and stared around at the dizzying maze of buildings. Though the sun was barely setting on the horizon, the lights had already been turned on, creating a blaze of neon. The street was lined with bars, restaurants and casinos, all shouting their wares to the passing tourists.

There was nothing quiet or elegant or dignified about this part of town. She wondered if all of Reno would be like this. Loud, coarse, vulgar. This was the biggest town she'd ever been in. It was also the first time she'd ever been on her own. The thought exhilarated her. And terrified her. This might be just the place where a girl with no past could carve a future for herself. If she was willing to work for it.

Shifting the suitcase to her other hand she dug the piece of folded paper from her pocket and studied the crudely drawn map, even though she had already committed to memory every street, every crossroad, every turn.

Squinting against the fading light she read the street signs, got her bearings, and started walking.

She followed the ribbon of sidewalk past the gaudy lights of a bar. Three men in jeans and cowboy hats pushed past her and shoved open the door. The twang of a guitar filled the air for a moment before the door closed, abruptly cutting off the sound.

She trudged up the street, toward the glittering lights of a casino. A sleek car pulled up to the curb and a uniformed employee raced out to take the keys and hold the door. Addy had to pause while a man in a tuxedo assisted a woman from the car. Taking his arm, the woman glided along beside him. The beading on her long gown caught and reflected the lights around them. The front doors were opened by another uniformed employee. The couple disappeared inside the quiet, plush interior.

On the sidewalk, Addy breathed in the lingering scent of the woman's perfume. She had looked so elegant walking beside the man. So dignified.

For long moments Addy continued staring at the gilt and marble facade, wondering what went on inside a gambling establishment. She thought of the scenes from movies, depicting beautiful women and sophisticated, worldly men, placing chips in front of a wheel of fortune.

She figured she'd probably never get to see the inside of any of these places. Shifting the suitcase to her other hand, she continued walking.

Deliberately avoiding the bars and fancy restaurants, she made her way along the street until the glitter and glamour were far behind. Here there was only an occasional light from a dingy bar or greasy restaurant. The people walking the streets weren't dressed in evening clothes. No exotic fragrances trailed in their wake.

Addy paused outside the door of a small diner. The smell of onions on a grill caused her to press a hand to her stomach to quell the hunger that gnawed at her. The job had promised room and board. Still, she might be too late for dinner. And breakfast was a long way off.

Pushing open the door she made her way to a small booth and took a seat. She was relieved to drop her suitcase at her feet and flex her stiff fingers.

A tired-looking woman shuffled over and took a pencil from behind her ear. "What'll it be?"

"Hamburger. Fries."

"Anything to drink?"

As Addy opened her purse to count her meager bills, she gave a gasp. "It's gone. My money's . . ."

She looked up to see the waitress staring at her with suspicion. "We don't feed panhandlers."

"But I'm not . . ." Addy clamped her mouth shut and reached for her suitcase. It had to be the drunk beside her in the bus. He'd leaned against her so many times, while he slept. Pretended to sleep, she corrected herself.

She straightened her shoulders and strode to the door, feeling the dark, unsympathetic stare of the waitress.

Outside the diner Addy swallowed back the tears that threatened. Now, more than ever, she prayed this job would work out. Studying the street signs, she made a left turn at the light.

The houses must have once been considered quite elegant, although now they showed the signs of years of neglect.

She followed the map, reading the numbers on the weathered old houses until she came to the one she'd been seeking.

It stood far back from the street, surrounded by a rotting wood fence that had fallen apart in several places, sagging into the dirt. The house rose to three floors, with a wide porch around the front and sides of each floor. The roof, like the house, had faded to a dull gray. Several shutters hung at odd angles. Except for a few sparse tufts of grass, there was no lawn, just a patch of dry, barren earth.

Addy swallowed back her disappointment. It definitely wasn't the house with the white picket fence that she'd hoped for. But it still wasn't a total loss. Though the house would be described by most as shabby, Addy felt that there

4

was a certain solidness about it that was comforting. It would, after all, be the first real house in which she had ever lived.

Rusty hinges protested loudly when Addy pushed open the gate. As she climbed the steps she was forced to move around a gaping hole in the rotting wood. Setting her suitcase down on the porch she wiped her sweating palms on her skirt and pushed the bell.

After long minutes a porchlight was thrown on and she steeled herself for her first glimpse of her new employer.

The door opened and Addy caught sight of a man seated in a wheelchair. A mane of white hair spilled over a wide, wrinkled forehead. His skin was the texture of aged leather. Bushy white eyebrows framed the darkest, most piercing eyes Addy had ever seen.

"Yeah? What do you want?"

Addy stuck out her hand. "I'm Addy O'Brien."

She swallowed in embarrassment when he didn't return her handshake. He merely stared at her. She dropped her hands awkwardly to her sides.

"You're expecting me."

"I am?"

"I answered your ad."

He glowered at her. "Another one. Is this some kind of a joke? When is that goddamned fool Witherspoon going to give up."

"I'm afraid I . . ."

"Sonofabitch." His gaze dropped to the suitcase at her feet. "I suppose it's too far for you to turn tail and walk back home."

"A couple of hundred miles. I . . ."

"Couple of hundred . . ." He swore, loudly, savagely. "Might as well come in." In frustration he slapped a hand against the wheel of his chair, causing it to turn aside.

Addy peered beyond him into the room. In the far doorway a man paused to study her. He was tall and lean, with an athletic body clearly defined in narrow jeans and a faded shirt. His dark hair was thick and shaggy, brushing

5

the collar of his shirt. A growth of dark beard covered his cheeks and chin. He leaned a hip against the doorway and lifted a glass to his lips.

She glanced at him hopefully. Maybe he could clear up this misunderstanding.

Picking up her suitcase she stepped through the doorway, making certain she left the door ajar behind her. If either of these men tried anything funny, she'd be out the door before they could get halfway across the room.

The man in the wheelchair was already rolling away from her.

"Is Mr. Witherspoon here?" she asked timidly.

"Here? Hell no. Witherspoon never shows his ugly face unless I order him to. He's probably treating himself to a weekend in Vegas, thanks to the generous retainer I pay him. That's all lawyers are good for. Collecting fees and spending other people's money."

"Look. Mr. . . . ." She stopped, realizing the man hadn't even bothered to introduce himself.

"Starr. Jake Starr."

"Look, Mr. Starr . . ."

"Jake." He spun the chair to face her. Again she felt the force of his gaze. "And this is my friend, Sam Money."

Addy nodded and the man did the same.

"Mr. Witherspoon sent a contract and demanded I sign it," Addy said. "Otherwise he wouldn't send me the bus fare."

"Goddamn it, he's getting cagey." Jake's eyes lit for a moment. "You signed a contract? For how long?"

"A year."

"A year!" His explosion of laughter was as unexpected as his anger had been only moments before. "Well, I'll be damned. And you were dumb enough to sign it sight unseen?"

Her tone rang with righteous indignation. "I need this job, Mr. Starr." He'd never know how much.

"Jake." He studied her with new interest.

Dark hair fell in untidy waves to her waist. The long

6

walk had worked up a sweat, and little tendrils stuck to her forehead and cheeks. Her skirt and blouse were neat and clean. And obviously bargain basement. Though she was small and slender, she didn't appear fragile. In fact, there was a certain strength in her. It was there in her eyes, along with something else he couldn't quite define. Pain maybe. Or anger.

She was scared. Her eyes kept darting toward the escape route behind her. He saw the way she kept close to the door, with the distance of the room between them. Ready to run like a rabbit if he made a move. Still, though she clutched her battered suitcase with a death grip that was turning her knuckles white, she stood her ground. He couldn't help but admire the way she faced him, holding her head proudly, keeping her spine stiff.

He'd known a gangly youth who had once faced the world in exactly that same brazen manner. He'd managed to fool everyone. Still did, if the truth was known.

"A year's contract." He pursed his lips. "Did he give you an advance?"

"No, sir. Just bus fare."

"Look." His eyes narrowed. "I don't answer to sir. Or mister. The name's Jake. Just Jake."

"Okay." She swallowed. "Jake."

"Good. Do you know anybody in this town who could put you up for the night?"

"No s . . . No."

"Sonofabitch." He thought a minute, then pointed to the doorway behind him. "I sleep in there. Sam's been using the bedroom upstairs. There's a bedroom on the third floor. I can't say what condition it's in. Haven't been up there in years. But at least it's a place to sleep for the night."

Only for the night. She felt as if the weight of the world had just dropped on her shoulders.

When she continued to face him he said, "Take your goddamned suitcase up. Have a look around. Then come back down and we'll see if you can at least earn your keep for the night."

"I can earn my keep." She picked up her suitcase and climbed the stairs.

Behind her, he merely watched until she was out of sight. Then he turned the wheelchair and stared out the window.

"Goddamned Witherspoon!" He let loose with a string of oaths guaranteed to curl the hair of a hardened drill sergeant. Even that didn't make him feel better. "This time he's scraped the bottom of the goddamned barrel with this useless, skinny female."

When Sam Money, who was standing across the room, cleared his throat loudly, Jake slammed a hand against the wheel, sending his chair whirling. And found himself face to face with a wide-eyed Addy.

Chapter Two

"I – need some sheets for the bed."

The string of curses lodged in Jake's throat. He swallowed them back. One more word and the damned fool kid was going to bolt out the door without even taking time to run back for her luggage.

"Linen closet's down that hall."

Addy spun away, eager to escape. A few minutes later she climbed the stairs, uncomfortably aware of two pairs of blackbird eyes watching her until she was out of sight.

In the bedroom Addy shook out a clean sheet and proceeded to make up the bed. As she worked she fumed. Jake Starr had made his feelings perfectly clear. He didn't want her here. In fact, he'd made it plain he hated her on sight.

She wasn't supposed to have witnessed that last angry tirade of Jake's. But she had. And now she knew exactly how he felt.

She shook out a pillow case and stuffed the old feather pillow inside. Her temper grew. She'd stay the night; she had no choice. But in the morning, she'd be gone, contract or no. It was clear that Jake had known nothing about this arrangement. Obviously a contract meant nothing to him.

Bottom of the barrel. The words still stung. That mean, miserable excuse of a man. Let him tear up the documents. She couldn't wait to get out of here. She didn't need Jake Starr or his rundown house. There'd be plenty of jobs in a town like this. And all of them better than the one she'd taken here.

She couldn't quiet the nagging little fear. She had no

money. What if she didn't find another job right away? Where would she go? There was no one to turn to.

Caregiver. She snapped the blanket, giving vent to her anger, then smoothed it into place and plumped the pillow. She was a fine one to think about giving care. She couldn't even take care of herself. And as for the old grouch downstairs, he probably just wanted a servant. One who'd bear the brunt of all that pent up fury. Well, she had news for Jake Starr. She was nobody's whipping boy. No matter how desperate she was.

"Kid."

Her head shot up at the voice that boomed from the bottom of the stairs. Walking to the landing she looked down at him.

"You done up there?"

She shrugged. "I guess so."

"You know how to cook, kid?"

She strode down the stairs. "My name is Addy."

"Addy then, goddamn it. Can you cook?"

"A little. What do you need?"

"I need a goddamned steak and baked potato; that's what I need. But I'll settle for anything that'll fill my gut."

"What's the matter? Doesn't your friend, Sam, know how to cook?"

"As a matter of fact . . ."

Sam shot him a look and Jake finished lamely, "I think his days as cook around here just came to a halt."

"I'm going back to uncorking a whiskey bottle." Though Sam's words were harsh, his tone was affectionate as he glanced at the older man.

Jake swiveled his head toward Addy. "Come on, I'm hungry."

"I'll have to see what you have. Where's the kitchen?"

He wheeled his chair through a doorway and she followed. The kitchen, like the rest of the house, was worn and neglected. Like the man who lived here, she thought as she made her way to the refrigerator and opened the

10

door. Inside she found two quarts of milk, one of which was so sour she winced when she sniffed it.

"How long has this been here?"

"I don't know. A couple of weeks."

She dumped it down the drain before he could stop her.

"Goddamn it, kid. Chester would have drank that."

"Chester?"

He pointed to a huge blob of gray and white fur stretched out on top of the refrigerator. Hearing his name, the cat looked up and switched his tail from one side to the other before closing his eyes again.

The ragged cat suited his surroundings, she decided, and wondered how many other surprises she'd find before the night was over.

"I guess he'll have to drink the good stuff." She placed the other quart of milk on the counter, along with a hunk of cheese, and began rummaging through the contents of the refrigerator.

"No steak." She unwrapped a butcher's paper and found several dry slices of salami.

In a vegetable bin she sorted through a pile of brown lettuce and dried up cucumbers and managed to salvage an onion and half a green pepper.

"How about an omelette?"

"It's not steak but it'll keep me from starvation." He turned. "How about you, Sam?"

"Nothing for me, Jake."

"If you're going to drink that rotgut, you need some food." Jake turned back to Addy. "He'll eat whatever you fix."

She located a blackened skillet and turned on the stove. From the freezer she took a package of sliced potatoes and placed them in the oven to brown. She fed bread into a toaster and began beating the eggs and slicing and chopping the vegetables.

She turned to glance at Jake. He sat in the center of the room watching her. Sam lounged in the doorway, watching both of them with a wary expression.

11

"Can one of you at least keep an eye on the toast?"

She saw the fire that came into Sam's eyes, but he said nothing as he walked to the counter.

She folded the ingredients into the egg mixture and carefully turned the omelette.

"What'll you drink?" she asked.

"Coffee. Hot and black," Jake said. "Sam's got his whiskey."

She shot a glance at the glass in Sam's hand, then measured out the coffee and filled the pot with water. Soon the kitchen was filled with a rich aroma as the coffee perked.

She found the dishes and quickly set the table for two. When Jake saw it he snarled, "We don't eat alone. Set three places."

She tried not to show her relief as she set another place at the table and poured the coffee.

Jake rolled his wheelchair across the room and picked up his fork, then began eating mechanically.

"Should have left out the green pepper. And next time add tomato."

"I had to make do with what you had, remember?"

"Yeah. I'm just telling you for the next time."

"There won't be a next time."

"That's right. There probably won't be. But I'll be the one to decide that." He glanced at the tiny portion on her plate. "When's the last time you ate?"

She shrugged. "I had a bowl of cereal this morning."

From the looks of her, he thought, that was all she'd eaten in days. She'd blow away in a good wind.

"Sam and I can't eat all this. You'd better help us or it'll go to Chester."

With the threat of all that good food going to the cat, she filled her plate and missed the satisfied gleam that touched his eyes for just a moment. So, the kid couldn't stand waste. Well, neither could he. That was one strike in her favour.

"I guess," Jake peered at her over the rim of his cup, "you've done a little cooking in your day."

"A little." She pushed back her chair and carried the coffee pot over to the table to top off Jake's cup.

He watched as she polished off the rest of her omelette and spread strawberry jam on a piece of toast.

The ball of fluff on top of the refrigerator moved, stretched, then leaped to the counter, and from there to the floor, in surprisingly graceful motions. Seeing him, Addy poured some of her milk into a saucer and placed it on the floor. The cat lapped it up and then began circling her ankles.

"Hello, you fat old blob." She ran a hand over his thick fur. "Looks like you're being well fed."

"Don't try to make friends with him," Jake cautioned. "Old Chester's not fond of strangers. Has a habit of digging his claws into them when they reach for him."

Addy started to lift her hand away. Immediately the cat stood on his hind legs and rubbed his head against her hand until she gave in and petted him again. His contented purring would have rivaled a motor boat.

Jake looked annoyed. "Damned cat never took to a female before. Must be getting senile. So where did you do this cooking?"

She finished her toast. "Home."

"Where's home?"

"Wherever I happen to be at the moment."

His eyes narrowed. "And where did you just come from?"

Her gaze met his across the table. Now that she was fortified with a good meal, she was feeling strong enough to play his game. And beat him. After all, she'd be out of here in the morning. She didn't need to answer his questions.

"I guess you'll just have to ask Witherspoon."

"Goddamn it." Whatever truce had been declared over dinner was already forgotten.

He brought his fist down on the table, causing his coffee

to slosh over the rim. "Don't think I won't. He works for me. He'll tell me anything I want to know."

"Fine with me."

He pulled a cigar from his pocket and thought about the doctor's warning to cut down. With a shrug he peeled off the wrapper, then held a match to the tip. Through a haze of smoke he watched as she pushed away from the table and carried the empty plates to the sink.

She was aware that both men were watching her. It only served to stiffen her spine, making her movements awkward as she cleared the table and loaded the dishwasher.

"How long has it been since this thing's been run?" She studied the dishes caked with dried food.

He shrugged. "Couple of weeks maybe."

"A couple of . . ." She clamped her mouth shut and ran the water until it was steaming, then started the wash cycle. "I'd better run them through a couple of times."

Jake puffed on his cigar while she scoured the sink and counter tops and scrubbed the table until it gleamed. Then he rolled his wheelchair over to a small china hutch and lifted a deck of cards from a drawer.

Addy folded the dishtowel and stood watching as Jake shuffled the cards.

"Do you play, kid?" He caught the sudden frown on her face and added lamely, "Addy?"

"Yeah. I know Fish and Crazy Eights."

"Fish and . . ." Jake's eyebrows knitted together as he deftly shuffled the cards.

Addy was fascinated. She'd never seen anyone handle cards like that.

"We don't allow kids' games here," he said, dealing the cards. "We play Poker, Blackjack, Pai Gow, Red Dog."

"But I only know how . . ."

"No Fish. No Crazy Eights." This was stupid, he thought with a feeling of exasperation. He must be getting feeble minded to bother with a greenhorn like this. He took a deep breath. "I'll teach you the rules. But you've got to pay attention. I'll only tell you once."

14

Addy listened as he explained the difference between a full house, a straight, a flush, a royal flush. He opened a box of matches and shoved a pile of them toward Addy and another pile toward Sam. "We'll play for matches, since I suppose you don't have any money you'd care to gamble."

At a shrug of her shoulders he picked up his cards and said, "This is five card draw. Ante up."

Addy watched as he and Sam each tossed a match in the middle of the table. She followed suit.

"Jacks or better will open." Jake studied his hand then glanced over at her. "Can you open?"

Addy shook her head.

"How about you, Sam?"

Sam shook his head.

A hint of a smile touched Jake's lips. "Well, I can." He tossed another match in the middle and Addy and Sam did the same.

"How many cards?"

Sam took three. Addy discarded four. Jake set aside three. When he dealt her the cards, Addy studied them carefully, then glanced up to find him watching her.

"The pair of Jacks are still in the game." He picked up another match and tossed it into the pile.

Sam did the same.

"How about you?"

Addy shrugged.

He nodded toward the pile of matches. "If you want to see these cards you have to pay."

She tossed her match next to the others.

"Two pairs," he said with a laugh. "Jacks and deuces."

Sam tossed in his cards.

Jake grinned. "Sorry, kid. Some nights, that's just the way the cards fall." His hand closed over the pile of matches. Almost as an afterthought he murmured, "What did you have?"

"Three nines."

For the first time he saw the gleam in her eyes.

"I believe you said that three of a kind beats two pairs."

Sam turned his head to study her more carefully.

Jake moved his hand away and watched through narrowed eyes as she drew the pile of matches toward her. In a tone of admiration he said, "You were paying attention, weren't you?"

"Yeah. Want to play again?"

He handed her the deck. "Winner deals."

He and Sam were forced to watch as she fumbled with the cards, dropping several while she struggled to shuffle. "Sorry." She glanced up and saw them wince as another card dropped from the deck. "I guess I'm not very good with cards. Would you show me again how you shuffled them, Jake?"

He took the cards from her. His big fingers curled around the cards almost sensuously as he cut them, shuffled, and let them fall from one hand to the other without missing a beat.

"Think I could ever learn to shuffle like that?"

"Don't see why not. It just takes time. And a lot of practice."

He handed her back the cards and she dealt. Again she won. And for the next three games in a row she beat her opponents.

With each loss Jake's scowl deepened. As she lay down her cards for yet another win she said with a laugh, "Sorry, Jake. But you said yourself, some nights that's just the way the cards fall."

"Shut up and deal." He saw her stifle a yawn and said, "The rule of the house is, no one goes to bed until I win at least one hand."

"Looks like we're in for a long night," Sam said with a scowl.

Jake picked up his cards and swallowed back a smile. "Not so long. I'll open." He tossed a match in the center of the table and discarded. "I'll take three cards."

Addy dealt three cards to him, three cards to Sam, and gave herself three.

"It's going to cost you five matches to see these."

Addy and Sam tossed the matches into the pile and waited.

"Jackpot time, kid." Jake tossed down three aces. "Now tell me you can beat this."

Addy shook her head. "Not this time. You win."

"Sam?"

The younger man shook his head.

With a little laugh of triumph Jake scooped up the matches and sat back looking flushed and happy. "You know what, kid?"

"Addy," she corrected.

"Yeah. Addy. Know what? You're not a half bad poker player. With a little time and coaching, you could be good. Of course," he added quickly, "you'd never be as good as I was in my prime. But you've got potential. Doesn't she, Sam?"

Sam said nothing as he studied the girl whose eyes were heavy with weariness.

"I don't care about potential." Addy yawned again and pushed away from the table. "I'm too tired to even see the cards."

"Yeah." Jake tried to hide his disappointment. The nights were always the worst. He would have enjoyed her company a while longer, just to pass the time. "It always seems like such a long day when you travel. You'd better get to bed."

"Can I get you anything before I go?"

"Nah. I'll be turning in pretty soon."

"Well then . . . ." She stood a moment, feeling suddenly awkward in the presence of two such intimidating men. "What time do you want me to be up and out of here?"

"Out of here?" He'd hoped she'd forgotten his earlier outburst.

"Look, Jake, you made your feelings pretty plain. You called me a skinny female who was scraped from the bottom of the barrel. You said I could spend the night before I left. I figure sooner or later you'll find someone who suits you."

"Yeah. You're right." He didn't want to look at Sam. He knew he'd see a frown of disapproval.

It was Sam who'd first rushed to Jake's side after the accident. If not for Sam, Jake knew he'd have died. And it was Sam who'd moved in when he found Jake living alone, unable to care for his simplest needs. Now, despite the string of housekeepers, it was Sam's company who made the loneliness tolerable. Sam Money was probably the most loyal friend Jake had ever known. But Sam was a practical man. Jake wouldn't be surprised if Sam had cooked up this little scheme with Witherspoon.

His voice roughened. "Don't bother to get up early. I'm a night person. Like to sleep in late in the morning. We'll talk tomorrow."

"Okay. Well, goodnight, Jake. Sam."

"Goodnight, kid. Addy," Jake corrected quickly.

Sam said nothing.

Both men watched as she pushed her chair neatly up to the table and made her way from the room. They listened to the squeak on the stairs as she climbed them. For a few minutes longer they heard the sound of her footsteps overhead, as she made her way from the bedroom to the bathroom, and then back again. And then there was only silence.

"Come on, Sam," Jake said, picking up the deck. "I'll beat you at blackjack."

"Just a couple more hands," Sam remarked. "The whiskey's getting to me. Pretty soon I won't be able to see the cards."

"Good. I prefer my opponents drunk or blind. Or both."

Above them, the cat lifted his head for a moment, then curled up in his favorite spot on top of the refrigerator.

The cards skimmed through Jake's fingers as he shuffled. Staring into space for a moment he muttered, almost to himself, "Funny kind of kid, isn't she? She put up a pretty good bluff. Of course, I could see right through her. Inside she was scared to death. But she wasn't one to back away. I liked that about her."

Sam kept his thoughts to himself.

Jake dealt the cards, but instead of picking them up he mused, "She can cook. That omelette was one of the best I've eaten. Even with green peppers and without the tomatoes. Hell," he mused, "I wonder what she could do with a pot roast."

Sam chuckled. "If she leaves in the morning you'll never find out."

The old man's scowl deepened. "How many cards do you want?"

In no time Jake was lost in the game. Thanks to the allure of the cards, and the company of his one good friend, he could hold back the lonely hours of the night for a little while longer.

Chapter Three

Addy stood in the darkness, watching the play of moonlight against the stark white sheets. She could have drawn the curtains, but she couldn't bear to shut out the moon and stars.

The room was bigger than anything she could imagine, with a fireplace made of stone along one wall. There were high, peaked ceilings and floor to ceiling windows that led to a porch that wrapped around the front and sides of the house. There was a big brass bed and two oversized dressers. In one corner stood a tall, old-fashioned looking glass, thick with dust. Beside the fireplace was a weathered rocking chair. Everything in the room looked old and neglected. But with the lights out, she couldn't see the dust and layers of dirt that had accumulated through the years.

The old rag rug was soft beneath her bare feet. Her toes curled into it, playing with the rough texture. The hardwood floor underneath was dusty and scarred.

A room of her own. Even though it was only for one night, it was a luxury she had never before experienced. A room and a bed without anyone else to share it.

She'd expected to feel lonely. Instead she felt pampered.

She climbed into bed and drew the blankets over her. The springs creaked slightly as she shifted. Soft. The mattress was old and soft, molding itself to every little movement. She rolled to her side and felt a new sense of freedom. She could turn as often as she wanted without worrying about disturbing anyone else.

With a sigh she closed her eyes and breathed in the cool

fresh air that wafted through the open window. Within minutes she was asleep and tumbling back, back, into the place that always seemed to beckon her when her mind was troubled.

* * *

"Look, Addy. A shooting star. Quick. Make a wish."

At her mother's command, eleven year old Addy O'Brien cradled her baby sister in her arms and squeezed her eyes tightly shut. When she opened them, her mother still had her face lifted to the night sky, her eyes closed, her lips moving in silent prayer.

Addy studied her mother's pretty face surrounded by wisps of straight blonde hair. Though Colleen O'Brien was pale and fragile since the birth of her baby, she was still a strikingly beautiful woman.

Addy adored her sweet, dreamy mother. The time spent with her was a delight. Colleen O'Brien seemed always to have a new, fascinating fact to share with her firstborn. The hot dry air of the Nevada desert seemed cleaner when she breathed it. The barren landscape seemed greener.

As Addy watched, her mother's eyes blinked open. "What'd you wish for, honey?"

"An A on tomorrow's math test."

"But you always get A's. Why waste a perfectly good wish on something you know you can have?"

Addy shrugged. "I guess I just wanted to make sure. What'd you wish for, Mama?"

Colleen leaned her back against the small porch railing of the mobile home and glanced down at her four year old daughter, Erin, dozing in her lap. The night breeze was too hot to be refreshing, but at least it moved her hair off her neck. "I wished for a real job for your daddy, something grand and important, and a house of our own, with a yard full of white roses."

Addy smiled in the darkness. She always loved her

mother's wishes. Her own were usually practical. It was her nature. But her mother was able to remove herself from the harshness of reality. Her dreams were lavish and wonderful.

"I've never seen white roses."

"We had them in our yard in Michigan. Big, fragrant blossoms that bloomed from early spring to late summer. Umm." Colleen breathed deeply, ignoring the stench of overflowing garbage piled near the curb for morning pickup. "I can still remember the way they smelled when I was a little girl. My father would pick a big bouquet for my mother, and she'd set them in a big cut glass vase on the dining room table, and for days the whole house would smell like springtime."

Addy loved her mother's stories of her childhood. The big old house in Michigan, filled with laughing, squabbling brothers and sisters, and loving parents who worked hard all week and took their brood to church every Sunday, sounded like a wonderful fairy tale. But sometimes she worried that it all seemed more real to her mother than her life here in Nevada with her often absent husband and three daughters.

"What does springtime smell like, Mama?"

"Oh, Addy." With a smile Colleen lifted her hair from her neck and piled it on top of her head. As soon as she dropped her hand the fine tendrils tumbled down her back again. "After a rain you can smell the earth, dark and sweet. And when the roses burst into bloom, they fill the air with the sweetest perfume. It's like nothing I can describe."

She glanced at her daughter and they shared a laugh. This certainly wasn't the kind of life Colleen O'Brien had envisioned for herself. Worse, it wasn't what she'd hoped for her daughters. But then, she'd learned that reality was never as good as fantasy, real life would never be as sweet as her dreams. Maybe that was why she remained a dreamer. Even though sometimes the dream became a nightmare.

Colleen's laughter suddenly died in her throat. They both looked up at the glare of headlights cutting a path through the darkness. Tires crunched on gravel as a battered truck came to a sudden, screeching halt alongside their porch.

"Take your sisters inside. Right away."

Addy heard the tension in her mother's tone. Without a word she balanced the baby on her shoulder and dragged her sleeping little sister to her feet. As Erin began to protest, Addy pulled open the door and shoved her inside ahead of her.

Outside she heard the voices, low with anger. It was always the same. Her father's long absences were followed by homecoming fights which more and more often erupted into violence. Every time her father got a paycheck, he disappeared. And when he returned, his pockets were always empty. And his despair grew.

This time he'd been gone for five days. Addy knew that he wouldn't be able to remember most of what had occurred during that time. But what was even worse, the next few days would be a time of anger and deep depression. Craving what he no longer had the money to buy, and suffering guilt over what he had done, would make him extremely volatile. A single word could set off his fuse, causing him to explode into a storm of violence. It was easier to rage against his family than to place the blame squarely where it belonged.

It took only minutes to settle the baby into the crib in her parents' bedroom, and press the sleepy Erin into the narrow bunk.

Addy undressed quickly and crawled in beside her sister, pulling the blankets up over her head. But nothing could shield her from the angry words that had started the minute her father had exited the truck.

Addy tensed at the sound of footsteps approaching. The walls seemed to shudder as the door was thrown open and heavy boots beat a tattoo toward her parents' bedroom.

Her father's deep voice was angry, slurred. Her mother's muffled voice filtered through the thin walls, protesting, then pleading.

In the room next door Addy heard a string of curses as her father's boots were hurled against the wall. She scrunched her eyes tightly shut and forced herself to memorize tomorrow's maths lesson. She thought about the brain teasers her teacher had offered to any students who wanted to earn extra credits. Addy had figured out all three of the challenges. Now she ran them through her mind, concentrating so hard, she was able to blot out everything. Or at least most of it.

Much later, when her mother had stopped crying, and her father lay snoring, Addy clung to her side of the narrow bunk bed and listened to the strange, muted sounds of the night. Beside her, four year old Erin rolled over, taking the blanket with her. Addy gently tugged a corner of it until her bare feet were covered.

Amid the static of a neighbour's tinny radio, Glen Campbell sang about a rhinestone cowboy. The music was suddenly smothered by the drone of jets from the nearby air base. When they passed directly overhead Addy lifted the edge of the frayed curtain and watched as the jet stream streaked the sky.

She wished she could fly. Fly far away. But only if she could take her mama and Erin and little Shannon with her. She searched the sky for falling stars, but there were none. It didn't matter, she thought as she dropped the edge of the curtain and curled up on her side. She didn't believe in magic wishes anyway. She struggled to hold the tears back but they wouldn't be denied. A cry escaped her lips, and then another.

* * *

Addy sat straight up in bed. Something had awakened her, but for a moment she didn't know what. And then she felt the wetness of tears on her cheeks.

"Hey, kid! You all right?"

She struggled to remember where she was. Then it all came rushing back to her. The ramshackle house. The grouchy old man. Home was a million tears, and a million years away. Home was gone forever. She'd have to invent a new one.

"Kid. Answer me."

She scrambled out of bed and padded to the head of the stairs. "I'm fine."

"I want to see for myself."

She walked to the landing. He sat in his wheelchair at the foot of the stairs. Bushy white brows were knitted together in a frown.

"You were crying."

"I was just dreaming."

"Some dream." Jake studied her in the light of the stairwell. She looked even younger in an oversized tee-shirt that fell to her knees. Toussled dark hair hung limply over one eye. Even from this distance he could see the gleam of moisture on her cheeks.

"Goddamn it. From the sounds of it, you had me ready to call the emergency services."

"Sorry."

He shrugged. "Not your fault. I know how it feels. Had a few of my own once or twice. Go back to bed."

She lingered, unwilling to face sleep and its accompanying dreams just yet. "Why aren't you in bed?"

"I don't need much sleep."

"But it must be awfully late by now."

He glanced at his watch. "Three fifteen."

"Where's Sam?"

"Out."

She sat down on the step, wrapping her arms around her drawn up knees. "What do you do at three fifteen in the morning?"

"Play a little solitaire, read, play a little more solitaire until I have to give up and go to bed."

"Sounds like you don't care much about sleeping."

"When you're as old as me, kid, you won't want to waste much time sleeping. 'Cause you'll know that someday you just won't wake up."

Addy shivered. "Want to play a little poker?"

He gave her a long speculative look. "Grab something warm. The air gets chilly this time of the morning."

She ran up the stairs and rummaged through her open suitcase. A few minutes later she returned wearing a battered old terry robe.

At the kitchen table the cards had already been shuffled. Jake dealt quickly. She picked up her hand and studied her cards, missing the smug look on Jake's face as he picked up his.

A tumbler of whiskey rested on the table beside him. The cards in his hand were unbeatable. And for the first time in more months than he could count, he had somebody new willing to join him in holding back the night. It didn't get much better than this.

Addy decided to chance a question. "Is Sam Money a relative?"

"No. Why do you ask?"

She shrugged. "I just wondered why he lived here."

"Sam's probably the best friend I'll ever have. He once saved my life. Now he continually saves my sanity."

"So he's here – permanently."

Jake glanced at her. "Don't let his drinking worry you. Sam's one of the good ones of this world. To me, he's like an angel of mercy."

Some angel, Addy thought. But she kept her thoughts to herself.

Minutes later Jake laid down his hand and collected the jackpot of matches. "Remember this, kid," he said with an odd little grin, "there's always a point where the cards turn in your favour, or turn against you. A gambler's got to be sharp enough to know the exact moment. That's how fortunes are won and lost."

He won the next ten hands. But by the time the dawn light streaked the sky, Addy had won twenty-two straight

26

hands. And had heard every rich, ripe curse in Jake's colourful vocabulary.

*   *   *

There was a crashing sound on the porch and then the sudden rush of air as the door was torn open. Sam leaned unsteadily against the doorway, studying the two figures at the kitchen table.

His gaze was fixed on the girl in the terry robe. It was pink, like Laura's. Laura always wrapped herself in it after her shower and he'd draw her close and breathe in the fresh, clean fragrance of soap and shampoo and White Shoulders, which he brought her every Christmas. White Shoulders. He frowned. He hadn't smelled it in such a long time, but even now, he could inhale and smell it in his lungs. In his heart.

"Didn't take you long to get drunk," Jake said without looking up from his cards.

"I worked at it." With a great effort Sam made his legs move and stumbled across the room. With unerring precision he located the cupboard that held the glasses and filled one from the bottle he'd bought. He hadn't planned to drink anything more tonight, until he spotted that pink robe. His hand shook as he lifted the glass to his lips.

"How're things at the casino?"

"Busy. You ought to go there some time."

Jake shot him a look. "I suppose all my friends asked about me?"

"Of course they did. They always do."

"But you're the only one who bothers with me."

"That's because you have such good whiskey."

Jake glanced at the sky, turning light outside the window. "Think I'll grab a couple hours sleep." He tossed down the cards and drained his glass.

"Yeah. Me too." Addy pushed quickly away from the table. She wasn't about to stick around with a drunk. "You need some help? I mean, with that wheelchair and all . . ."

Her voice trailed off. She felt her cheeks redden. She knew why she'd been hired. Caregiver. She wasn't going to be paid to just sit around playing cards.

"Yeah." Jake rolled through the doorway ahead of her and led the way to his bedroom. "I can manage most things by myself. But there are a few things I just can't do."

Addy stopped in the doorway. A hospital bed had been rigged with an overhead railing that allowed Jake to pull himself from the chair to the bed and back again.

As she watched, Chester padded past them and curled up at the foot of the bed. He licked his paws while keeping an eye on them.

"I can dress and undress myself, as long as I keep it simple," Jake explained with a frown. "But socks and slippers are another matter."

"How about . . ." She swallowed. "Bathroom facilities."

He gave her a probing look. "What do you think? I need someone to change me?"

"No. But . . ."

"The bathroom's through there." He pointed and Addy was glad for the chance to escape his probing stare.

A series of cleverly designed railings around the shower allowed him the same freedom as the bed. He could lift himself from the anchored wheelchair to a chair positioned in an open tiled shower. Or from the chair to the toilet, outfitted with a similar railing.

"There's one little problem," he said, rolling his chair up behind her. "I have to get in the shower and then turn it on and sit in the goddamned cold water until I get it to the temperature I want. I've been freezing my ass off lately."

"I could turn it on early and get it just the right temperature before you climb in."

"You want me to lie here waiting for you to come in and turn on the shower like I was some helpless little kid?"

"You're not helpless. But there are some things I can just do easier than you. I guess that's why you hired me."

"I didn't hire you, kid. Witherspoon did. But I'll be the one to do the firing. Remember that."

She swallowed. "Well? Do you want me to get your shower ready in the morning?"

He thought a minute. "Yeah. If you're awake early enough."

"I will be." She turned to him. "Do you need anything tonight before I go upstairs?"

"No. Nothing. Goodnight, kid."

"It's Addy."

"Right."

When he said nothing more she called, "Night, Jake."

She closed his door and looked up in surprise. Sam was standing just beyond the door, barring her way to the stairs. Though he'd watched and listened, he said not a word. His silent, watchful attitude disturbed her more than she cared to admit. There was something about Sam Money. He reminded her of a hunter. Watching. Listening. Stalking.

As she started to move past him his hand snaked out to stop her. She reacted as if she'd been burned, jerking her hand away and shrinking back against the wall.

So, he thought, she didn't like to be touched.

"I just want you to understand something." Though his eyes were bloodshot, she had the distinct impression that he was very much in control. "Jake Starr talks a tough game. But he's the finest man I've ever met."

"So?"

"So I'm warning you. If you're some kind of creampuff, you won't make it through the week."

"And if I'm tough enough to take it?" she challenged.

"If you're a con, I'd better find you gone in the morning." His eyes were dark and challenging. "Do you get my drift?"

When she didn't speak he caught her by the shoulders. He realized at once his mistake. Through the thin fabric of her robe he could feel the tremors. And something more. The heat, the softness of her flesh.

29

He dropped his hands to his sides and took a step back.

"Just what are you to Jake?" Her eyes smoldered with anger.

"Let's just say I've appointed myself his guardian angel. So if you cross me, lady, you'll find out I'm an avenging angel. Do we understand each other?"

"Oh, yes." She shoved past him quickly. "I think we understand each other very well."

Addy climbed the stairs and stood for a minute, taking long, calming breaths.

She stared at the sunrise far off on the horizon. Soft pink light filled the sky and flooded the bedroom. With a shiver she made her way to the bed and climbed in, pulling the blanket over her head.

Even with her arms around herself, she couldn't seem to shake off Sam's touch.

Chapter Four

Addy lay a moment, completely disoriented. Sunlight filled the room. A glance at the bedside clock showed her that it was half past noon.

Noon. She had never slept this late in her life. If Jake was waiting for a warm shower, he'd be furious.

She slipped from bed and rummaged through her suitcase. She was showered, dressed and downstairs in ten minutes.

She hesitated outside Jake's door. There was no sound from within. What did it mean? Was he still asleep? Or was he lying there in misery, waiting for his new ex-employee to come to his aid?

Tentatively she opened the door and peered inside. The curtains had been drawn against the world outside. The room was in semi-darkness.

She could make out a dark mound in the bed, moving in quiet, steady rhythm. She closed the door and let out the breath she'd been holding. Thankfully, he was still asleep.

Past noon and he was still sleeping. Addy shook her head as she made her way to the kitchen. It had been a long time since she'd known anyone who stayed up all night and slept all day.

"If you'd asked, I could have told you he was still asleep."

At the unexpected sound of Sam Money's deep voice she froze. "I didn't know you were downstairs."

He was standing by the window, drinking a cup of coffee. He hadn't shaved. His lower face was covered by several days' growth of beard. But it was his eyes that held her, even when she wanted to glance away. Eyes that seemed to question, to challenge.

He wore faded jeans and a denim shirt under a baseball jacket that had seen better days. But even the baggy jacket couldn't camoflage the muscles of his arms as he lifted the cup to his lips.

His gaze flicked over her, noting the clean skirt and blouse, the face free of makeup. If only she didn't appear so artless, so innocent. All the same, he mistrusted her. Why would a pretty young woman want to spend her days caring for an invalid she didn't even know? He turned away to stare at the dusty landscape.

It didn't compute. She probably had a motive. If she did, he'd uncover it. It was just a matter of time.

Noting the fresh pot of coffee, Addy poured herself a cup and rummaged through the cupboards for something to eat. Except for some stale cereal and half a jar of peanut butter, the cupboards were as bare as the refrigerator. But she knew she could make do. Hadn't she always?

She made toast and spread it with peanut butter. While she ate she opened the windows wide to rid the room of the musty smell of mildew and stale cigar smoke. She filled a trash bag with the remains of soggy crackers and moldy bread and some things, black and fuzzy, that could no longer be identified. Then she tackled the floors and countertops, scrubbing and disinfecting until they gleamed.

"I don't think Jake expects you to do all this." Sam leaned a hip against the doorway and watched as the sunlight played over her hair. "He's never been one to be impressed by a clean environment."

"I'm not doing this to impress Jake."

He arched a brow. "You're telling me you just like to work for the fun of it? Or is it because you need to be busy?"

"If you must know, I'm doing it for the money. If Jake decides to send me away, he'll still have to pay me for yesterday and today."

"The money's important to you, is it?"

"Yes." She turned away. He'd never know how important.

"Kid."

She heard the raspy, tobacco-roughened voice and hurried to the doorway of Jake's bedroom.

"So, you're already up ahead of me."

With his hands wrapped around the bar over his head, he'd pulled himself to a sitting position in the bed. He was wearing a pair of loose fitting boxer shorts and nothing else.

"Get the shower started."

She turned on the water and waited, adjusting the temperature until it was perfect. When she walked from the bathroom she saw him lift himself from the bed and move across the bar, hand over hand, until he was positioned over the wheelchair. Then he lowered himself into the chair and slapped a hand against the wheel, turning it toward her.

She carefully avoided looking at him. He was practically naked. "Your shower's ready."

"Thanks, kid. What's for breakfast?"

She glanced at him and immediately felt a wave of sympathy. The exertion had cost him. Sweat beaded his forehead and upper lip. The powerful muscles that corded his arms were slick with sheen.

She shrugged and averted her gaze. "The eggs are gone. But there's some bread for toasting. And peanut butter."

"Good enough."

She watched as he disappeared into the bathroom. Without any modesty he began slipping off his shorts. She beat a hasty retreat past Sam, who was standing in the doorway, grinning.

"Why don't you help him instead of standing around watching?" she asked in an accusing tone as she picked up Jake's clothes from the floor.

"In case you haven't noticed, Jake likes to think he

can take care of himself. And most of the time he can."

She held the clothes as far away as she could until she reached the laundry room, where she dropped them into the washer before measuring out detergent. The clothes hadn't seen soap and water for a long time.

Maybe, she thought as she moved back to the kitchen, it was just as well if this job didn't work out. She was extremely uncomfortable around these two. She wasn't quite certain just what Jake wanted his employee to be. Was she a housekeeper? A cleaning woman? A cook? Or was she a glorified baby-sitter, staying up at night with him and passing the time learning how to beat him at poker? Maybe she was supposed to be all those things. Not that it mattered all that much to Addy. All she'd ever known was hard work.

If the job itself hadn't been spelled out in the contract his lawyer had drawn up, everything else had. The document stipulated that she would have free room and board in exchange for duties to be defined by her employer. In addition she would be paid two hundred dollars a week. Two hundred dollars. That was more than Addy had ever seen. And the money was everything to her. It was the thing that drove her. With enough money she could begin her quest. A quest that had been her obsession since she was twelve years old.

Addy leaned her elbows on the sink and stared out the window at the patch of dried earth encircled by a rotting fence. It was no more bleak than the view she'd had in her childhood. She had only to close her eyes and she was there again.

*   *   *

Eleven year old Addy lay in her bunk, aware that something had roused her from sleep. She heard it again. The bleating of the baby in the next room. Slipping from her bunk she padded into her parents' bedroom and lifted the squalling infant into her arms. Her mother sat up, shoving her hair from her eyes. When she saw that the baby was being tended, she gave her daughter a weak smile and fell back against the pillow. The man lying beside her never moved.

Addy tiptoed to the cramped kitchen and turned on the stove. While the bottle heated she changed the baby's soaked diaper. She filled a bowl with cereal and milk and managed to feed herself and the baby at the same time. That done she escaped the confines of their tiny home. She crept outside and walked barefoot through the sand until she found the single tree in the center of the mobile home park. This was her favorite spot. This tiny oasis of green. With a blanket spread on the hard-packed earth, she lay the baby down and knelt beside her. Shannon gurgled and cooed, and at Addy's coaxing, gave a smile. Addy hugged her, and wondered again at the love she felt for this tiny creature who was so helpless. Shannon was hers, she thought fiercely. From the day her mama had brought the baby home, she had become Addy's responsibility. And her joy. She never thought about the extra work that had fallen on her shoulders. Caring for Shannon, as she cared for four-year old Erin, was a simple fact. She couldn't imagine life without them.

An hour later, with the sleeping baby nestled at her shoulder, Addy headed back home. Fifteen minutes later she raced between the crowded mobile homes to the main entrance, where a yellow school bus was just drawing to a halt amid a cloud of dust.

She found an empty seat in the middle of the bus.

"Got your homework done?" Eddie Stewart, red hair plastered to his head, wearing faded denims and a soiled tee shirt, paused beside her seat.

"Sure, Eddie. Come on, I'll help you finish yours."

As the bus jostled over ruts in the road, two heads bent over a maths workbook. Eddie was failing just about every subject. And Addy was the only one who seemed to care enough about him to help. But she was glad for the distraction. At least, she reasoned, it would keep her from worrying about Erin and Shannon, and wondering who was looking after them while she was at school. She brushed aside the nagging fear that they probably looked after themselves until she returned.

At the end of the school day, Addy faced the beginning of more chores.

"Your daddy said he'd do the laundry, honey." Colleen sat weakly in a chair, balancing the baby in her arms. "But something came up and he had to leave."

Addy glanced at the dollar bills lying on the kitchen table. Her dad must have been paid. Her mother didn't have to explain any more. He always left after he got paid. And he usually didn't return until the paycheck was spent.

"It doesn't matter, Mama. I'll take the clothes to the laundromat."

"There's money on the table, honey. If you want to take Erin along, buy her a can of soda."

Addy stuffed the money into the pocket of her shorts and picked up the heavy basket. "Come on, Erin. Let's take a walk."

Erin needed no coaxing. She adored her older sister. And she loved any excuse to escape the four walls of their dingy home.

"How do those flowers grow, Addy?" She pointed a stubby finger at the blossoms growing neatly beside Mrs. Bentson's trailer.

"You put seeds in the ground, and the rain and sunlight make them grow into pretty flowers."

"But how?"

"I don't know. They just grow."

A bird passed overhead and the little girl stopped to watch. "Why can't we fly, Addy?"

"'Cause we don't have wings."

"Why?"

"We just don't. We got a brain instead, so we can invent our own way to fly."

"How come we have a brain and the birds don't?"

Addy grinned and led her sister inside the laundromat, situated on the far side of their mobile home park. "We have a brain so we don't have to peck in the dirt all day for our dinner."

She sorted the clothes and filled three washers, then got change from the attendant and bought Erin a can of soda.

"Just one?" the attendant asked.

Addy counted her change and mentally figured out what she'd need to run the dryers for an hour. "One's enough."

Erin took a long drink and then offered it to Addy, who took a sip before handing it back. Circling the room she found an old colouring book and some crayons that somebody had left behind.

"Look, Erin. Want to colour?"

The little girl knelt down on the dirty floor and began filling in the pictures. Addy walked to the door and watched a game of baseball being played in a small open field across the street.

The attendant flipped the pages of her magazine and glanced at the girl standing wistfully by the door. "If you want to join the kids playing ball, I'll keep an eye on your little sister."

"Thanks." Addy was surprised by the offer. But she quickly shook her head. Mama had warned her about leaving Erin or Shannon unattended. There were bad people out there. People who took babies because they couldn't have any of their own. "I've got to keep an eye on the clothes."

The attendant shrugged her shoulders. "Suit yourself."

It never occurred to Addy that she was different from most kids her age. They'd be more than happy to leave the laundry and the little girl and join their friends. But she had always been different. Like a little old woman, Mama said. She'd stay and tend her duties. And by the time she left, the clothes would be dried and carefully folded. And she and Erin would go straight home. No detours. Ready to tackle even more work, until, exhausted, she would fall into her cramped bunk beside Erin.

*   *   *

"You look like you're a million miles away, kid."

Addy spun around, guilty of being caught daydreaming. "Toast and peanut butter coming right up."

Jake remained in the doorway, watching her nervous, hurried movements as she prepared the toast and filled a cup with coffee. Sam walked up behind him and pushed Jake's chair to the table.

"Oh. I forgot a spoon."

As she started to turn away Jake caught her by the wrist. He was surprised at how slender it was. His fingers could have easily wrapped around both her wrists with room to spare.

Addy felt the strength in his grip. It shouldn't have surprised her. She'd seen how he lifted himself from his bed. The muscles in his upper body made up for the paralysis in his legs. Still, his strong grasp caught her by surprise.

"Slow down, kid. Around here nobody races to do anything. Slow and easy. That's the rule at Starr's."

She swallowed and shrank back.

Behind Jake's chair Sam watched in silence. So, it wasn't just his touch that repelled her. It was obvious to him that Addy O'Brien didn't like being touched by any man. He watched as she fled across the room. When she returned with the spoon, she set it down and retreated to the far side of the kitchen.

"What've you been up to in here?" Jake pinned her with a challenging look. "It smells different. Looks different too."

She shrugged. "I just cleaned it up a bit. And opened the windows to let in some fresh air."

He drained his first cup of coffee and waited for more. "I don't believe in fresh air."

"Give it a try, Jake," Sam said softly.

"Hell, these old lungs wouldn't know how to breathe it in after all these years of cigar smoke and stuffy saloons."

They both looked up at the sound of the doorbell.

"See who's there," Jake said.

Addy dried her hands on a dishtowel and hurried to the front door.

"You must be Adelia O'Brien." The man was tall and distinguished looking, with dark hair just beginning to gray at the temples. He wore a perfectly tailored dark suit and carried an expensive briefcase.

"About time you showed your ugly goddamned face, Witherspoon," Jake's voice bellowed from the kitchen. "Don't you think you should have prepared me for your latest little surprise?"

The lawyer studied the girl in the simple cotton skirt and blouse. She was younger than he'd expected. And prettier. "As you just heard, my name is Andrew Witherspoon. I'm the one who sent you the contract."

"How do you do, Mr. Witherspoon." Addy held out her hand and it was grasped in a firm handshake.

Stepping past her Andrew said in a hearty tone, "And good morning to you, too, Jake. I see you're in top form this morning."

"I expect my lawyer to take care of business, especially since it's my money that keeps him in those goddamned eight hundred dollar suits."

Chester leaped down from the refrigerator and began rubbing himself against the lawyer's trousers. Witherspoon nudged him away with the toe of his Italian leather shoe.

"Which is exactly what I've been doing. You told me to find someone to take care of you. I suppose Addy told you she's signed a contract for one year."

"She's a goddamned kid, for Christsake. What does she know about taking care of a goddamned cripple?"

"Have you told her what her duties will entail?"

"You mean have I told her that she'll do the work of

39

ten mothers, nursemaids and cleaning women? That she'll be nothing more than a goddamned indentured servant for the next year? Is that what you want me to tell her, Witherspoon? And should I tell her that the last six lucky employees have all quit before the first week because they couldn't stand the pressure? And that's why you forced the poor dumb kid to sign a binding contract sight unseen. Because it's the only way left to keep anybody around this goddamned sweatshop."

Addy's face flushed clear to her hairline. He was talking about her as if she wasn't even in the room.

The lawyer's voice was calm, reasonable. "You make it sound so tempting, Jake. No wonder there are thousands standing in line to work for you." He turned. "Miss O'Brien, would you mind going to your room while Jake and I have a private discussion? And maybe you'd take Jake's mangy cat with you. He loves shedding his hair on my legs."

Eager to escape, Addy picked up Chester and raced up the stairs, closing the bedroom door behind her.

In that same calm tone Andrew Witherspoon said, "It's a good thing I didn't let you write your own ad, Jake. We'd have had to settle for a convict instead of a girl from a shelter."

"Shelter?" Jake's tone hardened. "What the hell's a shelter?"

Across the table Sam said, "It's a place for girls who've been neglected, abused, or are in trouble with the law."

Jake swiveled his head to study his lawyer. "Which category does the kid fit into?"

"The first, I believe."

"You believe? You mean you don't even know her background? She could be an ax murderer? Or a goddamned little thief? And you brought her into my home? Me, a helpless . . ."

"You're hardly helpless, Jake." The lawyer took a chair and opened his briefcase. "Here's the file on Addy O'Brien. What little there is. They won't make the psychiatric reports available, but they do give a little background information. I guess you can draw your own conclusions."

Jake read quickly. With each paragraph his eyes narrowed perceptibly. He muttered aloud. "Mother – dead. Father, addicted to drugs and alcohol, suspected of neglecting three little girls until his death." He looked up. "Three? The kid has sisters?"

"There's more," Witherspoon said softly.

"The two youngest were adopted out," Jake read from the paper. "The oldest, Adelia, was abandoned. No known next of kin. Sent to shelter for abused, neglected and wayward girls, where she lived until released by the State of Nevada at the age of twenty-one."

When he finished the report, Jake's face reflected his inner rage.

"Some life. It's even lousier than mine. I wonder why no one adopted the kid?"

"Too old," the lawyer said dispassionately. "You can see from the report that she's above average intelligence, and, despite some lingering problems, comes highly recommended by the counselors. Now that she's of age, she's been cut loose by the state. This is the first time she's been on her own since her family disintegrated. She would have taken anything just to prove to herself that she can make it on the outside. Even a job as indentured servant."

"Cut the crap, Witherspoon. How the hell am I supposed to act around a kid like this? The first time I yell at her she'll probably run like a rabbit."

"Are you telling me you haven't yelled since she got here?"

Jake grimaced, thinking about their introduction. "Maybe a little."

"It looks like she's still here," the lawyer said reasonably.

"But hell." Jake slammed his hand down on the arm of the wheelchair. "How am I supposed to treat a kid that's been hurt like that?"

41

Andrew Witherspoon shrugged and replaced Addy's file in his briefcase. He closed it with a snap and got to his feet. "She's been wounded by an uncaring father, and victimized by a system that simply can't cope with all the problems of society today. But the wounds weren't mortal, Jake. I suppose they're a little like yours. Just enough to slow you down and cause a lot of pain, but not enough to count you out yet."

"Who knows?" Sam said, draining his coffee. "Maybe the two of you will be good for each other. Sort of like the blind leading the blind."

"Maybe you should say the lamb leading the lion. Although in the case of our Miss O'Brien, I could hardly call her a meek little lamb. From what I just saw, I'd say there was fire in those eyes. And maybe a temper to match your own, Jake."

"Get the hell out of here," Jake hollered. "And take your fancy goddamned words with you."

"Does this mean you're going to honour the contract?"

"Hit the road, Witherspoon. And don't let the door hit you in the ass on the way out."

"I guess that means yes."

Andrew Witherspoon was smiling as he made his way to the new Porsche parked beyond the gate. He was one of the few people in the world who knew Jake Starr well enough to understand that he was all bluster.

Chapter Five

"Kid. Get down here."

Addy stiffened her spine as she walked slowly down the stairs. She'd heard the door slam behind the lawyer and had seen him take off in his shiny new sports car, leaving a cloud of dust in his wake. She figured she already knew the outcome of their meeting.

"Before I start to pack, you owe me for yesterday and today. And don't think I'm leaving without my money." She spoke quickly, hoping to finish before she lost her nerve.

"You think I'm going to let you get away after just two goddamned days? What kind of fool do you think I am? Hell, no, kid. You signed a contract, remember?"

Across the room Sam watched her face as she struggled not to show her emotions. Surprise? he wondered. Or relief? It was hard to say. She was a damned good actress.

Turning his chair around Jake called over his shoulder, "Let's make a list of what we need from the store."

Addy took a moment to compose herself. She hadn't lost the job. She didn't know whether to rejoice or despair. A whole year of seeing to all the needs of a mean-mouthed old grouch.

Two hundred dollars. Her fear was quickly dispelled by the thought that she would earn two hundred dollars a week. By the end of the year she'd have ten thousand dollars saved. She'd be able to start the quest that had become her obsession. She could put up with anyone, even Jake Starr, to follow her dreams.

She took a deep breath and trailed him into the kitchen.

43

"For breakfast I like eggs," he said, "and potatoes and sausage or bacon. And for supper I like meat and potatoes. Any kind you can cook. And Oreo cookies. And donuts. Jelly filled." His eyes softened just thinking about them. "And a big bottle of whiskey. The cheapest brand. Never did care what the label said, as long as it packs a punch."

Addy wrote everything, then looked up. "How about fruit? And vegetables and salad stuff?"

"What the hell am I going to do with rabbit food?"

"It's good for you."

"Look at me. You think I'm going to magically get young and healthy again? As long as I'm still alive, I want the things I like. To hell with healthy. Here." He reached into his pocket and withdrew a couple of fifties. "This should be enough. The keys to the car are hanging over there on a peg beside the back door."

"I can't drive," Addy said.

"Can't drive? Twenty-one and can't drive?" Jake seemed thunderstruck. "Where the hell you been living? On the moon?"

The minute the words were out of his mouth he regretted them. Living in a state shelter was probably worse than being stranded on the moon.

From the stricken look on Addy's face he knew he'd cut her deeply. But it was too late.

He'd have to bluff his way through this mess. "Look, kid, the store's at least a couple of miles from here. You can't walk."

"A couple of miles is nothing. I do it all the time. I don't mind."

"Well I do. It isn't the walk there. It's the walk back with your arms full of heavy bags."

"I can manage, Jake."

"The hell you will!" he thundered, slapping the arm of his chair.

Addy stiffened her spine and lifted her head in that way he'd come to recognize. Carefully folding the bills, she stuffed them into her pocket and picked up the list. "I'll be back in an hour. Do you need anything before I leave?"

"Hell, no. I can take care of myself."

"So can I. I'll see you later."

He watched as she let herself out the back door.

"You'd better go after her, Sam. It's too far to walk."

"Did you see her face, Jake? She's determined to do it her way. Let her go."

Jake rolled his chair to the window and watched as Addy made her way along the sidewalk.

*　　*　　*

As she walked, Addy studied the sagging old houses that lined both sides of the street. Last night, she had traveled this route without really seeing it. Now, in full daylight, she could take the time to study the people. The laughter of two small children playing under a hose caught her attention. Their young mother held the hose while they raced through the spray. Just seeing it, Addy was transported back in her mind to her own childhood.

*　　*　　*

Summer in the desert regions of Nevada was a series of hot, shimmering days spent searching for relief from the relentless sun. Heat rose up in waves from the pavement and sticky asphalt, and those foolish enough to walk barefoot in the sand, blistered the bottoms of their feet.

The children of the Paradise Mobile Home Park splashed in plastic pools or ran under hoses. The air was filled with their screams and shrieks and giggles.

Behind the closed door of Addy's home, the silence was punctuated by the hum of the small electric fan that managed to move the stale air around.

Shannon slept fitfully in her crib. Erin, after a morning spent playing with neighbouring children, dozed in her

45

bunk. Addy dropped ice cubes into a glass of water and carried it to her mother, who was still in bed.

"Mrs. Bentson said you should see a doctor, Mama."

"You had no right to discuss our business with Mrs. Bentson."

"I didn't. She just asked why she hadn't seen you lately."

"You tell everybody I'm fine, you hear?"

Addy nodded her head. "But Mrs. Bentson was right. You should see a doctor."

"There's no money, Addy."

"You could pay the doctor later, when Daddy comes back."

Colleen's lips thinned. She shook her head and sipped the cold water. The look didn't escape Addy's notice. She felt a rush of fear at the familiar question. What if he never came back? What would they do then?

A part of Addy wished he would stay away forever. When Daddy was gone, they all seemed to breathe a sigh of relief. For a few hours or days, the lines of tension would leave her mother's forehead and eyes. For a few precious hours or days, they would all laugh, and talk, and dream. But then he would return, and the terrors would begin again.

But if he never returned, she thought with a shiver, how would they get by? What would they do for food and diapers and medicine? Addy knew what such things cost. It was she who walked to Wally Jobar's store whenever Mama needed something. It was nearly a mile each way. The walk there was easy. The trip home, with a heavy bag of groceries in her thin arms, took considerably longer. Especially if Addy brought Erin along. It wasn't that she wanted to, but sometimes she knew Mama could sleep while they were gone.

Mama always insisted that they pay their debts. Once, when Addy had been fifty cents short, and Wally had told her to pay him next time, Mama had made her walk all the way back to pay him. Wally had been horrified.

"It's getting dark out. Doesn't your mother know there's danger for little girls in the dark?"

"My mama said she couldn't get to sleep knowing she owed you money."

Wally bit down on his anger. Though he admired the woman's honesty, he considered this just foolish pride.

"Now she owes me nothing." He tucked an extra quart of milk and a can of infant formula into a bag. As an afterthought he handed Addy a Snickers Bar. "Something sweet for the walk home. Now go," he said, shoving her out the door. "And next time, you wait until daylight to come here. I got enough to worry about without worrying about my best customer, too."

When she turned to look over her shoulder she saw him standing at the window. It gave her a good feeling to know that Wally was watching out for her. In her young life, he was the only kind man she'd ever known.

*   *   *

Addy was pulled from her reverie by the grocery store just ahead. It was much bigger and cleaner than the one from her childhood. And the clerks in their green and white uniforms looked bored.

She bought all the things Jake had requested. And she bought the vegetables he'd scorned as well. She wouldn't force him to eat the healthy things. But maybe if they were there on the table, he'd eat a few of them anyway.

When she handed the clerk the money, the girl tucked the fifties under her drawer and handed Addy the change without a word.

Addy pushed the cart out the door and moved along the dusty sidewalk. A hot breeze blew through the trees lining the road, causing the leaves to sigh. Instantly Addy was reminded of her mother's soft sigh. And once again she was back in her childhood. Remembering. Always remembering.

*　*　*

Mama had grown steadily weaker, Now, she almost never left her bed.

"Sit here awhile, Addy," Colleen said softly, patting the edge of the mattress.

Addy slid up beside her, hugging her knees to her chest.

"You've got your Grandma's pretty dark hair." Colleen lifted a hand to her daughter's head, smoothing, stroking. "You're like her, you know. That's why I named you Adelia. You would have loved my mother."

Addy nodded, loving her mother's stories, knowing she was about to launch into another. It seemed to make her mama happy to talk about her family. It was one of the few things that eased Colleen O'Brien's pain these days, even though the mother and father she'd loved were dead now for years.

"My mother was amazing," Colleen said proudly. "The day the doctor told her that my father was dying of cancer, she came home and canned two dozen quarts of tomatoes from the garden." She gave a weak laugh. "Two dozen quarts."

Looking up at Addy she said, "When a neighbour asked her how she found the strength to go on, she said, 'You just do what you have to, and you don't stop to think about it." Colleen's eyes softened. "Mama said, 'With no man to help, I'll need to put in an even bigger garden next summer.' And she did. I don't know how, but she always managed."

Addy saw a flicker of pain come into her mother's eyes.

"Mama always said the smartest thing a woman could do was learn to take care of herself. And the second smartest thing was to marry a man who was a real helpmate." Her voice lowered. "Mama must be turning over in her grave when she takes a look at what a mess I've made. She must be so ashamed of her weak daughter."

"You aren't weak, Mama. You're sick."

Colleen nodded slowly. Her voice took on a dreamy note. "I wasn't always sick. There was a time when I could do anything I set my mind to. Like my mama. But I did have a weakness for Danny O'Brien. Only your daddy wasn't at all like he is now." She smiled. "Oh, he had dreams. Big dreams. And he was kind, and sweet. And so handsome."

Addy watched the transformation in her mother's face as she remembered. "Everyone said he was the best mechanic in our town. Danny O'Brien could fix anything. He said one day he'd get a car dealership. Danny's Deals. Doesn't that have a nice ring?"

Addy nodded.

"A car dealership was a big thing in Michigan. Danny's Deals. It would have been so wonderful." Colleen's smile faded. "Mama always said she saw a flaw in his personality. But I don't know. I think something happened to him when he realized he'd never see his dreams come true. He doesn't want to be the way he is, Addy. It's the drugs and the drink that have changed him."

In the silence they listened to the ticking of the clock on the bedside table. A tear welled up in Colleen's eye and she blinked rapidly. Her voice lowered to a whisper. "He's getting worse. I know he doesn't like himself, but he just can't stop. He doesn't have the strength. And neither do I. One of these days he's going to . . ."

"I can take care of you, Mama. I can take care of all of us," Addy whispered.

Colleen pulled her close and pressed a kiss to her temple. "I know you can, honey. You make me so proud."

She looked away a moment and her lips trembled. "But I should be the strong one."

"You get some sleep now, Mama, while Erin and Shannon are sleeping."

"Addy." Colleen clutched her daughter's arm. Her eyes went wide with a sudden flare of passion. "Promise me something."

Addy swallowed.

"Promise me you'll look out for Erin and Shannon if anything happens to me."

"Nothing's going to happen to you, Mama."

"Promise me, Addy."

The little girl gave a solemn nod of her head, then scrambled off the bed and drew the sheet over her mother's thin body. "I'll take care of them. I promise I won't let anything happen to them."

Colleen squeezed her daughter's hand and gave a nod of approval. "You're strong, Addy. Just like my mother."

Addy waited until her mother's eyes closed and her breathing became slow and even. As she made her way from the bedroom, she couldn't shake the cold fear that had settled around her heart. A fear that became reality just days later.

*   *   *

Addy tossed her head and studied the houses as she passed. Though neglected, they were large and rambling, with ornate woodwork around the large porches. It was plain that this had once been a prosperous neighbourhood. These old houses, that had once been so loved, were now sadly neglected.

Why did people neglect the things they ought to love? she wondered.

She didn't pay any attention to the sound of an engine idling at the curb until a voice said, "Jake was worried about you. He sent me to pick you up."

Addy turned. Sam got out of the car and unlocked the trunk. For a moment Addy could only stare at him as he moved toward her. He was so tall. And his walk was slow and fluid in the way of a man very self-assured.

She let him take the sacks of groceries from her arms.

As his fingers brushed her hand, she felt a rush of heat. She glanced up, afraid that he'd felt it too.

Sam's face never changed expression. "Go ahead and get in. I'll put these in the trunk."

She nodded her head and turned away quickly.

Sam was relieved when she removed her hand. It had been a long time since he'd felt anything quite like this, and for a moment he wondered if he'd imagined it. Last night, when he'd caught her by the shoulders, he'd blamed the heat on his anger. Now he knew better.

Once in the car he drove faster than he'd intended. He wanted to get her back to Jake's and be done with it. He glanced at the girl. She didn't even notice the speed. From the way she kept her face averted, she wasn't interested in small talk. That suited him just fine. The less said between them, the better. He figured he'd made himself very clear last night. She'd better watch herself, because he'd be watching her.

Addy stared at the houses slipping past her line of vision. Though her eyes were open, she didn't really see them. In her mind, she was slipping back to her childhood.

*   *   *

Addy climbed from the school bus. The first thing she noticed when she approached her shabby little mobile home was Erin, seated on the front porch, still wearing her pyjamas. Her hands, face and front were covered with brown, sticky chocolate.

"Where's Mama?" Addy asked.

"Sleeping." The little girl shoved the rest of the chocolate bar in her mouth and chewed.

Even with the door closed Addy could hear the baby wailing. "What's wrong with Shannon?"

The little girl shrugged. "She just keeps on crying. Mrs. Bentson hollered over for Mama to feed her. But Mama didn't get up."

A tiny shiver of fear curled along Addy's spine. Throwing open the door she raced to her mother's bedroom. The curtains were still drawn. In the gloom, she could see her mother tangled in the sheets, one arm flung out on the pillow beside her.

"Mama." Addy touched a hand to her mother's shoulder, then drew back with a shudder.

The baby began to wail louder.

As if in a trance Addy picked up the infant and patted her back as she shouted, "Mama. Wake up. Come on, Mama. You have to wake up."

The figure in the bed didn't move.

Addy pressed her cheek against the baby's temple and knelt down beside her mother's bed. "Please, Mama. You can't . . ." She felt the tears well up in her eyes and blinked them back. "You can't leave us alone, Mama. You have to wake up."

"I'm hungry, Addy," came a little voice from the doorway.

Addy turned and stared for a moment at the little girl in the dirty pyjamas, with matted hair and pouty lips.

"Go next door, Erin, and ask Mrs. Bentson if she'll come over."

When her sister disappeared, Addy made her way to the kitchen and found a bottle for the baby.

Cleo Bentson shuffled up the steps and into the kitchen. An enormous pink flowered mumu covered her bulk. The tops of her arms jiggled as she steadied herself against a chair. Her hair, bleached nearly white, stuck out in wild little tufts like cotton balls glued to her head.

"Erin said for me to come over." She stared around suspiciously. It was the first time she'd ever been permitted beyond the front door. Everyone in the neighbourhood knew how the O'Brien's guarded their privacy. Like people did who had something to hide. She wondered what it was they didn't want anyone to know.

"Where's your mom?" Her gaze centered on Addy, who sat stiffly in the kitchen chair, feeding the baby.

"She's in the bedroom."

Mrs. Bentson made her way down the narrow passageway toward the bedroom. When Erin started to follow, Addy grabbed her by the back of the shirt and drew her against her lap.

"Don't go in there now, Erin."

"But Mama . . ."

"Just stay here." Addy's voice was strangely calm.

She heard the sudden shriek, and a moment later watched as Mrs. Bentson backed from the room and raced to the phone. As the woman's voice rose hysterically, giving the address and directions to their section of the mobile home park, Addy continued holding the bottle. While Shannon clutched at it with greedy little hands, Addy found herself wondering how they were ever going to find Daddy. And what would happen to them when he learned that Mama was dead?

*   *   *

The car pulled through the gates and glided along the driveway. Addy wiped at her burning eyes. It wouldn't do to let Sam or Jake see her crying. It was odd that even now, after all these years, the thought of her mother's death could bring tears to her eyes.

Maybe it was this old house, with a fence, and big rooms with windows overlooking the yard. Of course there wasn't any garden with white roses. In fact, there wasn't even a yard. Just a patch of brown earth. But to Mama, it would have been heaven.

She studied the peeling paint, the sagging fence. With hard work it could be the place of her mama's dreams.

"You go ahead in." Sam swung his long legs from the car. "I'll carry in the groceries."

"Thanks."

When she entered she saw Jake seated at the kitchen table. A deck of cards was in his hands.

"You made good time."

He was staring at her again, with that piercing look that made her think he could see clear through her.

Addy struggled to find her voice. "I got everything you asked for, Jake." She took the change from her pocket and placed it in front of him.

"Good. I can't wait to see what you'll fix for supper."

When Sam deposited the bags, Addy was happy to busy herself unloading them. That way she could cover her uneasiness around him.

"So what's for dinner?" Jake called.

She laughed. "You just finished eating breakfast a couple of hours ago."

"Yeah." Jake frowned and glanced at his watch. "I guess we do have a little while before suppertime." He shuffled the cards. "Hurry up and put the groceries away. We can get in a few hands before you have to stop and cook."

"Is that all you think of? Eating and playing cards?"

"No, kid. Winning. That's all I think of. Come on. I feel lucky. You and Sam can contribute to my retirement fund."

Chapter Six

Addy looked down from the chair on which she was standing to clean the bookshelf. When she caught sight of the lean, muscled man, her pulse rate accelerated.

"Hello, Sam."

"Addy." He felt a strong sexual tug and was annoyed. He'd managed to convince himself that he'd imagined it the first few times he'd come close to her. Now there was no doubt. He was definitely attracted to her. But it wasn't something he wanted to feel. Not about this woman. In fact, not about any woman. There was no room in his life for a permanent relationship. Ever again.

He glanced beyond her to where Jake sat. "Thought you'd need a stiff drink while I challenge you tonight."

"Good thinking." Jake turned. "Addy, why don't you get us some glasses and join us for a hand."

As he followed Jake to the kitchen, Sam glanced around in appreciation. With every passing hour of each day the place was improving. Although the furniture was the same, the house was different. There was a fresh, clean airyness about it that he'd never seen. Curtains billowed at the windows. The furniture gleamed under a coat of polish. There were fresh flowers in a vase on the kitchen table.

"The place looks good, Jake."

Jake frowned. "Addy walks behind me with a goddamned rag and disinfectant. I swear, the minute something gets dirty around here, she's there cleaning it."

"Am I hearing right? Are you actually complaining about somebody who likes to keep this dump clean?"

Jake bristled. "It's not a dump. Well, maybe it is.

55

But it's my goddamned dump. And I'll make a mess if I want."

Sam grinned. For all his doubts about the girl who'd taken charge of Jake's house, she seemed to be doing something right. He'd never seen Jake so lively. Still, he intended to reserve judgment a while longer. He was a man who took his time to study a person closely before putting on any labels. But once he did, he was rarely wrong. It was probably all those years of training and working undercover. Even now, when he'd turned his back on the department, he couldn't turn off the instincts. And all his instincts told him the girl was hiding a lot of secrets. He didn't intend to trust her yet. Especially with a friend like Jake Starr. Jake had endured enough pain for one lifetime. Hell, so had he. Maybe that's why he'd taken such an interest in the old rebel. Though he'd rather be at a casino somewhere, hearing the sound of voices murmuring around him, blurring the harsh edges of his isolation, he couldn't stand to see Jake so alone.

Chester leaped down from his perch on top of the refrigerator and made figure of eights around Sam's feet. Sam leaned down and scratched the old cat behind the ears until Chester's purrs filled the room like a rusty old engine.

Addy poured two glasses of whiskey and watched as Sam Money drank his in one quick swallow. Reminded of her father, she felt a flash of sudden irritation. No matter what he did to her heartbeat, she had no use for a drunk. She was determined to keep him at arm's length.

"I think I'll pass on cards today. You two play without me."

Sam felt himself relax when she left the room. At least for a while he'd be able to concentrate on the game.

*   *   *

Addy answered the bell to find a tall, bespectacled man standing at the front door. Despite the heat he wore a navy

56

blazer and tan, wrinkled slacks. His shirt was rumpled, his tie loosened. In his hand was a briefcase.

"I'm Milton Carver to see Jake and Sam."

"Hey, Milt. Come on in," Jake called behind her.

Addy moved aside and the man hurried across the room with his hand extended.

"How're you doing, Jake?"

"Not bad for an ornery old coot. Milt, this is Addy O'Brien. Addy, Milt is my accountant."

As the two shook hands Jake added, "And the most honest man on the face of this goddamned earth, next to Sam. Come on, Milt. We'll all work at the kitchen table."

Milton followed him to the kitchen, noting the changes in the house as he did. Dropping his briefcase on the table he snapped it open.

"Here're the monthlies. You're not going to like the latest figures."

Jake studied the papers carefully, handing each to Sam when he'd finished. He read quickly, stopping occasionally to question a figure. While Sam read, Jake said absently, "Addy, would you mind making a pot of coffee?"

Milt watched as the girl moved comfortably around the kitchen. He'd seen a parade of housekeepers come and go in the last couple of years. But none had done for this old place what this slip of a girl had managed to do.

A few minutes later Addy carried three cups to the table. Jake lifted a pair of reading glasses from his nose and rubbed his eyes. "I must need new glasses. These columns of figures are beginning to blur together."

"I'll read them to you." Sam took the paper from Jake's hand and quickly scanned it.

"No. Leave 'em. I'll have a go at them later. I saw the most important figure at the bottom. It was a hell of a lousy month."

"I don't know why business is down. This is the height of the tourist season. If figures are down now, what'll it be like when the tourists are gone, Jake?"

"You've been warning me for months that the place was falling apart. How bad is it?"

Milton stirred cream into his coffee and glanced at Sam before saying, "It's true that it's shabby. And compared with some of the casinos that are going up these days, it just can't compete. But it's always had its regular customers, plus those people who like the feel of a good, old-fashioned saloon. But Jake, what it really lacks is someone watching over it. Without you there, the figures are just going to keep sliding. Nobody else cares about the place like you."

Jake's tone was bleak. "Witherspoon's been warning me that I ought to sell it before it all goes to hell."

Milton drained his cup and stood, clapping a hand on Jake's shoulder. "I know how much you love that old place. I think instead of selling it, you ought to come back."

"You know I can't do that, Milt."

The accountant's voice was filled with sadness. "I'm sorry you feel that way, Jake." He turned to Addy. "Thanks for the coffee, Miss O'Brien. I'll let myself out." He shook hands with Sam.

When he heard the door shut, Jake picked up the papers and studied the figures again. Then he rolled his wheelchair into the living room and sat, staring out the window. Sam remained alone at the kitchen table, brooding.

* * *

Jake didn't show much interest in dinner, even though Addy had fixed stuffed pork chops and a fruit salad with fresh baked biscuits.

Across the table, Sam ate in silence, respecting Jake's obvious need to be left alone.

Addy tried three times to draw the two men into conversation, without success. Finally she decided to use a direct approach.

Turning to Jake she remarked, "I didn't know you

owned a business." She broke open a warm biscuit and spread it with butter.

"Not much of a business these days."

"What business are you in?"

He glanced up. "You mean Witherspoon never told you?"

Addy shrugged. "Why would he tell me that? He wasn't hiring me to work in your business."

"I just figured he'd have told you. It's an old saloon and casino."

"What do you call it?"

"What else? Jakes." He drained his cup and watched while she refilled it.

"Jakes. I like it. How come you never go there?"

"I haven't since . . ." He looked away. "It's been a couple of years."

"But why?"

"I don't want the regulars seeing me like this."

"Like what?"

"In a goddamned wheelchair." He tossed down his napkin. "I want them to remember me the way I used to be. Hell, I was the life of the party before all this." He pounded his fists on his deadened knees. "You think I want them to feel sorry for poor old Jake Starr?"

She couldn't picture anyone ever feeling sorry for a man as vital and alive as Jake. But she kept her thoughts to herself.

"Who's looking out for the business now?" She picked up the plates and headed for the sink.

"I've got good managers. Been with me for years."

"I guess it's not the same as having the owner there, looking out for his own business."

"Don't you think I know that?" He brought a hand down hard against the wheel and turned away, rolling slowly into the living room.

Addy glanced at Sam. He sat very still, watching her with a frown. Then he picked up his cup and made his way to the living room.

He was bothered by Addy's questions. There were too many women preying on old men with more money than brains. He'd never figured Jake Starr to be a fool. But, just in case, he'd be even more diligent about Addy in the future.

*　　*　　*

Addy took her time rinsing the dishes and loading the dishwasher. Then she took even more time scrubbing the sink and counter tops and the table.

She didn't need to know how Jake had been injured to know that it had hurt him much more deeply than he let on.

When he rolled back into the kitchen an hour later, she was seated at the table shuffling the deck of cards.

She looked up with a grin. "I'm feeling lucky tonight. How about you?"

He nodded and took his place across from her. Without a word Sam pulled out a chair and sat.

By the time the clock struck midnight, Jake's good humour had returned. It hadn't been hurt by the fact that he'd just won ten hands in a row.

"I've been keeping track of the matches, kid. Now that you're earning money, it's time we exchanged them for the real thing." His smile grew. "I know I'm going to enjoy our card games even more now that we're playing for cash."

When they'd tallied all the matchsticks, it turned out that Sam owed Addy fifty cents. He reached into his pocket and handed it to her with an admiring grin. "You caught on fast."

"I was always a fast learner."

She thought how handsome he was when he smiled. In the same instant she scolded herself for such thoughts. He was nothing more than a drunk. She turned to Jake. "You owe me two dollars and sixty-seven cents."

He tossed the money down on the table and turned his wheelchair away.

"You act like it's a thousand dollars," she said, counting it.

"Might as well be, kid. I hate losing."

She carefully folded the money and smiled as she bid them both goodnight.

* * *

"How're you at maths?" Jake asked.

Addy looked up from the clean clothes she was folding. "It was my favourite subject in school."

"Good. Take a look at these figures. See what you think."

Sam paused in the doorway. A tiny frown line appeared between his brows.

Addy scanned the first paper, mentally adding the columns of figures, then turned to the second page, and then the third. "What is this?"

"A printout of our volume of business for the past three years, showing the percentage of losses in each successive year."

"It doesn't take a maths whiz to figure out that you're losing money, Jake."

He nodded. "But look at the drop from last year to this year."

"Almost thirty percent. Are the other businesses in the area losing that heavily?"

"I don't keep up with them anymore. But from the rumours I've heard, I'd say the others are all up, not down."

"So it's just at Jakes."

"Yeah."

"I think you'd better talk to your managers."

"You sound like Sam." Jake glanced toward the figure in the doorway, who turned away. A moment later the back door slammed.

"What the hell am I supposed to say to them? One of you guys is on the take?" He gave a bitter laugh. "If they weren't stealing from me before, they will be after I accuse them of it."

"What else can you do?"

"Resign myself to less profit." He took the papers from her hands and turned away.

Addy watched him stare broodingly out the window. She was going to have to find a way to get him out of this house and back into the world he'd left behind. But how?

She went off in search of Sam and found him on the back porch, repairing a squeaky hinge.

He looked up as she approached.

In the heat of the day he'd taken off his shirt. She stared at the dark hair that covered his chest and dipped to below his waist. As he struggled with the heavy door, she watched as his muscles bunched and tightened. Seeing him like this gave her a funny feeling in the pit of her stomach. It was unlike anything she'd ever felt.

Sam worked without acknowledging her. He needed the release of hard, physical labour. The thoughts he was entertaining were too dark, too confusing. He resented Jake's trust of this woman. More and more, the old man was taking her into his confidence.

When he was through he mopped his forehead, then turned to her and leaned a hip against the porch railing. "I don't think you came out here just to watch me work."

"You're right. I wanted to talk to you about Jake. Why won't he leave the house?"

"It's pretty hard to do in his condition."

"Come on, Sam. There are plenty of people in wheelchairs who live a normal life. Why is Jake a prisoner here?"

He took his time pulling on his shirt. She watched as he tucked it into the waistband of his pants. When he looked up he saw the way her gaze was locked onto him. Her cheeks darkened.

"I guess you'll have to ask Jake."

"I'm asking you."

"Jake Starr is a proud man. I guess he doesn't want anyone staring at him, making him feel like less a man than before his accident."

Addy seized on the one word. "Tell me about his accident."

"Nothing much to tell. He was struck by a car when he left Jake's one night. When he came to, the doctors told him he'd never walk again."

She started to turn away, then turned back to ask, "Where do you fit into this?"

Sam opened the door and seemed to take a long time studying the hinge before closing it. Turning his head he said, "I like to play poker. I figured Jake needed a partner."

"But what are you to Jake?"

"I hope I'm a friend."

"A friend? Or a leech who likes to drink his whiskey?"

His reaction was instinctive. Without thinking he caught her arm. Instantly he realized his mistake. She hated being touched. But her skin was so incredibly soft. "You'd like to drive a wedge between us, wouldn't you?" he growled, "Then you'd have the old guy right where you wanted him. Alone. Defenceless. Then you'd have it all."

He saw the way she flinched. But instead of pulling away, his perverse nature made him keep his hand on her arm, though his earlier anger was forgotten. His voice was low with feeling. "Okay, Addy, who was he?"

Her head came up sharply. "What do you mean by that?"

"You know exactly what I mean." His tone softened. "You wouldn't flinch like that unless you expected to be hurt every time somebody touched you. Who did that to you?"

When she refused to answer, he clenched his teeth. What the hell was the matter with him? This girl and her past were none of his business. Jake was his only concern.

He dropped his hand to his side. He had to put some distance between them. In fact, he'd have to see that he gave her a very wide berth.

He opened the door and walked inside, leaving Addy alone on the porch.

Even after he was gone, she could still feel the imprint of his fingers on her flesh. She drew her arms tightly around herself and leaned weakly against the porch.

*   *   *

Jake looked up as Addy pulled on an oversized yellow rainjacket she had found in a hall closet.

"Where are you going?"

"To the bank and the store."

"In this storm? Are you crazy?"

"I've collected my first week's paycheck. I want to open an acount at the bank. Besides, we're out of eggs and milk and bread and . . ."

"I wouldn't care if the cupboards were completely bare and we were starving to death. In case you haven't been paying attention, that's thunder and lightning out there, kid. It's not the time for a goddamned romantic walk in the rain."

"I need to open a bank account. It's important to me."

His eyes narrowed. "You're a greedy little thing. I don't know why you couldn't have waited until Monday to get that paycheck."

"It's been a week, Jake. The contract said I'd be paid two hundred dollars a week. That's today. And I want it in the bank where it's safe."

"If somebody breaks in and steals it, I'll make it up to you."

"That's not the point. I want to have my own bankbook, and watch the amount grow."

"Not today. Tomorrow.

"Today."

"At least wait until this storm passes. Sam should be back by then. He can drive you."

"No. I need too many things at the store. I can't wait until the storm blows over. It may last all night." Her tone deepened with anger. "And you never know when Sam will come back. Sometimes he doesn't come back until morning." She pulled open the back door and stalked outside.

Inside, Jake watched her go and turned the air blue with curses. By the time she'd returned an hour later, he had worked himself into a rage.

"You're the only goddamned female in the whole country who doesn't know how to drive a car. And we're going to change all that tomorrow."

"What do you mean?"

"I mean that you're going to learn how to drive. I'm going to teach you."

"You? How can you . . . .?"

"Before I was confined to these goddamned wheels I knew how to drive. And just because I don't drive anymore doesn't mean I've forgotten how. Tomorrow morning, kid, you and I are going for a ride."

Addy removed the dripping coat and turned away to hide the smile that tugged at her lips. This wasn't at all what she had planned. But it would have the same result. Whether or not he knew it yet, Jake Starr was about to rejoin the real world.

*   *   *

"The first thing I'm doing Monday morning is calling a contractor to come over here and build a ramp for this porch."

"He'll want a fortune."

"I don't care."

"That's just the heat and exhaustion talking. Tomorrow you'll forget all about this."

Addy pushed the wheelchair frantically while Jake's

muscles strained against the porch railing, until, at last, they had made it down the stairs. Both their faces were flushed with sweat.

"I don't know why Sam picked today to be gone," Addy complained.

"Sam has a life. Just because he spends a little time with me doesn't mean he owes me anything."

"But he didn't come home last night, either."

It crossed Jake's mind that Addy spent entirely too much time thinking about Sam. "What Sam Money does is none of our business. Now quit your fussing and push me to the passenger side of the car. I can get myself inside."

"You'd better take a few minutes to rest."

"Push the goddamned chair, Addy, and quit arguing."

With a hiss of anger she pushed his chair around the car that was layered with dust and grime. But all the dirt in the world couldn't hide the fact that it was a Mercedes. A very sleek, very expensive Mercedes.

"When's the last time this car was driven?" she asked.

"Whenever the last housekeeper quit."

Addy opened the door. After long minutes of struggle Jake managed to settle himself inside.

"Get in the car," he ordered.

Addy hurried around and climbed in the driver's side.

"Now first you fasten your seat belt."

"I know that much."

"Don't get lippy. Just do it."

Addy fastened her belt while Jake fastened his. She noticed that his hands were trembling, and blamed it on the exertion of getting into the car.

"Those dials on the dashboard tell you everything that's going on under the hood."

"I don't care what goes on under there. I only care whether or not I can keep this car in the right lane."

"But you have to pay attention to everything on that dashboard. It'll tell you how much gas you have, how fast you're going, whether or not you need oil, even whether the engine's overheating."

"Look, Jake . . ."

"Shut up, kid. Now, turn the key."

Addy did as she was told and listened as the engine purred.

"Put it in reverse."

Addy moved the gearshift and stepped on the gas. The car shot backward so hard they felt their necks snap.

"Gooddamn it. You almost backed into the fence. Keep that foot off the gas pedal and shift into drive."

Addy did as she was told. The car crept forward.

"Now put your foot down gently."

She stepped down on the pedal and the car jerked forward. Instantly she hit the brake and the car stopped so abruptly it stalled. "Now look what you made me do."

"Slow and easy, kid. Remember that. Slow and easy. Now try again."

Jake gripped the edge of the door and waited while Addy started the car and shifted into drive. She cleared the open gate and pulled onto the street. But at the corner, when she saw a car coming toward her, she panicked and hit the brakes again, causing a car behind her to skid to a screeching halt.

She sat there trembling while the approaching car passed and the car behind her swerved around her, the driver shaking his fist and yelling obscenities. She was outraged. "Did you hear what he said?"

"Yeah. My sentiments exactly. Only he said them nicer than I would have. Now, kid. Pay attention. You can't just stop dead in the middle of the street, or you're going to cause an accident. Got it?"

She nodded.

"Now start again. And this time, no matter what, keep the car going in a nice straight line. Think you can do that?"

Addy started up again. This time she made it the length of the block. At Jake's command she turned right and proceeded another block or two before he ordered her to turn left, into oncoming traffic. She waited until a car, nearly a block away, had passed. Then, just as she started to make her turn, she saw a truck heading their way. She jammed her foot down on the accelerator and the car shot through the intersection and screeched along the street for half a block.

"Slow down, goddammit, or I swear, Addy, I'll jump out right here."

Addy slowly brought the car to a reasonable speed. Then, trembling, she pulled to the curb and turned off the ignition. Her hands were shaking. So were Jake's.

"I'm no good at this, Jake. I just wasn't meant to drive."

"For Christsake, kid. Everybody has to learn. You're doing fine." He struggled to pry his fingers from the door handle, where they were frozen in place from gripping it so hard. "Now start again. And this time, you find your own way home. I'll just sit here and keep my mouth shut."

Addy took a deep breath and started the engine. When the traffic cleared she eased away from the curb and started along the street. She drove for nearly a mile before she was forced to merge into a double lane of heavy traffic. For a minute she felt a rush of panic. But then, with a glance at the man seated silently beside her, she managed to keep the car between the lines. And though several cars blew their horns in frustration at the slow-moving vehicle in front of them, she managed to keep her wits about her and turn at the street that would lead to Jake's house.

When she started to pull up at the curb Jake said tersely, "Might as well drive to the back door. I've got to face that goddamned chair again."

Addy swung the car through the gate and felt the scrape of metal against the passenger door as she misjudged the distance between the car and the opening.

"Oh dear. Sorry." She chanced a look at Jake, but though his mouth was a grim tight line, he said nothing. "Would you like me to . . .?"

"Keep going. It's too late to do anything about it now."

Addy swung the car around to the back porch, barely missing Jake's wheelchair. When she turned off the ignition, they both sat silently for several long minutes.

It was Addy who finally broke the silence. "Thanks for the lesson, Jake. But I just don't think I was meant to drive. I'm sorry about the gate. If you know somebody who can fix the car door, you can take it out of my wages."

"Help me into my chair, Addy."

She handed him the keys and got out of the car. By the time she had his wheelchair in position, he was struggling to lift himself from the seat. Once he was in the chair she pushed him to the porch, where he spent nearly ten minutes struggling hand-over-hand to the top, where Addy stood waiting with his chair. It took her even longer to manipulate the heavy wheelchair through the narrow doorway and over the threshhold. When they were finally in the kitchen, they both felt exhausted from the effort.

"That does it," Jake said, slamming his hand down on the arm of his chair. "That goddamned does it."

"Does what?"

They both turned toward the porch, where Sam was just coming up the steps.

With a streak of curses Jake rolled to the living room.

"What's Jake so hot about?" Sam asked, strolling into the kitchen.

Addy sank down into a chair and wiped the sweat from her brow. "We've been out for a drive," she said.

"What?" Sam stopped in his tracks to stare at her.

"Well, I drove and Jake barked orders. But I don't think I was cut out to drive. It was one of the most frightening things I've ever done. And I never want to do it again."

Sam shot her an incredulous look. "Jake actually left this house and went with you in the car?"

She nodded, feeling the trembling in her legs begin to subside. "Yeah. So much for all my wonderful dreams of getting Jake out of the house. After a day like this, I'm sure he'll never venture out again."

Sam found himself looking at her with new respect. Addy had just done what no one else had been able to accomplish. She'd persuaded the prisoner that there were no bars on his cell. Maybe, he thought with sudden interest, he'd stick around a while longer, just to see what other surprises she had up her sleeve.

Chapter Seven

Addy watched as an old battered car turned up the drive-way. The man who alighted wore a rumpled suit the colour of mud. He reached across the seat and picked up a bulging black bag, then turned and walked to the porch. He was slightly stoop-shouldered, and his stomach protruded so far over his pants he couldn't button his jacket. He climbed the stairs and knocked on the front door.

"Hello." Glancing at the bag Addy asked, "Are you Jake's doctor?"

"Yep. Boyd Wilton. And you are . . .?"

"Addy O'Brien. Nice to meet you, Doctor Wilton. Jake's in the kitchen."

He moved past her with surprising grace.

"So, what've you been up to, Jake?" he called in greeting.

"Not a hell of a lot. How about you, Boyd?"

"Same as ever. Everybody I see is sick or dying."

"Not around here they aren't. I'm fit as a fiddle."

"I'll be the judge of that. Give me your arm." Without further small talk the doctor wrapped a blood-pressure cuff around Jake's upper arm and proceeded to test him.

"Pressure's high, but that's nothing new. You were always excitable, Jake."

"Especially when you beat a pair of aces with three lousy fours."

The doctor chuckled as Jake asked softly, "How high?"

"Too high. You been taking your medicine?"

Addy's mouth dropped open. Jake hadn't said a word to her about any medicine. She'd never seen him swallow

71

a pill of any kind. Unless he counted the nightly cigar and whiskey as medicine.

"'Course I am. Now what the hell else to you want to check?"

Doctor Wilton shot a glance at Addy, then back at Jake. "I guess we'll do the rest in the bedroom, for the sake of privacy."

"Just make it quick, goddamnit. I've got things to do."

"Like what?"

Jake shrugged. "I stay busy."

"Yep. I can see that. Let's go." With the doctor following, Jake wheeled himself past Addy and into the bedroom.

The doctor closed the door and Addy busied herself at the kitchen sink. But even with the door closed she could hear Doctor Wilton's voice raised in righteous anger. "I've warned you about the dangers of eating everything you want, Jake. You knew one of these days it would catch up with you. A man in your situation should be drinking at least eight glasses of water a day."

"If I did, I'd be spending the whole goddamned day in the bathroom."

"Your kidneys are delicate, Jake. I'm telling you . . ."

"Delicate, my ass. You listen to me, Boyd Wilton. There's nothing delicate about this body."

"You've been damaged, Jake. You aren't the man you were before the accident. You need to . . ."

"Cut the crap, Boyd. Are you through?"

Addy heard the door open and turned to see Jake wheel through the doorway. Behind him, the doctor's face was flushed from shouting.

"You ought to get out of this mausoleum, Jake."

"Where the hell would I go?"

The doctor lifted his shoulders. "I don't care if you just wheel up and down the street. At least you'd be away from these four walls for a few hours."

"I think you're the one who needs to go for a walk,

Boyd. Look at you. With Ellen gone you've forgotten how to laugh."

Boyd Wilton brightened. "That woman could make me forget all the misery of the day with a single word."

"Yeah." Jake's tone softened. "Ellen was one of a kind, Boyd. You were lucky to have had her for all those years."

"Forty-two years we were married. And I still miss her every day." He turned to Jake. "I don't care if you don't want to hear it, I'm going to give you some advice anyway. Get out of this house, Jake. You've locked yourself away long enough."

"Get lost, Boyd. Go and inflict your stethescope and your goddamned needles and your little vials of poison on some other poor unsuspecting jerk. But don't bother me for another month."

Boyd Wilton turned to Addy. "It was nice meeting you, Miss O'Brien. I won't tell you to take good care of Jake. I know that's a mountain no one could climb. But take care of yourself."

He gave her a warm smile and walked to the door. Without turning he called, "Eight glasses of water a day, Jake. Your new prescription is on your night table."

As soon as he was gone, Addy raced into Jake's bedroom and shoved the prescription into her pocket. She would pick up his medicine tomorrow and find a way to make him take it. Along with eight glasses of water a day. Even if he threatened murder.

*   *   *

Addy awoke to the sound of hammering. She glanced at the clock on her nightstand and saw that it was only nine o'clock. What could Jake be pounding at nine on a Monday morning? He'd taught her the intricacies of dice until nearly four o'clock. She'd expected him to sleep until at least noon.

The pounding was louder now. Padding to the window

she peered outside and saw a truck parked in the driveway. A team of workmen swarmed around the house, measuring, sawing, hammering.

"What in the world . . .?" Addy watched as a man in overalls took a swipe at the front of the house with a sledgehammer. The old house shuddered at the assault.

Dressing quickly, Addy hurried down the stairs. A peek in Jake's room showed him to be sound asleep, oblivious to the noise outside his window.

She glanced up as Sam strode down the stairs. His hair was mussed, his lower face darkened with a shaggy growth of beard. His eyes were still heavy-lidded from sleep. The whole effect was strangely appealing, and Addy had to struggle to keep from staring.

"What's going on?" he asked.

"That's what I intend to find out." Addy opened the front door and stepped around two men who were measuring the front porch.

Sam trailed behind her.

"Who's in charge here?"

"I am." A burly man in jeans and a denim jacket looked up from a blueprint he was studying. "What can I do for you, miss?"

"What are you doing here?"

"Ramping your porches, ma'am."

"Did Mr. Witherspoon order this?"

"No, ma'am. Mr. Starr."

"Jake?" Addy turned in time to see the surprised expression on Sam's face.

"What is that man doing?" Addy pointed.

"We're taking out the doors, ma'am. They're not wide enough to accomodate a wheelchair. We'll replace them with wider doorways and new doors. And we're going to have to take down this entire porch. The wood's rotted clear through. You're lucky somebody didn't break a leg on this old thing."

As the foreman walked away, Addy and Sam watched for a few minutes more, then made their way inside. In the kitchen, Addy glanced out the window and realized that another crew was at work on the back porch.

She filled the coffee pot and then, with a feeling of dread, glanced at the car keys hanging beside the back door. Following the direction of her gaze, Sam read her thoughts.

"If Jake's going to all this expense, it looks like there's no way you'll get out of learning to drive now."

"Yeah."

Sam watched as she sank down in a chair and listened to the pounding going on outside. Her troubling thoughts were transparent.

"This is what you wanted, isn't it?"

She nodded. "A chance to get Jake out of this house and back into the world he'd left behind. But I hadn't really thought it through. It never occurred to me that driving could be so terrifying. Still," she mused as she got to her feet, "if I want to ease Jake back into his old life, I'd better get used to the idea. If it kills me, I'll learn to drive that car."

She dragged out the blackened skillet and began to chop vegetables and grate cheese. "I'd better make Jake the best darned breakfast he'd ever had. I think he's going to need it before this day is over."

"If that's the case, you'd better let me help."

"You cook?" Addy's brow arched.

In his best falsetto Sam said, "You just set the table, dearie, and leave the omelette to me."

* * *

For days the house was rocked by the sound of electric saws and drills. Workmen invaded, removing doors and parts of the walls.

Jake was so pleased by the changes, he actually had Addy push him outside to look over the house. That was when he became aware of the shocking difference between the old house and the new additions. The new

75

wood gleamed richly in the sun. The old peeling paint on the rest of the house looked ever more shabby by comparison. He decided then and there to have the entire house sanded and painted.

"With all that new lumber out here, I might as well clean up the whole thing. What do you think, Sam?"

They were in the yard, watching as the workmen put the finishing touches on the back porch. Addy and Sam had stood back while Jack manoeuvered his wheelchair down the front porch ramp all by himself. His face was flushed and happy with success.

"Sure, Jake. Why not?"

Addy was already mentally planting flowers and grass. "What about the fence?"

"What about it?"

She shrugged. "I just thought you might want it repaired and painted while they're here."

The foreman's eyes brightened as he calculated how much more his crew could earn. "It wouldn't be much of a job, Mr. Starr. I think for about five hundred more we could make it as good as new."

"Five hundred's too much. Make it three hundred."

"Four-fifty," the foreman said.

"Four hundred."

"Done."

Jake winked at Addy before turning his attention to the foreman. "Go ahead then. But that's it. I want everything finished by the end of the week."

"You got it, Mr. Starr." The foreman walked off to speak to his men.

Seeing the smug, happy look on Addy's face, Jake reached into his pocket and held up a set of keys. "I figured, since we're already outside, we may as well take advantage of it. Did you read that booklet I gave you the other day?"

"The one the state gives out to new drivers? Yeah."

"Good. Let's go for a ride. It's time you got your driver's license."

Addy groaned. "I knew the day was too good to last."

He turned his wheelchair toward the car. "You think you've got it bad, kid. I'll probably be canonized as a goddamned saint for putting my life on the line like this. How about you, Sam? Want to go along for the ride?"

"No, thanks. I don't think I could stand any more excitement."

"Coward."

Trailing along behind Jake, Addy missed the gleam of laughter in his eyes.

*   *   *

Addy saw the red Porsche pull up in the driveway and dried her hands on a kitchen towel. She reached the front door just as the doorbell rang.

On the porch stood Andrew Witherspoon, looking tanned and fit. And extremely puzzled.

"Hello, Addy. What in the world has happened here?"

She smiled. "Ramps. For Jake."

"Ramps? A gross understatement, my dear. I didn't even recognize the place. Where is Jake?"

"Out back. Arguing with the landscaper."

"Landscaper?" The lawyer burst into laughter. "I don't believe it."

Addy watched as he strolled through the house, admiring the changes as he went. With the front door widened, the workmen had taken out a small window as well, replacing it with floor-to-ceiling glass that filled the room with light.

Witherspoon paused at the back door as Jake easily rolled his chair through the new wider opening.

"What's going on, Jake?"

"Start a fresh pot of coffee, Addy," Jake called to her. To his lawyer he said smugly, "Made a few changes in the old place. How's it look?"

"Wonderful. But aren't you the guy who told me you'd

never allow a ramp, because that would shout to the whole world that a 'cripple' lived here?"

Jake removed three cigars from his pocket and offered one to Sam and one to Witherspoon.

"Let the dumb bastards say what they want about the old coot who lives here. What the hell do I care?"

"But how did all of this come about?" the lawyer persisted.

"I had to teach Addy to drive. And it was too much hassle getting up and down that goddamned porch. I had no choice," Jake said, pulling the wrapper from the cigar.

"Wouldn't it have been cheaper to call a cab?"

Sam chuckled. "Yeah. But not nearly as challenging."

"And the fresh paint?" Andrew took a chair and leaned over, holding a light to the other two cigars and then to his own.

Ignoring the sarcasm, Jake grinned. "Figured, since I had the crew here, I might as well get my money's worth."

Andrew drew on the Havana, enjoying the smooth, rich taste. Jake was such a contradiction. He drank the cheapest whiskey, but insisted on smoking the most expensive cigars. He wouldn't spend two cents on new clothes, but he insisted on a new Mercedes every year, even though he hadn't driven in over three years, since his accident. And now he was remodeling a house in an old seedy neighbourhood, when it would be cheaper to sell and move to a brand new, barrier free apartment in an upscale neighbourhood.

"Coffee, Mr. Witherspoon?" Addy asked.

"Thanks, Addy." Andrew leaned back, studying the old man in the wheelchair. "And the landscaper? Did he just happen to be working nearby, too?"

"Naw. That was sort of an accident." Jake glanced at Addy's back as she filled another cup. "You see, Addy kept running all over the goddamned yard with the car. And I realized she needed straight lines."

"I'm afraid I still don't understand." The lawyer glanced from Jake's face to Sam's.

Addy's cheeks, Sam noted, had reddened considerably.

"After a rain, Addy buried the wheels in mud. It took a goddamned wrecker to pull her out. So I decided she needed a lot more driveway." Jake pointed to the ribbon of concrete that now lined the driveway and back yard. "And some areas of green grass to show her where she shouldn't drive."

"Amazing." Andrew Witherspoon smoked his cigar and drank his coffee, and marvelled at the changes wrought in the short time since the girl's arrival.

"You'd better hope Jake never decides to teach Addy to fly." Sam grinned as Addy's cheeks took on a becoming shade of scarlet. "Or the whole town might get a facelift."

They all shared a laugh.

"You didn't come here to admire my house," Jake said, "What's up?"

Andrew set his cigar in an ashtray and snapped open his briefcase. "I have some rather interesting news. I was approached by a group of businessmen who'd like to buy Jake's."

With his head bent he missed the way Jake's mouth dropped open. But Sam saw it.

"They've asked me to present their offer." Witherspoon lifted out a sheaf of documents and handed them to Jake, who chomped down hard on his cigar.

"I might add, it's a very generous offer, considering the condition of the place."

Jake set the documents on the table without reading them. "Why didn't they contact me directly?"

The lawyer shrugged. "Maybe they've heard of your reputation as a tough-talking businessman, Jake, and they were afraid of dealing with you. Or maybe they just thought they ought to do it through legal channels. At any rate, they've set a time limit on their offer. It's good for one month. After that, they'll make a similar offer to another small-time casino owner nearby. But I happen to know that yours is the one they really want."

"Should I be flattered?"

The lawyer smiled. "It's a good offer, Jake. A damned good offer. They'll pay you more money than you could spend in a lifetime."

Jake snorted. "I've already got more money than I can spend in two lifetimes. One month, you say?"

Andrew Witherspoon finished his coffee and closed his briefcase. "I have to run, Jake. Call me when you've had a chance to look over their offer."

He shook hands with Sam and then glanced toward Addy. "I'll let myself out."

When the front door closed behind him, and the Porsche roared up the street, she turned to study Jake. He was sitting very still, smoke curling over his head. The documents were lying on the table. He made no move to read them.

*   *   *

"Jake wants the monthlies, Milt." Sam's tone was brisk. He cradled the phone between his ear and shoulder, holding a pen and paper in his hands. After a moment he handed the phone to Jake.

"I know it isn't the end of the month yet, goddammit. But I want the figures you have so far." Jake listened a minute, then snapped, "Yeah, you could say something's come up. Read them to me."

He wrote furiously, then listened, then wrote again. "Thanks, Milt. We'll see you next week as usual."

Addy watched as he replaced the phone and sat staring at the paper.

"Bad news, Jake?" Sam asked.

"Nothing I didn't expect."

"Profits are down again?"

"I knew they wouldn't start to climb. But I never figured them to be down this much."

80

In an effort to distract him, Addy picked up the deck of cards but he waved her away. "Not tonight, kid. Got too much on my mind."

Addy went out to the kitchen and picked up the brochures left by the landscaper. Pouring herself a cup of coffee she began to leaf through the pages, planning the white roses she would plant around the base of the house and around the big pine tree in the back yard. The landscape architect had told her to stick to hardy plants native to Nevada, that could withstand the hot sun. But she could see only roses. White roses like the ones her mother had always loved.

She pushed back her chair and returned to the living room. Jake was still staring at the darkness beyond the window. Sam sat in the corner, nursing a glass of whiskey.

"How far is Jake's from here?" Addy asked without taking time to think.

"Couple of miles."

"Let's go."

"What?" Jake turned to look at her. "Now?"

"I just want to see it. In the dark. I saw all the lights of the bars and casinos when I got off the bus. They lit up the sky. Does it have bright lights like the big casinos?"

"Naw. There's a sign. A small one. But that's all."

"Come on, Jake. I want to see it."

"Hell." He sat a few moments longer. "Okay." He rolled his chair toward the back door. "But just for a minute. I don't want anyone to see me. Come on, Sam."

Reluctantly Sam drained his glass and followed them.

When they were in the car, Addy turned the key and hesitated a moment, fiddling with the switch for the headlights. She'd never driven after dark. She was already beginning to wish she'd taken more time to think this through.

"What's wrong, kid?"

"Nothing."

She took a deep breath and engaged the gearshift. When

the car started rolling, she prayed she'd make it through the newly widened gate. That accomplished, she stared at the white lines that seemed to leap up at her in the darkness.

She had to keep reminding herself that she was doing this for Jake. Otherwise, she'd turn around and head back to the safety of the big old house.

In the back seat, Sam sat back, determined not to interfere. It would have been a simple matter to take the keys from her and insist on driving. They'd all have relaxed more. But Addy needed to do this, if she was ever going to get rid of her fear of driving.

He studied the two slender hands gripping the wheel, and found himself wondering what they'd feel like on his skin.

Dangerous thoughts, he realized. He needed a drink.

*　　*　　*

"There it is."

Addy pulled over and stared at the wooden saloon with the gaudy yellow, red and green neon sign that flashed the word "Jake's".

"My gosh, Jake. You can see it for miles."

"Yeah." His voice was rough. He cleared his throat. "Location, kid. That's everything in this business. This corner is the choicest location in all of Reno. The Interstate dumps all the traffic here. You can't get in or out of this town without passing Jake's."

"Is that why you built it here?"

"Hell," he said with a laugh. "I didn't build it. I won it."

"You did? How?" She turned to him with a smile and watched his face in the glow of the neon.

"It was nineteen forty-five. Found myself in a high-stakes poker game. There used to be a mansion up on that hill. It's gone now." He pointed and Addy peered through the darkness, but could see nothing.

"When the game started, there were a dozen of us. A bank president, a smart-ass young lawyer who later went on to become Governor of Nevada, a bunch of successful businessmen from the area, and me. I was twenty-five years old and full of piss and vinegar. I never doubted I could beat every man in that room. I guess that's why I kept on playing." He leaned back, caught up in the memories.

"The game started at nine o'clock. By midnight six of the players had dropped out. By three in the morning, there were only two of us left. Me and old Horace Belcher. I had slowly won a few bets until finally, all the money was piled up in front of me. It was more money than I'd ever had at one time. Another man would have quit while he was ahead. But I couldn't. You see, Horace owned a couple of girlie joints, and I always thought it'd be fun to own one. So, on the last hand, when he didn't have enough to match the bet, I told him if he'd throw in one of his sporting houses, I'd put up the whole jackpot. Everybody knew Horace was a greedy man. I knew he couldn't resist the chance to win back all that money."

"But you could have lost everything."

"It wouldn't have been the first time." Jake shook his head. "After the deal I got a little bit worried. I knew he was holding a pair of kings."

"How could you know that, Jake?"

"Intuition, kid. He was sitting loose and easy, the way a man does when he's confident of winning. I'd caught sight of the edge of one king when he picked up his cards. Figured he had to have a pair of 'em."

"Were you sitting on a pair of aces?" Addy asked.

"Hell no. The highest card in my hand was a six of clubs. So when he fattened the pot and discarded three, I did the same, holding on to the six and a two. Every man at that table watched while Horace dealt me three cards and gave himself three, too."

"What did you get, Jake?"

A slow, satisfied grin spread across his face. "The highest card in my hand was still the six of clubs."

"Then you lost."

"No, kid. I won. The jackpot. And Horace's girlie saloon."

"You beat a pair of kings?"

"Yeah," he said with a low rumble of laughter. "I laid down a six, five, four, three, and deuce. Of clubs." He laughed again, his spirits definitely higher than an hour ago, and Sam joined in.

When they fell silent again, Jake said, "How about it, Sam? You going in? Or do you want to go back and play against the toughest poker player in Reno?"

"You're on," Sam said. "I never could walk away from a challenge."

Jake turned to Addy. "Okay, kid. You've seen Jake's. Now let's go home."

Chapter Eight

"What's this?"

Jake stabbed at a piece of green vegetable on his plate.

"Broccoli. The store had a special. Ninety-nine cents."

"I can see why. That's the only way they can get rid of it. Even Chester wouldn't eat that stuff."

"Cats don't eat vegetables."

"They're smarter than I thought."

"You don't have to eat it," Addy said, lifting a forkful to her mouth. "I'll just toss it out with the garbage."

Sam held his silence and watched the two of them. Addy played the old man like a fish on a line. She knew her threat would work. She'd learned that the one thing Jake Starr hated most was waste.

Jake swallowed the hated vegetable in three bites.

"That's goddamned disgusting."

"You know you like it. Besides, it's better for you than that steak."

"Listen, kid. I've been eating steak and potatoes for as long as I could afford them. Even before I could afford them. And there's nothing wrong with my health that two good legs and a new spine couldn't fix."

Addy's interest was piqued. Jake rarely mentioned his infirmity. Seeing the question that formed on her lips, he immediately changed the subject.

"What's for dessert?"

"Strawberry shortcake." She pushed away from the table and returned with three glass bowls filled with angel food cake topped with fresh strawberries and mounds of white confection. Addy didn't bother to tell Jake that it was fat-free, sugar-free frozen yogurt instead of ice cream. But it was a ploy to get him to eat fruit.

"Goddamn it, if I don't think I died and went to heaven."

Jake dug into his shortcake, unaware of the way Addy winced at his words.

"If you keep on swearing like that, you'll never get to heaven," she said sternly.

He looked up, his eyes narrowed on her. "You think I give a good goddamn whether or not I go to heaven?"

"You ought to. My mama said . . ."

She stopped, realizing what she'd just revealed.

Jake grinned. She was as tightlipped about her early life as he was. "Go ahead, kid. I don't think quoting your mother is quite the same as spilling your guts about your life story."

She swallowed and glanced at Sam, who was watching her carefully.

"Well, my mama used to say that the only way we'd see all the people we loved was by going to heaven. In that other place . . ."

"You can say it. Hell," Jake put in.

"Yes. In hell, nobody will recognize anybody else. That's what'll make it hell. Even if you walk up to your own mother, you'll just walk right on by without ever knowing who she was."

Jake fell silent. Strange, but he'd never heard that before. And he thought he'd heard everything.

"What else did your mama teach you?"

"That people who swear are just too lazy to find a better way to express their anger."

"Sounds like you had a smart mama, kid. But there's another reason for swearing. Where I grew up, that was the only way anybody talked. It's the only way I know."

He leaned back, sipping strong coffee.

A rare smile touched Sam's lips. Jake was about to launch into a story from his past. Though he'd heard most of them, Sam never tired of hearing them again.

"I came out here in the spring of nineteen-twenty-seven. I was seven years old, and I already knew more about hustling than most men learn in a lifetime. My father was a gambler. He made his living going from town to town, ranch to ranch, hustling anybody with a buck."

"What about your mother?"

He shook his head. "My mother left us somewhere between Houston and Dallas. Thought she'd found herself a big-time rancher who'd give her a better life than the one she was stuck with."

"She didn't take you with her?"

"Me?" He gave a snort of laughter. "I was my father's son. Didn't want anything to do with my mother or her rancher. So my daddy just said good riddance to her and off we went to find bigger fish in Nevada. And we found plenty of 'em. Why, kid, this was virgin territory."

"What did you do while your father gambled?"

"Anything I could. Hustled a free meal or a free bed. I sat in on the games and watched for cheaters. Kept an eye on anyone going to his pocket for a card or maybe a gun."

"A gun?" She paused in the act of refilling his cup.

He grinned. "This was still a wide open wilderness, kid. Every man in Nevada carried a gun. Even me."

"But you said you were only seven."

"Some kids grow up fast." He grew silent for a moment, thinking about the girl across the table. In some ways she seemed much younger than twenty-one. But in a lot of other ways she was old beyond her years. She'd probably been old at seven.

"That's how my father finally died," he said softly. "At the end of a gun."

"Somebody shot him?"

He nodded. "Took me better'n two weeks to find the bastard. He was hiding out at a cabin high in the Sierras. Tracked him through the snow with nothing but a pair of Indian moccasins and a thin jacket to keep out the cold. Never been so cold in my life. Thought I'd freeze to death.

But I knew one thing. I wasn't going to die until I kept the vow I'd made before God and every man in that town. I vowed to make him pay for what he did to my father."

"You killed him?"

Jake set down his coffee cup and met her shocked look squarely. "Yes."

She turned to Sam. His hand had tightened around the stem of his glass. But he said nothing.

"Do you believe this?"

He nodded. "There are some things a man has to be willing to kill for, Addy. Or to die for."

It was probably the longest sentence Sam had uttered in her presence. She had the distinct impression he wasn't just talking about Jake. She was silent for a moment. Then she turned back to Jake and asked softly, "How old were you?"

"Thirteen." An intense look came into his eyes. A look of pain and something more. "Nobody ever treated me like a boy again. They knew me to be a man of my word. And in the seventy-two years I've been on this earth, I've never broken a promise."

For long moments the only sound in the room was the sigh of the wind in the trees. Then Jake waved a hand at the clutter of dishes and picked up a deck of cards.

"Clear the table, kid. I'm feeling lucky tonight."

* * *

The cards were good to Jake. And, as always, that made him mellow. He felt like talking tonight. Maybe one reason was because he had an audience. Sam had always listened to his stories. And now Addy. She was easy to talk to. In a lot of ways, he realized, she was like him.

"I can see now, in hindsight," Jake said, picking up the hand Addy dealt him, "that my father had a lot of flaws. Of course, when I was a boy, I'd have fought any man who suggested such a thing. But now, looking back, I can see more clearly. In a lot of ways, I was the strong one, because I had no choice. It was a matter of survival. You know?"

Addy nodded her head. If Jake only knew how much his words touched a chord inside her.

Across the table, Sam watched and listened.

"I was always out hustling. For food, a place to stay the night, someone who'd take us in when we needed clean or mended clothes. For some reason, my father never gave a thought to those things. He just cared about the next game, the next challenge. So I became the sensible one. I was his eyes, his ears." Jake chuckled. "His goddamned conscience."

Jake watched as Addy shuffled.

"I remember one night, I must have been about eight years old, and I fell asleep in the corner of the saloon while my father was engaged in a high-stakes poker game. When I woke up, the place was empty. Everybody had gone home. I looked around, thinking my father would never have gone off and left me. But, by God, he had." Jake chuckled, remembering. "I panicked. I mean absolute, goddamn terror. I knew if I didn't find my father, I'd be an orphan. And the thought left me paralyzed with fear. I knew what happened to orphans in these towns. I'd seen the work houses. So I took off, racing through the deserted streets, not knowing where the hell I was going, just determined to find him. The only thing was, a cold wind had blown in across the mountains, and the air was frigid. And all I had on was a thin shirt and pants, and shoes with holes in the soles. After about an hour I was shivering so much my teeth were rattling, so I gave up and went back to the saloon. There was a cozy fire burning in the fireplace, and my father and one of the saloon girls were cuddled up in front of it, toasting each other with whiskey." Jake shook his head. "They'd been there the whole time, upstairs in one of those cheap rooms, while I'd been running through the town scared out of my mind."

He laughed again, a bitter sound, before he glanced

across the table. At the look on Addy's face his tone grew soft. "Something I said?"

Without a word she pushed back her chair and walked to the sink where she filled a glass with water. She drank, slowly, giving herself time to compose her features, then turned, leaning against the sink. "I didn't realize other kids went through that, too."

"Went through what?"

"Feeling alone and scared. Especially when their parents didn't act like grown-ups."

"You too?"

She nodded.

"Want to talk about it, kid?"

She glanced at Sam, then away. "No."

In the silence of the room she returned to the table, but didn't sit. Instead she began to pace nervously.

Sam leaned back, watching. So much pain and anger bottled up in one little female. It wasn't his nature to prod. But it was Jake's.

"Was your father a gambler, Addy?"

She shook her head. "A mechanic. When he could get work. He got fired a lot from his jobs because of . . ." She swallowed. She'd never spoken the words aloud before, and found she couldn't say them. Such ugly words. She shrugged. "Mama said it helped him forget for a little while."

Sam paid as much attention to the things she didn't say as to the things she did. Booze and drugs. He'd seen it destroy so many lives. Wasn't that why he'd poured himself into a bottle after . . .?

"A lot of men can't handle what life dishes out," Jake said softly.

Addy nodded. "My father kept promising my Mama he was going to quit. But each time he got a paycheck, it happened again."

Restlessly Addy walked to the counter and put on a pot of coffee. When she turned, Jake saw the years of sadness in her eyes. "Mama said the drugs helped him with the pain. But she was wrong. They just caused more pain. To him and to us. The worst came when my mama died. After that, he didn't have any reason to come home except to change clothes."

"How old were you?" Jake asked.

"Twelve."

Sam sipped his whiskey and watched her eyes. Such wise young eyes.

"How old were the other kids?" Jake asked.

"Erin was five and Shannon was just a baby." Addy looked up, suddenly aware of how much she'd revealed. "I think I'd better go to bed now, Jake."

Jake sat quietly at the table, running his index finger around the rim of the glass. "Sure, kid. It's late. Think I'll turn in, too."

"Need anything before I go up?"

"No. I'm fine. See you tomorrow."

"Yeah. Goodnight, Jake."

"Goodnight, kid."

"Goodnight, Sam."

Sam noticed that she didn't look at him. It was probably because of the drink in his hand.

"'Night." He shoved it aside and watched as she headed toward the stairs.

*   *   *

Addy crawled into the big bed and pressed her eyes tightly shut, hoping to blot out the thoughts and images that filled her mind. But they wouldn't be denied. Even as she drifted into sleep, the memories came rushing back.

Later, though Addy wasn't certain if it was hours or only minutes, she sat up and rubbed her eyes. Peering into the gloom she felt the trembling subside. She wasn't at the Paradise Mobile Home Park. She was in the upper bedroom of Jake Starr's big old house. And her father could no longer hurt her. But he did. He still did. Maybe he always would.

Chapter Nine

"That's the fourth time I've held the goddamned queen, hoping for a pair. And it's the fourth time you beat me." Jake tossed down his cards and glared at the queen of hearts lying face up on the table. "Never did have any luck with the goddamned ladies. They were always bad luck for me."

"Some men just can't handle the ladies." Sam shoved the jackpot of pennies toward Addy, who grinned and picked up the cards.

Jake noted with satisfaction that her shuffling technique was much improved. She handled the cards almost as smoothly as a professional dealer.

He leaned back in his wheelchair, watching as Addy dealt. "My father hooked up with a real lady once. One of those la de da do-gooders who decided that I needed a firm hand and a thump over the head with a Bible every night for good measure. She decided to reform both of us. Even tried to haul him over to a preacher's house, to make it legal. That was when my father came to his senses. He told her to get lost. And then he went out and got roaring drunk."

Jake poured himself a glass of whisky and sipped. It was two in the morning, and this was his second glass. He didn't need alcohol the way some men did. He just liked having it there at his elbow, knowing he could drink it if he wanted to.

Addy glanced at Sam. Though he'd been drinking steadily since dinnertime, there was no change in him. But his drinking worried at the edges of her mind.

"There was another one. A real lady. Worked at a

saloon. Had a body that . . ." Jake glanced up and stopped, embarrassed at what he'd almost said. Sometimes he forgot that Addy was there.

"My father fell head over heels for her the minute he laid eyes on her. I hated her on sight. And as the days wore on, I hated her more. She whined and complained about everything. His job, or rather, his lack of one. His money. Most of all, his kid. She hated me as much as I hated her." He chuckled, low and deep in his throat. "Maybe we were both jealous of the other. Who knows? But, by God, I hated her. I knew she was no good from the day she walked in. And by the time she walked out of his life, she'd pocketed everything of value she could carry. Goddamned classy lady, that's what she thought she was."

He picked up his hand and set aside three cards. "This is one hell of a hand, kid. There's no way you can beat it. Give me three."

Addy discarded three cards and dealt, giving Jake three and Sam two. She found herself holding a pair of aces. But her mind wasn't on the cards. Something Jake had said had triggered some memories of her own.

He glanced at her. "What's wrong. Did you knock the spots off the cards?"

"Huh?" She looked sheepish. "Sorry. What've you got?"

"Three deuces. Beat two aces anytime. Where are you, kid? Your mind sure as hell isn't here."

"I was thinking . . ." She set down the cards and watched as Jake greedily hauled in the pile of pennies. "Isn't it funny how, after a while, some things don't hurt as much as before? But other things still hurt, no matter how long it's been."

"Yeah. I guess it's like falling down. Sometimes you just get a bruise. But sometimes you break a leg, and even years later you feel the twinge on rainy days."

"Yeah."

Sam and Jake remained silent, watching as Addy struggled with old demons. From the expression on her face, they knew exactly where she'd gone. Everyone had a private hell.

Suddenly she picked up her cards and studied them with a frown. "I think it's going to be a long night, gentlemen. I'm feeling mean. Mean and lucky."

Jake threw back his head and roared. Damned if she wasn't beginning to sound a lot like him.

Across the table, Sam watched her with grudging respect. She was tougher than she looked.

*   *   *

Addy tossed and turned. For so long she had held these terrifying secrets at bay. All during her years at the shelter she had adamantly refused to talk about her sisters. But now, released in sleep, the memories came rushing back.

*   *   *

It was a Wednesday night when Danny returned. Shannon and Erin were already asleep.

Addy heard her father's footsteps on the porch, then the sound of the door opening. When she turned, she was shocked at her father's haggard appearance.

A dark stubble covered his cheeks and chin. His eyes were bloodshot. He was wearing the same clothes he'd been wearing six days earlier. The stench assaulted her.

He took off an old baseball cap and tossed it on the table. Underneath, his hair was plastered to his head.

"I figured you'd be asleep."

"I . . ." She scrambled from her chair, eager to escape. "I was just going to bed."

"You forgot your homework." He picked up the slip of paper, then glanced down at the words. "What's this?"

"It's a note for my teacher. I was just . . ." She swallowed. ". . . explaining why I couldn't be at school all week."

94

He read the words aloud. "Addy has been sick. The doctor diagnosed it as strep throat." He shot her an admiring glance. "Pretty slick, kid. I'd believe a note like this."

"My teacher won't. But she can't prove it's a lie."

"How many times have you done this?"

"Every time I have to stay home with Shannon and Erin."

She held out her hand for the note. As he handed it to her, she noticed the way his fingers trembled. In fact, his whole arm seemed to jerk with some kind of spasm. When he saw her watching him, he jammed his hands into his pockets and rocked back on his heels.

At the sound of a vehicle approaching, they both looked up.

"Who's here?" Addy asked.

Danny peered out the window. "Go to bed."

"But somebody's here."

"They're here to see me. I got a little – important business to attend to." When she hesitated, he snarled, "Get lost, Addy."

She hurried to the bedroom. As she climbed between the covers she heard the rumble of masculine voices in the kitchen. None of them sounded familiar.

At a word of caution from Danny, the voices were reduced to whispers. Addy strained to make out the words, but they were spoken too softly. Each time a word or a laugh became too raucous, Danny would issue a sharp command about waking the sleeping children. Then they would whisper again.

At last, drained by the effort to hear what was being said, Addy drifted into sleep. When she awoke, she glanced at the clock and gave a little gasp. Seven o'clock. She heard Shannon gurgling happily in her crib.

She woke Erin for school, then picked up the baby and changed her before heading for the kitchen for a bottle.

She halted at the sight of her father seated at the kitchen table. At the sound of her footsteps, his head

95

came up slowly. His eyes were glazed and he moved as if in slow motion when he caught sight of his daughter in the doorway.

"Is it morning already?" he asked.

Addy nodded and took a bottle from the refrigerator.

"I'll do that." He snatched the bottle from her hand and reached for the baby. "Get Erin ready. See that's she's cleaned up." A sly smile caught the corners of his mouth. "I want her to look extra special for school today."

Addy hesitated, watching her father feed Shannon. A tiny thread of fear coursed along her spine. He moved as though he were sleepwalking.

She pushed aside her fears. He'd been away for six days. And probably hadn't had much sleep. He could grab a nap in another hour or two when the baby went back to bed.

"Erin has a little pink dress with rosebuds on the sleeves. It used to be one of mine that Mama saved."

"Good. See that she wears it."

Addy made her way to the bedroom. "Come on, Erin." Addy's bright smile was reflected in her eyes. "You're going to get a shower and have your hair washed before school."

The little girl rubbed her eyes. "Is it my birthday, Addy?"

"No. But it's something just as exciting." As Addy ran the water and added shampoo to Erin's wet hair, she whispered, "Daddy's back. And I think he wants to take care of us again."

The little girl giggled as Addy made soap sculptures out of her long blonde hair, before rinsing all the shampoo out. When she was beautifully washed, combed, amd dressed, Addy led Erin to the kitchen.

"What do you think, Daddy?"

Danny O'Brien's smile grew as his daughter twirled for his inspection. "I think she's as beautiful as a princess. Now clean up the baby."

"Why?"

"Because all my little girls deserve to look like princesses."

Addy bathed the baby and put on the only outfit that still fitted her. It was pink and frilly, with white lace frosting the collar and cuffs.

"Here, Daddy. Doesn't Shannon look sweet?"

"Yeah."

He surprised Addy by opening his arms. Almost reluctantly she handed the baby over. Her father's slow, measured movements worried her. But at least he was home. At least he was trying.

"What about me, Daddy?" Addy straightened. "Is this skirt okay?"

"Huh? Oh yeah, Addy. It's fine. You're just going to school."

"So is Erin." She shot him a puzzled glance before pulling on a sweater and picking up her books. "Come on, Erin. We've got school buses to catch."

"You go ahead, Addy," Danny said, sticking the nearly empty bottle back into the baby's mouth. "I'll see that Erin catches her bus."

"But it'll be here in a couple of minutes. We always walk to the corner together."

"Hey." His tone was sharp. "You're not in charge anymore. I'm here, remember? I said I'll see to it. Now get out of here and stop playing mama."

"Okay." Addy gave her sister a quick kiss. "You look pretty, Erin. I'll see you later."

"Bye, Addy," the little girl called as Addy planted a kiss on Shannon's bald head and made her way to the door.

That was the last glimpse Addy had of her two sisters.

*   *   *

Addy sat up in bed and ran a sweating palm across her eyes. Fighting a wave of nausea she raced to the bathroom and knelt beside the toilet. This happened whenever she remembered that horrible day.

Erin and Shannon were gone. Without a word of goodbye. Without a chance for Addy to tell them how much she loved them. Without telling them of her promise to Mama that they would always be together.

She had promised. And even now, with no records to prove where they had gone, she was determined to find them. One day, when she had saved enough money, she would hire a professional to find her sisters. And they would never be separated again.

She leaned over and retched again and again, until, drained, she crawled back into bed and lay trembling beneath the covers. Her hands were balled into fists. If it took her a lifetime, she'd find them.

Chapter Ten

Addy answered the phone on the second ring. She recognized Witherspoon's voice.

"Afternoon, Addy. Let me speak to Jake."

She handed the phone to Jake.

"Yeah." Jake motioned for Addy to take away the remains of his breakfast. He'd noted the dark circles under her eyes and wondered if she was coming down with something. But what did he know about females? Maybe it was something she ate, or in her case, didn't eat. At any rate, she looked like she'd put in a rough night. Sam didn't look much better.

"Sure I'm up." He glanced at the clock and saw that it was one fifteen. "Been up for almost an hour. What do you need?"

At the sink Addy heard the tension creep into Jake's tone. "No. I haven't made a decision yet. There's a lot to consider. Besides, you said I had a month."

He listened a moment before adding, "I know it's a good deal. And the price they're offering is more than fair. But, goddamnit, Witherspoon, that place was my whole life for a lot of years. I'm not going to walk away from it without giving it careful consideration."

Addy loaded the dishwasher and wiped down the countertops. When she walked to the table she saw the frown line between Jake's brows.

"Yeah. You'll hear from me as soon as I've come to a decision."

He dropped the receiver onto the cradle and sat, drumming his fingers on the table.

Addy hated seeing him so pensive. Thinking quickly she said, "I have to go to the bank, Jake. Want to go along for the ride?"

"I don't think so, kid. You go alone."

"I'd like some company."

"I'm afraid I'm not very good company today."

"That's all right. You don't have to talk. Just look out the window."

He and Sam glanced up at the same moment.

Arching a bushy white brow Jake said, "Don't try to con a con, Addy. What are you up to?"

"I just thought we could drive by Jake's again. I'd like to see what it looks like in daylight."

He broke into a smile. "Yeah?"

"Yeah."

He shrugged. "Why not? How about you, Sam? Want to trust Addy's driving again?"

"Why not? I don't have anything to lose."

"Just your life," Jake said with a laugh.

"That's what I said. I don't have anything to lose."

Addy raced up the stairs then returned a moment later, carrying her bankbook.

"Planning a big shopping spree soon?" Jake asked.

"Shopping?"

"Isn't that what all women do when they get a little money saved up?"

Addy shrugged. "I don't know what other women do." She stuffed the bankbook and her pay in her purse and walked behind Sam, who pushed Jake's wheelchair down the ramp. "I only know I have no intention of spending a dime of this money."

"Never?"

"Never," she said firmly.

Sam helped Jake into the car, then folded the wheelchair and placed it in the back seat.

When she turned on the ignition, Jake continued as though they hadn't been interrupted. "What in the hell are you going to do with your money?"

"I have plans, Jake." Addy manoeuvered the car, turning smoothly into the flow of traffic.

Jake leaned back and watched as she handled the car. She'd taken to driving as easily as she'd taken to cards and dice. The kid was a natural at everything she tried. All she needed was a good teacher.

Shopping was another matter, however. She definitely needed some more clothes. As far as he could determine, she owned three blouses and three skirts. They were always spotlessly clean and perfectly pressed. But they were inexpensive and nondescript. A sparrow's clothes. And she could be a goddamned peacock in the right hands. If there was one thing Jake had learned in his years on this earth, it was how to tell the sparrows from the peacocks. Clothes. Though he had no use for fancy clothes for himself, he'd always admired them on beautiful women. Like Lil. His mouth curved into a contented smile. Now there was a woman who knew how to dress to please a man.

Addy pulled the car into a parking slot at the bank. "I'll only be a minute."

"Take your time. I'm not going anywhere."

Addy shot Jake a quick smile and hurried away.

From his vantage point Sam watched her walk away. She probably wasn't even aware that she had a way of walking that made a man itch. Careful, he warned himself. Some itches weren't meant to be scratched.

When she returned, she placed the bankbook carefully in her purse before fastening her seatbelt.

Jake was dying of curiosity. What was it that drove Addy to save every dollar, without spending any on herself? It had to be something dear to her heart. But she apparently had no intention of sharing the secret with him. And he'd be damned if he'd ask again. Even if the curiosity was killing him.

She pulled into traffic and drove several blocks until they came to Jake's.

"Well, here's what it looks like in daylight, kid." Jake

drank in the sight of the old wooden saloon as the car pulled up to the curb.

It bore no resemblance to the elegant glass and steel casinos that lined both sides of the street. The building was two stories of dark, aged wood, with peeling letters on the side that spelled out, "Food, Spirits, Games of Chance."

Knowing the history of the building, Addy could almost see a grizzled old prospector pulling up on his mule and hurrying inside, eager for a glimpse of a woman in a low-cut gown who would share a glass of whiskey and bring him luck at the tables.

"Can we go inside, Jake? Please?"

A harsh refusal sprang to Jake's lips. But before he could utter a word, he caught sight of the look in her eyes.

She was hooked. Just the way he'd been all those years ago. It was there in the dreamy smile, the eyes gone wide as she tried to take it all in at once.

"All right," he said, surprising himself as much as Addy. "But I'm warning you, kid. This goddamned old place cast a spell over me the first time I laid eyes on it. And I've never been free of it since."

She gave a delighted laugh and hurried around the car to retrieve his wheelchair. Before she could open the door Sam took charge, smoothly helping Jake into his chair and pushing him toward the curb.

"You don't have to worry about me, Jake," Addy said solemnly. "I just want to see the inside of a real casino. When we leave, I'll still have both feet on the ground."

Before Addy reached the front doors, they were opened by a short, wiry man in jeans and leather vest over a crisp white shirt. His face bore the lines and wrinkles of an old man, but his eyes danced with the excitement of the very young.

"Sam, I don't believe it. How'd you talk Jake into coming back?" He shook Sam's hand, then caught Jake's hands in both of his. "Jake, you're looking so fine."

"Thanks, Shorty. Say hello to Addy O'Brien."

"Miss Addy." The old man whipped the cowboy hat from his head in a courtly gesture and offered his hand.

"Shorty's been with me since forty-seven."

"That's right. Came out of the war and couldn't face going back to the city. When I got to Reno I found Jake's place, and I've been here ever since." He turned to Jake with a big smile. "It's so good to see you back here. Welcome home, Jake."

"Thanks, Shorty."

As Addy stepped through the front entrance it was like stepping back in time to a rough, turn-of-the-century saloon. A long wooden bar ran the length of the room. Mounted behind the bar was a huge portrait of a nude, reclining on yards of scarlet satin.

The walls were gray, weathered wood. Mounted here and there, with no apparent eye to design, were the heads of deer and mountain goats. There was even a mountain cat, the largest Addy had ever seen, looking as though it could leap off the wall to attack some unfortunate creature below.

The rough wooden floorboards were scarred by the scuffle of boots from miners and ranchers, adventurers and ordinary citizens, searching for a pot of gold.

Addy's ears were assaulted by the sound of slot machines. Bells were ringing. Someone had just won a jackpot. She paused a moment to watch as coins spilled down until the tray was nearly overflowing. A woman in tight pants and a sweatshirt was scooping the coins into a paper cup as fast as her fingers could move. Her eyes were bright with greed.

Beyond the banks of slot machines were several dice tables. A crowd ringed one of the tables where a man's hand could be seen throwing the dice. The crowd roared its approval when the dice landed. Since she had been taught the game by Jake, Addy knew what was happening. The man had just made his point. And the crowd was with him.

"Listen, Addy," Jake said as Sam pushed his wheelchair silently among the tables. "It's a sound like nothing else in the whole world. Smell it." He breathed in air heavy with stale whiskey and cigar and cigarette smoke and occasionally, unwashed bodies. "I didn't realize how much I've missed this goddamned place."

"Jake." A dealer at a blackjack table looked over the heads of the people who sat facing him in a semi-circle.

At his call heads swiveled.

"My God, it's Jake. How are you?"

"Hello, Tony. Fine. Just fine."

"Wonderful to see you, Jake."

"Thanks, Calvin."

A bar waitress, wearing cut-off jeans and the tightest tee-shirt Addy had ever seen, stopped in her tracks.

"Jake Starr. Oh, Jake. You look so good." She came to a stop in front of him and balanced a tray of drinks while bending down to drop a kiss on his cheek. "It's great seeing you here."

"Thanks, Brenda. How're the kids?"

"Billy's in third grade now. And Joey started first grade this year."

"Already? Where did the time go?"

"I don't know. Isn't it amazing? If you promise to come back tomorrow, Jake, I'll bring their pictures."

"I can't promise." He seemed momentarily uncomfortable, then seemed to come to a sudden conclusion. "Hell, I'll be here. I'd like to see those pictures."

"Great. I'll bring them."

As quickly as she hurried away, another young woman, with a tray of cigars and cigarettes, stopped.

"Jake. I can't believe how good you look. We'd heard that you were confined to your bed."

"An ugly rumour, Kate."

"So I see. Are you going to be back from now on?"

"Maybe. I guess I'll just take it a day at a time."

"I hope you're back for good. The place hasn't been

the same since you left." She blew him a kiss and hurried away.

As he rolled past the blackjack tables toward the poker tables situated near the back of the casino, Jake took hold of the wheel of his chair, causing it to brake.

Hesitating, Addy leaned down. "What's wrong, Jake?"

"Nothing. I just don't want anyone to push me, kid. I'd like to look like I can handle things myself."

"Of course." Moving along beside Sam, Addy watched as the men at the poker tables looked up from their cards.

"Why, you old sonofabitch," one of the men called.

The others turned. Several of them dropped their cards in surprise and shoved back their chairs to hurry toward him.

"Jakie. I knew some day you'd be back." A man so thin his ribs could be counted through the red golf shirt he wore, clapped Jake on the back.

"That's more than I knew, Fingers. What's going on? It's not like you to drop out of a game."

"What do you mean? You think I could concentrate on the cards at a time like this? It isn't every day my old pal comes back from the dead. Besides," he added sheepishly, "I was holding all losers."

Jake threw back his head and roared. "That's more like it, Fingers. Shake hands with Addy O'Brien."

"Hi, Addy O'Brien." When the man extended his hand, Addy understood his nickname. His fingers were long and delicate, and as graceful as a woman's. But when he shook her hand, his grip was firm.

"Good to have you back, Jake," said a man in a beautifully tailored suit.

"Thanks, Henry." He turned to include Addy. "Henry Carstairs, this is Addy O'Brien."

"Miss O'Brien." The man's voice was as cultured as a university professor.

"Mr. Carstairs."

"I don't believe it. Jake." A fat man in a jogging suit

with a designer logo on the jacket hurried toward them. After clapping Jake on the back, he reached into his pocket and dropped a hundred dollar bill in Jake's lap.

"What's this?"

"The last time I saw you, Jake, you staked me to a game. Don't you remember?"

Jake merely stared at him.

"You left before I had a chance to repay you."

"If that's the case," Sam said with a laugh, "what about the interest?"

"That's right," Henry Carstairs said. "Don't forget, Bennie, it's been three years since Jake loaned you that hundred. By now you probably owe him another hundred in interest."

Without missing a beat, Bennie dug into his pocket and withdrew another hundred and handed it to Jake. "Bennie Stone always pays his debts."

"Especially if he's winning," Henry Carstairs said with a laugh.

"Thanks, Bennie. Meet Addy." Lifting his hand in a signal, Jake waited until the waitress, Brenda, hurried to his side. "Buy a round for everyone at these tables," Jake said, dropping a hundred on her tray. "How about you, Addy?"

"Just a soda," she said, fascinated by the sights and sounds and blur of colours.

Brenda took everyone's order and hurried away, returning minutes later with a tray loaded with drinks.

Addy slowly sipped her soda and drank in the flavour of the place Jake Starr had called home for the past half a century.

In the corner a wheel was spun, moving in dizzying circles until it gradually slowed, then stopped. A man in crisp white shirt and black pants picked up the money from the losers, then payed off the winners. Afterward he paused while more bets were placed. With a quick flick of the wrist, the wheel was spun again.

Beside her, Sam Money watched the way her eyes

followed the action. It was plain to see that she'd never been in a place like Jake's before. And from the way her eyes danced, it was obvious that she was hooked.

"Hey, Jakie," Fingers called. "You going to join us for a few hands of poker?"

"In a while," Jake said, accepting the handshake of a cluster of dealers who were just returning to their shift. "Just give me a few minutes."

"Sure. Sure. Take all the time you want. Of course," Bennie Stone said, shuffling the cards, "there are a few guys here who've been waiting over three years to win back the money they lost to you on that last night."

Addy's attention shifted to the men around the poker table.

"Yeah, Jakie," Fingers said. "You walked out of here with a hell of a jackpot that night. Remember?"

Jake shook his head. "I'm afraid not. That whole night's a blur. I woke up in a hospital bed unable to remember anything at all. It was days before I knew my name. And weeks before I could recall my past. But the time immediately before and after the accident has been completely wiped from my memory."

"Such memory loss is often associated with a blow such as the one you suffered in your accident, Jake," Henry Carstairs explained in his best professorial tones. "In my practice I often dealt with the victims of post traumatic distress. Occasionally the memory of the exact moment of impact is often gone for good."

Jake turned to Addy. "Henry was a clinical psychologist before he answered the siren call of the cards."

Addy took a step back from Henry Carstairs. Seeing it, Jake's eyes narrowed in sudden realization. She must have had an unpleasant experience with one or more of the psychologists on the staff of the shelter.

Jake went on as though he hadn't noticed. "Now Henry analyzes all of us while he tries to win our money."

Jake wasn't the only one who'd noticed Addy's reaction

to Henry. Sam, standing beside her, had noted it as well. He stored it away in his memory for another time.

Giving her an engaging smile Henry Carstairs said, "They are rather easy subjects to analyze, Miss O'Brien. As transparent as glass. And every one of them a thief."

"You only call us that when we win," Bennie cut in. Turning to Jake he said, "I've heard about amnesia before, but never knew anybody who actually had it. You're a damned medical miracle, Jake."

"Yeah. Some miracle." Jake's words were harsh, but Addy saw the light in his eyes as more and more employees came forward to welcome him back.

"You've been really missed around here," said a woman in white uniform and chef's hat. "The old place hasn't been the same. I hope you're back for good."

"I don't know, Theresa," Jake said, accepting her warm hug. "But at the moment I'm wondering what kept me away so long."

Addy found herself wondering the same thing. She'd never seen Jake looking so happy. Or so at ease.

When the crowd of well-wishers finally thinned, Jake turned toward the circle of men around the poker table. "Okay, boys. Deal me in. How about you, Sam?"

"No thanks. Think I'll find my usual seat at the bar."

Addy felt a wave of irritation as Sam walked away. Of course he'd want to sit at the bar. That seemed to be his favourite occupation.

Turning her attention to Jake, she watched as he picked up his cards and studied them before discarding three. Soon she was so absorbed in the game, she forgot about everything else. Except the man who sat across the room at the bar, drinking and watching. Though she tried to ignore him, he was never far from her thoughts.

*   *   *

"I need some of Theresa's chilli," Jake said, tossing down his cards.

Addy glanced at her watch and was shocked to discover that it was past seven o'clock. She and Jake had been at the casino for six hours. Yet it seemed like only minutes had passed.

"Hungry, kid?"

"Yeah." She laughed. "I think I'm starving. But I just didn't notice until now."

"This place has a way of doing that to people. Come on," he said, using his powerful hands to propel the chair forward. "It's time you saw something besides the goddamned poker tables."

Addy watched as the crowd parted for Jake's wheel-chair. As he rolled along, he was constantly forced to stop to greet old friends.

"Jake," said a beautifully dressed woman. "I'm so happy to see you here."

"Thanks, Dinah. And thanks for the cards and letters. They meant a lot to me."

"You never answered them, or returned my calls, Jake," she scolded. "I was so afraid. Everyone here thought you must be close to death."

"I guess I was dead for the last couple of years." He caught her hand and lifted it to his lips in a courtly gesture. "But I've joined the living again, Dinah. So don't count me out yet."

"Will you join me for a few hands of blackjack later?"

"Wouldn't miss it." He rolled on, pausing to accept handshakes, pats on the back, hugs.

At the entrance to a small coffee shop he paused while the hostess and waitresses hurried forward to greet him warmly. Addy watched as Jake basked in the light of their smiles.

"Find us a table in the corner, Rosetta," he said to the dark-haired hostess.

"And let you hide from all the people who are dying to tell you how much they've missed you? Not on your life," she said, leading the way to the first booth. "This has always been your table, Jake. I've been waiting a long time for you to come back and claim it."

She set down two menus and walked away. Instantly a waitress arrived with a cup of black coffee for Jake.

"Thanks, Charlene. I see you haven't forgotten."

"No, sir, Jake. Are you having the chilli or the steak and eggs?"

"Chilli."

"And you, miss?"

"Charlene, this is Addy O'Brien."

"Hi, Addy. It's nice to meet you. What'll you have?"

"I'll have the same. But bring me a soda instead of coffee."

The girl walked away and returned within minutes with their order. "The rumour is you're back for good, Jake. Is it true?" she asked.

Jake shrugged. "The rumours seem to fly faster than my brain. But it's not a bad idea."

"That's wonderful." The waitress's smile was genuine. "We've really missed you around here. The place just wasn't the same without you."

Without a word Jake ducked his head and bent to his food. But not before Addy caught sight of the flicker of emotion that crossed his face.

They were nearly finished when a handsome man in a dark business suit made his way to their booth.

"Jake, you sly old dog." The man stuck out his hand and Jake grasped it. "The whole place is buzzing about Jake Starr being here. To tell you the truth, I didn't really believe them at first. I know how you feel about being seen in that wheelchair. But finally I figured I'd have to see for myself." He looked Jake up and down. "I still can't believe my eyes."

"Believe 'em." Jake nodded toward Addy. "Addy O'Brien, meet Hamilton Davis. Ham is my casino manager."

"Mr. Davis."

"Call me Ham," he said, shaking her hand. "Everyone does."

"Addy is the one who finally coaxed me into coming back," Jake said.

"Really? How did you manage what others have failed to do for more than three years, Miss O'Brien?"

"I just told Jake that I wanted to see the inside of a casino."

"Ah. Your first time?"

When Addy nodded he said, "What do you think of Jake's?"

"I like it. A lot more than I expected to, in fact."

Her remark made Jake flush with pleasure, though he didn't know why.

"Then I take it you intend to come back?"

"As often as Jake wants."

Ham turned to Jake with a look of concern. "What did the doctor say about coming here?"

"How the hell should I know? I didn't ask his permission."

"I think you should check with him before you take on anything new, Jake. You've been through a lot."

"Yeah. Yeah. I'll call him." Jake handed his empty bowl to the waitress. "One more refill. Be sure and tell Theresa that that was the first good chilli I've had in over three years."

With a laugh the waitress walked away and returned with another steaming bowl.

"Theresa says there's plenty more where that came from. She's been saving up her best cooking for when you returned, Jake."

Addy and Ham watched as Jake dug into a second bowl of the hottest, spiciest chilli in the state of Nevada.

"While I'm here," Jake said between mouthfuls, "I'll want to take a look at the books."

"Sure thing. You won't mind if I take care of a few things first, will you, Jake? I just came on my shift, and there are a couple of things that require my attention."

"Fine. Addy and I are going to have a piece of Theresa's pecan pie before we leave here. How about meeting me in the office in about an hour?"

Ham nodded, then hurried away.

* * *

Addy sat beside Jake while Hamilton Davis pulled out several ledgers and spread them out on the desk in front of Jake.

"You can see from these just how bad business has been. In the past six months alone, we've watched business decline by nearly ten or fifteen percent."

"Why?" Jake demanded.

Ham shook his head. "I wish I knew, Jake. I've had my floor men watch the dealers. I can't find any of them skimming. I think it's just the competition. How can we compete with those big new casinos, with their hotel rooms and pools and golf courses? Who wants to come into a place like Jake's when they can have all that glamour?"

Jake shook his head as he studied the rows of figures. "It doesn't make any sense. We had that same competition three years ago. Hell, ten years ago. But we always managed to hold our own."

"People are becoming more sophisticated. They want more than a chance to gamble. They want men in tuxedos and girls in something low-cut and clinging. They want champagne and caviar, not beer and hot dogs."

"Maybe you do, Ham, but there are still a lot of plain people out there who just want to go out for a good time. And they used to come here to drop their paychecks. But lately, I'm paying more to my help than I'm taking in. It doesn't take a genius to figure out that I'll soon be dipping into the profits. And pretty soon, there'll be nothing left of this place."

Ham closed the ledgers and replaced them in a drawer, turning the key and depositing it in his pocket. "Maybe it's time to fold our tents while there's still something left

112

in the bank." He walked to the door. "I've got to get out on the floor, Jake. Call me if you need anything else."

"Yeah. Sure. Thanks, Ham." When the door closed, Jake sat drumming his fingers on the desk for long minutes. Finally he looked up to find Addy watching him. "Let's go, kid. I think I've had enough for one day."

As Jake rolled through the casino, more players and employees hurried up to him to extend their happiness at seeing him back.

At the bar they found Sam nursing a double scotch.

"Ready to go?" Jake asked.

Sam's gaze flicked over Jake before settling on Addy. He saw the look of disapproval on her face. That only made him more determined than ever to stay and drink. Hell, he brooded, he wasn't her father. He'd get roaring drunk if he wanted.

"No. I think I'll stay awhile. I'll see you tomorrow."

Addy took up a position behind Jake's chair and pushed him away without a backward glance. She wouldn't allow herself to think about Sam Money. Or his drinking.

When Jake had struggled into the car, and the wheel-chair was stowed, Addy turned the key in the ignition.

"Well, what did you think?"

"I loved it, Jake. I hope we can go back again soon."

"You mean you'd be ready to do it all again tomorrow?"

She nodded. "And tomorrow. And tomorrow."

"You might be sorry, kid. I used to be here all day, every day. And sometimes far into the night."

"That would suit me just fine."

Jake threw back his head and roared. "You know, kid, I think you mean it."

"I do."

He turned to watch her as she manoeuvered the car through downtown traffic. Goddamnit if she wasn't becoming more like him every day. But behind her careful smile he thought he detected a hint of pain or anger. And from the way she'd glowered at Sam earlier, he be willing to bet that Sam had something to do with whatever was bothering her now.

Chapter Eleven

"You two are becoming fixtures around here," Kate called as Addy pushed Jake's wheelchair through the front doors of the casino.

"Yeah. Maybe I could get a job dealing," Jake said with a laugh.

"The pay's not bad. And the tips are good. But I think you'd better stick to being the boss." Kate hurried away when she saw a man at a blackjack table signal to her.

"She's a great girl," Jake said to Addy. "Her husband-to-be was killed by an armed robber the night before the wedding. He was in his last year of college and working nights in a convenience store. That was four years ago and Kate hasn't gotten over it yet."

Addy glanced at the beautiful young woman, laughing and joking with a customer. Who would ever guess she was hiding a broken heart?

"I guess everybody has a story."

"You'd better believe it, kid. You ought to hear his sometime," he added as Sam Money walked toward them.

Addy felt her palms begin to sweat and wiped them along her skirt.

"Hi, Jake. Addy."

"You're here early tonight."

"Some nights I need a drink earlier than others." He glanced at Addy as he spoke and she cursed the way her pulse rate accelerated.

"Hey, Fingers," Jake called as they neared the poker tables. "How're the cards treating you?"

"Bad, Jakie. I need a break." The skinny man tossed

down his cards and pushed away from the poker table. "I shouldn't have started so early today. I'm running out of steam already."

"Come on. I'll buy you a cup of coffee."

Addy walked along beside the men. She and Jake had an unspoken agreement. When they reached the poker tables, she no longer pushed his wheelchair. It was a source of pride to him that he could manoeuver his own chair while his friends were watching.

She knew the effort that little vanity cost him. But, as Jake had explained, it was a good feeling to be tired after these last few years of doing nothing. He was sleeping better. And waking earlier, now that he had something challenging to look forward to each day.

Rosetta greeted them warmly and led them to Jake's booth. Within minutes, Charlene, their usual waitress, had placed coffee in front of the four of them and stood waiting for their orders.

"Steak, well done, eggs, over easy, and hash browns," Jake said.

Charlene glanced at Addy, who simply smiled. Addy, Fingers and Sam declined to order, and sat sipping their coffee.

When the waitress returned she placed a half a grapefruit in front of Jake.

He looked at it, then up at the waitress with a scowl. "What's this?"

"It's a grapefruit."

"I goddamned know what it is. Why is it here?"

"I'm just following orders."

"Orders? I ordered . . ." Jake turned to glower at Addy. "What did you tell her?"

"That no matter what you ordered, this was what you should get."

"Oh yeah? Well you can take this . . ." Jake turned to find Charlene already gone.

After a few well-chosen words, he took a bite and winced. "It's sour."

"Then it ought to suit you just fine." Addy bent to her coffee, but not before she saw Sam and Fingers stare at her with matching looks of stunned surprise.

"I think you may have met your match, Jakie."

"Shut up, Fingers, and drink your goddamned coffee."

Beside him Sam studied the girl who calmly sipped her coffee. Cool. The girl had guts. He found himself watching her with admiration.

Jake finished his grapefruit and watched as the waitress approached with a tray. She placed a plate in front of him and beat a hasty retreat.

He studied the contents. "What the hell is this?"

"A hard boiled egg," Addy said, "some baked chicken, and a piece of wholewheat toast."

His eyes narrowed. "You've gone too far, kid. I already had my mouth ready for steak and eggs. I'm not eating this slop."

Addy shrugged. She'd expected this fight. For the past two weeks she'd watched as Jake ate everything on the menu that was unhealthy for him. She'd already caught him late at night taking something for the pain in his stomach.

"I can't stop you from eating things that are bad for you, Jake. But you ought to consider giving yourself a steak and egg breakfast as a reward once a week, instead of eating it every day. That way, you'd have something to look forward to, and you wouldn't have to pay the price every night."

He gave her a long, piercing look. "Did anyone ever tell you you were like an old woman, Addy? I didn't realize I was hiring a goddamned nagging nanny."

She grinned. "Just doing my job."

"Yeah. Well see that you don't do it too well, kid, or you'll find yourself out on the street." He picked up his fork and began to eat.

Across the table, a slow satisfied smile crept across Fingers's mouth. Damned if the kid didn't bully old Jake into doing something he didn't want to do. In all the years that he'd known Jake Starr, this was the first time Fingers could recall such a thing.

Beside him, Sam Money fought back a grin. Despite his reservations, Addy was proving to be an amazing woman. She just might accomplish the impossible.

* * *

"Jake, could I see you a minute?"

Jake looked up from his cards toward Hamilton Davis, who was standing just behind him.

"Sure." Jake handed his cards to Addy. "Play this hand for me, kid. I'll be back in a minute."

Addy took the cards and studied them.

"How many, Addy?" Bennie Stone paused, watching her.

"Three." She discarded three cards and picked up the three the dealer slid toward her.

The six men around the table studied their cards as they were dealt. Addy glanced at each one, watching their expressions. After all this time spent as an observer, she'd had plenty of time to figure them out. Fingers was holding something good, she knew. His eyes were dancing. Bennie, on the other hand, didn't get what he wanted. It was there in his eyes and the downward curve of his lips. Henry Carstairs was harder to read. He was studying the cards closely. At that precise moment his glance moved up, and he caught her eye. She looked away quickly.

"Well, gentlemen. And Addy," Fingers said grandly. "I'm raising the pot. If you want to stay in, it'll cost you another five dollars."

"I'm out," Bennie said, dropping his cards.

"I'm out too," Henry Carstairs said.

The three other men at the table dropped out as well.

"I'll see you." Addy tossed in one of Jake's five dollar chips.

"Uh, kid . . .," Bennie began, but Fingers shot him a look that silenced him.

"Read 'em and weep," Fingers said, spreading his cards for all to see. "A pair of Jacks and a pair of lovely ladies."

Bennie whistled. "That's one fine hand, Fingers."

"Indeed it is." Fingers glanced at Addy. "Well, what've you got that made you want to stick around for the finale?"

"Three little deuces." She dropped her cards and watched his expression go from triumphant to defeated as he realized that she'd won.

Bennie scooped the jackpot toward her. "I'd say Jake's luck was changing, wouldn't you, Henry?"

Across the table, Henry Carstairs watched Addy's face as she waited for the dealer to shuffle the cards. He was man enough to appreciate the perfection of her features, the small, turned up nose, the slightly arched brows over eyes that were more green than blue, the high, rounded cheekbones. But his training caused him to see beyond her physical beauty. She rarely ever met his direct stare, choosing instead to look at a point over his left shoulder. Whenever she caught him looking at her, her cheeks reddened and she looked away. Secrets, he thought. That sweet little face hid a million secrets.

Beside him, Sam Money had come to the same conclusion.

*　　*　　*

Jake rolled toward the poker tables and stared at the stack of chips in front of Addy.

"You ought to bring along a substitute more often," Fingers said without looking up from his cards. "I've never seen anyone have such luck."

Jake watched as Addy discarded, then picked up the new cards that were dealt to her. "All right, gentlemen," she said in that soft, sultry voice. "I believe Henry opened. How lucky are you feeling now? Would you like to up the ante?"

"Yes, indeed." Henry tossed a five dollar chip in the pot and watched as the others followed suit.

"A pair of aces," Henry said proudly, displaying his cards. "Can anyone beat it?"

Fingers and Bennie shook their heads and folded their hands. The other three did the same. Only Addy remained.

"Two pair," she said, dropping her cards on the table.

"Two pair! Can you believe her luck?" Fingers looked up at Jake, who was beaming like a proud grandfather.

"Hell, yes. She learned from the master, gentlemen."

Addy moved aside and Jake settled his chair into place. Quickly counting the chips, he gave out a low, appreciative whistle. "I should just have you play for the house, kid, and I'd soon make back all the money this dump's been losing."

"Just try not to lose any of it while I'm gone," she said with a laugh.

Jake watched as she strolled away. Then he returned his attention to the cards.

*   *   *

Addy walked slowly through the casino, watching the action. She'd never expected to feel so comfortable in such an alien place. But from the moment she had first walked through the door with Jake, she'd felt as if she'd come home.

Home. What a strange word to apply to a saloon. But since she'd never truly had a home, it didn't seem so strange after all.

Jake had begun allowing her to fill in occasionally for an absent dealer. And she had even worked the dice tables, though Fingers had complained that it wasn't a proper woman's game.

"The dice don't care if a man or woman handles 'em," Jake said. "So why should you?"

"It isn't right. She's too young and pretty to be working the dice pit in this dump."

"Watch your mouth," Jake growled. "I can call it a dump if I want. But if I catch any man saying it, I'll have him barred from the place."

Jake beamed with pride whenever he received a glowing report about Addy's work. Every day she learned more about the operation of the casino. And every day he received more praise for her work.

* * *

Addy stood to one side, out of view of a row of blackjack players, watching as the dealer snapped the cards down. The play was swift, efficient. When it was over, only one player at the table had beat the dealer. The others all lost.

The dealer quickly scooped the money into the various slots in his tray and dealt again. Fascinated, Addy continued to watch. Within minutes the hand was over. Again, only the one lucky player had won.

Addy found a seat at an empty table and continued to watch for an hour. The dealer, whose name tag read Hobie, was fast and efficient. He wasted no time on small talk with his players, as some of the dealers did. He seemed disinterested in the people who sat facing him, never studying them or even making eye contact. He merely dealt the cards, turned his own over, and collected the money.

Addy studied the one man at the table who kept winning. He was slight of build, with brown hair and brown pants and beige shirt. He sat very still, never moving, never interacting with the others, who often talked or laughed among themselves. When he won he showed no pleasure. When he lost, which was rare, he showed no trace of anger or frustration.

It took Addy a while to figure out what puzzled her about him. And then it dawned on her. He was so deliberately bland. Absolutely nothing set him apart. As though, she realized, he was determined not to call attention to himself.

When the dealers shifted to other tables, and Hobie moved on to the table to his left, the player who had been winning cashed in and walked to the bar.

Later, when the dealer, Hobie, had moved to yet a third table, the player left the bar and took a seat at Hobie's table. Within minutes he was winning.

Deep in thought, Addy watched him for a few minutes longer. Then she made her way to the poker tables to see how Jake was doing.

* * *

"Where's your mind tonight, kid?"

Addy turned her attention from the white lines flashing past the car on the rain-swept street. The windshield wipers beat a steady rhythm in the darkness.

"I'm not used to driving in rain. I need to concentrate."

"I've told you before. Don't con a con. Your mind isn't on your driving. What's wrong? Did something happen today at the casino?"

"I think so."

She turned into the driveway and brought the car around to the back door. Ignoring the rain that pelted her, she walked around to Jake's side and struggled with the wheelchair. When it was in place, he lifted himself out of the car and she wheeled him up the ramp.

Once inside she went around snapping on lights and returned to hand Jake a towel. "Would you like a robe?"

"Hell, no. You think a little rain is going to melt me? Kid, there were nights when the only thing between me and the rain, sleet or snow was an old sheepskin jacket.

122

Now," he said, flinging the towel on the table, "tell me what's bothering you."

"I think I spotted a dealer cheating today. But the only way it would work is if the guy who was winning was his partner." She glanced at Jake and saw the scowl on his face. "Do you think he'd risk asking someone to cheat with him?"

"Risk?" Jake thundered. "If they're both part of the scheme, what's the risk?" His voice lowered. "Tell me what you saw, Addy."

She quickly detailed what she had seen, and watched Jake's eyes darken.

"It's the oldest scam in the world," Jake said. "Pulled it a few times myself. What I can't figure out is how it got by Ham."

Addy thought back over the hour she'd spent watching the blackjack table. "Hamilton Davis came over once, with another man, to count the money at the table."

Jake frowned. "And then what?"

Addy paused. "He wrote some figures on a sheet of paper and left."

"Tomorrow," Jake said, "I want you to point out the dealer to me."

"Okay." She stifled a yawn. "His name is Hobie. Want a bedtime snack?"

"No." He glanced at the clock and saw that it was after two in the morning. "I'm heading off to bed. I want a clear mind when I confront our clever dealer, Hobie, with what I know."

As she started up the stairs he called, "You caused quite a stir at the poker tables today, kid. The guys couldn't stop talking about you. Especially Henry Carstairs. He thinks you're fascinating."

"That's – nice." She didn't turn around. "'Night, Jake," she called over her shoulder.

"Goodnight, Addy."

Addy listened to the sound of Jake's wheelchair below as she made her way to her room. She had been feeling pleasantly tired. But now, at the mention of Henry Carstairs, she felt the old familiar hitch in her breathing. A clinical analyst. Counselors. There had been too many to count at the shelter. She crawled into bed and squeezed her eyes shut, hoping to blot out the thoughts that she knew were hovering on the edges of her mind.

She resisted drifting back to that terrible day when she learned that her father had died when his truck stopped on the tracks of an oncoming train. As if that tragedy wasn't enough for a frightened girl of twelve, her trailer was destroyed that very night by a mysterious explosion, and she was taken to live at a state shelter. The only things she'd manage to salvage from the debris was a photograph of herself with her two sisters, one of her parents in their courtship days, and a book of bedtime stories that had belonged to Erin.

Addy sat for several moments in the dark, listening to the soothing sounds of the night. A plane droned overhead. Down the street a car's engine purred into life. In the distance was the mournful cry of a train.

She drew her knees up and wrapped her arms around them. These were the sounds of freedom. She had survived the state shelter, and the probing questions of the counselors, trained to help her through the maze of childhood traumas. All their poking and prodding had been designed to help heal the wounds. But they hadn't understood that she didn't want them healed. She wanted to keep the memories alive and festering, so that she wouldn't be lulled into forgetting her ultimate goal. She couldn't rest until her quest was completed, and her promise to her mother was fulfilled.

Chapter Twelve

"Forget breakfast, kid." Jake wheeled out of his bedroom. "Just some coffee to start my engine, and then we'll head downtown and deal with our thieves."

He'd taken pains with his appearance this day. His mane of white hair was carefully combed. He wore a crisp white shirt and dark slacks. Balanced on his lap were dark socks and a pair of beautiful black loafers.

While he sipped his coffee Addy unselfconsciously bent and pulled on his socks and shoes.

"How do I look?" he asked.

"Different." She straightened and studied him with a critical eye. "I've never seen you look so . . ."

"Handsome?"

"I was about to say professional."

"Oh." His little frown turned into a smile. "What the hell. I'll settle for professional. After all, that's what they're all going to see today. The old goddamned Jake. The one who used to hire and fire and crack the whip whenever anybody stepped out of line. When it comes to a showdown, kid, I'm the last guy to blink."

"I think you're looking forward to this," she said, filling his cup again.

"Damned if I'm not. Nothing I ever liked better than a good fight." He drained his cup and set it down. "Come on. We've got work to do."

"What about Sam?"

"Let him sleep. He didn't get in until this morning."

Addy realized that she'd feel a lot better if Sam was with them on this. There was something about

Sam that inspired trust, despite all his flaws. She dismissed the thought and concentrated on what they were about to do.

*   *   *

In the early afternoon the casino had more than the usual number of tourists, as well as the regulars that Addy had come to recognize.

Besides Jake's cronies, there were the slew of senior citizens who trickled in to play the nickle slots before gathering in the coffee shop, and the people who worked nearby and spent their lunch hours feeding quarters into the video poker machines. There was the church secretary who made the rounds every Monday afternoon, exchanging casino tokens that had been dropped into the collection basket. While in each casino, she would drop several of her own quarters into the slot machines, hoping for that magic jackpot that would let her retire in comfort. And there were more than a dozen bearded, grizzled old men who still worked the creeks nearby, panning for gold just as their fathers and grandfathers had. Several times a month they came into town and gathered at Jake's to talk about the old days, and possibly to seek a different pot of gold.

This day Jake and Addy made their way through the casino, stopping only to chat with an occasional employee. Heading directly to the office, Addy closed the door while Jake rolled to the desk. Taking a key from his pocket he opened the locked drawers and began going through the personnel files until he came to the one he'd been seeking.

"Here it is. Hobie Graves," he said, withdrawing a work application. "Age forty two. Worked in Vegas at the Sahara, the Riv, Caesars." Jake looked up. "I'm going to be busy for a while. Need to make a few phone calls."

Addy listened while he spoke with the casino managers of the Las Vegas casinos listed on the application. When he finally hung up the phone, he drummed his fingers on the desk.

"It seems our Hobie has pulled this scam before. He's been fired from every casino within a month or two of being hired."

"How long has he been working here?"

"Too long." He snapped the folder shut and carefully replaced it in the files before locking the drawer.

Addy watched as Jake scanned the work schedule posted on a sheet of paper on top of the desk. "Hobie has the evening shift. Come on," he said with a sudden burst of energy. "Let's see if any of the guys are feeling lucky. Looks like I have time for a game or two before the fun begins."

"You mean you can actually play poker before this confrontation?" Addy held the door open while Jake manoeuvered his chair through the doorway.

"Hell, yes. Makes me feel like the old Jake. Remember," he said, waiting for her to reach his side. "You're my eyes and ears in this casino. Let me know when you spot Hobie's partner. I need to catch them in the act."

Addy nodded.

"See. I told you I saw them heading toward the office," Fingers called when he spotted them moving between the poker tables. "Jakie, come here. You have to settle an argument between us."

"Hey, Jake. You're looking mighty fine today," Bennie Stone said.

The others muttered their approval.

Addy couldn't help smiling as Jake puffed out his chest before gripping the wheels of the chair and propelling himself forward. It was hard to believe that scant weeks ago, he had refused to even leave his house for fear of being seen in a wheelchair.

"I'll see you in a while," she whispered. "Think I'll take a turn around the casino first."

"Okay, kid. Just don't wander too far. I want to

catch those bastards before they get any more of my money."

"Don't worry. The minute I spot them, I'll tell you."

She waved to the guys at the poker tables and hurried away.

*   *   *

The early evening brought a crowd. Addy watched as a cluster of tourists streamed from a bus and shoved their way through the front doors. Fascinated by the memorabilia that hung on the walls of the old room, they wandered slowly around, studying the photographs of bearded old prospectors and famous gamblers who had once sat at these very tables. Soon, like all the others who'd come before them, they were lured to the games of chance. The blackjack tables were filled, with people waiting for an empty chair. They stood three deep at the crap tables. The neon lights of every slot machine danced and whirred with the sound of money.

Addy watched the change of shifts and found herself observing the blackjack dealer named Hobie from the moment he started. But it wasn't until the casino was crowded that the other half of his team showed up. Addy almost didn't recognize the man as he took the chair vacated by a woman who had been losing heavily. At first glance he didn't even resemble the man Addy had watched on the previous evening. But as she studied him, she was convinced he was the same man. Tonight he wore black pants and a dull gray shirt with the sleeves rolled to his elbows. And he was wearing glasses. But after studying him carefully, she was convinced he was the same man. There was that same stillness about him, as he sat quietly, looking neither left nor right as he studied his cards. Someone at the table made a funny comment that caused everyone to laugh. Addy glanced at the man's face. He never even smiled. To the others at the table this was a game; to this man, it was all business.

Addy watched him win three hands in a row before she went in search of Jake.

Leaning close she whispered, "It's time, Jake. They're both together at the same table."

He tossed down the cards he was holding. "I'm out, gentlemen. Be back in a few minutes."

As he turned his chair from the table, Addy moved along by his side. They positioned themselves so that they could observe the blackjack table without being seen. For long minutes they remained there, watching.

"Pretty smooth," Jake murmured. He turned to Addy. "Did you see the signal that passed from the dealer to the player?"

"Signal?"

"Watch the next hand," Jake said.

Addy watched as the dealer flipped down the cards, then paused to allow each player time to look at the cards and make a decision. When the dealer came to his partner, who was showing a king and a five, the dealer tapped a finger on the deck he was holding. The player signalled for a card and drew a six.

"Twenty-one," Addy breathed.

"That's the name of the game." Before Addy realized what Jake was doing, he rolled his wheelchair up behind the dealer and tapped him on the arm. "You're through, Hobie."

The man's eyes went wide. "My shift just started."

"Nope. It just ended. Come with me." Turning to the player, who had stuffed his money in his pocket and was scrambling off his chair, Jake said, "I'd like you to be my guest in my office."

"Sorry. Got to run."

"I don't think you understand." Jake's hand shot out, catching the player by his sleeve. "That wasn't an invitation. It was an order."

The man twisted free and started to run. Before he'd

gone three feet he was confronted by a beefy security guard. "You heard Mr. Starr," he hissed. "Allow me to accompany you to his office."

The guard locked his hand around the man's arm and escorted him away.

Before the other players could react, a new dealer had stepped up and began methodically shuffling the cards. Addy and Jake disappeared through a doorway and led the dealer to Jake's office.

Inside the office Hamilton Davis looked up in surprise. "What's going on, Jake?"

"I might ask you the same thing, Ham." He watched in satisfaction as the security guard released his hold on the dealer and his accomplice before placing himself squarely in front of the closed door.

To the player who had been winning Jake said, "Empty your pockets."

"I will not. This is a free . . ."

"Nothing is free here, sonny. Empty your goddamned pockets," Jake thundered.

Startled by his outburst, the young man began emptying piles of folded bills and chips. When his pockets were empty, Jake said to Addy, "Count it."

Addy quickly tallied the amount. "Two thousand, four hundred seventy-five dollars."

"Not bad for half an hour's work," Jake said in a dangerously soft voice. Turning to Ham he said, "I see by the personnel records that Hobie's been here for almost six months."

"Yes, but . . ."

"In six months, working eight-hour shifts with a partner, a clever con could net more than a hundred thousand dollars. Now multiply that by a couple of other clever dealers, and you can see where my profits are going, Ham."

"I'm sorry, Jake. I swear I didn't even guess. How did you find out?"

"A single phone call to Vegas this morning told me all I

needed to know about our Mr. Hobie Graves. He's been fired from every casino for this same goddamned scam. And in every one of them he was caught within the first three weeks. But not here."

Jake's next words, spoken in a dangerously soft tone, had his casino manager trembling. "What's happening, Ham? Is no one watching out for my interests anymore?"

"I . . ." Ham swallowed. "I got bogged down, Jake. I guess I just wasn't ready to take over so many responsibilities at once."

"Then why didn't you ask for help?"

"I didn't want to bother you. You had enough to deal with."

"Not good enough, Ham." Jake rolled his chair closer, and took a key from his pocket. Unlocking the drawer he removed a sheaf of papers. "Your take makes Hobie and his partner look like goddamned pikers. I figure, in the three years since I left you on your own, you've helped yourself to about half a million of my money."

"You're crazy." Ham pushed back his chair and jumped to his feet. "There aren't any papers in that drawer that would incriminate me."

"These do." Jake held up a handful of old telephone bills. "It was something that Addy said earlier that made me check you out. You called Vegas, Ham. You checked their references thoroughly. You weren't looking for honest employees. You were looking for partners for your little scheme. And you found the perfect ones. They'd help you steal from me, and they'd keep their mouths shut as long as they got a piece of it."

"You think there are others?" Addy asked.

"Two more, to be exact. Both working the midnight shift."

Addy was stunned. "How do you know that, Jake?"

"Simple," he replied. "I made a couple of phone calls to Vegas to check out two other dealers who'd worked in the same casinos as Hobie. All were confirmed as having

131

been fired for running a scam. And all were hired here as soon as they arrived in town." Jake turned to Hobie and his partner, who had remained silent throughout the entire exchange. "How much did you two get a week for this little scheme?"

"It sure wasn't half a million," Hobie snarled.

"Shut up." Ham startled everyone by pulling the guard's gun from his holster and hitting him on the head, sending the guard dropping heavily to the floor. In one quick movement Ham dragged Addy in front of him like a shield.

The moment his hands touched her Addy was overcome with a wave of revulsion. Feelings long buried came rushing to the surface, and she felt, as she had so many times in the past, that she was being forced to surrender control of her life. Never again, she had vowed. Never again.

Waving the gun at his two accomplices Ham shouted, "Lie on the floor, your hands above your heads. Do it," he hissed when they hesitated.

The two men did as they were told.

"Now the girl and I are walking out of here, slow and easy, as if nothing's happened. And if you want to see her alive, Jake, you'll do nothing. No police. No crazy heroics. As soon as I'm over the border into Mexico, I'll turn her loose unharmed."

He took a step toward the door, dragging Addy with him.

Jake saw the look of terror in Addy's eyes and felt a great black rage begin to churn inside him. This whole thing had suddenly gone very wrong.

In a deadly calm voice he said, "The kid isn't a bargaining chip, Ham. Let her go."

"Are you crazy?" Ham's voice rose. "She's my only ticket out of this mess. And if you call the cops, I swear, Jake, I'll kill her."

"You still don't understand, do you, Ham?" Jake's voice frosted over. "This was supposed to be between you and me. I was going to let you pay back what you'd stolen. But now, it's no longer only about money. And I can't let you walk out of here with Addy."

"How're you going to stop me, Jake? Are you going to get out of that wheelchair and chase me?"

As he shoved Addy roughly ahead of him, Ham let out a high, shrill laugh. "It wasn't half a million, Jake. It was more like a million. And where I'm going that'll buy a lot of tequilla."

Ham started to walk over the burly guard who was lying on the floor. At that moment Addy took a deep breath and knew that she had to risk everything, even a bullet from his gun, rather than submit. Once he was free of the others he'd have no use for her. And he would kill her anyway.

Jake saw the look of sudden determination cross Addy's face, and with a sinking feeling realized that she was going to dig in her heels.

Ham was distracted by the body lying on the floor. Seizing that moment, Addy turned and gave him a shove. At the same instant Jake pushed himself from the wheelchair and launched himself against Ham. The force of the collision sent Addy sprawling against the wall.

The door to Jake's office was thrown open and Sam Money charged through the doorway. He looked toward Addy, to assure himself that she was unharmed. Then he plowed into the fight.

Jake and Ham were struggling for the gun in Ham's hand. The casino manager's soft hands were no match for Jake's strength. But Jake was pinned, unable to put up a fight.

It was Sam's hand that reached in to wrench the gun from Ham. There was a single shot.

Addy heard the sound of someone screaming, and realized it was her voice.

Without thought to her own safety she threw herself between Jake and Ham and wrapped her arms around Jake's neck.

Against his cheek she cried, "Are you hit?"

"I can't tell."

Over her shoulder she saw the blood ooze from Ham's chest and spread in widening circles across the once crisp white shirt. Sam knelt beside him and touched a hand to his throat. Finding no pulse he glanced at Addy and shook his head.

Addy felt a bubble of hysteria rise in her throat. "What do you mean you can't tell? You either are or you aren't wounded." She touched a hand to Jake's chest, his arms, his back, to assure herself that there was no blood. Then she held him a little away, searching for some sign of a wound.

"Listen, kid," he muttered thickly. "You've got me in such a goddamned death grip, I can't feel anything at all." He lifted a hand to her cheek in a gesture of rare tenderness. In a softer tone he asked, "Are you all right?"

"Yeah." She let out a long shaky sigh. "I'm fine."

"You sure as hell are. I could tell you were going to resist, and I couldn't let you stand up to that gun alone." He let his hand fall away. "Now get me up off the goddamned floor."

With Sam's assistance she got Jake into his chair. She watched as Sam examined the guard and helped him to a sitting position.

"How'd you happen to be here, Sam?" Jake asked.

"If it hadn't been for Fingers I'd have missed all the action. He just told me what you were planning. Thought I'd lend a hand."

"I'm grateful. You saved my ass again. If it weren't for you, I'd be the one lying there. I'd better call the cops," Jake said wearily. "See that these two don't move."

As Jake phoned the police station, Sam kept an eye on Addy, whose unusual pallor worried him.

Falling back on old habits Sam took the guard's handcuffs and secured the two accomplices. Then he left and returned with hot coffee for Addy and Jake, and forced Addy to drink it even though her hands were shaking.

She was grateful for his quiet competence.

134

Sam stayed beside Jake and Addy for the next few hours, as they answered the police questions. There was no time to think, no time to reflect on what had happened.

Following Jake's orders, two more teams of cons had been picked up on the midnight shift. And all were eager to implicate Hamilton Davis as the brains behind the scam that had netted over a million dollars.

As the police began another round of interrogation, Andrew Witherspoon arrived, having been summoned by Sam.

Jake turned to Sam. "Would you mind taking Addy home? She's been through enough."

"What about you?" she asked.

"Looks like I'll be here through the night. Witherspoon can bring me home when we're finished."

Sam took one look at the weariness etched on Addy's face and decided to cut off any argument she might have. "Come on."

His grip was firm on her arm as he led her from the office. Without a word they walked to the car. When he started the engine she leaned her head back against the seat and closed her eyes. It felt so good to let someone else take charge for a few minutes. But only for a few minutes, she promised herself as she struggled against an almost overpowering feeling of exhaustion.

Chapter Thirteen

The lights of the city moved past in a blur of neon. Addy's eyes felt heavy but she was afraid to close them again. Instead she fastened her gaze on Sam's hands, steady and competent, on the wheel.

"You okay?" He barely moved his head but she felt the force of his gaze.

"I'm fine. You didn't have to drive me home. I could have waited for Jake."

"Jake will be there for a couple more hours. There'll be more questions to be answered and documents to be filled out."

"You seem to know a lot about police procedure."

He said nothing, but she saw the way his jaw clenched.

The car swerved into the driveway and Addy unfastened her seatbelt and sat a moment, feeling slightly disoriented.

Sam came around and opened her door. They walked up the ramp and Sam unlocked the door and threw on the lights.

"How about some coffee?" He felt her shrink back as she brushed past him.

"No thanks. I think I'll just go up to bed." She turned, feeling suddenly awkward in his presence. "Thanks for bringing me home, Sam."

"Sure." She was still too pale, and he could see that she was holding herself together by sheer will alone. But she would resent his help, or anyone's. "I'll be right here if you need me."

He listened to the creaking of the old floor as she moved around in her upper bedroom. Soon the footsteps ended and he knew that she was in bed.

He filled a tumbler with whiskey and stood by the window, staring out into the darkness.

It had felt good to leap back into battle. It was the first time his adrenalin had pumped like that in a long time. Too long. And the feel of handcuffs and a gun in his hand seemed right too.

He'd told himself that he didn't miss police work, and in truth, there was a lot about it he didn't miss. The endless paperwork, the tiresome stakeouts were things he could live without. But he missed the thrill of the hunt. And most of all, he missed the close friendships. There was a bond between men and women who put their lives on the line every single day. His friends at the NYPD had been the best.

He lifted the glass to his lips and drank deeply. Now he was alone. Completely alone. He'd cut himself off from everyone who'd ever known him. It was his choice. This was the way he wanted it. He wanted no reminders of that other life. He couldn't have tolerated another kind word about Laura and Timmy, and the bright, beautiful lives that had been snuffed out.

Their images flashed through his mind and he felt a moment of searing pain. He lifted the tumbler to his lips and drained it, then walked to the kitchen for more.

*   *   *

Addy tossed and turned in her bed, unable to shake the terrible memories. Memories triggered by Ham's arm around her throat, the gun in his hand.

*   *   *

In the state shelter, Addy lay on the bunk that had been assigned to her. Inside she felt frozen, paralyzed. She'd been cut adrift. Floating. Or sinking. She'd never felt so alone. So afraid.

The room at the children's shelter had twelve bunks, six against each wall with an aisle between them.

The girls ranged in age from eight to twelve. Addy, who was just a week shy of her thirteenth birthday, was one of the oldest in the group.

The days had been filled with a succession of stern-faced men and women who asked countless questions and wrote the answers on documents. Addy was checked by a doctor, a nurse, a dentist. All had given their stamp of approval. She was, despite her sullen withdrawal, and her exessively thin body, considered reasonably healthy.

When the bell rang for dinner, Addy followed the others into the gray dining hall. What the food lacked in taste it made up for in volume. Most of the girls, who had never known three meals a day, ate until they were full.

The girl seated next to Addy curled her left arm protectively around her plate while with her right hand she shoveled food into her mouth. She barely took the time to chew and swallow before the gesture was repeated again and again until her plate was empty. Then she sat in silence, watching the others eat. Addy had never heard her utter a single word. She spent her days curled up on her bunk, snarling or whimpering whenever anyone got too close.

Deep in thought, Addy moved the thick orange mass of spaghetti around her plate.

"You don't want that?"

Addy turned to the girl on the other side of her. Jet black hair had been piled into an enormous bouffant hairstyle. Her eyes were outlined with heavy black lines. Jutting breasts strained the buttons of her blouse. If it weren't for her round babyface, she'd be mistaken for a twenty year old.

"No. Want it?"

"Sure." The girl slid it onto her plate and began devouring it.

Addy watched without interest.

"My name's Savannah." An impish grin split the girl's

lips. "Actually it's Shirley, but I hate my name, so, since this is the start of a new life, I figure why not a new name too? So, from now on my name's Savannah. What's yours?"

"Addy. Addy O'Brien."

"Your own name? Or did you just invent it?"

"My own."

"Great name. If I had yours, I wouldn't change it either."

When Addy didn't reply she went on. "You're new. But you'll get used to the food."

"I'll never get used to anything about this place."

Savannah glanced beyond her to the girl who was now licking her plate like a dog. "It's not that bad. Was your life so great on the outside?" She helped herself to Addy's hard bread roll and mopped up the sauce on her plate.

"My life was . . ." Addy shrugged. ". . . my own."

"I'll take it here anytime over life at my house. Want your milk?"

Addy shook her head and watched as Savannah drank it down in one long gulp.

Savannah caught her arm and lowered her voice. "Look. I know I talk a lot. Most of the girls can't stand my mouth. My caseworker says I'm a smartass. I guess I am. But I figure, since you haven't talked to anybody since you got here, and all I ever do is talk, why can't we be friends? That way I can do all the talking and you can just listen."

Addy shrugged, eager to get away by herself.

"Come on," Savannah said. "I need a friend. Nobody here wants to talk. And look at you. I've been watching you ever since you got here. You need a friend too. Otherwise you're going to forget how to talk. Like Gurney there."

"Gurney?" Addy glanced at the girl to her left, who was now licking the last drops from her empty glass. Her long tongue went around and around the glass. Then she dipped her finger in, wiping, licking, until the glass was as clean as the plate.

"Ida Gurney." Savannah laughed. "Ida rather had any name but that." She giggled at her little joke. "Now that's a girl who needs to invent a new name. And a new life. I've heard the caseworkers talking about her. Enough to make me gag. She spent most of her ten years chained in a cold, damp basement. She's not sure if she's a girl or a dog."

Addy shuddered and felt a wave of compassion. She studied the girl more closely.

"Don't go feeling sorry for her, or thinking you can help her. The last person who tried to be nice to her still has Ida's teethmarks in her arm for her trouble. She's crazy. And as vicious as a mad dog." Savannah's tone lightened. "See? You need me. I've been around long enough to show you the ropes."

"I'll learn by myself." Addy pushed back her chair.

"Sure. Okay." Savannah flashed her quick smile. "Want that pudding?"

Addy turned back. "No. But I think Ida would." She placed the dish in front of the silent girl, who growled a warning low in her throat.

When Addy walked away, the girl wolfed down the lumpy pudding without even taking time to taste it.

In the days that followed, Addy began to read aloud from Erin's book of bedtime stories. At first, Addy told herself, it was to keep the memory of Erin alive. But now, she was forced to admit, she did it as much for Ida, whose bunk was beside hers, as for herself. Her voice seemed to soothe the girl. It was true that Ida's eyes never blinked; her head never turned toward the sound of the voice. But Addy noticed that Ida's breathing seemed to grow calmer when she read the familiar stories. And Ida's hands, which were usually balled into fists, would open like flower petals while Addy's voice washed over her.

An aide entered, followed by two burly men who were carrying several mattresses. One of them, a youth, with long, stringy blonde hair and a straggly Fu Manchu moustache, stared pointedly at Addy, sizing her up. He wore his pants low on his hips and had a cigarette pack rolled into the sleeve of his tee-shirt.

Addy turned away, uncomfortably aware that the youth had shifted his attention to her. As always, she needed to become invisible.

Drawing her knees up she opened a textbook and hid behind it. An image of her mother flashed through her mind. Mama. It had been a long while since Addy had allowed herself to think of her beautiful mother. Now the memories washed over her. Mama's gentle voice, her soft laughter, the look of love in her eyes when she'd kissed her daughters.

"The most important thing a woman can do is learn to take care of herself." She could hear her Mama's voice, repeating her grandmother's rules. "And the second most important thing is to marry a man who can be a helpmate to her."

Addy sighed as the aide followed the workers from the room and ordered lights out. In the darkness she rolled to one side. She had no intention of ever marrying. But she was surely going to learn to take care of herself and not trust that job to anyone else. Not even the people here who said they wanted to help. She stifled a yawn and drifted into sleep.

Addy didn't even know what had roused her from deep sleep. She only knew that she was suddenly wide awake, staring into the darkness. Something, or someone, was standing over her. Though she couldn't see, she sensed it.

As she started to sit up, a big hand closed over her mouth and another hand grasped her roughly by the shoulder, dragging her from her bunk.

The scream that bubbled to the surface died in her throat. Struggling for breath, she clawed at the hand that covered her nose and mouth. But she was no match for the strength of the person who dragged her through the doorway and into the darkened hallway.

When the hand dropped away from her mouth she

dragged precious air into her lungs. She was hauled roughly to the floor and hands caught at her flannel nightgown, ripping the fabric away.

"No." She fought, but the hands were quick, practiced, cruel.

"I've been watching you," he said in a terrifying whisper. "I don't think you know what this is all about yet. So I've decided to teach you."

"No. Please . . ."

"Shut up. Just lie back and enjoy yourself."

Addy heard a chilling laugh as he tore away the last of her nightgown and pressed himself down on her.

In desperation she kicked, bit, scratched, raking her fingernails down the side of his face.

"Little bitch." His hand swung out in a wide arc, snapping her head to one side.

His hands grasped her shoulders, pressing her against the cold hard floor. His breath came in short gasps as he struggled to subdue her.

Suddenly Addy heard a snarl, like the sound of a mad dog, and the youth rolled away from her. Addy watched in astonishment as Ida Gurney attacked him, biting his face, drawing blood with each vicious snap of her jaws.

His cries of pain and rage soon awakened the entire building. When an aide turned on the lights, Ida was still attacking the long-haired worker, her teeth so deeply embedded into his arm, it took three more aides to pry her loose.

* * *

"Addy. Addy, are you all right?"

Addy sat up in bed and recoiled from the figure of the man beside her. His hands were on her shoulders and she shook them off with a shudder.

"No. Don't . . ."

He carefully clenched his hands at his sides to keep from

142

touching her. "It's Sam Money. You've been having a bad dream."

At his words Addy stopped struggling and lay back, her breath coming in short gasps.

"Sam." Her eyes widened, trying to see him in the dim light that spilled through the doorway from the hall.

The mattress sagged when he sat on the edge of the bed. He was shirtless, and it was obvious that he'd pulled on a pair of jeans in great haste. His hair was mussed; his voice sleep-roughened.

"I'm sorry. I . . . I woke you."

"It's all right. Just so I know you're awake now and okay."

She was trembling violently and he wished there was something he could do to offer comfort. But it was obvious that she hated being touched.

His voice grew stern. "I think it would help if you talked about it."

"No. I can't. You don't understand . . ."

He understood a lot more than she knew. He'd over-heard what she'd been saying in her sleep. He knew she'd had to fight for her honour and her life. His eyes narrowed. From what he'd heard, she'd won.

"It's over now, Addy."

"It'll never be over." The simmering anger in her tone left him no doubt as to the rage that still lingered.

"Listen to me," Sam said through clenched teeth. "Sometimes you just have to let go of the past and get on with your life."

"Like you?"

She saw the quick flash of his teeth. "I had that coming." Without realizing it, Sam placed a hand over hers.

He had forgotten how dangerous it was to touch her. As soon as their fingers brushed, he felt a rush of heat.

He needed to get out of here. Fast. Before whatever vestiges of honour he had left deserted him.

She sighed. Just the smallest of sounds, but he found he couldn't turn away. Instead he lifted a hand to her face.

Soft. Her skin was as soft as the underside of a rose petal. He knew, in that instant, that he had to touch her lips. It was the most compelling need of his life.

Addy felt the gentleness of his touch and for a moment forgot to breathe. No one had ever touched her with such tenderness. For the moment her fears were forgotten. How good it felt to be touched like this. How right. As his fingertips skimmed over her face she saw him bend closer and her heart stopped.

He framed her face with his hands before touching a thumb to her mouth. With soft, feathery caresses he traced the outline of her lips, the curve of her cheek.

His unexpected tenderness was almost her undoing. She moved against his touch and stared into his eyes, seeing something there she'd never seen before. The world-weary cynicism was replaced by a gentle smile.

"You have to go now," she whispered.

"I'd rather stay."

She sat very still, struggling to find the strength she'd always been able to call upon. But with his hands so soft and gentle against her face, her firm resolutions fled.

"Please, Sam. Please go."

Struggling against the needs that tugged at him, he dropped his hands to his sides and moved away from the bed. For a long moment he stared down at her. Then he turned and left without a word.

Outside her door he clenched his hands into fists and made his way down the stairs. There was no point in going to his bed. He wouldn't be able to sleep now. The taste of her was still on his lips. The need for her was still so urgent, he felt his entire body vibrating with desire.

Chapter Fourteen

Addy heard the slam of a car door and knew that Witherspoon had finally brought Jake home.

On trembling legs Addy made her way down the darkened stairs. As exhausted as she was, she knew there would be no more sleep this night.

Her feelings for Sam brought a new dilemma. She had deliberately locked all men out of her life. Until Sam, it had been easy. But Sam's touch unlocked strange, new feelings. Feelings she didn't like to admit to. Maybe, if it had been some other man, she might have accepted, even encouraged, these feelings. But after her experience with her father's addiction, she wanted nothing to do with a man who spent his days and nights with a bottle. Whatever feelings Sam stirred in her, she would fight them. She had to.

She felt the sting of tears. Strange. She hadn't cried that night, when she'd been attacked by the youth at the shelter. And earlier tonight she'd been completely dry-eyed while she had faced Ham's attack, and later the police questioning. But now, thinking about a simple touch from Sam, she had an overpowering need to weep.

Padding into the kitchen she started a pot of coffee.

"Can't sleep either?"

Addy whirled at the sound of Sam's voice. He was standing by the window, watching Jake's progress up the ramp.

"Too much excitement, I guess." Her hand trembled as she held the spoon.

"Yeah. Me too."

Jake rolled his wheelchair through the doorway.

"Well, look at this. The goddamned welcoming committee." He glanced from Sam's dour expression to Addy's frown. "The coffee smells good."

"Want a cup?"

"Yeah."

She was glad to have something to do. As soon as the coffee was ready she filled a cup and brought it to the table, where Jake had rolled his chair.

"I'm glad you're up, kid," he said, sipping the coffee. "You handled yourself well tonight with the police." He paused, sipped. "That wasn't your first experience with them."

"No." She waited, bracing for the questions.

Instead Jake said, "I've had my share of dealing with the police through the years." He glanced up. "I told you that I killed a man when I was thirteen."

Addy nodded and filled a cup for Sam. When she handed it to him their fingers brushed and she pulled her hand away quickly. His frown deepened.

"I didn't tell you what happened after."

She tried to pull her thoughts together and watched as Jake took another long drink of coffee.

"I tied his body on the back of a horse and climbed into the saddle. Don't ask me how," he said with a half smile. "I was so far gone, I don't even remember most of the trek down the mountain. I guess I blacked out in the saddle. But I remember riding into town, and people shouting, and a sheriff's deputy hauling me off the horse. And there was talk about hanging me because I'd killed a man in cold blood. While they were deciding about a trial, a doctor was brought to tend my wounds and he discovered that I'd been shot in the back. That's when the whole story came out. The sheriff realized that my father's killer had shot me and had intended to leave me for dead. But just as he bent over me to steal my gun, I managed to fire off one last shot and caught him in the chest."

Jake gave a chuckle. "It's funny how something so terrible can bring about such amazing changes. The only

146

thing that saved me from the gallows" he said, meeting Addy's direct gaze, "was a gunshot in the back that damned near finished me off."

His voice softened. "What saved you from the gallows?"

His question startled her. For a moment she could only stare at him. Then, careful not to look at Sam, she said, "A girl who could only growl like a dog."

Puzzled, Jake held his silence.

"It was a long time ago," she said with a sigh. "I try not to think about it. And I try not to be afraid." In halting tones she said, "But I'm such a coward. I was scared tonight, when Ham grabbed me."

"Bullshit. I saw your eyes, kid. You'd already made up your mind to fight. That's when I got scared."

"You, Jake?"

"Yeah." He set down his coffee and stared at her across the table. "I can't remember ever being that scared, kid. If he'd have hurt you . . ." He clenched his fists. "But I knew our only chance was stopping him before he got out of that office. I had no choice. I had to act before he got away."

"Even if it meant being shot?"

He grinned. "Haven't you heard? I'm faster than a speeding bullet."

She felt the tears burn her eyes again and walked to the stove. With her back to him she said, "Sam was the only calm one. As though he'd seen it all before."

"He has," Jake said. "Didn't he tell you?"

"Tell me what?"

"Sam used to be an undercover cop in New York."

She turned and found Sam staring at her.

"I quit," Sam said abruptly. "Thought it would be more fun playing poker in Reno, Nevada. And drinking gallons of cheap whiskey."

He saw the dark look that came into her eyes.

Jake glanced out the windows at the pale pink light that streaked the sky. "I've been thinking. Sam, you said you'd never go back to New York."

Sam nodded.

"And you've put your life on hold for a long time now, so you could help me deal with . . ." Jake glanced down at his lifeless legs and then back at Sam. "I'd like you to consider taking over the security operations at Jake's."

When Sam said nothing, Jake added, "I really need you, Sam, or I wouldn't ask."

"Thanks. That makes it damned hard to refuse."

Jake's eyes lit. "You'll do it?"

For several long, tense moments, Sam said nothing. Finally he nodded. "Sure. Why not? I can certainly do a better job than Ham did."

"You'll be good for the place, Sam." Jake turned to Addy. "Well, now that that's taken care of, I feel hungry. How about the two of you?"

She started to laugh, a clear rich sound that relieved Sam of his last remaining tension. "I guess I could arrange to fix some breakfast before you go to bed."

"I'd like that. As long as it's real food, like bacon and eggs and potatoes, and not that healthy fruit and nuts crap."

"You've got it." Addy busied herself with pots and pans and paring knives.

A short time later the three of them tucked into the first real food they'd eaten in hours. They enjoyed their meal in companionable silence.

"Now that we've put away a breakfast dripping with fat and cholesterol, I guess I'll sleep like a baby."

Addy watched as Jake drained his coffee and rolled his chair toward the bedroom. "Get some rest," he called. "We're going to have a busy night."

"Doing what?"

"Running Jake's." He paused in the doorway and turned. "Oh. Did I forget to tell you, kid? You and I are going to take over the day to day operation of the place. How do you feel about being casino manager?"

Addy's mouth dropped open.

He chuckled. "With Sam in charge of security and you

in charge of the casino, I've already got a winning team. See you in a few hours."

* * *

Casino manager. Addy hadn't believed it at first. In fact, she'd thought Jake was just teasing. But now, with her name on the door and a badge pinned to her blouse, it had become a fact.

She patrolled the casino, watching the dealers, talking with the players. It was Addy, along with an armed guard hand-picked by Sam, who halted play to count the money. And Addy, Sam and Jake went over the daily sheets, tallying the profits and losses for Jake's accountant, Milton Carver.

Within days, the profits were up, the losses down. And every week the profits were growing. When Milton Carver arrived for his monthly meeting with Jake and Sam, he couldn't hide his enthusiasm.

"Ah, this is more like it," he said, finalizing his figures.

He polished off a second cup of coffee and watched as Addy tidied up before going upstairs to dress for work.

"How much longer can she keep this up?" he asked.

Jake glanced at him over the rim of new glasses. "Keep what up?"

"This double duty. She was hired to take care of you. Now she not only does that, but she helps run the casino too."

"She likes it."

"I'm sure she does. But I'd call that a little more than she bargained for, wouldn't you?"

Jake sat drumming his fingers on the table while Milton snapped his briefcase shut and walked to the door.

"See you two next month."

"Yeah. Next month." Jake watched him walk out the door, then turned to stare at Sam.

Two days later Addy saw the red Porsche turn into the driveway. She opened the door before the lawyer had a chance to ring the bell.

"Hi, Addy," he said, stepping inside. "Jake asked me to drop by before you two left for the casino."

"Come on in," Jake called from the kitchen.

"I guess I know why you summoned me," the lawyer said as he shook Jake's hand in greeting. "Now that Jake's is making a profit again, I'm certain you have no intention of selling."

"That's right. And you can tell the investors that. But that isn't the only reason I wanted you here. Take a seat, Witherspoon. Coffee?"

"Yes, please."

Addy brought him a cup of coffee while he made himself comfortable across the table from Jake.

"I'd like to talk to Andrew alone," Jake said to Addy.

Taking her cue, she made her way upstairs and took her time getting ready for the evening.

Downstairs she heard the lawyer's voice raised in anger. Addy grinned and ran a brush through her hair. She'd give a lot to know what they were fighting about this time. But it wasn't in her nature to eavesdrop. If Jake wanted her to know, he'd tell her. If not, he had a right to his privacy.

* * *

"You can't be serious, Jake," Witherspoon said.

"I am. And you'll draw up the papers exactly the way I say."

"It's true that Addy has made some rather amazing changes in your life. And I'll agree with Milt that she's now pulling double duty, taking care of you and the casino too. I even agree that Sam Money is a fine choice to head your security team, even though he has a reputation for loving his liquor. But to even suggest that they're worth the salary you were paying Hamilton Davis is beyond belief."

"Why? They're doing Ham's job. What's more, they're two of the most honest people I've ever met. If they can do the job, and bump up the profits, why shouldn't they reap some of the benefits?"

"I don't object to Sam's salary. He'll earn it. But fifty thousand dollars a year is a bit much for a twenty-one year old with no college education. There are plenty of young MBA's who'd sell their own mother for a chance like this."

"Your chauvinism is showing, Witherspoon."

"For God's sake, Jake, she doesn't know the first thing about running a casino. If it weren't for you, she'd be lost and you know it."

"Maybe. But I know this, Witherspoon. If I had to trust anyone with Jake's, it would be Addy O'Brien and Sam Money. So quit arguing and draw up the contract."

"Why does it have to be in writing? Why not just tell them what you'll pay them and let it go at that?"

"You're the one who came up with the idea for a contract, remember? Now that I've gotten used to it, I sort of like the idea of something legal and binding between us."

Andrew Witherspoon nodded. "All right, Jake. If it'll make you happy, I'll draw up a contract. The documents should be ready in a couple of days."

"Good. Thanks."

The lawyer shoved the notes into his briefcase and snapped it shut. As he let himself out, he noticed the beds of carefully tended white roses around the base of the trees. He had to admit, the two people in question had made a very big improvement in Jake's life.

*   *   *

Addy waited until she heard the Porsche roaring down the street before descending the stairs.

"Come on, Jake. We're running late."

He grinned. "It's okay, kid. I own the joint, remember?"

* * *

Addy had one routine that never varied. On payday, she insisted on going to the bank and the store before returning to the house to pick up Jake for their evening at the casino.

The first time she saw her new paycheck, she'd been absolutely speechless. Jake watched with delight as she'd torn open the envelope, only to stare in open-mouthed surprise at the figure on the check.

"This can't be right," she said, studying the amount.

"What's wrong with it. Not enough?"

"Not enough? Jake, you've given me someone else's check." She handed it over. "See?"

He read the amount and handed it back to her. "Nope. That's yours, all right."

"But . . ."

"Oh. And this is yours, too." He handed her an official looking document. "I'll need you to sign it."

"What's this?"

"Read it, kid."

She read quickly, then looked up at him with eyes as big as saucers. "I don't understand."

"It's your new contract," Jake explained. "I asked Witherspoon to draw up a new one, since you've taken on new duties with the casino."

"But Jake. Fifty thousand dollars?"

"That's the going rate for young casino executives. Since you're now doing the job, the pay is yours."

"You can't be serious."

"That's exactly what my lawyer said. Now shut up and sign. Unless, of course, you're thinking about quitting."

"Jake . . ."

"Sign it, Addy. Quick now, before I change my mind."

She snatched up a pen and signed her name.

"Heading for the bank and the store?"

"Yeah. Need anything?"

"Nah. See you in a couple of hours."

"Okay."

Addy swung her bag over her shoulder and headed for the car. A few minutes later she drove into the bank's parking lot. As she started to get out of the car she remembered that, in the excitement, she'd left her bankbook on the dresser upstairs. With a sigh of impatience, she fastened her seatbelt and headed back to the house.

She hated inefficiency. But her mind had been on other things. Like the sudden changes in her life. With the kind of money Jake was paying her, there was no reason to put off her quest any longer. She'd be able to start right away. The thought had her quivering with excitement.

She turned the car up the drive and ran lightly up the steps. In her bedroom she snatched up the bankbook and stuffed it into her purse, then headed down the stairs. As her foot found the last stair she heard Jake's low rumble of laughter, followed by a higher-pitched trill of feminine laughter.

Addy stopped dead in her tracks.

Where were the voices coming from? She glanced toward Jake's bedroom. The door was ajar. She stepped closer and heard Jake's voice, low, satisfied.

"Ah, Lil, you're the best. I don't know what I'd have done all these years without you."

The woman's voice had the intimacy of blues singer in a smoke-filled room. "You'd have found yourself a wife and settled down with two kids and a dog like everyone else."

"That life was never for the likes of us, Lil."

"Not for me, certainly. Three times I've tried, and three times I've regretted my actions. But you were a different story, Jake." There was the slightest French accent to her words. "You know you regretted missing out on all that."

153

"Maybe I did, once upon a time. But not anymore. It would mean giving up all that you and I have shared through the years. I don't know of another woman who would dash over at noon to sip whiskey in my bed and make an old fart like me feel like a frisky young pup again."

"By the way, where is that whiskey?"

Jake chuckled. "You were in such a hurry to tell me all your latest news, you probably left it on the kitchen table."

"I'll be right back."

Addy had no time to react. When the door opened, she stood there, her face flushed, her eyes wide.

The woman was tall and elegant, with steel gray hair swept back from a face that, though lined with age, was still exquisite. Her eyes were a vivid shade of blue. Her perfectly tailored suit was a lush shade of plum. The shoes dangling from her left hand were Italian leather. The gold at her throat and ears was expensive and tasteful.

For one long terrible moment the two women stared at each other in silence.

Knowing that she had intruded on something very private and very precious, Addy turned and fled without a word.

Chapter Fifteen

Addy's cheeks continued to flame all the way to the bank. Every time she thought about what she had walked into, she felt a fresh wave of embarrassment. Right now Jake and the elegant woman – Lil – were probably sharing a laugh over the stupid girl who had blundered into their little tryst.

Oh, why had she stayed around to listen? If she had left as quickly as she had entered, no one would have been the wiser. How could she face Jake again, knowing what she knew?

As the teller handed her the receipt of her deposit, a new thought left Addy trembling. What if Jake flew into a rage over her discovery of his indiscretion, and fired her? What would happen to all her grand plans then?

She drove to the store and stumbled around, trying to concentrate. But the rows of boxes and canned goods only added to her confusion. How could she possibly think about food when her whole life was turned upside down? What if she was returning to no job? What if she found her clothes waiting on the front porch?

With her mind in a fog she went through the check-out line and paid the cashier. Wheeling a cart through the parking lot she loaded the bags into her trunk and headed back to Jake's.

By the time she turned into the driveway, her palms were sweating and her heart was pounding. How could she face him? What could she possibly say in her defense?

Picking up two heavy bags, she nudged a hip against the door and backed into the kitchen.

"I hope you picked up some steaks," Jake said from the doorway. "I'm in the mood for red meat today."

Startled, she dropped a bag and watched helplessly as cans and bottles rolled across the floor. She scrambled around retrieving them, grateful that she didn't have to meet Jake's gaze.

"I'm glad you didn't have a dozen eggs in that one." He rolled his chair across the floor.

"Yeah." She swallowed and ducked outside to fetch the last two bags of groceries.

When she returned, Jake was digging through the bags on the table. His hair was wet. It was obvious he'd just had a shower. Did Lil get the water temperature just right for him? Or did she shower with him?

Addy looked away quickly, afraid he'd catch her studying him. "I don't see any steaks. Did you get some?"

"I got a pot roast and some chicken." She peeled off her sweater and busied herself putting away the things.

"Then don't make dinner tonight. We'll eat at the coffee shop before we get to work. I'm dying for a steak. What do you think?"

Addy nodded. "Whatever you say, Jake."

"Good. I'm ready to go whenever you are, kid." He rolled his chair through the doorway, whistling a happy little tune.

Addy finished putting away the groceries, before making her way to her room. As she paused on the stairway, Jake called, "Give me a hand with these goddamned shoes and socks."

Addy turned back and entered his bedroom. She tried not to look, but she couldn't help glancing at the bed. It had been carefully made. Nothing seemed out of place. But the fragrance of expensive French perfume lingered in the air. Addy realized that she'd often smelled it here in Jake's room. But until today, she'd never given it a thought.

"Thanks, Addy." Jake gave her a bright smile as she slipped on his socks and shoes and straightened his cuffs.

156

"I've got a feeling it's going to be one hell of a great night."

"Yeah. I'll be right down." She fled his bedroom and raced up the stairs. Once there she sank down on the edge of her bed and took in several long gulps of air. He was acting like nothing had happened. Could it be that the woman – Lil – hadn't told him about her untimely return?

Addy walked to the dresser and ran a brush through her tangled hair. Pausing, she stared at her reflection in the mirror. Could it be that Jake had no idea that Addy was on to his little secret? If that was the case, she would have to continue to pretend she didn't know. But wasn't that far better than having to admit what she knew?

She dropped the brush with a clatter and picked up her purse. This whole thing was so confusing. But for now, she'd just have to let Jake play out his hand. And she'd follow suit.

*   *   *

Fingers tapped Addy on the shoulder and said in a whisper,

"Better keep an eye on that guy in the baseball cap."

Addy studied the man standing at the dice table. "Why?"

"I've watched him in this town for years. He carries loaded dice in his hip pocket. He's tried his scam on so many casinos, he's been barred from most of them."

"Why isn't he barred here?"

Fingers shrugged. "Maybe he hasn't worked Jake's before. Or maybe he just hasn't been caught. But if I was you, kid, I'd worry if he gets the dice. He'll clean out the tables before he leaves."

"Thanks, Fingers."

As she watched, the dice were passed to the man in the baseball cap.

Positioning herself so that she could observe every

move, Addy watched as the man brought his hand back to toss the dice. In that split second she saw him exchange the table dice for a pair in his hip pocket. It was an old trick that Jake had taught her early one morning, around four o'clock when they were both unable to sleep. Only an amateur would miss it, Addy thought with scorn.

The dice rolled across the green felt. When they stopped rolling they came up four and three. The players around the table let out a shout as they collected double their bets.

Addy saw the shooter place five one hundred dollar chips on the line. Immediately a crowd began to form around the table as fresh players scrambled to place their bets on a hot shooter.

Moving with the crush of people, Addy stepped directly behind the man in the baseball cap and bumped him as she pretended to reach over his shoulder.

"Sorry," she said.

He turned and gave her a wide smile. "My pleasure, Ma'am. You can press that lovely body against mine any time. In fact, you just stay close. Maybe you're my good-luck charm."

With a disarming smile Addy moved back and stepped around the table to whisper something in the box man's ear. Immediately he lifted the dice from the table and examined each one. Without a word the old dice were removed and fresh dice put in the game.

Seeing it, the player gave a smug look and picked up the fresh dice. As he selected two, he brought his hand back to toss again. In that instant, his look of confidence disappeared, to be replaced with a look of amazement. His back pocket was empty. He tried to cover his blunder by tossing the dice so hard they landed off the table. As the others turned toward the direction of the dice, he stared around until he spotted Addy, who was still standing next to the box man. She opened her hand to reveal the dice she'd lifted from his hip pocket.

In that moment a burly guard positioned himself beside the shooter and said discreetly, "Excuse me, sir. You have an appointment with the owner."

As the two men walked away, fresh dice were passed to the next player in line. The game continued without a pause.

"That was as smooth an operation as I've ever seen."

At the deep tone of Sam's voice, Addy whirled.

He was staring at her with genuine interest. "Where'd you learn to pick a pocket like that?"

"Just one of my many talents." She cocked her head to one side. "If it was so smooth, how'd you spot it?"

"Just one of my many talents." He ran his index finger along the curve of her cheek and felt the jolt clear to his toes. "In my other life I was trained to spot hands that were quicker than the eye."

"I'd better remember that." She took a step back, breaking contact. "Well, I'd better get back to work."

"Yeah."

He watched until she melted into the crowd. His first instincts, he realized, had been correct. She was a con. He walked resolutely to the bar and ordered a double.

Addy went in search of Fingers.

Leaning over him at the poker table, she brushed a kiss to his cheek. "I owe you one for this," she whispered.

"Hell, kid," he muttered, "that's what friends are for."

When she walked away he touched a hand to his cheek. It had been a long time since a sweet little girl had kissed him like that. No wonder Jake was putty in her hands. And Sam Money, he noticed, wasn't as immune to her charms as he pretended to be.

*   *   *

Addy had the feeling that someone was watching her. It was past midnight and the casino was crowded. She glanced around the blackjack tables. Everyone seemed absorbed in the game. Still the feeling persisted. Turning, she allowed her gaze to scan the circular bar that dominated the corner of the room.

Sam sat alone, a glass in his hand. For the first time that she could recall, he'd been absent from the casino and from Jake's house for two days. Two long days. She didn't miss him, of course. And she had no intention of counting the days.

But now he was back.

Even from this distance she could see his eyes, red-rimmed and weary, focused on her. With a shiver she forced herself to turn away. But even as she crossed the casino, putting distance between them, she could feel his gaze burning into her back. Even when she made her way to the office, the sad, haunted look in his eyes remained with her.

*　　*　　*

"I've been thinking, Addy." Jake parked his chair at the kitchen table and watched as she cracked eggs for an omelette. "That is, the guys were talking and . . ."

Addy set the heavy skillet on the stove and grated cheese. "And what?"

He cleared his throat and looked to Sam for help. But Sam seemed busy with his own thoughts.

How did he handle this without hurting her feelings?

"You're young and beautiful and you're in a position of authority in the casino, but . . ."

She poured in the eggs and added chopped fresh tomatoes. "But what?"

"You still dress like a goddamned schoolgirl."

She sprinkled on a topping of cheese and watched as it began melting down into the egg mixture. Then she dropped the bread into the toaster. "So?"

"I'd like you to . . . shop for some new clothes."

Addy turned, crossing her arms over her chest. "I don't

know anything about shopping. I've never bought new clothes."

"What? That's impossible," he thundered. "I thought females were born with a need to shop."

"Maybe other females. But I've never shopped, except in thrift shops and second-hand stores. I wouldn't know what to do in a fancy department store."

"Well I'll be goddamned." He thought a minute, then brightened. "I never thought I'd say this, but I guess someone has to teach you how to be a credit to your sex."

She crossed the room and caught his hand. "You mean you're taking me shopping, Jake?"

"Hell, I may be old, but I'm not senile yet. The day Jake Starr goes into a fancy store, you'll know it's time to put me away. No, I have someone else in mind, kid. Someone who knows all about spending money and turning out fine ladies."

They all looked up as a pall of black smoke rolled through the kitchen.

"Oh my gosh. The toast. The omelette."

Addy shot across the room and lifted the blackened skillet onto a cool burner, then flipped up the charred toast. She turned on the fan and opened the door, but the smoke billowed around the room, burning their eyes, clogging their throats.

"Never mind," Jake said as Addy tried to salvage their breakfast. "We'll eat at the coffee shop. Sam, get me out of this goddamned smoke."

A short time later, as they headed toward the casino, Jake muttered, "It's a good thing I own the goddamned coffee shop. I'd hate to be giving somebody else all that business and making some other damned fool rich."

*   *   *

Addy took a final look in the mirror and fluffed her hair. Jake's friend, Mrs. Miccelli, would be here any minute to take her to the fanciest shops in Reno.

161

For long minutes she studied her reflection with a critical eye. The dark skirt and white blouse were neat. Addy thought they suited her. The black pumps were servicable. The earrings, black and white disks she had bought in the casino gift shop, were her only jewellery. She wore her long dark hair tied back with a plastic clip.

"Shake a leg, kid. Company's here."

Addy grabbed up her shoulder bag and hurried down the stairs. "I'm warning you, Jake. She's going to have her hands full with . . ."

Addy froze on the bottom step. Her words died in her throat. Standing just inside the front door was the beautiful woman who had been with Jake the day Addy had returned unexpectedly. The woman she had seen stepping out of Jake's bedroom.

Jake didn't even notice the shocked look on Addy's face. He was too busy beaming at their visitor. "Addy O'Brien, I'd like you to meet Lillianne Miccelli."

The woman walked toward her with her hand outstretched.

"Addy, how do you do?"

She heard the lilt of just the slightest French accent.

"Mrs. Miccelli." Mechanically Addy accepted her handshake. Her own hand had turned to ice.

"Please. Call me Lil. Everyone does."

"If anyone can help you shop, it's Lil," Jake said with a trace of pride. "She's dressed more ladies than anyone I know."

Addy glanced at the fashionable suit Lil was wearing. The pale peach skirt and fitted jacket hugged her trim figure. She wore a double strand of pearls with a cameo clasp in pale peach, and matching earrings. Her shoes and bag were taupe leather.

Even in a crowd of beautifully dressed women, she would stand out. "You two have fun," Jake said. Reaching into his pocket he withdrew a roll of bills and handed them to Addy. "Here, kid. Don't come back until you've spent all of it."

"But Jake, I have money."

"I know. But I've seen the way you hoard it. This way, you won't be tempted to look at the price tag before you buy. Just enjoy yourself."

"Jake, I . . ."

"Get out of here. I'll see you later."

Addy followed Lil outside and was astounded to see a chauffeur driven limousine parked in the driveway.

"I thought we could relax and get acquainted," Lil said, accepting the driver's assistance into the back seat. "And we wouldn't have to be distracted by traffic."

Addy's eyes widened as she stared around the luxurious interior. The seats were softest leather. A tray between the seats held a crystal decanter and several goblets.

"Champagne?" Lil asked as they settled in.

"No, thank you."

Lil poured one for herself and sipped.

In the background, a stereo played Chopin. An open window separated the driver from the passengers. Lil touched a finger to the button, closing the window, assuring their privacy.

Addy felt stiff and awkward, waiting for whatever was to come. "Jake has told me so many good things about you, Addy. I feel as though I already know you."

"You've . . . talked about me?"

"But of course. You have become the most important person in Jake's life. Why, the changes you have wrought are remarkable."

"Changes? Oh, yes, the changes." This wasn't what Addy had expected. She couldn't seem to focus on the conversation.

"It is not only the physical changes in the house, though they are amazing. The house is almost as beautiful as it was when it was first built." She paused. "Did Jake tell you why he built that house?"

Addy shook her head.

"He built it for a lovely young lady named Miriam. She was the daughter of one of the wealthiest families in Reno.

163

From the moment he met her, Jake fell madly in love. And so he courted her with flowers and jewellery and exotic gifts. During their courtship he commissioned a house that would be worthy of a young woman of her background. And when the house was completed, he moved in and prepared a lavish party in her honour. At that party he intended to ask her to marry him."

"I didn't know Jake was married."

Lil's voice lowered. "He wasn't. The night of the party, Jake learned that Miriam had run off to San Francisco with a young lawyer she had just met."

Addy was surprised at the anger she felt. After all, this must have happened nearly forty years ago. But knowing Jake, and feeling as she did about him, she found herself hating the young woman who had broken his heart.

"What did Jake do?"

"What could he do, chérie? He remained in the house and buried his pain beneath layers of hard work. It is what we all do, is it not?"

Addy nodded. It was what she would do.

In brisk tones Lil said, "I was speaking of changes. The most remarkable changes are in Jake himself. I didn't think anyone would ever get him back to his casino. God knows, I tried. But he wouldn't hear of it. And now." She gave Addy a dazzling smile, "I think Jake is happier than I have ever known him. And it is all thanks to you." She sipped champagne before saying, "But that is not what you want to hear. You want to know who I am, and what I am to Jake."

"It's none of my business, Mrs. . . . ."

"Lil. You must call me Lil. I think it is your business, Addy. You are in Jake's life now, and you need to know all you can about the others who share that life."

"You didn't tell him I was there that day."

"No. It wasn't necessary."

"I'm sorry that I surprised you. I didn't mean to eavesdrop. I forgot something and had to come back for it. And when I did . . ."

"There I was. Yes. I could see that it was awkward for you."

Addy nodded, thinking there would be an explanation. But Lil merely sipped her champagne before saying, "Jake thinks you should look sophisticated and professional. What do you think?"

"I think he's trying to make a silk purse out of a . . ."

"I think that is not the proper comparison, chérie. You are far too pretty to call yourself a sow's ear. Trust me. This should prove to be an easy task." She glanced up as the limousine glided to the curb. "Ah. Here we are. I guess we will have to continue our girl talk over lunch. For now, take a deep breath, Addy. I think you will enjoy."

Addy didn't know what piqued her interest more; shopping, or resuming her talk with this fascinating woman.

Chapter Sixteen

"We'll start here," Lil said, leading Addy to the beauty salon.

The hairdressers smiled their greetings to the woman who was apparently well known and much admired.

"Lil. We've been expecting you." A tall, rugged man wearing a plaid shirt and narrow jeans tucked into ornate cowboy boots hurried forward. Except for his smooth skin and soft hands, he could have looked more at home on a ranch than in a hair salon.

"Hello, James." Lil accepted his kiss on the cheek and said, "This is Addy O'Brien. She's hoping to look polished, sophisticated."

"If that's what you want." His gaze flicked over Addy before he turned to a young assistant. "Margo, help Miss O'Brien into a gown and see that her hair is shampooed."

The girl nodded and led Addy to a small back room where Addy slipped into a shapeless smock.

"So." James approached when her hair was washed, armed with comb and scissors. "You're managing Jake Starr's casino."

"Yes. At least that's what he tells everyone. The truth is, Jake does most of the work. I'm just his legs."

James winked at Lil. "Humility. It's a most refreshing trait. I'd thought it had vanished from the American scene."

Addy watched as he lifted a strand of hair and began to cut.

"I think Jake Starr's legs should have a dash of glamour as well as sophistication."

"I'm afraid I'm not the glamorous type."

James shared a laugh with Lil. "If you think that, Miss O'Brien, then you haven't been looking in the right mirror. You have all the makings of a very glamorous woman." Before she could protest, he draped a long piece of hair over her eyes and commanded, "Bend forward please."

Addy endured the cutting and shaping, the jelling and blow-drying. And when she finally stared in the mirror at the finished product, she was astounded. James had left her hair long enough to just brush her shoulders. It swung in a soft pageboy, pulled back on one side with a jewelled comb. A few wispy hairs dusted her forehead.

When James had finished fussing with a stray hair here, a certain wisp there, and the final spray applied, Addy was led to a makeup booth, where two pretty young women applied foundation, blusher, eye liner, mascara. One of the women showed Addy how to line her lips and fill in the rest with gloss.

"Such beautiful eyes and lips," the girl said. "With just a touch of colour at the lids, we can highlight the deep blue of your eyes. And with such full lips, you need only a trace of lipstick."

When they were finished, the face looking back at her in the mirror was flushed with eagerness. Or was it merely the blusher that had been added to her cheeks? No matter. Addy left the shop feeling beautiful.

"Now to your wardrobe," Lil said, leading Addy toward a designer salon.

A fashionably dressed young woman greeted them and led them to a private room, where suits, dresses, shoes and even undergarments were brought in for Addy's inspection.

With Lil's encouragement, Addy began to sort through the clothes, deciding which ones she wanted to try on and which ones she absolutely didn't like. She found herself passing up the pastels for strong, vibrant colors. Soft,

167

feminine dresses were discarded. Sleek, tailored clothes suited her.

"You have excellent taste, Addy," Lil said when they were alone for a moment. "You had no need of my help."

"Are you kidding?" Addy paced the room, running her hand over the lapel of a deep purple suit, stopping to study the lines of a bright crimson dress and jacket. "I would have never tackled this by myself."

"But you will after this. You see, there is nothing to fear from this place. The people are eager to please you."

Addy lifted the price tag on an emerald cashmere jacket and rolled her eyes. "This certainly isn't the thrift shop. Jake was right. I'd better not look at the prices, or I'll never buy anything."

A clerk returned with the undergarments Lil had suggested. With her assistance, Addy began slipping out of her skirt and blouse.

"Silk," she murmured, running her hand over the teddy as she felt it skim over her flesh. "Don't you think it's too extravagant to wear with business suits?"

"Not a bit. Wait until you see what it does for the inner you, chérie. In no time you will wonder how you ever wore anything else."

Addy studied her reflection in the mirror. "Who'd have ever dreamed . . .?"

Lil saw the soft look in her eyes and wisely kept her thoughts to herself.

Addy tried on a succession of suits and dresses, each one more beautiful than the last.

"If you ever decide to try your hand at a new line of work," the young salesgirl said, "you could be a model."

"Me?" Addy laughed aloud.

"You have a wonderful figure," the girl said, turning Addy so that she could see her reflection.

The red wool suit worn over a simple black chemise was stunning.

"You must take that," Lil said.

Addy nodded. This was starting to be fun. Unselfconsciously she stripped and tried on the next outfit.

*   *   *

"We'll break for lunch," Lil said. "Then we'll tackle shoes and handbags. And some jewellery."

They took a seat in a small, private booth and ordered. Sipping iced tea, Addy leaned back. "I never dreamed shopping could be so tiring."

"I find it exhilarating." Lil accepted a cup of coffee from the waitress and stirred in cream.

"Jake said you dressed hundreds of young women. What was your job?"

"I thought he would have told you. I was responsible for dressing all the girls who worked in Horace Belcher's saloons."

"You – dressed the showgirls?"

Lil laughed. "It was not an easy task. Every girl wanted to look her best. And every girl had a different figure. I was kept very busy trying to please so many tastes. I had to please not only the girls, but the customers who came in to see them. The men, many of whom lived very simple lives and worked hard for their wages, wanted a world of fantasy when they entered a saloon."

"Did you – recruit the girls too. Or just dress them?"

"I never advertised for girls, Addy. There were always dozens of them knocking on my door. Don't forget, fifty years ago there weren't many jobs open to girls who left home. But there were just as many reasons to leave home then as there are now. Though we often never spoke about it, many of the girls had escaped a very unhappy situation. They had to flee with nothing but the clothes on their backs. And they had to find a place to sleep and food to sustain them, or they would be forced to return to the hell of their home."

These were things Addy could easily relate to. She leaned across the table. "How did you get a job like that?"

"I was a costume designer in Paris."

"For movie stars?"

Lil chuckled. "No. For the Follies."

"So you had experience dressing showgirls."

"Yes. That's where I met my first husband, Henri." She leaned back. "I was only seventeen, and he was thirty-five. He was very wealthy, and called himself a patron of the arts." She smiled. "I suppose he was considered a wealthy playboy. But what did I know? At seventeen, I saw only the glamour, the excitement of life in the fast lane. So I married him and thought I would live happily ever after."

Addy knew by her tone that it hadn't worked. "How long were you married?"

"Almost two years. Two years of living hell. But he was very generous when we parted. My second husband, Jérome, was even richer than the first." Her voice lowered. "And even more cruel. I didn't know there were such people in the world. By the time I found the courage to leave him, I had a child. A little boy. It was for him that I vowed to flee to a better life."

Addy sat up straighter. Her iced tea was forgotten. When it came to children, she seemed electrified. "What was your son's name?"

"Raul." Lil's tone softened. "I named him for my father. I adored him." Her tone slowly hardened. "But Jérome decided that his son should be raised by servants in the country, until Raul was old enough to attend the same private schools that his father had. He told me that I could have my freedom, but that I could never have my son."

"What did you do?"

Lil stared into her coffee. "You must remember that it was fifty years ago, Addy. I hired a solicitor, but once Jérome proved that I had worked for the Follies, my reputation was ruined. I was considered a woman of loose morals, unfit to raise his son. I was forbidden to see the boy unless I was accompanied by Jérome." She pushed aside the cup. "I couldn't bear to be so near my son and unable to see him. So, at the tender age of twenty-one, I sailed for America."

"How did you happen to come to Reno?"

"I knew the money from my settlement wouldn't last forever. I went to San Francisco, and took a job designing costumes for the opera. But one night, a group of us went to a burlesque house nearby to hear Veronica Henry, who was a famous singer. After the show she admired my gown, and I told her that I had made it from one of my own designs. She hired me on the spot to design all her gowns for her show. I traveled with her for the next three years." Lil's eyes sparkled, remembering. "Oh, those were grand times. She knew governors and senators. And wherever she went, she wore the gowns I had made for her. I was certain I would one day own one of the finest design houses in the country."

Addy saw the flash of pain in Lil's eyes.

"One night, while Veronica Henry was performing at Horace Belcher's finest saloon in Reno, I received word that Raul had died." She shook her head. "He had died, and I wasn't even notified until after he'd been buried. I must have gone a little crazy. I wept buckets and buckets of tears, and finally, at Veronica's insistence, drank a tall glass of whiskey and fell asleep." She sighed. "It was the first whiskey I had ever tasted, and it was horrible. Until then I had only tasted champagne. But it did the trick. I slept for several hours. When I awoke, Jake, who introduced himself as the new owner of the saloon, told me that he was sending me home to Paris to visit my son's grave." She looked up to see Addy watching her. "I was in no condition to argue. Besides, I needed to see for myself where my son was lying."

"So you went back to Paris?"

"Yes. But only for a week. At the end of that time I booked passage for America. I knew that I would never again return to the place of my birth. My home was now America."

"And you went back to work for Veronica Henry."

"No. Veronica had gone to New York, and left word that she no longer needed my services. She had signed up to do a lavish review on Broadway. All her costumes would be provided. When Jake found out that I needed a job, he asked me to dress the girls he had inherited with his saloon. I was grateful for the work. And even more grateful to meet a man like Jake Starr. He was so solid. So good. So different from the men I had always seemed to attract. I ended up staying on for many years, creating the costumes I loved. I gave up the idea of starting my own shop. I guess I realized that I would miss being part of the excitement of Jake's saloon if I were to leave. You will see, Addy." Her eyes sparkled with the memories. "There is never a dull moment at Jake's."

A waitress brought their lunch, and for several minutes they were silent.

"Oh, this is wonderful," Lil said between bites of a crab filled crépe. "I had forgotten how much fun it is to shop with another woman. Especially a woman who has definite ideas about what she likes and looks good in. Addy, you must go back and try that crimson dress and jacket. I thought it was perfect with your colouring."

Addy threw back her head and laughed. Though she hadn't admitted it until this very moment, she was having the time of her life.

Within the hour they were back in the salon, where she tried on a dozen more outfits before making a final decision.

Three hours later, as the driver and clerks loaded the vehicle with boxes and bags, Addy and Lil slipped into the back seat of the limousine.

Addy kicked off her shoes as Lil handed her a goblet filled with soda. Both women leaned back against the leather cushions and sipped.

When all her purchases were loaded, the vehicle slipped soundlessly away from the curb. For a moment Addy had a flash of memory, of her two little sisters being taken by a nurse and uniformed chauffeur. The sudden wrenching pain left her breathless.

Lil refilled her glass and watched her. There was something there, just below the surface, that had suddenly brought a flash of pain to Addy's eyes.

Lil realized that though she had revealed much about herself, Addy had said very little. It was plain that the young woman had secrets. Secrets she was not yet ready to share.

As the car sped toward home Lil said, "You have not asked me the obvious question, Addy."

"Which is?"

"Why I never married Jake."

Addy looked down. "It's none of my business."

"No. I suppose it is nobody's business except mine and Jake's. But as I said before, you are now in Jake's life. And you have a right to know. I love Jake like a brother, like a father, like my dearest friend. And I believe he feels the same way about me."

Lil saw the questions in Addy's eyes. Questions she was too polite, or too shy, to ask.

Lil's tone was gentle. "Perhaps, at your age, it is difficult to understand. We are good for each other, Jake and I. And for many years we had no one else. And after his accident . . ." She shrugged. ". . . he had no one but me, would trust no one but me to see him like that." She gave a low, easy laugh. "We are still good for each other. Two old fools who make each other feel, for a little while, that we are young again."

As the car pulled into the driveway of Jake's house Lil put a hand on Addy's. "But we have never lied to each other or ourselves. Jake and I will never be anything more than good friends."

The driver walked around the car and held his hand toward Addy. Accepting his help she stepped out, then turned to find Lil still seated. "Aren't you coming in, Lil?"

"No, chérie. It is late. I cannot stay. But I would love to do this again some time."

"So would I. I had a wonderful time, Lil. I don't know how to thank you."

"Thanks are not needed between friends. But I hope you will call me in a few weeks and arrange to shop and have lunch again. It would make me very happy."

"Consider it done. I'll get your number from Jake."

"Goodbye, chérie. Wear the red suit tonight." Lil's eyes crinkled with warmth. "You will knock them dead."

Addy held the door while the driver carried in the boxes and bags until the living room was overflowing with packages. She stood in the doorway waving to Lil until the limousine was out of sight.

Then she turned to find Jake sitting in the doorway between the living room and kitchen, watching her closely.

"Looks like you girls had a successful shopping day."

"Oh, Jake. It was wonderful. I've never seen so many beautiful clothes. I tried on suits and dresses and shoes and things I can't even mention."

Jake threw back his head and laughed. "I told you Lil would show you around. Did you get everything you wanted?"

"I bought things I'd never even dreamed of."

"You look different. I like your hair."

"Thanks. It was Lil's idea."

"How did you and Lil hit it off?"

"She's great. I really enjoyed being with her. In fact, I promised we'd do it again in a couple of weeks." Addy began methodically picking up the packages. "I wanted her to come in to visit for a few minutes. But she said she had to go."

"I'm not surprised." Jake lifted the lid on a shoe box and held up a strappy little high-heeled sandal. "Sexy. I like it." Still examining the shoe he added, "Lil doesn't usually stay out past dinner time. She likes to be home when her husband gets there."

Chapter Seventeen

Jake, still examining the shoe, didn't see the stunned look at Addy's face. When she could recover her voice she said, "Husband?"

"Yeah. Didn't she tell you?" Jake glanced up to find Addy staring at him in surprise. "Lil married for the third time a couple of years ago."

"But you . . ." Addy swallowed back the words and turned away to snatch up bags and boxes until she couldn't hold any more in her hands.

"What, kid?"

"Nothing." Addy raced up the stairs. "I'd better get ready. It's time to get to work."

"Yeah." Jake watched until she disappeared up the stairs. Then he lifted the shoe again and gave a long, low whistle of approval. Placing the shoe back in the box he wheeled his chair into the bedroom.

Upstairs, Addy needed to be busy. Tearing the plastic bags from the clothes, she hung suits and dresses neatly in the closet.

How could Lil be married and still be whatever she was to Jake? And why did she still come around? Did her husband know about her regular visits to Jake? Did he approve? Or was he blissfully unaware of what his wife did while he was otherwise occupied?

As she slipped off her old skirt and blouse and dressed in the red suit, Addy decided that whatever Jake and Lil meant to each other, it wasn't her business. She'd been hired to work for Jake, not to intrude on his personal life. And as for Lil, she'd really enjoyed her company.

She would like to get to know her better, and if possible, call her a friend.

Addy gave herself a quick spray of the perfume she'd chosen from among the dozens she'd sampled. She studied herself in the mirror and couldn't help but smile. This was an entirely new Addy looking back at her.

She thought again, as she so often did, about what Savannah had said so many years ago. If you don't like the person you are, just invent a new one. Addy walked to the door and pulled it open. As she started down the stairs she began to laugh softly. The old Addy O'Brien had just been tossed aside. The crowd at Jake's was about to meet a stranger. If it killed her she'd show them a polished, sophisticated, capable casino manager.

*   *   *

"Addy. What the hell have you done to yourself?" Fingers pushed back his chair and got to his feet so fast he dropped his cards.

Everyone at the poker table looked up, then stared in surprise.

"Oh my God." Bennie Stone straightened the jacket of his jogging suit and sucked in his stomach. "You've got class written all over you, Addy. You look like . . ." He struggled for the right word.

"Like a superstar, Addy," Henry Carstairs injected smoothly. "You look absolutely beautiful."

"Thank you." Addy felt her cheeks flame. She'd hoped someone would notice her. But now that she was the center of attention, she felt the old shyness taking hold. Especially since Sam Money was sitting there staring at her without saying a word. This night he wore a white fisherman's knit sweater over his faded denims. A two-day growth of beard gave him a rough, dangerous appearance.

"Well, I'd better get to . . ."

"You're not going anywhere for a few minutes." Jake

rolled his chair to the poker table and smiled like a proud father. "These old geezers don't get too many chances to ogle pretty girls. So sit a minute and let them feast their eyes. Of course," he added with a chuckle, "Sam's too young to fall into their category, but he can enjoy too."

He signalled to Brenda, who hurried over. "A round of drinks. And cigars."

When Brenda had taken their orders, Jake said, "Change Addy's from soda to champagne."

"Jake, I've got a long night of work ahead of me."

"One little glass of champagne won't hurt. Besides, this is a special day, kid. Enjoy."

When the waitress returned, Jake lifted his glass. "Addy, this old joint has seen a lot of pretty women in its day. There was a time when over a dozen beautiful ladies danced the length of that bar, to the cheers of hundreds of love-starved ranchers and prospectors. But I don't think, in all the years this old place has been standing, that it's ever had a prettier woman under its roof."

"Amen," Fingers muttered.

The men lifted their glasses and solemnly toasted Addy. Sam allowed his gaze to linger, loving the way her cheeks flamed.

Jake watched closely as she sipped her champagne. "Well? What do you think?"

She took a second taste. "It's nice."

"Nice? Champagne is nice?" He laughed. "Addy, that's like saying a royal flush is an interesting hand."

"Or Niagra Falls is a little wet," Fingers said.

They all laughed. Still laughing, Addy tipped up the fluted glass and sipped again. "It fizzes. And it's so smooth. Yes, I think I like champagne." She drank again. "I definitely like it."

"Now you're in trouble, Jake," Bennie Stone said. "She'll have you ordering cases of the stuff."

Addy grinned and took one last sip before standing. "You may be right, Bennie. But the next time I drink it, it'll be at the end of a workday, not at the beginning. Now if you'll excuse me, I have a casino to run."

With a look of pride, Jake watched as she made her way through the tables. He saw the way the dealers turned and watched her as she passed by. Their looks of appreciation weren't lost on him.

"What the hell did you do, Jake?" Fingers asked. "Summon her fairy godmother?"

Jake threw back his head and roared. "That's what I did, Fingers. That's exactly what I did."

*   *   *

"Lil, it's Addy. I know it's been almost a month, but I honestly don't know where the time goes. How about lunch tomorrow?"

Addy could hear the pleasure in the woman's tone as she accepted.

"Why don't I pick you up this time? Noon? I'll get directions from Jake. See you tomorrow."

Addy replaced the receiver and hurried up the stairs to dress for work.

*   *   *

Addy expected Lil's home to reflect the woman. Elegant, refined. She wasn't disappointed. At the closed iron gates she announced herself to a black box mounted on a post. Moments later the gates swung wide to admit Jake's freshly polished Mercedes.

As Addy drove up the curving drive, she admired the two story house of gleaming white stucco and Spanish tile roof. A crew of workmen swarmed over the carefully manicured lawns and gardens.

When Addy stopped the car at the sweeping front porch, a houseman opened the double doors and stood at the top step to admit her. Before Addy could ascend the steps Lil was rushing forward to greet her.

"Addy. Welcome." She linked her arm through Addy's and led the way. "Did you have any trouble finding my place?"

Addy laughed. "No. I just followed Jake's directions. He told me to look for the biggest house in town. Now I see that he wasn't kidding."

As they swept through the front entrance, Addy paused, unable to take it all in at once.

The walls, the floors, the massive sofas, were all dazzling white. A white granite fireplace dominated one wall. On one side of the room was a white grand piano. The only touches of colour came from the bouquets of fresh flowers that were massed in front of the fireplace and in low bowls on every table. The air was perfumed with their fragrance.

"Come, Addy. You must see the view from the terrace."

Lil led her past a grand dining room with walls of glass overlooking a formal rose garden. French doors led to a lovely terrace, paved with brick. Dozens of clay pots filled every corner with colorful blooms.

"Below us, chérie, is the city of Reno. Above us are the majestic Sierras."

"Oh, Lil. What must it be like to wake every day to this?"

Lil smiled, but the smile froze on her lips as a man came into view.

"Company, darling?" He crossed the terrace and stood beside her.

"Giovanni, this is Addy O'Brien. Addy, my husband, Giovanni Miccelli."

Addy had a quick impression of a man who, though over seventy, had barely a line or wrinkle on his tanned face. His hair was steel gray. His charcoal suit was impeccably tailored. He was as handsome as Lil was beautiful. They would appear the perfectly matched couple.

He took Addy's hand and studied her closely. "Jake Starr's new companion? You've astounded everyone by

179

lasting longer than any of the others. Tell me your secret. Are you just tougher than Jake, or has the old grouch stopped being so obnoxious?"

"Jake's tough," Addy said with a smile, "but I'm tougher."

A maid placed a tray on a glass-topped table. Giovanni opened a bottle of champagne and filled three fluted glasses. He handed one to Addy and one to his wife. Lifting a glass he said, "I suppose we should drink to Jake. After all, even though he isn't here with us, he's hardly ever far away. Wouldn't you agree, darling?"

"To Jake," Lil said, avoiding her husband's eyes.

After they had sipped, Giovanni said, "My wife couldn't stop talking about you after your day of shopping. It would seem that she has made a new friend."

"I'm glad. I had such a good time."

"We should go," Lil said, setting down her glass. "I made reservations for noon."

"Where are you eating, darling?"

Lil dropped her cocktail napkin. "Nikko's."

"Good food, if you like Greek. I'll see you at five." He leaned forward and touched his lips to Lil's cheek. His fingers tightened around her arm for a fraction. "I'm off to the club." Straightening, he gave Addy a cool smile. "It was nice meeting you, Addy."

She watched as he walked from the terrace. Lil, she noted, was still staring at the view of the city below.

"Well, I'll just get my purse." Lil linked her arm through Addy's once more and led the way through the opened French doors. Minutes later they were heading along the curved driveway. As soon as they passed through the iron gates and turned toward the city, Lil's mood seemed to lighten.

"Oh, Addy," she breathed, "I am so happy you asked me to lunch. I can't think of anything I'd rather do today."

With a little sigh she leaned back and watched as the rows of beautiful houses slipped past her line of vision.

"For a little while I'd like to talk and laugh and think of nothing more serious than what wine to drink with my lunch."

Addy made a mental note to keep their conversation light.

* * *

". . . and the old man was so excited about tossing the dice to make his point that when he leaned over the table his false teeth fell out."

Addy's stories about the casino had kept Lil laughing for the past hour. Now, wiping tears of laughter from her eyes Lil asked, "What did you do?"

"I just stared at the poor dear. But old Wendle, who's been dealing craps for Jake for over thirty years, never even batted an eye. He just pulled out his own false teeth, tossed them down on the table and yelled, 'You're faded.' While everyone else was still laughing the old man tossed the dice, made his point, shoved his teeth back in his mouth, and graciously offered to let Wendle keep his."

Lil and Addy were still laughing when the waiter brought the bill. Addy snatched it away before Lil could touch it. "This is my treat."

"But I can so easily afford it, Addy. Jake tells me that you save every penny you earn."

"Yes." Addy thought about the bank account that was growing steadily every week. Soon, very soon, she could begin the search.

"Where did you go just then?"

Addy mentally shook herself. "Sorry. I was just think-ing."

"About the money?"

Addy nodded. "About what it will buy."

"And what is that, chérie? Diamonds? Minks? Fast cars?"

"Oh." Addy gave a short laugh. "I don't want those

things, Lil. All I've ever wanted is . . ." She stopped when she realized what she had almost revealed.

Lil waited, watching her eyes.

When Addy remained silent, the older woman said softly, "We all want things that sometimes seem beyond our reach." Her tone grew dreamy. "There was a time when all I could think of was getting my son. When I was finally forced to admit that it could never be, it was the most painful episode in my life. Everything since then has been anticlimactic."

"How would your life have changed if you'd been granted custody of him?" Addy suddenly asked.

"Ah, chérie. Don't you think I have asked this of myself a million times or more? The thought of it tantalizes me. I tell myself that I could have kept him alive. That he would have grown to be a fine man, with a wife and children of his own. My grandchildren." Addy saw the light go out of her eyes as she added softly, "There was a part of me that died with him in Paris. A part of me that no one else can ever fill." She put her hand over Addy's and said, "How can I expect one as young and beautiful as you to understand such heartache? It is beyond explanation."

"But I do," Addy said suddenly. "I do because it's happened to me."

Lil studied her in silence. "Are you saying that you had a child, Addy?"

"I had two little sisters. They were like my own." Her voice took on an edge of steel that Lil had never heard before. "I loved them more than anyone else ever could."

"What happened to your sisters, chérie?"

Addy struggled desperately to compose herself. It was so tempting to unburden her heart. But she had kept the secret for so long now. And she wasn't yet ready to trust. Not even Lil.

Seeing the waiter hovering, Addy dug into her purse and removed a bill. Placing it on the tray, she signalled to the waiter. "Keep the change."

When he walked away she said, "They were sent to live with strangers. I was taken to a state shelter."

"Ah," Lil said with a trace of sympathy. "They were adopted. And I suppose the adoption agency is reluctant to give out any information they consider secret. Have you any way of finding the names of the people with whom they now live?"

Addy shook her head. "I don't know. But as soon as I have enough money saved, I intend to try."

"You mean you will launch an investigation into your sisters' new identities."

"Yes."

"I wish you luck." Lil glanced at her watch and picked up her handbag. "I must leave, Addy."

They drove most of the way in silence. When they turned into the curving ribbon of drive that led to Lil's magnificent house, she cocked her head to study Addy. "I think we were fated to meet, chérie. We now discover that Jake is not our only link. We have both been denied the love of those closest to us. And we both know it is a pain that never goes away."

When Addy brought the car to a stop Lil caught her hand and pressed it between both of hers.

"Thank you for lunch, my dear. And even more, thank you for telling me about your sisters. I know it is painful. But I think you are much stronger than I. You will find them. And you will make them a part of your life again."

"Do you believe that, Lil?"

"I truly do, Addy." She leaned over and kissed Addy's cheek. "Call me soon."

"I will."

Addy drove along the curving drive and glanced in the rearview mirror. Lil was still standing where she had left her, on the steps leading to her home. Even when Addy drove through the metal gates, she could see Lil standing, watching. Looking very much alone.

Chapter Eighteen

Addy walked out of the bank and sat down in the car. But instead of turning on the ignition, she sat staring at the figures in her bank book.

Five thousand dollars. That was more than she'd ever dreamed she could have in her possession.

It was time.

She opened her purse and studied the ad she'd torn from the newspaper: Gordon Schechter, Private Investigator. All services confidential.

She read the address, then turned on the ignition and began to thread her way through traffic.

Yes, she thought again as she pulled up to a row of brand new office buildings. It was time.

She sat a moment, studying the elegant gold letters on the door, then forced herself to get out of the car. At the entrance to the office she stopped again, feeling her heart begin to pound. Before she could lose her nerve she knocked, then opened the door.

The furniture was new, and as elegant as the man behind the massive faux marble slab that served as a desk. Two ornate chairs flanked the desk. Behind each chair was a huge potted plant.

The man was talking on the phone. When he caught sight of Addy he slowly swiveled his chair and mumbled something into the phone before replacing it.

His desktop was bare except for several important looking forms. A crystal ashtray was littered with cigarette butts. In one slick motion he emptied it into a wastebasket.

His hair was sleek, razor cut, giving him the appearance

of an actor or a model. Gold cufflinks glinted beneath the sleeves of a beautifully tailored dark pinstripe suit.

He looked very prosperous. Very successful. That was good. He probably had hundreds of satisfied customers.

"Are you Gordon Schechter?"

"I am. And you are . . .?"

"Addy O'Brien."

"Hello, Addy." He stood to offer his hand and she saw the glint of gold and diamonds on his finger. "What can I do for a pretty little thing like you?"

In one quick glance he took in the designer suit, the simple but elegant jewellery, the businesslike approach.

"No," he said quickly when she opened her mouth to speak. "Let me guess. You want me to follow your husband. That's what I do best. Evidence for divorce cases. All I need is his name and a photo if you have one. And the last place he worked."

"I'm not married."

"Oh. I see." He gave a sly smile. "You think the boyfriend is up to a little hanky-panky, huh?"

Addy glanced at the door. This had been a mistake. She needed time to think over what she was about to do.

When he saw the way her gaze darted to the door Gordon Schechter moved swiftly around the desk and led her to a chair. "Why don't you tell me why you're here."

She looked up at him. Despite the slight hint of arrogance about him, she decided that he had a nice smile.

Taking a deep breath she said, "I'd like you to find my sisters."

"How long have they been missing?"

"Ten years."

"Were they snatched by a parent in a messy divorce?"

Addy shook her head.

"Given up for adoption?"

Again she shook her head.

"Look, Miss O'Brien, I need a little help here. Why don't you start at the beginning and tell me everything."

She looked away. This was going to be a lot more

185

painful than she'd expected. When she looked up, Gordon Schechter was leaning a hip against the edge of his desk, watching her.

"Go ahead. Just tell me everything."

Addy did. Quickly. Without emotion.

When she was finished Gordon Schechter let out a long, slow whistle. "That's some story. But after all these years . . ."

"I can afford to pay you," she interrupted.

"Yeah?" He was silent for a minute. "You know what you're asking? I'd have to start at the beginning, where you grew up, people who knew you, and follow maybe a hundred false leads before I find one solid one."

"I don't care. And I don't care how long it takes, or how much money it takes. I want my sisters back with me."

"We're talking – thousands of dollars."

She nodded.

His eyes narrowed slightly. "Maybe twenty-five, thirty thousand."

"I don't have that much yet."

"Then I . . ."

"All I have is five thousand."

He stood and walked behind the desk to hide the gleam that had suddenly appeared in his eyes. When he turned to her his manner was subdued. "Five thousand's a start, of course. And I'll need it all up front for the expenses I'm going to incur."

"All of it?"

"You want those sisters, don't you?"

She blinked at the harshness of his tone. "I said I did."

"Then don't start our business association by quibbling over dollars. I'll take a check for five thousand and get started right away. Here," he said, passing a blank form across the desk. "Fill this out carefully. I'll need this information for my investigation."

Addy filled in all the blanks with the name of her childhood home, the names of neighbours who might still live in the Paradise Mobile Home Park, the names of teachers who might remember her. When she was finished, the private detective read it over and said, "Very thorough, Miss O'Brien. This should be a big help. And now the check."

"I'll need a receipt."

"Of course."

Addy made out a check for five thousand and waited while he wrote out a receipt. Tucking it carefully into her purse she stood. "When do you think I'll hear from you, Mr. Schechter?"

"I can't say. A case like this might keep me away from my office for days, weeks, or even months." Moving smoothly around the desk he guided her toward the door. "I'll phone you once a month, to keep you abreast of what I've discovered." Opening the door he took her hand. "I'll get back with you. But it will be at least a month before you hear from me. Keep a good thought, Miss O'Brien."

Addy found herself standing outside the office, feeling slightly dazed. Walking to the car she got in, fastened her seatbelt, and sat staring at the name on the door. Gordon Schechter, Private Investigator. It wasn't like her to put her trust in a man. Especially a stranger she'd just found in a newspaper ad. But she had no choice. Someone had to find Erin and Shannon. Someone had to help her make them a family again.

She was pinning all her hopes on this man. She felt the old familiar pounding in her chest.

As she drove away she tried to do as he'd instructed and hold a good thought. Soon. Soon it would all be over.

What would Erin and Shannon look like now? Shannon would be ten and Erin fifteen. Had someone given them love and affection? Oh, what a joyful reunion they would have. She hadn't allowed herself to indulge in such fantasies, for fear of having her heart broken. But now . . .

As she stopped for a traffic light, she found herself weeping uncontrollably. With the help of Gordon

Schechter, Private Investigator, her dream was about to come true.

*   *   *

It was a Friday night, traditionally the busiest night of the week. The locals had collected their paychecks and couldn't wait to spend them. The tourists were out in droves. Addy found herself dividing her time between the blackjack tables and the craps tables.

As she watched a game in progress at the dice table, a grizzled old man with a gray beard and shaggy gray hair pushed his way between two players and tossed a hundred dollar bill on the table. Immediately the dealers greeted him warmly and handed him his chips.

He didn't play until the dice were directly in front of him. Then he placed all one hundred dollars on the pass line and picked up the dice. He held the dice for less than fifteen minutes. But in that time he'd turned his hundred dollars into two thousand. When he finally threw a seven, he politely thanked every dealer at the table, then cashed in his chips and walked to the bar where he ordered a double shot of whiskey without ice.

Intrigued, Addy went in search of Jake, who was playing poker with the others.

When she'd described the old man to him, Jake gave a knowing smile. "That's old Joey the Horse."

"Joey the Horse?"

He grinned. "Next time you see him, look for the bulge in the hip pocket of his faded old overalls. He carries a horseshoe for luck. He's been coming in here every Friday for as long as I can remember. Nobody knows his real name. But he has a couple of nicknames. Some of the dealers call him Horseshoe Joe. I've always called him Joey the Horse. He never plays for more or less than a hundred dollars. If he's winning, he keeps playing until he loses. If he loses the first bet, it's all over. Either way he walks to the bar and has one drink, then leaves."

"He looks like a grizzled old prospector," Addy remarked.

Jake shrugged. "Could be. Or a rancher. Or maybe just an oldtimer from the town.

"I'll bet he has some great stories to tell," she sighed.

"Maybe. But he's never made an attempt to strike up a conversation with anybody, and we've always respected his privacy."

A short time later Addy saw the old man make his way to the front entrance, where Shorty doffed his hat respectfully as he held the door for him.

Addy envisioned him climbing on the back of a horse and riding off to his claim somewhere high in the hills, where he would continue his search for gold nuggets until the following Friday night.

*   *   *

Addy heard the ringing of the phone and dashed down the stairs. But before she could reach it, Jake had picked up the receiver.

"Jake Starr here. Yeah, Milt. Sam says the monthlies are ready to be picked up. Okay. See you tomorrow."

As he replaced the receiver he glanced at Addy, who was still catching her breath from the run. "What's with you and the phone lately? Every time it rings you almost kill yourself to grab it." He gave her a long narrow look. "You expecting something?"

"No, I . . ." She felt tears threaten and blinked furiously. "It's been over a month and I haven't heard a word."

"Over a month of what?"

Across the room Sam looked up.

"Oh, Jake." She dropped down on the bottom step and drew her arms around her knees. Despite the designer suit she'd just put on for work, she looked like a sad, frightened little girl.

"Come on, kid. Tell old Jake."

"I can't."

"You'd better share it with someone before you bust a gut. Come on. What's this all about?"

"I hired a private detective."

Sam's hand tightened on the tumbler. It was the only sign that he was listening.

"What!" Jake looked alarmed. "Why?"

"To find my sisters."

"What do you need with a detective? Why not just call the State of Nevada? They'll put you in touch with the adoption agency that placed them."

"They weren't adopted."

"Come on, Addy. I read your record. The one Witherspoon got from the shelter. It said you had two sisters who were adopted."

She took a deep breath. "That's what everybody thinks. But that's not what really happened."

"What did happen?"

"I can't tell you. I can't tell anybody."

A muscle started to work in Sam's jaw. "Did you tell this detective you hired?"

She glanced at him, then back at Jake. "I had to. He wouldn't take the job until he had all the facts. But I can't tell anyone else. I just can't."

"Look, kid." Jake was struggling to hold his temper at bay, but there were times when all the willpower in the world couldn't help. "If you can't tell me what happened to your sisters, you can at least goddamned tell me who you've hired to find them."

"His name is Gordon Schechter. He's in a fancy new building downtown."

Jake glanced at Sam. "Gordon Schechter, huh? And you say you haven't heard from this guy in over a month?" His eyes narrowed with a sudden thought. "How much did you pay him?"

She couldn't meet his eyes.

"Come on, kid. How much."

"Five thousand dollars."

"What!" He slammed a hand against the wheel, sending

the chair racing toward her. When he was mere inches away he thundered, "Are you telling me you took everything I've paid you and gave it to some lousy, oily thief?"

"He's not a thief, Jake. He's a private investigator."

"My ass. If you haven't heard from him in a month, you're never going to hear from him again. He's already half-way across the country with your money. The sonofabitch saw you coming."

"Jake, I . . ."

"Come on," he said, wheeling his chair toward the door. "Get the car, Sam. Let's pay a visit to Addy's Mr. Schechter."

While Sam drove, Jake brooded in silence. Five thousand dollars. Everything she'd managed to save. He thought of how hard she'd worked, how many hours she'd slaved to earn that money. He couldn't think of another human being who was as devoted to making money as Addy. She never spent a dime of it for her own pleasures. She'd probably do without food if she had to, before she'd spend any of her money. But she'd stupidly given all of it to a smoothtalking thief. Jake thought of a few choice oaths and swallowed them back.

The car pulled up to the row of shiny new office buildings and parked in front of the one that Addy indicated. As she started out of the car her eyes widened and she slumped back.

"Oh no."

"What?" Jake studied her stricken face. "What's wrong?"

"His name is gone from the office. It was right there, Jake. And now it's gone."

He clenched his hands in his lap. "He's skipped with your money."

"No."

She flew out of the car and raced to the door. Sam followed more slowly.

The door was locked. She peered through the window and saw that the office was completely empty. All the fancy furniture was gone. The desk, the chair, the elegant gold telephone, were all gone. Pasted to the window was a sign offering the office for lease.

Through the car window Jake watched helplessly as Addy pounded her fists on the door in impotent rage. For long minutes she stood staring through the window, as if willing everything to be right. Finally, her head lowered, her eyes red-rimmed, she allowed Sam to turn her toward the car.

"You were right, Jake. He's gone. And so is my money."

She slumped in the back seat while Sam turned the key in the ignition. "We'd better get to the casino."

"We're going home, kid."

She glanced at Jake. "We're already late for work."

His voice was chilled. "I don't give a good goddamn about the casino right now. Drive us home, Sam."

They rode the entire distance in silence. When they reached the house, Jake waited until Sam had his wheelchair ready, and manoeuvered himself into it. When they entered the house he went around switching on lights. Addy followed behind them and stood in the middle of the room.

"Now," Jake said, swiveling his chair to face her. "You're going to tell me the whole story."

"You already know it. I paid a man five thousand . . ."

"I don't give a crap about the money. I want to know what the hell is going on with your sisters. If they weren't given up for adoption all those years ago, what really happened to them?"

"I can't talk about it, Jake."

"You will, goddamn it. We're not leaving here until you tell me the truth."

Her voice rose to near hysteria. "It's none of your business."

"I'm making it my business. Now spill it, goddamn it, before I shake it out of you."

"No."

He wheeled his chair closer and snaked out a hand, holding her when she tried to pull away.

She'd forgotten how strong he was. He'd honed the muscles of his upper body to compensate for the loss of power in his legs. There was no way she could wrench herself free.

"Let me go, Jake."

"Not until you talk to me."

"I can't."

His hand trembled with frustration but he kept his tone deliberately calm. "You will. It all starts with your father, right?"

She nodded and felt the tears sting the backs of her eyes.

"He was a junkie, you said."

Addy felt the lump start in her throat and threaten to choke her.

"Did he need money, Addy? Was that it?"

She swallowed. In a trembling voice she said, "He was always losing his jobs. And always blaming us. And then one morning, when he'd been gone for days, he returned and seemed – different. Excited, like something big and wonderful was about to happen."

When she stopped Jake squeezed her hand. "Go on, Addy."

She stared down at their joined hands and felt the power in his. Almost as if he was willing her his strength.

In a halting voice she whispered, "I trusted him when he told me to get Erin and Shannon all cleaned up. I bathed them and dressed them in their best clothes. But I knew he wasn't acting right. I knew. But when he told me to go to school, I was too afraid to argue. So I left." Her eyes filled but she blinked away the tears. "I left them with him, Jake. I just left them there at his mercy. They were being driven away in a limousine when my school bus dropped me off. And when I got home from school I learned that he'd sold them."

Jake's hands tightened on hers. For a moment he

couldn't believe what he'd heard. "How do you know he sold them?"

Tears flooded her eyes and began to spill over. "There were piles of money on the table. He was counting it. And when I confronted him, he admitted it. He said they'd have a better life where they were going."

She tried to pull her hands away but Jake held them tighter.

"Come on, kid. Get it all out."

Her voice trembled with sobs. "He wouldn't tell me where they were going, or even if they'd be together. All I know is he sold them. And when I told him he was no longer my father, he knocked me down and left me lying on the kitchen floor." The words were coming faster now, as if she had a terrible need to get them all out before the flood of tears. "And he never came back. Jake, he never came back to tell me where Erin and Shannon were. He died before he could tell me. His truck was hit by a train that night, and all that money drifted all over the tracks for strangers to pick up. And the secret died with him." Her voice lowered. "I have to find them. Don't you see? I have to find them. We're family. I promised my mama before she died that I'd always hold us together. Oh God, don't you see? I left them alone with him and he sold them. It was my fault as well as his. I knew he was weak. And I just left them alone with him."

She fled up the stairs.

Jake and Sam listened to the sound of her footsteps as she took the stairs two at a time in her eagerness to escape. They heard the creaking of the old mattress as she flung herself across the bed.

Sam could picture her, lying across the big old bed like a small, broken bird. He thought about going to her. But what comfort could he really offer?

With his hands clenched he fought the feeling of outrage that simmered inside him.

Finally he'd learned the secrets she'd kept in her heart for so long. At last he was beginning to understood the

194

mystery of Addy. She was carrying wounds as deep as his own.

He glanced at Jake. The old man sat, stiff and unbending, deep in thought. And Sam knew that, somehow, Jake was already figuring a way to put all the pieces back together.

Chapter Nineteen

"So the guy was using an alias."

Sam nodded. "He's been pulling this scam all over the state. He's used so many names, his rap sheet fills a dozen pages."

"Got a picture of the rat?"

"A couple." Sam handed them to Jake. "But he never looks the same. He's a master of disguise. He sets up shop, reels in a couple of rich fish, and moves on before they can blow the whistle. Most of the people he's conned are women hoping to get evidence against cheating husbands. They're not likely to come forward and admit what they were up to."

Jake's eyes narrowed as he studied the handsome face in the photographs.

"So what'd he do to you, Jake?" Bennie asked.

"He made me mad, Bennie. And you know I never forget."

"Yeah." Bennie grinned. "I don't think I want to play poker with you tonight. In this mood, you won't quit until you've drawn blood."

Jake forced himself to relax as he shoved the pictures down into a pocket of his wheelchair. "Yeah. You're right. Maybe I'd better just mingle tonight and forget about the game."

"If I hear any more about this Schechter guy I'll let you know," Sam said. "I don't have the connections in the Reno PD that I had in New York, but I've still got a few markers I can call in."

"Thanks, Sam. I appreciate it."

Unlike Jake, Sam kept his temper under wraps. But just below the surface, he was seething with rage.

*   *   *

Addy left the bank and got into the car, then opened her bankbook and studied the balance. It was nowhere near five thousand dollars. Five thousand. Every time she thought about how easily she'd been duped, she wanted to cry. But out of that ugly situation had come a new respect for money. If a thief could use her money for his own pleasures, she could learn to enjoy it herself. From now on, she vowed, if there was something she really wanted, she wouldn't put it off. She'd buy it, even though it meant dipping into the fund she'd set up to find her sisters.

Turning on the ignition, she headed toward the store. While she drove, she thought about the brochure she'd clipped from a magazine. Her birthday was coming up, and she wanted to buy a special gift. Only this time, before she parted with a large chunk of her money, she'd get a look at the merchandise first. She'd ordered it to be shipped C.O.D. She hoped the package arrived some morning while Jake was still sleeping.

*   *   *

"Don't plan any dinner tonight," Jake said as he sipped his afternoon coffee. "I want to eat at Jake's tonight."

"Okay." Addy continued scrubbing the counter tops and cabinets until they gleamed. It was such a special day, she needed to keep extra busy so she wouldn't jump out of her skin from sheer excitement.

"Why are you doing that?" Jake asked.

"Doing what?"

"Scrubbing. You're always scrubbing everything."

Addy paused to give him a quick look, then turned back to her work. "I like things clean. Does it bother you?"

"I don't like seeing you working all the time. Don't you ever just sit down and relax?"

She crossed the room and took a seat across the table, still clutching the dust rag in her hand. "Okay. I'm sitting down. Now what's bothering you?"

"You're sitting, but you're not relaxing. What do you do to relax, kid?"

She shrugged. "I don't know. I never had time to think about it. What should I do?"

"Hell, I can't tell you how to relax. But I always figured most women your age would rather sprawl on the sofa and watch soaps, or sit and read love stories. All you ever do with your spare time is work."

"I like it, Jake. I really do."

He drained his coffee. "Yeah. I think you mean it. We're two of a kind. We both love to work. Give me an hour to go over the books with Sam and then we'll go to the casino."

She headed up the stairs to shower and dress. Excitement had her fumbling with the buttons of her dress, and dropping an earring twice before she managed to get it on. She couldn't wait to see Jake's face when he saw her surprise.

Two hours later they were being greeted by Shorty, who gallantly doffed his cowboy hat and held the double doors while Addy wheeled Jake inside.

When they reached the poker tables, Addy moved aside as Jake took over the chair, leaning his strength into the wheels until he rolled to a stop beside his friends.

"Evening, Jakie," Fingers called over the rim of his cards. When Addy turned away to speak to Bennie Stone, Fingers winked and whispered, "Everything's ready."

"Good." Jake greeted Henry Carstairs, then asked, "How about the others?"

"They're all here."

Jake nodded and looked up when Addy and Bennie joined them. "I'm feeling a little bit hungry. How about an early dinner?"

Addy gave him her brightest smile. "I was just thinking the same thing. How about if Fingers, Bennie and Henry join us?"

Jake relaxed. This was even easier than he'd hoped. "Sure. Why not? How about it? You guys want to have some dinner with us?"

"You bet. Wouldn't miss it," Fingers said.

With his friends by his side, Jake rolled his chair toward the coffee shop. Addy trailed behind, looking very smug.

When they entered the coffee shop Rosetta led them past Jake's regular booth, stopping at a round table set up in the center of the room. A centerpiece of bright balloons danced above it. Seated at the table were Shorty, Andrew Witherspoon, Milton Carver, and Jake's doctor, Boyd Wilton. And Sam Money, wearing a blue denim shirt.

Addy's mouth dropped open. She'd planned a surprise, but not this surprise. She hadn't ordered balloons. And she definitely hadn't thought to invite Jake's doctor, lawyer and accountant.

"How did you . . .?" She stopped and tried again. "Who told you about . . .?"

"What's the matter, kid? Cat got your tongue?"

Addy glanced at Jake, who was grinning from ear to ear. "I don't understand. How could you possibly know about today?"

"Hell, you think I'd forget? This is our first anniversary. It was a year ago today that you came to work for me, kid."

"You mean that's what this is all about?" She started to laugh. When she glanced at Bennie's beaming face, she laughed even harder. "Oh, Jake. This is wonderful."

"I don't get it, kid. What's so goddamned funny?"

"It's just that . . ." She took the seat next to him and said to everyone at the table. "Today is special for another reason. Today is my birthday."

"You're kidding?" Jake turned to look at her, then glanced around the table. "Isn't that something? I planned a surprise dinner, and didn't even realize it was Addy's birthday. Rosetta," he called, "this is an extra special occasion. Bring out the champagne."

As the waitress filled their glasses, Shorty presented Addy with a bouquet of red roses. "Jake wanted you to have these in honour of your first anniversary, Miss Addy."

"Thank you, Shorty." She pressed a kiss to his cheek and his face turned as red as the roses before he returned to his seat.

Then Addy leaned over and kissed Jake's cheek. "You're not the only one who can plan a surprise, Jake," she murmured. "In honour of my birthday I wanted to buy you something special."

"Me? Why the hell should you buy me a gift when it's your birthday?"

"Because I don't know when your birthday is. And because I thought it would be fun to give a gift instead of getting one."

She lowered her face to the roses and inhaled their fragrance.

"Although I must say I love these."

Jake was actually twitching with excitement. "Where's my present? What'd you buy me?"

"Settle down, Jakie," Fingers called from the other side of the table. "You're worse than a little kid."

Addy nodded to Bennie, who left the table and returned a moment later riding a motorized wheelchair.

"I thought you might enjoy your own sportscar," Addy said with a smile.

"You mean that's mine?"

"It is if you like it."

With Bennie's help Jake slid from his bulky wheelchair to the trim little motorized scooter. For a few minutes he studied the buttons and read the directions, then threw it into reverse and backed away from the table. For long minutes he cruised around the room, dodging tables and waitresses. When he returned to the table, his face was flushed with pleasure.

"I'll be goddamned if this isn't the finest invention since sliced bread."

"You like it?" Addy asked.

"Like it? Kid, I love it." He brought the scooter in close and framed her face with his big hands. "I'm crazy about it. And about you."

While the others cheered and shouted, he kissed her soundly.

"Sam helped me keep the surprise," she said softly. "He kept it hidden here in the casino until today."

"I thought you two were up to something," Jake said innocently. "I've seen the way you two look at each other when you think nobody's looking."

Addy felt her face flame.

Sam felt distinctly uncomfortable.

"Now," Jake said, unaware of what he'd just revealed. "Let's drink a toast to Addy." He turned to her. "How old are you today?"

"Twenty-two."

"Twenty-two?" He shook his head, trying to remember all those years ago when he'd been that young. "Gentlemen, here's to Addy, and to the bright, beautiful future that stretches out before her. What a life you've got left to live, kid."

Everyone lifted their glasses and drank. Sam's gaze never left her face as he lifted his glass and touched it to the others.

"And here's to our first year together. May there be many, many more."

They drank again.

Addy lifted her glass. "And here's to Jake. I think I'll have to buy roller skates to keep up with him now that he has new wheels."

They all laughed before they drank again. But as the others talked and laughed among themselves, Jake surprised Addy by catching her hand and lifting it to his lips. "You've made me one hell of a happy man, kid."

Before she could respond, Andrew Witherspoon pushed away from the table and approached them. "I drew up the new contract you requested, Jake. Would you like me to give it to Addy now?"

"Yeah, you might as well." Jake watched as the lawyer handed Addy a sheaf of documents.

She read them, then looked up in surprise. "This can't be right."

"Why's that?"

"It says that I'm to direct the housekeeper in her duties, as well as serve as casino manager and assistant to the owner."

"So. What's wrong with that?"

"Jake, we don't have a housekeeper."

"Oh, did I forget to tell you? I thought we'd hire someone to take care of the shopping and the household chores. I think you and I are going to be spending even more time here from now on."

She couldn't think of a thing to say.

"Well? Are you going to sign it, or am I going to have to send Witherspoon out for your replacement?"

She took the pen he offered and quickly scratched her name. As she handed it back she said, "No replacements, Jake. I wouldn't miss this for the world."

"Men either, kid." He signalled to Rosetta, who instructed the waitresses to begin serving. As he tucked into his favourite meal of steak and potatoes, he paused a moment to mutter, "I wouldn't have missed a single day of it."

Addy glanced across the table toward Sam, who lifted his glass in a salute. In a slightly slurred voice he said, "You're a lucky man, Jake. Here's to a long and happy partnership to you both."

Addy watched as he drained his glass. A waitress approached immediately with a refill.

*　　*　　*

At lunch with Lil a week later, Addy described the new housekeeper.

"Her name's Verna. She was widowed a year ago. No children. She said she didn't need the money, but she needed to find something to do or she'd go crazy."

"Is she pretty?" Lil asked.

"Uum, no. I guess you'd call her plain. And she's kind of cranky, especially when Jake wakes up in one of his moods. But she's neat and clean, and she's a great cook. She has a place nearby, so she's not worried about driving home late at night."

"I'm glad you have help now, chérie," Lil said, sipping hot tea with lemon. "More than once I told Jake that he was asking too much of you."

"I didn't mind."

"Of course not. But now you can concentrate on your duties at the casino. How is it working out?"

Addy gave her a wide smile. "I love it. Oh, Lil, there are so many exciting and funny things that happen every day. Sometimes I wonder what my life would have been like if I hadn't accepted this job with Jake. How dull it would have been without Jake and the casino."

Lil gave a knowing smile. "I see you have fallen under the spell, chérie."

"The spell." Addy nodded. "Jake warned me. And it's happened."

Chapter Twenty

Since Addy and Jake and Sam had taken over the operation of Jake's, profits began to soar.

Jake was pleasantly surprised to learn that Sam was methodical in his paperwork.

"I spent a lot of years filling out documents in triplicate," Sam explained dryly.

Since Sam was willing, he and Milton Carver took over the monthly statements, freeing Jake for other things.

Jake was equally pleased at how quickly Addy learned all that he wanted to teach her. With Verna now assuming all of the household chores, Addy was free to study Jake's book-keeping methods and to reorganize the personnel files. Jake often allowed Addy, Sam and Milton Carver to handle the bulk of the paperwork.

One evening Addy found Jake pouring over some papers. When she peered over his shoulder he grinned.

"I've always wanted to build a hotel alongside the casino. In fact, I had the plans drawn up years ago, before my accident."

He spread the papers over the kitchen table and called to Sam. "Take a look at these. I thought we could duplicate the old Western theme, but incorporate the latest technology. The architect's renderings have already been approved and the necessary permits were drawn up years ago."

Sam and Addy studied the drawings, and at the same moment turned towards each other with similar smiles.

Jake gave a delighted laugh. "You see. It's got you hooked, too. Admit it, it's a great idea, isn't it?"

Addy slowly nodded, while Sam began talking excitedly

about even more changes they ought to make.

"That goddamn does it. I'm going ahead with it." Jake shot them a sideways grin. "We're going ahead with it," he amended. "And we're going to change the name from Jake's to Starr's."

Life couldn't be much better, Addy thought as she drifted off to sleep that night. She hugged the thought to her heart. She had a job she loved, a house that felt like home, and a man who fulfilled every fantasy she'd ever entertained about a grandfather. And now they were starting an even greater adventure.

As sleep overtook her, her lips curved into a smile.

* * *

It was two months before Addy thought she had enough saved to attempt another search for her sisters. This time she decided, since Jake and Sam were already familiar with the facts, she would take them into her confidence.

"I'd like to hire another private investigator. What do you think?"

Jake and Sam looked up from their paperwork.

Jake peered at her over the rim of his glasses. "Who'd you have in mind?"

"I've been checking the ads in the Yellow Pages. There's one, Francis X. Turner, who claims to be a former F.B.I. agent. His ad says he's licensed by the State of Nevada, and bonded."

"Now you're starting to use your head, kid." Jake read the ad and nodded. "Okay. Tomorrow we'll go and meet Francis X. Turner." He turned to Sam. "Okay?"

Sam nodded.

"How about right now?" Addy prodded.

Jake closed his ledger. "Why not?" Seeing the smile that touched her lips he held up a hand in caution. "Just one thing. Since Sam was once a cop, I want him to make the final decision. If he doesn't like the looks of this bird, we walk. Understood?"

Her smile faded slightly. Since they'd begun construction on the new addition, Jake was beginning to treat Sam like some kind of genius. "Whatever you say, Jake."

Addy made a quick phone call and turned with a smile. "He said he'd see us now."

"That's one really busy guy," Sam said sarcastically.

Jake led the way to the car. While Sam drove he said, "Now don't go getting your hopes up, Addy. I want to take a good look at this guy before you hire him. And if we decide to trust him, you're only going to give him a retainer. A couple hundred dollars. No more until he delivers the goods."

Addy nodded as their car turned into a row of nondescript offices. A few minutes later the three of them opened the door to a small office.

"Good afternoon," a pleasant woman said.

"Hello. We're here to see Francis X. Turner. He agreed to meet me now."

"You must be Miss O'Brien. Please go in."

The woman pressed a buzzer and they entered an inner office which was small and sparsely furnished. There was an old scarred desk and a leather chair. Two black chairs were positioned in front of the desk. The only other item of furniture was an ancient grandfather clock showing the wrong time.

A stocky, middle-aged man stood just inside the door waiting to greet them. His suit was rumpled, his tie loosened.

"Addy O'Brien?"

"Yes. And this is Sam Money and Jake Starr."

"The owner of Jake's?"

Jake nodded.

"Nice to meet all of you. I'm Francis Turner. Everyone calls me Fran."

As he walked around his desk he said, "I've been in Jake's a couple of times. I like it. Nice atmosphere. Friendly dealers."

"Thanks. Addy here is my casino manager. She has

need of the services of a private detective."

"Why don't you tell me about it, Miss O'Brien?"

While Addy relayed her story, Fran crossed his hands on the desk and listened. Occasionally he reached up to adjust his glasses, which would immediately slide back down his nose.

"You have had no contact with these sisters since you were twelve?"

"No."

"You're certain that they were driven away in a chauffeur-driven limousine with a uniformed nurse?"

"Yes."

He made a steeple of his fingers and stared at her.

"The state would never resort to such methods to pick up children, even in extreme cases. They would send an official car and a caseworker. So we can rule out official adoption. I've never heard about private agencies that use limousines and nurses, but I can look into it further. Barring the usual adoptive routes, I think it's safe to assume that your father was telling you the truth. He saw a way to make money and simply sold your little sisters to someone who was willing to pay."

"If it was a private party," Jake said, "what makes you think you can ever find them? Isn't it a lot like looking for a needle in a haystack?"

"Exactly. Except that, very often, someone will offer a clue that makes the search easier."

"Someone like . . .?"

Fran shrugged. "A neighbour maybe. A service station attendant who filled the tank and was intrigued by a limousine in his area. A cop that might have stopped the limo for speeding. A costume company that may have rented a chauffeur's uniform and nurse's uniform."

"Look, this didn't just happen last week. We're talking about something that happened years ago."

Fran removed a small notebook from his desk and turned to Addy. "I'd like the address of your childhood home, and the names of any neighbours who might have

207

witnessed this incident. Also any other information that might be helpful."

As Addy talked, he wrote, occasionally looking up to inject a question. At length he nodded.

"I think I have all I need for now, Miss O'Brien. If you want me to handle this case, I'll leave for Dry Creek in the morning. No matter what the outcome, I'll phone you one week from today. But if I have any leads, or if I require any new information, I'll need a number where you can be reached."

"You haven't talked about money yet," Jake said tersely.

"I'll require a retainer, of course, to cover my initial expenses. Let's say two hundred dollars, Miss O'Brien."

Addy and Jake glanced at Sam, who had watched and listened in characteristic silence. Sam gave a slight nod of his head. He'd sized up the man and decided he liked what he saw. No pretentions here. No slick sales pitch. The man didn't make any wild promises. Just offered to do his best.

Seeing Sam's approval, Addy took a checkbook from her purse and made it out for the amount required and handed it to Fran.

"My wife, Betty, will give you a receipt when you leave," he said. Getting to his feet he added, "It was nice meeting you, Miss O'Brien, Mr. Starr, Mr. Money. I'll be in touch within a week. I hope, of course, that I can call with some good news. But even if all the leads are cold, you musn't lose heart. It's been a few years now. It may take a long time. But nobody vanishes for good, Miss O'Brien. Your sisters are somewhere. It's only a matter of time before they're found."

"I hope you're right. Thank you, Fran."

When they were again in the car Addy turned to Jake with shining eyes. "I know you told me not to get my hopes up, Jake. But I have a feeling about this man. If anybody can find my sisters, it's him."

He grudgingly admitted, "You may be right."

Addy fastened her seatbelt and felt her heart thundering. Her palms were damp. She'd been so afraid to allow herself to think she had a chance. But now she couldn't hold back the wild rush of hope. With Francis X. Turner, former F.B.I. agent on the job, she would find her sisters at last.

* * *

When Boyd Wilton arrived with his little black bag, Jake bellowed a stream of curses before following him into the bedroom. With the door closed Addy could hear their voices raised in anger.

"I warned you if you kept eating all that junk . . ."

"Goddamnit, Boyd. You like torturing me, don't you?"

"Come on, Jake. You're a big boy now. You know the score. Your kidneys can't take this abuse."

"My kidneys are going to fail me anyway. You said so right after the accident, if you'll recall."

"I told you that kidney failure is a distinct possibility if you were forced to spend too many years in a wheelchair."

"There you are. It doesn't matter what the hell I eat, I'm still going to suffer. It isn't the food, it's my condition, Boyd. So leave me the hell alone."

"Look, Jake. Let's be reasonable."

"You think that medical degree gives you the right . . ."

There was silence and Addy knew that Boyd had shoved a thermometer in Jake's mouth to shut him up. With a grin she walked upstairs to get ready for a night of work.

* * *

"Phone call, Addy."

Addy left the casino floor and raced to her office. She arrived flushed and breathless and lifted the phone.

"Addy O'Brien here."

"Fran Turner," said the voice on the other end. "I'm in

209

Dry Creek. I've been interviewing your neighbours, and I've come up with something interesting."

Addy's heart nearly stopped. "Interesting?"

"Do you remember a neighbour named Cleo Bentson?"

"Of course. She lived right next door."

"Yes. That's what she told me. She also told me that she saw the limousine that took your sisters away. She thought it was odd that such an elegant vehicle would stop at your place, so she wrote down the license number."

Thank heavens for busybodies. Addy felt tears spring to her eyes. "Are you saying that she still has it?"

She could hear the mirthless laugh on the other end of the phone. "After being in her mobile home, Miss O'Brien, I'm convinced that Cleo Bentson has everything she ever owned since the age of one."

He'd watched the obese woman pick her way through the litter to clear a place for him to sit. The room was stacked with old newspapers and magazines, especially movie magazines. Hanging at the door was a pair of binoculars. Positioned at the window was a telescope. The woman admitted that she no longer left her home. Even her groceries were delivered. It was obvious that her entire life centered around these four walls and the comings and goings of the people in the Paradise Mobile Home Park.

"It took our Mrs. Bentson two days to find it, but she came up with the license number and the notation she'd made at the time. It read, 'Danny O'Brien's up to something. Call Department of Social Services again.' She had it stapled to the newspaper account of your father's death."

Addy couldn't speak over the lump in her throat. At length she swallowed and said, "That's very good news. The best. When will you have a name to go with the license number?"

"I'm heading home now. I'll check with the Department of Motor Vehicles. I'll be back to you tomorrow with the results."

"Oh, thank you, Fran. Thank you. Thank you." Addy hung up the phone and then sat staring at it.

Tomorrow. By tomorrow she would know how to find her sisters. She put her head down on her arms and began to weep, silently at first, and then great, gulping sobs.

Tomorrow she would at last see an end to her quest.

*   *   *

"I can't believe he hasn't called." Addy had paced the floor all afternoon, waiting for the phone to ring. Now, dressed for work, she was reluctant to leave, even though Jake was waiting at the back door.

"Come on, Addy," Sam said gently. "He called you last night at the casino, so you know he has the number. Give the guy a break. He's probably been at the Department of Motor Vehicles all day. He'll phone as soon as he has something."

"He should have called by now."

"He's got a lot of old records to plough through. Are you coming?"

Addy picked up her purse and followed Jake's scooter out the back door. As she turned the lock she strained for any sound of a telephone ringing. There was only silence.

"We ought to get a car phone."

"Yeah. Sure. We have so many goddamned people calling us, we need another phone."

She shot him a quick grin. "Sorry. I'm so jittery."

"I can tell. Just let Sam drive tonight. You won't be able to keep your mind on the road."

They pulled up in front of the casino and Addy helped Jake into his scooter. Shorty held the door for them and tipped his cowboy hat.

"Beautiful evening, isn't it, Jake?"

"Yep. And it's going to get even better, Shorty."

As they entered, Addy left Jake and Sam at the poker tables with their friends and hurried to the office.

211

"Any calls?" she asked the girl in the reception area.

"No, Addy."

She fought down her nerves. "I'm going to be out on the floor. When I get a phone call, I want to be paged immediately. Got that?"

The girl nodded.

Addy immersed herself in work, determined not to dwell on the call that would soon come for her.

For the next several hours she mediated a dispute between a dealer and a player at the blackjack table, summoned a burly guard to remove a drunken patron, and filled in at the dice table for a dealer who was suddenly taken ill. It was nearly midnight before she had a chance to return to the office.

"Did I get a call?" she asked the receptionist.

"No, Addy. No calls."

Jake watched as she paced the office. "Why hasn't Fran called, Jake?"

He shook his head. "Let's give him until morning, kid."

"I can't wait another night. I'll explode if I don't hear from him."

She dialed the investigator's office number and heard the message machine click on. She left a terse message before hanging up. "It looks like I have no choice. But if he hasn't phoned by the time we're up tomorrow, I'm driving over to his office."

"Sam and I will be right there with you," Jake said, chewing down hard on his cigar.

*   *   *

Addy awoke feeling sluggish and disoriented. It had been nearly four o'clock in the morning before she had gone to bed. Now, with the mid-morning sun slanting through her windows, she sat up and glanced at the bedside clock.

It was almost noon. She had taken the precaution of

setting the cordless phone on the nightstand beside her bed before retiring. There was no way she could have missed Fran's call.

Within minutes she was showered and dressed. When she made her way downstairs she heard Jake's voice summoning her to prepare his shower. Although Verna had assumed all the other household chores, this was one that Addy still took care of. She personally saw to Jake's water temperature and laid out his clothes for the day.

"No call?" He hadn't really needed to ask. He could tell by the look on her face.

"No."

She started his water and then began rummaging through his drawers for clean clothes, which she laid out on the bed. She had long ago discarded any embarrassment for Jake's distinct lack of modesty. When he rolled toward the bathroom, peeling off his shorts as he went, she merely looked the other way.

"Only coffee, Verna," she called as she entered the kitchen.

The woman turned from the stove and eyed Addy critically. "You ought to eat breakfast. Didn't anyone ever tell you it was the most important meal of the day?"

"No. I guess my education was sorely lacking in that area."

"Well, you can't fuel your body with nothing but caffeine. How about steak and eggs with Jake?"

"Is that what you're fixing him?"

Verna nodded. She wore her dark hair cut short like a man, and wore no makeup. Had it not been for her pendulous breasts, which were encased this day in a man's baggy sweater, she wouldn't even be suspected of being a woman. She wore pleated trousers and thick, ugly walking shoes.

"Jake left a note that he wanted steak and eggs and fried potatoes."

"Fix him half a grapefruit and a bowl of cereal."

"He'll skin me alive."

Across the room, Sam lowered his newspaper and swallowed his smile.

"No, he'll just make a lot of noise. When are you going to learn that his bark is worse than his bite?"

"Then he can bark at you," Verna said, putting away the heavy skillets and reaching for the fruit and a bowl. When it was ready, she placed the grapefruit and cereal on the table and busied herself in the laundry room. "I'm not coming out until I hear all of you leave," she called over her shoulder.

Addy chuckled and picked up her cup of coffee. In a whisper she said to Sam, "For all her tough appearance, Verna's terrified of Jake's temper."

"I'm glad you finally noticed." He lifted the paper and continued reading.

When the shrill ring of the telephone shattered the silence, Addy was so startled she froze. Then, forcing herself into action, she picked it up on the third ring.

"Miss O'Brien?"

Addy heard an unfamiliar feminine voice on the other end.

"Yes."

"This is Betty Turner, Fran's wife."

"Yes, Mrs. Turner. Do you have a message from Fran?"

"Forgive me, Miss O'Brien." The woman's voice trembled, then stopped. After a long pause she said, "I'm calling because you left a message on our service last night, and I thought it only fair to inform you as soon as possible." She paused, as though unable to speak. Then, in halting tones she said, "Fran is dead."

"Dead!"

"He was killed in an automobile accident last night, on the way home from the Department of Motor Vehicles."

"How terrible." Addy swallowed. "Do you know what happened?"

"I'm afraid the report has been very sketchy. The police said that Fran appears to have fallen asleep at

214

the wheel of the car. There were no other vehicles involved."

Addy could hear her choking back sobs as she added, "I'm sorry, Miss O'Brien. I just can't bear to talk any more. This is all such a shock to me."

"Yes. I understand. Thank you, Mrs. Turner. And please accept my condolences."

Addy was still holding the telephone when Jake rolled up behind her. He'd only heard the last words she'd spoken, but they were enough to alert him that something terrible had happened to Fran Turner.

"Condolences?"

Addy whirled to face him. For a minute she struggled to control her churning emotions.

"Fran is dead."

She set the receiver down, then continued to stare at it, as if certain that, somehow, it would ring again, and Fran's voice would tell her it had all been some horrible mistake. But the phone didn't ring. And the silence stretched out for what seemed an eternity.

She drew her arms around herself and began to pace.

"Fran had a license number. He was this close to having an answer."

"We'll hire someone else." It was Sam's voice, hard as flint.

She didn't seem to hear as she continued pacing.

Jake glowered at the grapefruit and cereal on the table and pushed himself away.

"It's almost as if someone doesn't want me to continue my search," Addy said.

At her words Sam looked thunderstruck and began frantically searching through the newspaper he'd been reading. His scowl deepened as he read about the robberies, the murders, the national and international disasters. And then his gaze fell upon a small item at the bottom of the page that he'd been looking for. It had caught his eye, but he couldn't figure out why. Now he knew.

He read quickly, then glanced up.

"Didn't you say that nosy neighbour of yours was a Cleo Bentson?"

Addy turned. "Yes. Why?"

"The paper says a Mrs. Cleo Bentson of Dry Creek was killed when an explosion ripped through her mobile home yesterday."

Addy raced across the room to read over Sam's shoulder.

"The cause of the explosion is still under investigation." Her face mirrored her horror. "Oh, Sam, this is like some terrible nightmare." Though she struggled for control, her voice broke. "This can't be happening again. It just can't be. We were so close to the truth. So close. And now, another explosion."

"What do you mean, another explosion?" Sam was instantly alert.

"My . . ." She swallowed, struggling for control. "After my father was killed, I went next door to stay with Mrs. Bentson. And that night, my trailer was destroyed in an explosion. That's when the authorities found out that I was alone and sent me to a state shelter. And now it's happened again. Another explosion. And whatever Mrs. Bentson knew is lost forever."

Sam chose his words carefully. "Did the authorities investigate the explosion?"

Addy shrugged. "I don't know. After I was sent to the shelter, I never heard from anyone." She studied him with new interest. "Why do you ask?"

"No reason." He dropped the paper, and in a determined tone said, "We'll start again. We'll find another detective."

"Do you really think so?"

He nodded. But when she'd composed herself and went off to find a handkerchief, his eyes narrowed in thought.

"You don't believe this was a coincidence, do you, Sam?"

Sam turned steely eyes to Jake. "This was just too much

of a coincidence. Police report or no, my instincts tell me that something about this whole thing smells."

He didn't bother to add that he was damned well going to uncover what it was.

Chapter Twenty-one

"I don't get it, Jakie." Fingers dealt the cards and leaned in close. "First you're mad at that P.I. Gordon Schechter; now you're asking me to find out what the police know about the death of another investigator. What's going on?"

Jake glanced at Sam. "I can't violate a confidence, Fingers. Just find out all you can about this guy's death."

"I already did. My friend down at the station said it's a simple case of a guy who worked too late and fell asleep at the wheel."

"They're already through with the investigation?"

"Yep. That's what I heard."

"What he means is," Sam interrupted, "that's all they're saying for publication. If you want to know the rest of it, you need some official documents."

"I might as well ask for the moon." Jake frowned and brought a hand to his stomach.

Seeing it, Henry Carstairs asked, "What's wrong, Jake?"

"Nothing. Probably just something I ate. I'll pass on the next game, gentlemen. Think I'll get back to my office."

When his scooter rolled away, Henry glanced at the others around the table. "I don't like the way Jake looks these days."

"What's the matter with the way he looks?" Bennie Stone asked.

Henry watched until Jake disappeared into the crowd.

"I don't know. Maybe it's just my propensity for finding a dark cloud under every silver lining."

"Psychologists and psycho-babble," Bennie Stone muttered. "Everybody ante. We're wasting time."

"I'm out." Sam pushed back his chair and followed Jake.

* * *

Addy had lost heart. Sam and Jake could see it in the way she absolutely refused to talk about hiring another investigator.

"Maybe later," was all she would say whenever they brought up the subject.

"But your sisters are still out there, kid."

"Yes. Thanks to me."

"You stop that. What happened to them wasn't your fault."

"How do you know that, Jake?" She turned on him with a look of fury. "Maybe I didn't do enough. Maybe I could have stopped my father."

"Look," Sam said patiently. "I think it would do you some good to talk to Henry Carstairs. Before he retired he was one of the country's top clinical psy . . ."

"I know all about his kind, Sam. I met a dozen like him at the shelter."

"Goddamnit it," Jake sputtered, "he isn't going to evaluate you. He'll help you sort through all this damned guilt . . ."

"No, Jake. I don't want to talk to Henry Carstairs. Or anybody else. Now if you don't mind, I'm going upstairs to dress for work."

The two men watched her walk away. While Sam continued to study her retreating figure, Jake pressed a hand to his stomach. The pain in his gut was getting worse. And the pills Boyd Wilton had given him were no longer doing any good.

* * *

Addy walked the floor of the casino, but she wasn't really aware of what was going on around her. The blur of customers, the clatter of slot machines, the chorus of voices, were no distraction this night. All she could hear was Fran's voice on the telephone.

"After interviewing Cleo Bentson, I've come up with something interesting."

Now Fran was dead. Cleo Bentson was dead. And the interesting information was lost forever.

Was there some terrible dark cloud hanging over her head that was programmed to rain on her every time she got too close to happiness?

"Addy?"

She was pulled roughly from her reverie by Henry Carstairs.

"What is it, Henry?"

"Jake asked me to talk to you."

"No. I'm . . . Not today, Henry. I'm afraid I'm . . ."

"Please don't think I'm meddling, Addy. But Jake is awfully worried about you. He made me promise that I'd talk to you. Could you join me for a cup of coffee for a few minutes?"

She gave a sigh of impatience. "All right. A cup of coffee. But I can't guarantee that I'll do any talking."

At the coffee shop she said to Rosetta, "A small booth in the back, please."

When they were seated, they both ordered coffee. Henry sat quietly. Addy stared pointedly at the table top.

Finally, in exasperation, she said, "I know that Jake thinks if I talk to you it will somehow relieve my guilt about something my father did. But he's wrong. All talking will do is open up old wounds. Besides, I've talked to enough psychologists in my lifetime to know that they can't do anything to help me. No one can help me. I have to help myself."

"Those are very wise words, Addy. Some people go through life without ever learning that fact. But sometimes, even though they can't directly help, psychologists can listen and help people sort through their problems to see things more clearly."

For the first time Addy allowed herself to look into his eyes. What she saw surprised her. Instead of the cold, calculating looks she'd become accustomed to at the shelter, or the usual boredom, she saw patience and wisdom, and more importantly, a man who cared deeply.

Taking a deep breath she began to answer his questions. Soon she was volunteering information. One hour and three cups of coffee later, she leaned back. Henry's hand rested lightly over hers. His eyes reflected compassion.

"The sins of the fathers," Henry muttered. "are visited upon the children."

"What?"

"It's only natural to feel responsible for the sins of our fathers," he said. "But the fact is, we can't go back and undo what was done by others. The only thing we can do, Addy, is go on. I'd say you've been doing an admirable job of getting your life together."

"But what about the pursuit of my sisters? Do you think this is some sort of sign that I should abandon my search?"

"Are you suggesting that these setbacks are signs from heaven? The answer is no, Addy." He didn't add that he thought the two deaths were highly suspicious. But he intended to privately voice his opinion to Jake.

Addy gave Henry a warm smile. "Thanks for listening. I – I guess Jake was right. You are a good listener. And I do feel better. But now, I'd better get back to work."

* * *

"What do you think, Henry?" Jake sat at a poker table, shuffling cards to Sam.

At a noisy table nearby, Fingers and Bennie were bemoaning their latest losses.

Henry pulled out a chair and sat. "Addy is a girl who

has been disappointed by everyone she's ever trusted. Her mother died, leaving Addy feeling responsible for her younger sisters. She blames herself for everything bad that's ever happened to them. Her father constantly let her down by his lack of self-control. This is a girl who has learned not to trust anyone but herself." He leaned forward to emphasize his words. "Now she hires two private detectives to locate her sisters, and one runs off with all her money and the other one dies suddenly, along with the only neighbour who has any recollection of that terrible day when her sisters were taken away. Is it any wonder she doesn't want to trust again?"

"What can I do, Henry?"

"Nothing. This is something she has to do herself." Seeing Jake's angry scowl he added more gently, "Just be patient, Jake. I think she's begun to trust you. But you can't undo in a couple of years what's been done to her for a lifetime."

"But I want to. Sometimes I want to just put my arms around her and tell her everything's going to be just fine. You know?" He looked up to see Sam and Henry staring at him intently. He looked down quickly. "Thanks, Henry, for taking the time with her. I really appreciate it."

"No thanks are necessary, Jake. I like that young woman. I'm happy to do anything I can to help her." He stood. "Just remember, it can't be done in a day. It all takes time."

"Time," Jake muttered somberly as Henry strode to the poker table to join his friends. He looked across the table at Sam, who had listened without comment. "My time is running out."

Sam looked up at him, but Jake was already turning his wheelchair away.

For long minutes Sam thought about what Henry had said. Then he shoved back his chair and went in search of Addy.

*　　*　　*

A long, dark hallway connected the casino with Jake's office. A burly security guard stood at the entrance to the hallway, to insure that only authorized personnel entered.

Seeing Addy headed in that direction, Sam nodded at the guard and hurried to catch up with her.

"Addy."

At the sound of Sam's voice she paused and turned her head. As always, her heart started working overtime at the mere sight of him. It was a most uncomfortable feeling.

"Are you ready to start a count of the tables?"

"Not yet. I just thought I'd get away from the noise and people for a while so I could think."

He fell into step beside her. "Thinking about hiring another detective?"

"No. Never again." She halted outside the office, then seemed annoyed at her sudden, fierce response. In a softer tone she said, "Maybe it's time to face facts and stop this foolish search."

Sam's voice was low with feeling. "It isn't foolish to want to find your sisters. You have every right to be a family."

"Maybe they won't want to be found."

"Or maybe you're afraid of what you'll find. Is that it, Addy? Have you decided to run from your past, for fear of what you'll find?"

Stung, she said without thinking, "Look who's talking. Big city cop has to find his courage in a bottle. What are you running from, Sam?"

The minute the words were out of her mouth she regretted them. But it was too late to take them back.

With his teeth clenched, Sam caught her roughly by the shoulders and shoved her against the wall. "That's none of your business."

"And what I do is none of yours. Now let me go." She fought against the hands that pinned her.

His anger got the better of him. The harder she fought, the more determined he was to hold her still.

"Don't touch me. You have no right . . ."

"I'm making it my right. When are you going to realize that not every man who touches you wants to hurt you?"

"Oh? And I suppose this is your way of looking out for me?"

"No." He went very still for a moment. The look in his eyes sent her heart tumbling. "This is my way of shutting you up so I can let you know I care."

He lowered his head. His lips hovered a fraction above hers. His breath was hot against her cheek. And then his mouth covered hers and she forgot everything. In the heat of the kiss her anger dissolved. The words she'd been about to hurl were forgotten. Her fears fled, to be replaced by a wild rush of feelings unlike anything she'd ever known.

He wasn't tender or gentle. He'd forgotten how to be. But he hadn't forgotten the hunger. His mouth was avid, seeking.

At the first taste of her he felt a storm of needs unleashed and wondered how he could have waited so long. He was like a starving man suddenly finding himself at a banquet. With a sense of greed he took, then wanted more.

Addy found herself caught up in something wild, and primitive, and frightening. She should fight him. And fight this demon inside her that caused her to respond with such abandon. But she found that she wanted what he wanted. This wild yearning, so long denied, struggled to be fed.

With a moan of impatience he dragged her against him and took the kiss deeper. He was acting like a fumbling teen on his first date, but he couldn't stop. He wanted her. Here. Now.

She wrapped her arms around his neck and clung to him. He could feel her breathing, laboured, shallow, and the little tremors that ripped through her.

"It's funny. There's just something about you that eats

at me, Addy." His words were muttered against her lips. "Ever since that day you walked into Jake's, looking like a refugee from a Girl Scout camp, I've needed to find out for myself if you were real."

Her words were choked. "I'm real, Sam."

"Yeah. God, Addy, I want you. Now." Still holding her against him he opened the office door and drew her inside. Then, pressing her against the closed door, he covered her mouth in a searing kiss.

There was no denying that she wanted what he offered. Her senses were assaulted by the touch of him, the taste of his lips. But though her body cried out for him, all the years of careful control would not allow her to trust. Or to yield.

"No. No, Sam." She put up a hand to stop him and he lifted it to his lips, pressing a kiss to her palm.

"Don't lie. At least not to yourself, Addy. You want this as much as I do."

"Maybe." She drew in a long, shuddering breath. "But I learned early in life that I can't always have what I want."

"But . . ."

"What I intend to have right now . . ." She swallowed and shrank back against the door, as if to evade any further touch. ". . . is some time to think. Clearly. Rationally."

She refused to look at him. If she did, he'd be able to read the truth in her eyes. Instead she stepped aside and indicated the closed door. "I'd like you to leave me alone now."

His eyes darkened with anger. "I will. For now. But sooner or later you have to deal with those feelings. You can't bury them away forever."

"I'll deal with them. In my own way, my own time."

He twisted the knob and yanked the door open. When he left he slammed it behind him.

Addy leaned against the desk. Her legs were trembling. In fact, her whole body was vibrating.

This was something she hadn't counted on. Odd, she

thought, touching a finger to her lips, that it should be the gruff, secretive Sam Money who would finally unlock the powerful emotions she'd kept so carefully hidden in her heart.

* * *

Boyd Wilton's old battered car chugged into the driveway and spluttered to a stop. Opening the door, Boyd reached for his black bag and made his way up the steps to the front door. Addy had the door open before he could knock.

"Hi, Boyd. You're a couple of weeks early, aren't you?"

He peered at her through his thick glasses before following her inside. "As Jake always says, what's a couple of weeks between friends. Where is he?"

"In his room. I'll get him."

"No. Don't bother. I'll just go in there."

Without waiting for Addy to announce him, Boyd shoved in the door to Jake's room and closed it behind him.

Addy waited a moment, expecting to hear the two voices raised in argument. Instead she heard only muted tones as the two men exchanged a few terse words.

"Addy," Verna said, coming up behind her, "I'm heading to the store. Is there anything you need?"

"No. Nothing."

"I'll be back in an hour or two."

"Okay." Addy walked to the kitchen to put the kettle on for tea. Boyd would want a cup, hot and black, before he left.

While the kettle was heating she ran upstairs to get ready for work. As she passed Jake's room, the door was still closed. The voices inside the room were unintelligible.

She dressed quickly, and, grabbing up her purse, walked down the stairs. When the kettle whistled she placed it on a cool burner and busied herself with the teapot, cups, saucers and napkins. Then she sat down at the kitchen table to wait for Jake and Boyd to emerge from the bedroom.

When Boyd finally walked out, he was alone.

"Where's Jake?" Addy looked up from her tea.

"He's – resting from the checkup." Boyd seemed distracted.

"I made you tea."

"No thanks, Addy. Not today."

"But you always . . ."

"I'm afraid I'm running late today." He turned away without meeting her eyes. "Sorry. Maybe next time."

"All right." Addy walked him to the front door.

He touched a hand to her shoulder and opened his mouth, then seemed to think better of it and turned away without a word. She watched him climb into his car and set his black bag on the seat beside him. For a moment he just sat there, staring into space. Then he started the engine and drove away.

"Addy."

At Jake's call she walked to his closed door and said, "Are you ready for work yet?"

"Come on in, kid."

She shoved in the door and stared in surprise. Jake was lying in bed.

"What's wrong? Aren't you feeling good?"

"I'm . . . No. I'm not feeling so hot today. Come here, kid." He patted the edge of the bed.

She walked closer and perched on the edge of the mattress, her hands folded primly in her lap. "Then we'll just stay home tonight."

"What's this 'we' crap. I'm the one who doesn't feel good. There's nothing wrong with you. Why should you stay home?"

"I'm not going to the casino without you."

"And why not? Aren't you the casino manager?"

"Well, yes, but . . ."

"Then you'll go. Verna can stay here with me. But first, there's something I need to ask you."

"Sure, Jake." She searched his face, wondering why his tone had suddenly grown so grave.

"I want you to marry me, kid."

"What?" She started to jump up but he was too quick for her. His hands pressed over hers on her lap, holding her down.

Her tone was offended. "That isn't funny, Jake. I don't think you should joke like . . ."

"I know it isn't funny. And I'm not kidding. I'm dead serious, Addy." He stared at her hands, so small in his. She had given up struggling, but she still looked as if she'd fly away the minute he let go. "I want you to marry me."

"You're not making any sense. You've never given me any reason to think that you thought about me . . . like that. You don't love me, Jake. And I . . ."

"Just shut the hell up and listen."

At his outburst she clamped her mouth shut and glared at him.

"Look, kid, this isn't going the way I'd planned it. It doesn't sound much like a proposal; it sounds more like a goddamned order. But hear me out. My name carries a lot of weight in this town. You might not have noticed but I wield a lot of power."

"I've noticed. So what?"

"Just listen, damnit. I was hoping for more time so I could look out for you. Now, the best way to do that is to give you my name. As Mrs. Jake Starr no one would dare to hassle you."

"Hassle . . .?"

He touched a hand to her lips to silence her and she swallowed back her protest.

"I've given this a lot of thought. It's the one thing I can do for you before . . ."

Her eyes narrowed. "This is about Boyd Wilton's visit, isn't it?" When he said nothing she felt her eyes fill and blinked furiously. "What did he say?"

"He said he'd see me in a week or so."

"Stop the games, Jake. What did Boyd come here for?"

When he refused to answer she leaned over and clutched his shoulders. Her teeth were clenched in anger. "Tell me. You have to tell me. You can't keep this from me."

His hands closed over hers. He looked up into her eyes. And in that instant she knew.

She tried to draw back but he held her firmly. "I'm not afraid of dying, Addy. And I don't want you to be afraid for me. I've known for a long time that this was coming. And now that the pain is getting worse, I'm actually relieved. I don't want to go on hurting like this." His voice lowered. "But I do ask this one favour before I go. Marry me."

"But why, Jake? Are you afraid of – dying alone?"

"Hell, Addy, don't you know that everybody has to die alone? That doesn't bother me. I just want to do something good for you before it's too late." He stared down at their linked fingers. "I give you my word. I won't touch you. It'll be like it is now. Only you'll have my name." He looked up into her eyes. "Deal?"

He saw Addy's lips tremble. "I don't know, Jake. I need time to think."

"There isn't any time left, kid. After what Boyd told me, I can't afford the luxury of time. I need an answer now."

"All right." Her voice was barely more than a whisper. "I guess my answer is yes. I'll marry you, Jake, if that's what you really want."

As she slid from the bed and started toward the door of his room he called, "You won't regret it, Addy."

As she rushed from the room she nearly collided with Sam, who stood in the doorway barring her way. He steadied her, then dropped his hands to his sides.

His face wore no expression at all as he said to Jake, "I couldn't help overhearing. I guess congratulations are in order."

"Yep. Addy's consented to be my bride."

"Well." Sam avoided looking at Jake or Addy. "I'd better get busy packing. I can be out of here in the morning."

"That's not necessary," Jake protested. "I don't want you to leave, Sam."

"I think you two need some time alone."

"Please, Sam. It's important to me that you stay. Especially now. I'd take it as a great favour."

Without a word Sam turned away and climbed the stairs.

With her eyes swimming Addy groped her way blindly up the stairs. She passed Sam's closed door, and for the briefest moment thought about knocking. But what could she possibly say?

It wasn't until she was safely in her own room that she allowed the tears fall.

Chapter Twenty-two

The wedding was a private affair, held in Jake's bedroom, with only Judge Thomas Sullivan, an old friend of Jake's, and Verna as a witness, and their closest friends in attendance.

The ceremony was originally planned for the lovely old living room, which Addy had transformed into a garden of flowers for the event. But during the night Jake's condition had worsened, until he was now too weak to leave his bed. He lay feebly against a mound of pillows, his hand resting in Addy's.

When the ceremony was completed the judge leaned over to kiss Addy's cheek. Then he caught Jake's hand and was shocked at the loss of strength in his old friend.

"Bet you didn't think I could still attract such a pretty young thing, did you, Tom?"

"You were always a ladies' man, Jake. I'm not surprised at all."

Jake's voice lowered, so the others wouldn't hear. "I want you to look out for her, Tom. My affairs are in order but . . ."

"Andrew Witherspoon is the finest lawyer in Nevada, Jake. And Milt Carver the best certified public accountant around." The judge glanced at both men, who stood with the others around the room. "Between them, they'll see that everything possible is done for your new bride. But you know I'll do everything I can for her as well."

"Thanks, Tom. Will you stay to drink a toast?"

"No. I have to get back."

"Our housekeeper will see you out."

Verna was crying as she hugged Addy and leaned over

the bed to brush her lips against Jake's cheek. Then she hurried out of the room to walk the judge to the door.

Their friends surged forward, eager to congratulate the bride and groom.

"You are a glowing bride, chérie." Lil kissed Addy fondly on the cheek. "And you, Jake, make a handsome groom. I think marriage suits you."

"I certainly waited long enough, didn't I?"

Jake and Lil shared the comfortable laughter of old friends. "You waited just long enough to find the perfect partner."

"Partner." Jake smiled, more to himself than to the others. "I like that. Addy is the perfect partner."

"You old devil," Fingers said, grasping his friend's hand. "You didn't even give me time to think of a gift."

"Your presence here is all the gift I want," Jake said.

Bennie Stone and Henry Carstairs kissed Addy's cheek before shaking Jake's hand.

"This is a switch," Bennie said. "No poker table. I don't know what to do."

"Just lift a drink to our happiness, Bennie," Jake said.

"Thank you for having me," Henry said formally.

"It wouldn't be a party without my friends here." Jake clasped his hand, then turned to accept the congratulations of Andrew Witherspoon and Milt Carver.

"You'll look out for Addy, won't you?"

Andrew placed a hand on Jake's shoulder. "Of course we will. But we expect you'll be around a long time to do that, Jake."

"Don't con a con, Witherspoon." Jake smiled to include his accountant. "Just be here for her. Both of you."

"You have our word on it," Milt said.

Shorty had positioned himself at the door of the room. Now he stepped forward and lifted Addy's hand to his lips. "You must be a special young lady, Miss Addy, to have won this old mule's heart." Turning to Jake he clasped his hand. "I wish you happiness, Jake."

"Then I already have your wish, Shorty. Right now I'm the happiest man in the world."

Out of the corner of her eye Addy saw Sam Money move toward her. She had deliberately avoided looking at him. Now she had no choice as he stopped beside her and caught her hand.

"Congratulations, Mrs. Starr."

Steeling himself, he bent and pressed a quick kiss to her cheek. He felt the flare of heat and stepped away, moving quickly to Jake's bedside. Taking Jake's weak hand in his strong one he said, "Now you have the best reason in the world to get well, Jake."

"Yeah. She'd inspire any man, wouldn't she, Sam?"

Sam nodded. "A man could probably give up any vice for a lady like Addy."

He squeezed Jake's hand again before moving away.

Addy watched him walk to the far side of the room.

Having accepted best wishes from all their guests, Jake held out his hand and Addy clasped it firmly between both of hers.

"You look beautiful, Addy."

She was wearing a simple ivory cocktail-length dress with a matching lace jacket. Just before their guests arrived Jake had asked her to go to the drawer of his nightstand. Inside was a jewellery box. When she opened it she found a double-strand pearl choker with a five-carat diamond teardrop, and matching earrings.

At his words she touched a hand to her throat. "This was so extravagant, Jake. I can't believe I'm actually wearing something this expensive."

"It made me happy to buy it for you, Addy." He grinned. "And it made the jeweller even happier."

His guests shared a laugh.

Addy had vowed to herself that there would be no tears. This wedding, which Jake had been so determined to have, would be a joyful affair.

She stood beside the bed and continued holding his hand. "I bought you something too."

"You did?" His eyes lit like a child at Christmas.

"It's not nearly as grand as your gift to me." Her glance fell on the motorized scooter parked across the room. How he'd loved that gift. She was so glad she'd thought of it. Tomorrow she would get him out of bed and take him for a long walk in the scooter. She didn't care what Boyd Wilton said; Jake was going to get better. He had to.

She pulled a tiny silver box from her pocket and handed it to Jake. He opened it to reveal a jewelled pin showing a royal flush; the ace, king, queen, jack and ten of hearts.

"To a poker player, it doesn't get any better than this, Addy."

"I know. That's why I bought it for luck."

She smiled as she pinned it to the collar of his tuxedo jacket. He'd insisted upon wearing a formal shirt, tie, and jacket for the wedding ceremony. But from the waist down he was dressed as always, in a pair of boxer shorts, hidden beneath the sheets.

"I've already had all the luck a guy can have. I've had a full, rich life, a handful of people I can call friends, and the most beautiful wife in the world. Now what more could I possibly ask for?"

"I can't think of a thing."

"Me neither, Mrs. Starr."

They both looked up at the knock on the door. Verna entered with a silver tray.

"I brought champagne for a toast."

Several opened bottles of champagne were poured into crystal goblets, which were passed among the guests.

Jake lifted his glass and Addy noticed that his hand trembled, causing some of the liquid to spill over the rim.

"Here's to my beautiful bride. Addy, I wish you long life, much happiness, and all the things your heart desires."

The guests lifted their glasses and drank.

Addy touched her glass to Jake's and sipped, enjoying the warmth that came over her.

"Here's to Addy and Jake," Henry Carstairs said in his most resonant voice. "May and December. Two of the most beautiful months in the year. And two of the most memorable people I've ever known."

Again the guests drank.

"To Jakie," Fingers said. "The best friend I've ever had. And to Addy, who brought sunshine and light into his life."

Sam Money sipped his champagne and studied the glowing bride. A band seemed to tighten around his heart. He filled his glass and drank again, and knew that within a few hours he wouldn't even be able to recall all the words of these grand toasts. But nothing, not even a gallon of champagne, would be able to erase the way she looked at this moment. The image of her determined smile, her eyes, so filled with secrets, her hand clinging tightly to Jake's, were burned into his memory.

*   *   *

Within an hour the guests were gone, and Addy and Jake found themselves alone.

A knock on the door revealed Verna, who entered carrying a silver tray.

"I brought your wedding supper."

She set it on a small table beside the bed and lifted the linen napkin to reveal Jake's favourite, steak and potatoes. An opened bottle of champagne rested in a crystal ice bucket.

When Verna left, Addy filled two goblets and handed one to Jake.

"Here's to Verna, bless her heart, for making me the only thing I really wanted for my wedding supper."

They drained their glasses. Addy filled them again.

"And here's to you, Addy. You're the best thing that ever happened to me. Now come on. Let's enjoy this good food before it gets cold."

Giggling conspiratorially, she climbed into bed beside

Jake and placed the tray between them. He managed only two bites of steak before he pushed his plate away. But Addy continued filling his goblet until the bottle of champagne was empty.

She felt deliciously light-headed and happy. Grasping Jake's hand she murmured, "I know most girls dream about their wedding day. But I honestly never thought about it. I guess I never really thought anyone would want to marry me. But you know what, Jake? It's been a beautiful day. And I wouldn't trade it for anyone else's big fancy wedding."

When he said nothing she turned her head to glance at him. His eyes were closed: his breathing slow and easy.

Bending close she brushed her lips over his cheek and smoothed a lock of his hair. Then she leaned back against the pillows and drank the last of her champagne.

It didn't matter that Jake was asleep. She had no place else she'd rather be. She would stay here in his bed and watch the slow, rhythmic rise and fall of his chest. And she would will him her strength to live.

*   *   *

A scant two weeks later, Jake was dead. Though Addy had kept her vow to take him out for walks in his prized scooter, he eventually became too weak to leave his bed.

News of his death spread like wildfire through the community. A priest, who claimed that Jake had given him the money to build his church, came forward to offer to conduct the funeral. A rabbi, who admitted that it was Jake who'd rebuilt his synagogue after it was leveled by fire, did the same. When several other ministers also came forward to praise Jake as the anonymous doner who kept their congregations going during hard times, Addy decided to invite them all to participate in the final service.

In order to accomodate the crowd, the funeral was held

in a banquet room of Jake's. Addy thought it only fitting that Jake take his final leave from the place that had for so long owned his heart.

To Andrew Witherspoon she wondered aloud, "I hope Jake doesn't mind all the fuss."

"Are you kidding, Addy? He's probably enjoying it. Jake always loved a party. And most of all he loved being the center of attention."

Milt Carver nodded. "Of course, it's hard to imagine all these religious leaders praying over Jake. I keep expecting to see the lid of the coffin open and Jake sitting up to tell everyone it was only a joke."

Addy swallowed her smile as the first minister began his eulogy. His kind, loving words were followed by more, until each religious leader had spoken about Jake's generosity, Jake's friendliness, Jake's gifts to the community, most of which had been done without any publicity.

At the end of the service the mourners filed past the casket to pay their final respects. The employees of Jake's, who'd all been given time off for the service, were visibly moved by the loss of a man who'd taken such interest in their personal lives. The neighbours and friends and the many curious who'd come to see the final act of a man who'd been a legend in their town, moved slowly past the bier. Many stopped to offer their condolences to Addy.

Several hours later, Addy, accompanied by Jake's closest friends, followed the hearse to a wind-swept hill overlooking the town. After a few words by a minister, the last of the mourners took their leave.

Lil, leaning heavily on her husband's arm, came forward to hug Addy. Lil's face was covered by a heavy black veil. But Addy could see the tears that streaked down her cheeks as she handed Addy a bouquet of roses.

"Before his accident, Jake always loved to wear a red rose in his lapel," she said.

"Thank you, Lil. I know he's smelling them right now, and loving the fact that they came from you."

"Oh, Addy." Lil fell into Addy's arms and the two

women clung to each other, sharing their sorrow, offering each other solace.

"He was the best thing that ever happened in my life," Lil whispered to Addy. "And I never told him."

"He knew. That's what friends are for." Addy wiped her friend's tears and noted idly how much Lil had seemed to age in the last few days. "I'll phone you soon, Lil, and we'll swap stories about Jake."

"Thank you. I'd like that." Choking back a sob, Lil was led away by Giovanni.

Milt Carver squeezed Addy's hand. "I still can't believe he's gone."

At his words Addy felt a terrible pain around her heart.

Milt seemed at a loss for words. Haltingly he whispered, "I'll drop by next week, Addy, when you've had a chance to clear your mind. We'll have a lot to go over."

She swallowed, fighting the tears that threatened again. She musn't allow herself to cry. Not now. Not yet.

Andrew Witherspoon caught both her hands and noted they were cold. "I'll phone you tomorrow. Jake left everything in order. No loose ends. But we'll have a lot to talk about."

"Thank you, Andrew."

"No, thank you, Addy, for making his last year his best."

As he walked away Boyd Wilton dug his hands in his pockets and stared at the ground. "I'm going to miss that old son-of-a . . ." He flushed. "Sorry. But I always enjoyed our battles."

"I know, Boyd." Addy touched a hand to his shoulder. "I'm going to miss fighting with him too."

He closed a big hand over hers. "You call me, Addy, if you need anything. Anything at all."

She nodded.

Jake's cronies formed a protective circle around her. Fingers, too overcome to speak, merely stared at the gaping hole in the ground. Bennie Stone, wearing a suit that was too tight to button, dabbed at his eyes. Shorty wore his familiar leather vest and jeans and boots and carried his hat in his hand. He was openly weeping.

Henry Carstairs spoke for all of them.

"Jake Starr was the best friend any of us ever had. He always had a funny story, or a trick to play on someone, or a loan when the cards turned on us. We'll never forget him. And Addy," he said, taking her hand, "we'd like to repay Jake by always being that same kind of friend to you."

"Thank you, Henry." Addy drew him close and kissed his cheek. Then in turn she kissed Bennie and Fingers and Shorty. "Thank you, all of you. I'm so grateful that Jake had friends like you. I will always treasure your friendship."

When they walked away Sam approached, wearing a dark suit, white shirt and tie. Though he had shaved, a dark stubble still clung to his cheeks, giving him a rough, ragged appearance.

"Jake Starr was a good man," he said. "He had a way of listening without judging. I valued his friendship."

"And he valued yours," Addy said softly.

"Well, if there's anything . . ." His voice trailed off. "You know."

"Yes. Thank you."

She offered her hand and he touched it for the briefest of moments before stepping back a pace. But he didn't leave like the others. He stood, just a few steps behind, keeping an eye on Addy.

Addy stood beside Verna and watched as Jake's casket was lowered into the grave.

Tears blurred her vision and she held out a hand as if to stop this final indignity. "Oh, Jake. I never had the chance to tell you this. You died too soon. But now, how could I let you go without telling you?" Her voice broke. "I love you, Jake. I love you."

Verna caught her arm but Addy pushed away to stand alone. She wouldn't give in to the need to be comforted. Not yet. Because if she did, she would collapse.

Her voice trembled with passion. "You were the grandfather I never had. And the father I'd wished for. And now my husband. And I never even told you how much you meant to me."

Lifting the roses to her lips she kissed then and dropped them, one by one, watching as they wafted down that long, dark space until they landed, sprinkling the lid with flower petals.

Then, remembering the small box in her pocket, she opened it and allowed the deck of cards to spill into the grave. The cards drifted down to rest on top of the casket, forming a pattern of spades and hearts, diamonds and clubs.

"I hope they play poker in heaven, Jake," she whispered, feeling the tears burn her eyes. "If they do, I know you're still winning."

Weeping, Verna made her way to the car. She watched as the two figures stood on the windswept hill, heads bowed, hands held stiffly at their sides. Finally Addy and Sam turned and made their way down.

When Addy returned to the car her eyes were red-rimmed, but there were no tears. She would do her grieving in private.

Sam took a seat behind the wheel. As the car moved slowly away from the graveside, a terrible fear clutched at Addy's heart, and two words played through her mind like a litany. Alone again. Alone again. All alone.

Sam glanced at her. Her head was turned, staring out the window. Her spine was stiff, her chin lifted. But he knew that she was holding on by a thread. When she finally allowed herself to cry, he thought, it would be a cloudburst.

Chapter Twenty-three

"Jake wanted you all here," Andrew Witherspoon said, glancing around the room at the assembled, "because you were all a special part of his life."

Addy sat stiffly on a kitchen chair that Verna had provided, her hands folded in her lap. She was glad that Jake's friends had been summoned. She didn't want to face this alone. For her this was the worst part. The documents, the official reading of the will, would make Jake's departing final.

Verna moved around the room, offering coffee. When all the guests were made comfortable, she took a seat in the back of the room.

Andrew Witherspoon retrieved a folded document from his briefcase. "Jake took the time to remember each of you in a special way. The words I'm about to read are Jake's words."

As always, Chester attempted to rub against the lawyer's legs, and Andrew deftly pushed him aside with the toe of his eelskin moccasin.

"To my wife, Addy."

Addy tensed as she felt the attention of the others shift to her.

"It was you who made me want to live again. So I guess you could say that you saved my life, kid. You brought back all the fun and laughter and challenge of my youth. You made me remember all the sweet dreams I'd let slip away."

Addy swallowed, and without realizing it, forgot to breathe.

"To Addy I leave this house, which she turned into a

home, and one-half of the controlling interest in all my holdings."

"To Sam Money."

Addy glanced across the room to where Sam stood leaning against the wall, his arms crossed over his chest. He seemed startled to hear his name.

"You saved my life. Any other man would have considered that enough. But you saved my sanity as well, by insisting on staying with me when I was alone. You don't know it, Sam, but I was thinking about ending it all until you moved in. Now, finally, I can show you how grateful I am."

The lawyer cleared his throat and said in sombre tones, "To Sam Money I leave my apartment above the casino, and half of all my holdings, the control of which is to be shared equally with my wife, Addy."

Sam's brows drew together in a frown. Addy couldn't tell if he was surprised or angry.

Witherspoon hastily turned to the next page of the document.

"Jake left personal bequests and messages to each of you." He cleared his throat. "To Lil, I leave a bottle of whiskey, to be savored, one glass a week, in my memory. And I leave the sum of fifty thousand dollars, to be spent foolishly."

Lil's eyes filled, and she lifted a lace handkerchief to her tears.

"To my old friend, Fingers."

Addy glanced at the man who sat with his cronies.

"When it comes to spotting a card shark, Fingers, you're the best. As a favour to me, I'd like you to stay on at the new casino, and keep an eye on the crowd. There aren't too many sharpies who'll get by you. The casino will pay you a salary, and part of your job will be to continue to play poker, so no one will know you're working there. I also leave you the sum of fifty thousand dollars. I've probably won that much from you over the years."

Fingers was flushed with pleasure as the lawyer turned the page.

"To Bennie Stone. You're the best card handler I ever met. Next to me, of course."

Bennie beamed with pride at the compliment.

"I'd take it as a personal favour if you'd stay on at the casino as a dealer at the poker tables. The chance to have you deal to them will bring in the best poker players in the country. As an incentive, I've added fifty thousand dollars. That ought to keep you in poker chips for a few years."

Bennie was grinning from ear to ear.

"To Henry Carstairs. You're good with people, Henry. You can read them like a book. I'd be most grateful if you'd consent to be a casino host. And whenever my old friends get together to reminisce about the old days, I'd like you to buy a round of drinks. Like the others, I'm also leaving you the sum of fifty-thousand dollars. Buy yourself a new tweed jacket."

Everyone laughed. But despite the laughter, their eyes were shiny with unshed tears.

"To Shorty. You've been the most faithful of employees. I ask that you continue your loyalty to my successors, and stay on to welcome everyone who passes through the doors of the new casino. And to make the job easier, I leave you the sum of fifty thousand dollars. Put it aside for your old age."

The old doorman chuckled and shook his head from side to side. "Only Jake Starr could be that generous."

"To Verna," the lawyer read.

The housekeeper began to weep.

"I hope you will consider staying on, so that my wife will be free to manage the casino and new hotel. See that she eats, and gets enough sleep. I leave a check for fifty thousand dollars, so that when you're tired of keeping house, you can retire in style."

Addy heard the housekeeper blow her nose as she hurried from the room.

"That concludes the reading of the will," Andrew Witherspoon said. He reached into his briefcase and removed two envelopes. "There is also a personal note to Addy and Sam from Jake. I thought you'd prefer to read them alone after everyone has left."

"Thank you, Andrew." Addy clutched the documents tightly. The wound was still too raw. At the least mention of Jake, she felt close to tears. She was grateful that Andrew Witherspoon understood and respected her feelings.

The guests got to their feet and began talking among themselves as they made their way to the front door. Addy followed more slowly beside Andrew Witherspoon. At the doorway they were joined by a scowling Sam.

"Did Jake give you any idea that he was doing this?" Sam asked her.

She shook her head. "Jake never mentioned any of this."

"One final note," the lawyer said as he paused at the door. "Jake left similar bequests of fifty thousand dollars to Milt Carver and to me. And a request that I always make myself available to both of you with the best possible legal advice. I want you to know that I would have offered my services to you anyway. The money was unnecessary."

"I know that. I'm sure Jake knew it too. It was his way of repaying you for all those years of loyalty. Thank you, Andrew."

"No. Thank you, Addy. For finding the key to Jake's heart. Since his accident, the rest of us had just about given up hoping that anything or anybody could ever get through to him. But you did what the rest of us had thought impossible. You're a hell of a woman, Addy Starr."

He turned to Sam. "I'll talk with you soon."

Sam nodded.

When everyone had gone, Addy turned to see Sam frowning as he read the note Jake had left him.

Sam carefully folded the note and returned it to its envelope before shoving it into his pocket.

At the look on his face Addy asked, "Did he hit you with another surprise?"

"It's a private thing between Jake and me. I don't feel like sharing it right now. I hope you don't mind."

She shrugged uncomfortably.

As he stood there, Addy realized that he hadn't once looked at her. Ever since the wedding, he'd avoided her.

"I'm glad you're going to share the operation of the casino with me, Sam," she said softly. "I don't think I'd know where to begin if I had to face it alone."

Sam jammed his hands into his pockets and shook his head from side to side. "My God. Hasn't it occurred to you yet?"

At the harshness of his tone she glanced up at him in surprise. "What are you talking about?"

"Jake. That old scoundrel. Don't you get it, Addy? He's playing games with us. He's up there laughing at the trick he's just played on us."

Sam tore open the front door, then said over his shoulder, "He's just handcuffed us together for a lifetime. And thrown away the key."

* * *

Sam had taken over the apartment above the old saloon, overseeing the construction of the new hotel and casino. Since Jake's death, he had seen to it that they were never alone together. Alone together, Addy thought. What a strange phrase.

There was a fresh pot of coffee and a slice of Verna's apple pie awaiting her in the kitchen. Dropping into a chair she took a bite of the pie, then shoved it aside and sipped strong, hot coffee.

The silence of the old house mocked her. She clicked on the television, but the jolly voices and phony laugh-tracks

245

annoyed her. She turned it off and decided to endure the silence instead.

Picking up a deck of cards she shuffled and glanced down as the cards moved deftly through her fingers. When had she begun to handle the cards so well? With a smile she remembered her early weeks with Jake, awkward and fumbling as she tried to shuffle.

"You taught me well, Jake," she muttered, dropping the deck of cards onto the table.

"Come on, Chester," she called to the huge ball of fur perched atop the refrigerator. "Lights out. Time for bed."

The cat leaped gracefully to the countertop, then to the floor, where he followed her through the rooms, as she turned out the lights. She saw him head for Jake's room and felt a fresh stab of pain, knowing the old cat spent every night searching in vain for the man who had for so long shared his bed.

Upstairs, she undressed quickly and climbed into her bed. As she did, she heard the rustling of paper beneath her pillow. Pulling out the documents, she plumped her pillows and sat down to read Jake's final words to her. As she tore open the envelope and unfolded the paper, she was unprepared for what followed.

"Dear Addy," he wrote. "I don't know when you started to take over my whole life. Was it when I first saw you standing in the doorway, a battered old suitcase in your hand, looking for all the world like one of those war-torn waifs I'd seen after World War II, scared but defiant?"

Addy blinked, astounded by the words he'd written. Eagerly she lifted the paper to the light and continued to read.

"Or was it when I discovered that, like me, you'd never had a home of your own before? I only know that you suddenly became the partner I'd always craved; the daughter I'd never had; the granddaughter I'd always dreamed of. I can tell you now what I'd never tell you in person. I love you, Addy. And I'm so goddamned proud of you."

Addy felt the tears burn her lids and blinked rapidly to stem the flow. She was determined to read it all before the tears blinded her.

"I saw so much of myself in you, and when the casino took hold of you, I realized that you were the perfect one to share my vision of building my saloon into all that it can be. This is your shot now, Addy. Make Starr's a reality. And use the profits to finish your quest. Take your life into your own hands, kid, and write your own happy ending."

With a sob Addy pressed the letter to her heart and finally allowed the tears to flow. She wept for the pain Jake had suffered and the loneliness he'd been forced to endure. And she wept for the dreams he'd left unfinished. She cried for the little girl who had trusted so many times, only to have that trust trampled beneath the feet of uncaring adults. And she cried for her sisters who were now strangers living among strangers they called family. And for the life together that had been stolen from them. She cried until there were no tears left. And then, drained by the weeping, she wiped her eyes and read the letter again.

He'd loved her. That foul-mouthed old curmudgeon had loved her. Like a father, a grandfather. And he'd said he was proud of her. The words would not have been easy for a man like Jake.

Her heart felt as if it would burst from happiness. Somehow, at this moment, it no longer mattered that her own father had failed her, and failed himself. All that mattered was that old Jake Starr loved her. And by coaxing her into marriage he had forever altered her life. She could put aside the past. Addy O'Brien was dead. She was Addy Starr now. The future was whatever she chose to make it.

She heard Chester padding up the stairs and knew that he had given up his vigil in Jake's room. At least for the moment.

"Come on," she said, lifting him to the pillow beside

her. "I know you prefer his bed to mine. But I promise not to take up too much space. Besides, Chester, we both miss him so much. The least we can do is keep each other company."

It gave her a small measure of comfort to feel the strong, steady heartbeat against her cheek. A contented purring lulled her to sleep.

* * *

This first evening back at the casino was difficult for Addy. Each time someone stopped her to offer condolences, or to mention Jake's name, she felt a fresh stab of pain.

How could she explain to anyone what Jake Starr had meant to her? His big old sprawling house had been her first real home. His casual acceptance of her, with all her flaws, had been a soothing balm to her bruised spirit. Jake was her haven, her best friend, her anchor. And now she'd been cut adrift.

What was worse, Sam Money had dropped out of sight. He wasn't in his usual place at the bar.

She didn't blame him. She wished she could go somewhere far away and pretend that none of this had happened. But it wasn't in her nature to hide.

Work was her solution. Hard work.

Henry Carstairs found her prowling the casino, after having been on her feet for hours.

"Come on." He dropped an arm around her shoulders and guided her toward the coffee shop. "Time for a break before you drop."

"I'm not tired."

"No. You're worse. You're practically dead on your feet. You need a shot of caffeine."

He led her to Jake's old booth and sat down across from her. When they'd ordered he studied her with a critical eye. "You ought to take a few days off, Addy. It's too soon for you to be here."

"You don't understand, Henry. I don't know how to do nothing."

"It's easy," he said with a smile. "You put your feet up, you open a good book, and you get lost in someone else's story."

"I guess I'm too busy living my own."

They sipped their coffee in silence for long, companionable minutes.

It was Henry who finally broke the silence. Placing a hand over hers he said, "Fingers, Bennie, Shorty and I want you to know that we'll always be here for you, Addy. If there's ever anything we can do, you just ask."

She felt the warmth of his touch, and the quiet strength. When had Jake's friends become her own? When had her life and his become so inextricably entwined? "I'm very lucky, Henry. Lucky to have found Jake. And lucky that he had all of you."

"Jake was the lucky one. You gave him something special, Addy. We'll never forget that."

Refreshed, renewed, Addy followed Henry from the coffee shop and returned to the casino. As she passed the Horseshoe Bar, she saw Sam seated in his usual spot, a glass in his hand. She felt her heart trip over itself. When he spotted her he inclined his head slightly, then tipped up the glass and drained it. Instantly a waitress arrived with another drink. Addy turned away and refused to look in his direction again. But she could feel his presence there as the night wore on, and though she struggled to deny it, she was happy to see him, no matter what his feelings about being stuck with her.

She berated herself for such thoughts. He was, after all, trying to lose himself in the whiskey. She'd learned from experience that a hard-drinking man like Sam Money would never bring a woman anything but grief.

Chapter Twenty-four

"I don't know anything about running a hotel."

"We'll hire experts. What did you know about running a casino until a short while ago?"

Addy, Sam, Andrew Witherspoon and Milt Carver sat around the kitchen table, going over the plans for the new project.

"Nothing. But that was different. I had Jake to take me by the hand."

"What we don't know, we'll learn," Sam said, studying the documents. "What we can't learn, we'll hire someone else to do."

"Big talk. Do you really think we can handle a hotel and casino?"

"Hell, we're planning on playing in the big-leagues now, Addy. We'd better be prepared to commit ourselves completely before we start this thing."

Addy thought about Jake, about how far he'd come from the first night she'd met him. And then she thought about her own life, and about her beginnings in the Paradise Mobile Home Park.

"Jake was right. It isn't just his dream. It's mine now." She glanced around the table. "I'm in. How about you, Sam?"

She felt the pull of his dark gaze as he looked directly at her. For a moment she held her breath, wondering if she could carry this off without him.

"Like I promised Jake, I'm in for the long haul."

"That's settled." Andrew Witherspoon stood and snapped his briefcase shut. "We have our work cut out."

* * *

"Addy."

Ignoring the chaos around her, Addy paused beside her secretary's desk.

"There are at least a dozen calls here that must be returned today." She handed Addy the list and added, "And I just took a call from Henry Carstairs. He's looking for Sam. He's down in the casino and needs to talk to one of you."

"Thanks, Paula. Have Henry paged, please. I'll take it in Sam's office."

She walked past her office to the security office next door. The door closed behind her, shutting out the babble of voices and the ringing of the phones.

Along one wall was a bank of monitors showing the players on the casino floor. The monitors could be adjusted to show every table and every row of slot machines, complete with close-up views of the players' hands. All were videotaped and studied closely by a team of professionals, all personally hand-picked and trained by Sam.

Addy smiled. Jake would have loved it.

She picked up the phone on the first ring.

"Henry." She turned as Sam walked in. Covering the mouthpiece she whispered, "Henry was looking for you." She turned on the speaker phone and asked, "Where are you?"

"Section three. Fourth dice table."

Sam switched on the monitor and Henry could be seen standing beside a bank of house phones.

"Smile for the camera. What's up?"

"Addy, do you remember old Horseshoe Joe?"

"Yes." She thought about the old man who regularly arrived to try his luck at the dice tables. Despite the upheaval during this time of renovation and building, the old man continued to show up once a week with his hundred dollar bill. He would either run it into a winning streak or lose it on the single toss of the dice.

"The old guy's acting funny," Henry said. "He lost his

first hundred and did what he's never done before; he took another hundred out of his pocket and lost that too."

"I'm sorry to hear it," Addy said, "but maybe he just doesn't feel like playing by his own rules tonight."

Henry shrugged. "Maybe. But so far, Addy, he's gone through a couple of thousand dollars. And he doesn't show any sign of quitting."

"Has he taken out any markers?" Sam asked.

"No. It's all coming out of his pocket."

Addy and Sam exchanged a glance. Addy said, "Then it's his business. I have to run, Henry. But I'll try to stop by later. Keep an eye on him."

"Will do."

Addy hung up and within seconds the phone rang again. This time Sam picked it up. As Addy started toward the door he caught her by the wrist. Immediately she felt the jolt.

He saw her eyes widen and gave her one of his rare smiles. "Stay a minute. You're always running off somewhere."

Did he know what his touch did to her? It would be so easy to forget the work and just stay here, with his hand on hers.

She pulled free. "Sorry. Can't keep the contractor waiting."

Sam watched her hurry from the office and heard only half of what the caller was saying. He mentally cursed the contractor. And the cunning old man who'd placed him in this hell.

*   *   *

It was after midnight when Addy walked onto the casino floor. These days she rarely found time to leave her office until the small hours of the morning.

She saw a crowd gathered around the dice table and heard a shout go up as the dice were tossed. Drawing closer she was amazed to see old Joey the Horse still

252

playing. He placed a pile of hundred dollar chips on the pass line and took the dice. As he tossed them, all eyes followed. A roar went up as he made his point. Instead of pocketing the winnings, he left them on the line. Picking up the dice, he tossed them again. The crowd groaned. Leaning closer Addy heard the stick man call the number.

"Seven."

All the money on the table was whisked away. In the blink of an eye, the old man's money was gone.

Addy watched as he lifted a glass to his lips and emptied it, then staggered away.

"Joe."

At the sound of her voice he turned and wiped at his bleary eyes.

"Mrs. Starr." He gave a courtly bow and almost fell.

Just as she went to grab his arm, another hand reached out to steady him. Addy looked up and was relieved to see Sam.

"How much money have you lost, Joe?"

He shrugged. "Do you mean how much of my money? Or how much of yours?" His voice was thick with the accent of Italy.

He thought a moment, struggling through the mist of alcohol that clouded his mind. "I had a strange feeling about tonight. It was going to be my lucky night. I believe I came here with two or three thousand dollars. But in the course of the evening I won several hundred times that much." He shook his head as if unable to believe that he'd won and lost a small fortune. Then he pulled out an empty pocket and staggered backwards. "But fickle old luck deserted me. I don't even have enough for another drink."

"Maybe it's a good thing you don't, Joe." Sam grinned.

"You don't need another drink. What you need is a bed. Can I take you home?" Addy asked gently.

He looked at her in surprise. "You would do that for me?"

"Of course. If you'll tell me where you live."

He seemed to think about that for a very long time. Then, like a boy, he gave a self-conscious laugh. "Sorry, Mrs. Starr. I cannot do that."

"Then how about accepting a room here at our hotel?" Sam asked. "The new hotel isn't finished yet, but there are still plenty of rooms available in the old saloon."

Joe stumbled and leaned heavily against the strong arm that held him. "I don't think so. Got to get home. Got to . . ."

With Sam on one side and Addy on the other, they led him gently toward the elevators. A few minutes later Addy opened a door and turned on the lights.

"Here, Joe," she said, while Sam eased him down onto the bed. She slipped off his dusty old boots and pulled the blankets over him. Reaching into her pocket she withdrew some money. "This is for breakfast." She peeled off several bills and placed them on the night table. "You're going to need some food when you wake up with a head that feels like it's splitting." Her voice lowered. "I saw my father like this more than a few times when I was little. And the mornings were always the worst."

Addy was stunned when the old man caught her hand and brought it to his lips. "In this cut-throat world, you are a rare and very fine lady, Mrs. Starr. An angel of mercy. I will never forget your kindness. I believe that tonight was my lucky night after all."

Bending down, Addy kissed his cheek. His eyes were already closed.

She followed Sam from the room. In the hallway he turned to her with a wicked smile, causing her heart to leap to her throat.

"That was a nice thing you did. How come you never put me to bed when I was that drunk?"

"Do I look stupid?"

"No. You look . . ." He paused and caught a strand of her hair. He watched as it sifted through his fingers. ". . . like a very wise, very compassionate woman." His tone deepened. "Joey called you an angel of mercy." He grabbed a handful of her hair and dragged her close. "But you're not an angel; you're a temptress."

She tried to pull away. "I don't mean to be."

His hand closed over her wrist, holding her still. "That's what makes you even more tempting. You don't even have to try."

She felt his thumb making lazy circles on her wrist. Heat poured through her.

He thrust both hands into her hair and drew her close, causing a ripple of pleasure. "Soft, Addy. Why am I always so surprised at how soft you feel? You try so hard to show the world your tough side. But I've discovered your softness."

She thought about escaping his touch, but it was already too late.

"I'm going to have to kiss you."

His lips brushed hers and she absorbed the first jolt.

How was it that Sam had only to touch her and she forgot every promise she'd ever made to herself?

He took the kiss deeper and all thought fled. His lips were warm and firm. His tongue tangled with hers, teasing, tempting.

He ran his hands along her spine, then slipped a hand beneath the jacket of her prim suit and encountered silk. Somehow he'd known she'd wear silk next to her skin. When his hand found her breast, small and firm against his palm, he heard her little gasp of pleasure. He felt the wild beating of her heart. It matched his own.

His kisses became more urgent. The thought of undressing her, of kissing every inch of her body, made him desperate. He'd never before known a woman who could make him mad with desire. His thoughts were jumbled as his mind filled with wild, forbidden fantasies. He feasted on her lips and knew that he wanted more. He wanted all.

With soft sighs and whispered words Addy moved in his arms. He felt her gradual surrender and was shaken by the sudden need to be tender.

With his hands on either side of her face he kissed her mouth again and again. "Come to bed with me, Addy. Now. There are empty rooms just waiting for us."

She surfaced slowly. What had she been thinking of? She pressed a hand to his chest, more to steady herself than to hold him at bay. "I'm needed in the casino."

"To hell with the casino." He caught her and drew her roughly to him. His body hummed with need. "Come with me now, Addy. You know you want this as much as I do."

She could no longer deny it. She wanted him. Desperately. But she had learned, a long time ago, that wanting was not the same as needing. She couldn't afford to need a man like Sam. "I have to go." She pushed herself free of his arms and took a tentative step back. Feeling stronger she took another step and another.

"This isn't finished." Sam's voice was rough with anger and frustration.

No, she thought. It was far from finished. But at least for now, she'd found the strength to walk away. She hurried along the empty hall, feeling his dark gaze follow her until she stepped into the elevator. She pressed a hand to the door to steady herself. By the time she reached the casino, she was back in control.

* * *

"Did you get the photo?"

The man speaking was olive-skinned, darkly handsome. He didn't look up until the golfball dropped neatly into the hole. Satisfied, he turned toward the doorway where a beefy man in a dark suit stood holding a Polaroid picture.

"Snapped it just as she walked out of the casino."

"She didn't see you?"

"Come on, boss. I know better'n that." He crossed the room and handed over the picture.

The younger man studied the photo. "So this is Addy Starr. Awfully young to be old Jake's widow. And prettier than I expected." He tucked the picture into his pocket and nudged another ball into position with his putter.

"What do you want me to do now?"

He gave a slow, easy stroke and watched as another ball dropped into the hole. "Pass the word. The lady and her casino are off limits."

"Why?"

He positioned a third ball. "I don't ask. When he wants me to know, he'll tell me. Just see to it."

He swore savagely when the ball circled the rim and rolled aside. The beefy man made a fast exit. He'd tasted his boss's vicious temper when the slightest thing went wrong.

* * *

"Addy, the decorator wants you to come up to the tower suite as soon as you can."

"Tell him I'll be there in fifteen minutes, Paula."

Addy and Sam were each having private suites set aside for their personal use. As she spent more and more hours at the casino, she found the drive to Jake's sprawling old house becoming impossible. Though Addy couldn't part with it, she intended to use it on infrequent weekends and holidays. Whenever Addy phoned to say she'd be there, Verna had a fresh pot of coffee and a piece of homemade pie ready. The old place sparkled under her care.

"Addy, the governor's office called from Carson City. The governor and his wife will attend the grand opening."

"That's great news." Addy continued walking through the new offices, on her way to her private office at the far end. "Paula, make a note to have flowers and fruit in the governor's suite an hour before he and his wife arrive. And a bottle of champagne. Find out how many of their staff will be here with them. We may have to book rooms in nearby hotels if we get many more positive responses."

Her head was spinning with all the details. It didn't seem possible, but the hotel and casino were actually finished. And the construction had gone off without a hitch.

*　　*　　*

Addy and Sam stood to one side and watched as the giant, glittering sign was hoisted into place atop the casino. Addy's eyes grew misty. Jake's casino. No, she corrected. Jake's dream; her casino. As unbelievable as it seemed, it was her casino. Hers and Sam's.

"By the time this day ends," Sam said dryly, "the entire city will be bathed in the neon glow of Starr's."

"I can hardly wait to see it shooting sparks high into a velvet sky, holding back the darkness." Addy thought about the day she'd arrived in Reno, watching the lights coming on all over town. It had seemed like another world.

"Congratulations, Addy, Sam," shouted one of the dealers as the morning crew arrived.

"Thanks, Ben."

"Looks good, Addy," called a woman in jeans and T-shirt, carrying her costume in a plastic bag over her arm.

"Thanks, Brenda. I'll see you inside in a few minutes."

Addy continued to stand beside Sam, watching as workmen swarmed over the roof, anchoring the braces into place.

"Jakie would've liked it." Fingers, his ribs showing through the fabric of his shirt, shook hands with Sam and dropped a hand on Addy's shoulder.

She laced her fingers with his and continued to watch the activity on the roof. "I'll bet he's watching right now. And chuckling."

"Naw. He's shuffling the cards. And getting ready to relieve the angels of their golden halos."

"Come on," she said, leading the way toward the front door. "I'll buy you a cup of coffee."

"Better lace it with something, Addy. I feel a cold coming on."

"Jake told me you never had a cold in your life."

"Did anybody ever tell you you've become a tough, cynical little broad?"

"Why, thank you, Fingers." She was laughing as she led him inside. "That's the nicest thing you've ever said to me."

As she moved through the plush interior, Sam saw the way the men stared at her.

Addy was aware of their respectful glances. She was tough, all right. They'd never know how tough. The woman they saw now, sleek, polished, professional, had been completely invented. She was a far cry from the kid who'd grown up just a couple of hundred miles from here. Or the scared girl who'd ended up on Jake's doorstep one night.

"What're you grinning about?" Fingers asked.

"Illusion, Fingers." She looped her arm through his and led him toward the coffee shop. "The magic of illusion."

* * *

Addy wore a slinky red beaded gown for the grand opening. She and Lil spent weeks of lunches and shopping to find the perfect dress. And when she tried it on, Lil insisted that it was the only gown for this special occasion.

"Oh, Lil, it's so expensive."

"How often do you open a new casino, chérie?"

Addy shrugged. "But it feels wicked to spend this much on a dress I may never wear again."

"The opening of Starr's will bring new jobs. And new jobs mean many more families earning a living. You are going to meet a lot of important, influential people who will only remember the glamorous woman in the red beaded gown. You must buy it, chérie."

Addy was glad she'd taken Lil's advice.

At Addy's insistence, a front table had been reserved for Jake's friends at the two-hundred-dollar-a-plate dinner that was to benefit the state's children's shelters. When she learned that the dinner was completely sold out, she consoled herself that it more than made up for the money she'd spent on the dress.

There were the usual dignitaries, mayor, governor, state senators. And to add an authentic western flavour to the affair they had invited movie stars who had made their mark in old westerns. It was a gala, glittery event.

The entertainment was a parade of the top three country musicians, followed by a lavish revue starring a magician who made horses, stage coaches, and an entire army of men dressed like soldiers in 1840 costumes, disappear.

The crowd was noisy and enthusiastic. The building of Starr's had, after all, been chronicled not only in the local papers, but had been reported in Time and Newsweek. Its success was of great interest to the financial segment of Reno and the state of Nevada.

In the crush of people, Addy saw Sam speak to a security guard. The uniformed man nodded respectfully, then moved away. When Sam turned, he caught her eye and for a moment their gazes locked. Then he turned to the governor and was soon deep in conversation.

Addy continued to watch him for a moment longer. He was unbelievably handsome in a black tuxedo. It was a far cry from his usual rumpled appearance, but the style suited him. Addy saw the admiring glances cast by many of the women in the crowd as they passed him.

When the dinner ended, the crowd surged toward the casino. As Addy moved through the crush of people, she felt a hand on her arm. Turning, she found herself staring into Sam's eyes.

"You toss a great party, Mrs. Starr."

"So do you, Mr. Money."

As she began to turn away his grip tightened on her arm. "Nice dress."

She felt his gaze burn over her and her cheeks grew hot. But as she tried to turn away he muttered thickly, "How does it feel to mingle with movie stars and entertainers and know that you outshine all of them?"

The crowd streamed around them, pushing and shoving. "What I'm trying to say, and doing such a lousy job of it, is - Addy, you look beautiful." He touched a fingertip to her cheek, then let it trail the curve of her jaw. "There isn't a woman in this place who can even come close to you."

"That's the liquor talking, Sam. If you were sober you'd be up ahead with Lil and the others, scoring points with the governor and the movie stars."

His eyes narrowed. His hands closed over her upper arms, drawing her firmly against him. "I haven't had a drop to drink yet. I've never been more sober in my life." He brushed his lips over hers, then, aware of the fire, drew quickly away. "Or more aware of a beautiful woman."

The crowd continued to surge past them. Neither of them noticed.

Sam had to fight an almost overpowering urge to draw her into his arms and crush her mouth with his. Instead, he lowered his hands to his sides and took a step back.

For a long moment Addy was too stunned to move. Where had these shocking, intense feelings come from? What power did Sam have that he could cause such paralysis? It hadn't even been much of a kiss; just a mere brush of lips on lips.

"Chérie, my husband's handsome nephew has been dying to meet you."

Caught off guard, Addy glanced at the man who stood beside Lil. He was indeed darkly handsome, with fine, even features and dark, curly hair. His perfectly tailored tuxedo displayed a trim, athletic body.

"Addy Starr, this is Gianni d'Angelo."

He took her hand and held it as he said, "Miss Starr. My friends call me Johnny D."

"I think I prefer Gianni. It's nice to meet you."

He continued holding her hand much longer than was

necessary. "I've waited a long time to meet you, Miss Starr."

"Actually, it's Mrs. Starr." She drew her hand away. "And this is my partner, Sam Money."

The two men shook hands and regarded each other stiffly for several seconds. Then the stranger returned his attention to Addy.

"You've done wonders with this old place."

"The design was my husband's, as was the dream. I'm just seeing to it that his dream becomes reality."

"You're doing a fine job of it. When the festivities are over, I'd like to meet with you. I have a business proposition to offer."

"Call my secretary. Paula will set up an appointment."

"Thank you. I'll call her next week."

Addy saw the governor and his party heading her way. "Excuse me. I see I'm needed. It was nice meeting you, Gianni."

"The pleasure was mine, Mrs. Starr."

He nodded toward Sam, and then escorted Lil across the room. As he walked away, Addy had the strange feeling that he was familiar to her. But it wasn't possible. She would never forget a man as handsome as Gianni d'Angelo.

She turned in time to see Sam's scowl of displeasure as he watched the stranger across the room. But before she could ask him why he seemed so angry, the governor took her arm and she was once again caught up in the festivities.

Chapter Twenty-five

Addy took the elevator to the penthouse suite. Inside, the curtains had been left open. She crossed the room and stood a moment in the pre-dawn darkness, staring at the lights of the city glittering far below.

At a knock on the door she crossed the room. "Who is it?"

"Your partner," came Sam's muffled voice.

Addy opened the door. He had loosened his tie and unbuttoned the top button of his starched shirt. In his hand was a bottle of Dom Perignon.

"I thought we'd toast the success of Starr's."

She gave him an easy smile. "Now that the party is over and the grand opening went without a hitch, I'd like nothing better."

He walked past her and stared around the suite, then gave an admiring whistle. "Not bad, Mrs. Starr."

Addy laughed. "I know it's not as comfortable as Jake's big old house, but I'll make do."

The living room was decorated in a sleek mix of black and white contemporary. Floor-to-ceiling windows on two sides offered a spectacular view of the city below. A comfortable white sectional sofa was arranged in a half-circle around a massive white granite fireplace. A slab of black and white veined marble formed the hearth. On a mirrored coffee table a black vase held an arrangement of white roses. Their fragrance perfumed the air.

The door to the bedroom stood open, revealing thick white carpeting and a king-sized bed covered in black and white satin and mounds of matching pillows. Sam could see more white roses on a bedside table.

"I'll get some glasses." Addy removed two crystal champagne glasses from a black lacquer cabinet.

Sam filled them and handed one to her. "Here's to Starr's."

"And here's to the man who made it all possible."

"God, I miss him," Sam muttered.

Addy nodded, for a moment too overcome to speak. At the oddest times she would find herself thinking about Jake and a lump would threaten to choke her.

They sipped, then moved together to stand in front of the windows. The lights of the city shimmered and glowed.

"I remember getting off the bus," Addy lifted the glass to her lips. "And feeling so anxious about this city. After Dry Creek, it was like being on the moon. And I remember passing all those big casinos, and wondering what they looked like inside. The glamorous people and their fine big cars seemed so far removed from reality."

"Haven't you caught on yet? None of this is real," Sam said with a laugh. "It's all make-believe. Tomorrow you're going to wake up and learn that it was all a dream." He glanced at her. "What would you do if that happened?"

"I guess I'd cry and pout and feel very sorry for myself. And then I'd roll up my sleeves and get a job."

"Yeah." His voice held a trace of admiration. "You would. I can't imagine anything taking you down for the count."

"How about you, Sam? What would you do if it was all gone tomorrow?"

"Hell, I've been there."

She saw the way his eyes narrowed and realized she'd hit a nerve.

He drained his glass and crossed the room to fill it. When he returned he lifted the bottle and topped off her glass, then set the bottle on an end table. "I've tried losing myself in a bottle and found it doesn't work. When I sober up, the pain's still there. So is the emptyness. It's funny . . ."

Addy waited, letting him choose his words carefully. The decision to finally talk about this private pain he'd carried around for so long had to be his alone.

"My life was so well-ordered," he said, staring at the streaks of pale pink that slashed the darkness. "Married my childhood sweetheart, Laura. Had a son. Timmy." The names, spoken aloud, brought a fresh stab of pain. "I was the youngest in my class at the Academy to make detective. I was a perfectionist. The brass knew if they gave the case to Sam Money, it was as good as solved. That determination to be the best is what killed my wife and son."

At her look of surprise his tone hardened. "I was working overtime, as usual, on a case, instead of being home with them where I belonged. You see, I've never been able to walk away from a case until I had it solved. It was my super ego. No crook in New York could outsmart Sam Money. If it took every waking hour, I'd solve the case." He drained his glass in one long swallow. "While I was parked in mid-town, on my time off, trailing a big-time drug dealer, a couple of two-bit hoodlums decided they wanted my stereo and TV and whatever else they could haul from my apartment. And a woman and little boy were just in the way, so they eliminated them. If I'd been home where I belonged, Laura and Timmy never would have died."

"You don't know that, Sam."

"Don't I?" His eyes glittered.

Addy understood the horror of coming face to face with the death of loved ones. But she couldn't understand his guilt. "How can you blame yourself for what happened?"

"I was the best shot on the force. There wasn't a petty thief alive who could have outshot me. Those thugs didn't stand a chance if I'd have been there. But I wasn't. I was out making a name for myself, playing super detective. And because of it, my wife and son are dead. That's my reward for being the best. Now

I've learned how to be another kind of perfectionist – a perfect drunk."

He drained his glass again and reached for the bottle. Addy placed her hand over his to stop him.

"Haven't you learned by now that that won't help?"

"Yeah." He shook off her hand and filled his glass. "But until I find something better, this will have to do."

"I wish you'd stop punishing yourself."

"Why should you care?"

Addy turned away. Why indeed? What was Sam to her, except a business partner forced on her by the sudden whim of a dead man? But though she tried to dismiss him, it wasn't that easy. There was something about Sam Money that tugged at her and wouldn't let go.

"I'm tired, Sam. It's been a long day. I think I'll turn in now."

She opened the door and stepped away, careful to keep some distance between them. The last thing she needed in her already exhausted state was to have him touch her.

He set his glass on the table and walked toward her. Pausing beside her he reached a hand to her cheek. They both felt the rush of heat.

"Better bolt your door, Addy. You never know when some drunk might get the notion to try to sweet-talk the beautiful owner of Starr's into bed."

"I see you take your job as head of security very seriously."

"Yeah." He dropped his hand to his side and strode quickly through the open doorway.

For long minutes after he heard the sound of the deadbolt, he stood staring at the closed door. Then he crossed the hall to his empty suite.

*   *   *

Addy strode to the bedroom and slipped out of the red gown. Within minutes she'd washed off her makeup and slid between the satin sheets. She switched off the lights and lay a moment in the darkness. The names and faces of so many people played through her mind. Entertainers and politicians, businessmen and opportunists.

But as she drifted to sleep, only one face remained – Sam Money's. Sam watching her from across the crowded room; walking beside her as she escorted the governor and the celebrities to the festivities; winking at her as they both endured the endless small talk.

She smiled as sleep overtook her.

*　　*　　*

"I need to talk to you, Sam."

He dismissed the two security guards with whom he'd been conferring. "Did somebody breach security?"

"No. It's personal."

"Let's go to your office."

"I'd rather talk right here before I lose my nerve again."

With his hand on Addy's arm he led her to a table in a deserted section of the bar. As soon as they were seated a waitress appeared with a drink.

"Scotch, rocks. Right, Sam?"

"Right." He tossed several bills on her tray and she sauntered away.

He tossed back the liquid and set the empty glass down.

He sat. Quiet, at ease, his legs crossed casually. Yet Addy had the feeling that Sam was a man who was never really at ease. Though she had his full attention, she would bet any amount of money that he knew everything that was going on around him.

He had a habit of watching all who entered or took a seat nearby. And though it was only a glance, Addy was certain he could describe everything about the people; their height, colouring, hair, manner of dress.

"Okay, Addy. What's up?"

"I don't know. One minute I think I'd like to hire

another detective to try to find my sisters. And the next minute I tell myself that it's too late. They could hate me for disrupting their lives. I keep asking myself if I'd be doing it for their sakes or for my own. By now they've certainly forgotten all about me."

His voice was low, intense. "They might forget. But there are some things the heart never forgets. If they heard your story, they'd know."

Puzzled, Addy stared into his dark eyes. She hadn't expected something so passionate from Sam. "How do you know so much about it?"

He gave a humorless laugh. "Haven't you heard? I'm an expert on hearts. Every night, when I get drunk enough, I think I've managed to mend mine. But every morning, when I wake up, there it is again. Broken in little pieces."

For a moment she felt his pain as surely as if it were her own. Then a realization suddenly dawned. Sam had spent too many years running away. She wouldn't repeat his mistakes. The only way to deal with the pain was to face it.

"I guess I've just made up my mind. I want to try again to find my sisters. I'd like you to recommend a private investigator."

He paused for a long moment before saying, "I might know someone."

She leaned forward. "Could he start right away?"

The waitress appeared with another drink. Sam accepted it and paid her, then looked up to see Addy's frown of annoyance.

"He'll need some time to – handle some unfinished business."

"How much time?"

"A couple of weeks. Maybe a couple of months."

He could see her disappointment. "A couple of months?"

"Is that so long?"

"It is when you've waited as long as I have. What's his name?"

268

He ran his finger around and around the rim of the glass. "Sam Money."

She looked up in astonishment. "What are you saying?"

He shrugged. "I know your story and background. I know where to begin. And I used to be a damned good detective."

"But what about your position here?"

"I have good people working for me, Addy. I personally trained them. I trust them to keep things running smoothly while I search for your sisters."

She gave him a long, steady look. "You said you'd need some time before you could start. Why?"

"I thought maybe I'd clean up my act first."

She caught her breath, then glanced at the drink in front of him.

He continued to run his finger around the rim of the glass, as if tempting himself. "After all this time in a bottle, I'm not sure I can climb out alone. I might need help." He shrugged. "Besides, I want you to trust me, and I know you can't trust a drunk. Hell, neither can I. So I guess it's time I found out if I can do it."

Addy watched as he studied the glass for long minutes before lifting it to his lips and draining it.

Her hopes tumbled. "I've got to get back to work, Sam."

He nodded.

She paused, about to say something more. Then she seemed to think better about it and walked away. When she was across the room she glanced at the Horseshoe Bar. Sam was already lifting another glass to his lips.

She turned away with a feeling of deep sorrow. When he awoke in the morning, Sam wouldn't even be able to remember what they'd talked about.

As she made her way to her office she couldn't help wishing things could be different. For a moment, she'd actually believed Sam. That was dangerous, she thought. If there was one thing she'd learned, it was that the only person she could trust was herself. And all the wishing in the world wouldn't change one fact. Sam Money was a drunk. She'd learned years ago what that kind of man could do to her life.

Chapter Twenty-six

"Addy, there's a Mr. Gianni d'Angelo waiting to meet with you."

"Thanks, Paula. Send him in."

Addy looked up from her desk as the handsome man closed the door firmly behind him. He walked toward her with his hand outstretched.

"Addy."

"Mr. d'Angelo."

"It's Gianni. I told you. Or Johnny D if you prefer."

It was obvious that he was accustomed to being charming in the company of women. He held her hand firmly between both of his and stared deeply into her eyes.

"How good of you to see me on such short notice. I just got back from Carson City. The governor sends his regards."

"How is he?" Addy withdrew her hand and indicated a chair.

"Still talking about your opening night celebration. He's convinced that Starr's will be an asset to Nevada."

He settled himself comfortably and pulled a thin, gold cigarette case from his breast pocket. When she declined his offer of a cigarette, he placed one in his mouth and held a gold lighter to the tip, inhaling deeply.

"Of course," he said, blowing out a thin stream of smoke, "I realize that you're a novice at running a hotel. For that reason I've come here to offer my assistance. There are many things I can do to make your operation run more smoothly."

She wondered why his words, spoken so casually, had her bristling. She managed to keep her tone even. "How kind of you. But, so far, everything seems to be under control."

He smiled indulgently. "There are so many factions that must be kept happy in an operation like this. A successful casino and hotel must depend upon linen supply, cleaners, garbage disposal, food and beverage, and, of course, the people to maintain all the services required. That is why you could use my influence. I'm what's called a fixer. If something is wrong, I fix it."

"You fix it?"

"Of course. I fix things with the unions, with the suppliers. Why should a beautiful woman like you have to deal with unpleasant details?"

Addy forced a smile to her lips. "I've had no problem with the unions. I pay a fair wage. And as for the other services, I'm managing to pay all my bills on time. I don't see why I should anticipate any problems."

He tapped ash into a crystal ashtray on her desk and leaned forward. "Of course you've had no problems. I put the word out that I would take it as a very personal favour if you are treated with the utmost courtesy."

For a moment Addy was speechless. When she regained her composure she said, "Are you suggesting that you . . . that I . . .?"

He nodded. "Think of me as a liaison between you and all those with whom you do business. For as long as you wish, you are under my protection. You'll be given very special treatment."

"And just what am I supposed to do for this protection?"

Ignoring the thread of anger in her tone, Gianni gave her his most charming smile. She was a beautiful, intriguing woman. He'd never had the pleasure of doing business with someone like her before. He was going to enjoy this immensely. A little business. A little pleasure.

"For openers, you can have dinner with me tonight."

Addy wasted no time pressing a buzzer on top of her desk, to signal her secretary. Getting to her feet she said briskly, "I'm sorry. I have an engagement this evening." She looked up as her office door opened. "Paula, would you show Mr. d'Angelo to the elevators?"

He didn't move. His smile remained in place. "Break the engagement."

"I'm afraid not."

He stubbed out his cigarette and leaned back in his chair, lacing his hands across his chest. So, she would not be easy. Mrs. Starr had just become even more intriguing. He loved a challenge. But of course, he'd win. He always won.

"Do you remember the bomb threat made to one of Reno's most popular casinos a few years ago?"

Addy felt her blood turn to ice. "Yes, I seem to recall reading about it."

"Nasty business. A disgruntled employee, as I recall. It would be a tragedy if something like that should befall Starr's." His gaze locked with hers. "I was the one called in to negotiate between the employee and the casino."

At the flash of fire in her eyes his own darkened with sudden passion. If she was afraid, she hid it well behind a mask of anger. He knew now that he had to have this woman.

He strode around her desk and caught her hands in a firm grip. He gave her his most charming smile. "I look forward to having dinner with you tonight."

His hands were strong, his grasp firm. She hoped he wouldn't feel the slight tremble in her hands as she pulled free.

"That's impossible. Goodbye, Gianni."

"Not goodbye; just good day. For now, Mrs. Starr."

Addy watched until the door closed behind him and thought of several rich ripe curses that Jake had taught her. Then she crossed her arms over her chest and stormed to the window. Far below, a steady stream of employees snaked from the parking lot to the hotel. She tried to imagine the horror and devastation if one of them planted a bomb in Starr's and threatened to blow it up along with everyone inside.

What in the world was the matter with her? She'd always been blessed – or cursed – with a wild imagination. Next she'd be convinced that Gianni d'Angelo was some sort of monster who'd just threatened her. How foolish could she get? Wasn't he a personal friend of the governor? Still, there was something frightening about him. Something dark and dangerous just beneath that smoothly cultivated image.

She pressed her heated forehead to the cool glass. If only Sam were here. He'd know what to do or say to calm her fears.

He'd been gone for over a month. She hadn't heard a single word. And she was beginning to fear that he'd dropped from the face of the earth. Or worse, that he'd poured himself into a bottle. This time for good.

*   *   *

Addy stepped back to survey her image in the mirror. The black cocktail suit with hand-beaded shawl collar projected the perfect image. She wanted to look elegant yet professional. Tonight was the meeting of the city's hotel and casino owners. Addy had hoped that Sam would accompany her, but in his absence, she had no choice but to go alone.

She looked up at the ringing of the doorbell. Adjusting an earring, she opened the door to admit several uniformed deliverymen who were carrying six dozen white roses in exotic black vases.

For a moment she was mystified.

"Where would you like these, Mrs. Starr?"

"Put them anywhere," she said, taking the card from a small white envelope.

The note read simply, 'I look forward to our dinner together.' She felt a trickle of fear along her spine. There was no signature, but she knew.

She waited until the deliverymen were gone, then she leaned against the door. Her brow knitted together in a frown. How could Gianni d'Angelo know the decor of her suite? And how could he possibly know that she had a weakness for white roses? The thought that he'd probed so deeply into her private life left her slightly shaken.

She glanced at her watch. There was no time to ponder this now. She was already late for the meeting.

Dropping the card on the table she picked up a small beaded bag and her key. She stepped into an elevator and exited at the second floor where a private dining room had been set aside for the dinner and meeting.

The men looked up as Addy entered, creating a brief lull in the hum of conversation. She realized at once that she was the only female.

She moved through the crowd, greeting the casino owners she had come to know over the past few months. There were no more oldtimers like Jake. They had all been replaced by aggressive young businessmen who headed corporations that were part of even larger conglomerates. The talk centered around marketing and theme parks and extravagant golf outings for high rollers.

"Have you thought about adding a golf course to your adjacent property, Mrs. Starr?" someone asked.

Addy shook her head. "At the moment I'm still getting my feet wet in the hotel and casino business. I don't think I'm ready for the next step."

"You need to consider the big picture," the president of Reno's largest casino said. "Old Jake dragged his feet for too long. A hotel is a step in the right direction, but you're already ten years too late. If you're going to compete, you need a longterm game plan."

"My thoughts exactly," came a voice directly behind her. "That's why Mrs. Starr and I are going to discuss her future."

Addy turned to find herself looking into the dark, laughing eyes of Gianni d'Angelo.

He smoothly steered her away from the cluster of

businessmen. When a waitress approached he plucked two glasses of champagne from her tray and handed one to Addy.

"I told you we would be having dinner tonight."

"I thought this was a meeting of casino owners."

"It is. But I was invited by the president of your association to lend my presence." His smile widened. "I see I've managed to surprise you. Good. I would hate to think I was predictable."

His presence was very unsettling. Still, Addy had to admit that this strange man fascinated her.

"The roses were another surprise." She sipped the champagne, needing something to do. His look was too piercing; his manner too possessive. "How did you know I love white roses?"

"A lucky guess."

"I think not. And the black vases?" She had a sudden, chilling thought. "Have you been in my apartment?"

He chuckled, evading the question. "I'm not nearly as interested in your apartment as I am in the woman who occupies it."

The chairman of the association pounded his gavel and called the meeting to order. The members began making their way to their tables, where waiters were already beginning the food service. Addy nodded to several of the men as she made her way to her table, with Gianni beside her.

"You seem to have gone to great lengths to get my attention. Why?"

"Why not?" Gianni held her chair. When she was seated, he took the seat beside her. Leaning close he murmured, "You are a fascinating, beguiling woman."

"And you merely wanted to take me to dinner."

"I didn't say that." His smile grew. "What I said was I would like to begin with dinner. Where we go from there will be entirely up to you, Mrs. Starr."

Before she could frame a curt response, he turned his attention to the others at the table, leaving Addy to stare in silent frustration at his handsome chiseled profile.

*　　*　　*

The business meeting that followed the dinner was an education for Addy. The presidents of several casinos voiced concern over the decline of tourism and the loss of players to Reno. The state of the economy and the number of armed robberies caused a heated debate. But when Gianni d'Angelo arose to speak, a respectful hush fell over the assembled businessmen.

"As you know, my family lives in this fine city. What happens to you, happens to me and my family. Though I have no vested interest in your establishments, I think it might be to your advantage if I put together a security force that would be trained to spot potential thieves even before they attempt to rob your businesses."

"At what cost?" one of the men asked.

Gianni shot him a cold stare before saying blandly, "What does it matter, if it curtails the robberies that are costing you millions? And if the cost is shared by all, it will not become a burden."

More than ever, Addy wished that Sam was here. Though Gianni's offer seemed innocent enough, it had a dark side. That same security force, trained and employed by d'Angelo, could be turned against the very people it had been hired to protect. The thought of this man's security force having free access to Starr's gave her an uneasy feeling.

After a quick, heated debate, it was agreed that the owners would turn to the city police for protection. If Gianni was angered by their decision, it wasn't evident. He merely smiled.

When the meeting adjourned, Addy hoped to steal away quickly, but she found herself cornered by several of the men who wanted to talk to her about her new venture.

"I understand you had no problems with the building trades, Mrs. Starr," one of her competitors said dryly.

"We've been very fortunate. Though we anticipated trouble, especially when the cement contractors went on strike in the state, they managed to settle peacefully in time to complete our work on deadline."

"How fortunate."

"I understand you managed to avoid the culinary workers walkout just before your grand opening as well," another said with a trace of sarcasm.

Addy thought about the panic she'd felt when it looked as though the opening would be marred by a messy picket line. Instead, the strike had been miraculously settled less than twentyfour hours before Starr's was due to open.

"That's true. As I said, we've been extremely lucky."

"Luck," one of the men said with a laugh.

The others exchanged knowing smiles.

Just then Gianni joined their circle. The men quickly shook hands and made their exit.

Addy fought down a sense of frustration. There was no escaping Gianni now, she realized. He looked as though he had no intention of leaving her side.

"May I buy you a drink in the casino, Mrs. Starr?"

"No, thank you."

"Then I'll escort you to your room."

"I think I'll take a turn around the floor first, and make certain there's no trouble."

"I'll accompany you."

"It may take me quite a while."

"I'm in no hurry."

With a sigh Addy led the way to the elevator. As they stepped inside, several men entered and took up positions on either side of the door. At Addy's arched brow, Gianni said softly, "They're with me. They see to my security."

They rode to the main floor in silence. As she moved among the dice tables, with Gianni at her side, Addy saw the two men trail slowly behind, always keeping Gianni in their sight.

"Hey, Addy." Fingers approached, and for a moment, when he caught sight of the man beside Addy, he stiffened.

Seeing his reaction Addy said, "Fingers, this is Gianni d'Angelo."

The two men nodded stiffly.

Addy was aware of the thinly veiled hostility between them. "What is it, Fingers?"

"Just thought you might join the old gang for a quick hand of poker, for old times' sake."

"I wish I could. But I've already put in fourteen hours today. I think it's time I turned in."

"Yeah. Sure." He glanced toward the man beside her, then muttered, "Heard anything from Sam yet?"

He saw the quick frown before she said, "Not a word."

"Don't worry." He patted her arm. "He'll be back."

"Yeah." She pressed a hand over his, then drew away. "Tell the others I'll see them tomorrow."

"Goodnight, Addy."

"'Night, Fingers."

She completed her turn around the casino, then headed toward the private elevator that would take her to the penthouse. She nodded to the beefy man who stood guard. "Good evening, Bruno."

"'Evening, Mrs. Starr."

She turned. "I'll say goodnight here, Gianni."

As the door slid open he took her arm and escorted her inside. "A gentleman always sees a lady to her door. You don't think I'd let you ride up alone, do you?"

When the two men made a move to follow, Gianni shook his head and they froze in their tracks.

She tried to dismiss him with a smile. "This isn't necessary. As you can see, I have all the security I need."

Gianni pressed the button to the top floor. As the door slid closed he turned to her. His voice held a hint of danger. "Do you really think a guard at the door to the elevator will keep you safe?"

"Well I . . ."

"Believe me, Mrs. Starr, a lot can happen between here and the penthouse. Even in an elevator."

Her gaze flew to the digital lights, indicating the floors as they sped past. Though they were ascending quickly, Addy felt a trickle of fear along her spine.

She knew nothing about this man, and he had already gained access to her private elevator. Once upstairs, they would be completely alone.

Beside her, Gianni was enjoying her discomfort.

When the elevator finally came to a smooth stop, she took a deep breath and stepped through the open door. Gianni followed a step behind. She removed the key from her bag and he smoothly took it from her hand and opened the door, then handed her the key.

She turned to face him, barring his way.

"Are you going to invite me in?"

"Not tonight. It's very late and . . ."

He dropped a hand on her shoulder. Though she seemed very determined, he could feel the slight tremble. "You may have noticed, Mrs. Starr, that I'm not very good at being refused."

Why hadn't she insisted on having her security guard ride up with her? Now she was alone, at the very top of the hotel, with a man who frightened her.

"Now will you invite me in?"

As she stood resolutely barring his way, a door opened across the hall. A deep voice behind Gianni muttered, "I believe the lady said no."

Chapter Twenty-seven

"Sam." Addy was so happy to see him it was all she could do to keep from rushing into his arms. Instead she said calmly, "Sam, I believe you know Gianni d'Angelo."

"We've met." Sam's tone was as cold as ice.

"I didn't think you'd remember." Gianni's eyes glittered with malice. "As I recall, you were drunk."

"Not quite drunk enough. Unfortunately."

Deliberately turning his back on Sam, Gianni lifted Addy's hand to his lips. "I enjoyed our dinner together. I'll call you."

With Addy and Sam looking on, he strode to the elevator and punched the button. The doors glided shut.

Sam turned on her with a fury she'd never witnessed before. "How could you have dinner with that slime?"

Her eyes narrowed. "You've been gone for over a month with no explanation, and you're yelling at me?" She turned toward the open door of her suite. "I don't even want to talk to you."

Before she took three steps he caught her by the arm and twisted her to face him. "You're going to talk to me, whether you like it or not. What are you doing with scum like d'Angelo?"

"What I do, and with whom, is none of your business." She lowered her voice, feeling the flare of anger suddenly dissipate at the nearness of him. "He showed up at a business dinner for the casino owners. A meeting, I might add, that I was counting on attending with you."

"Yeah. Sorry." He released her and followed her inside her suite. "I'd hoped to be back in time, but I got hung up."

Addy took the time to really look at him, noting the close-cropped haircut, the beautifully tailored dark suit. He looked tanned and fit. "I hope she was worth it."

"She?"

"It's pretty obvious that you've been off somewhere exotic enjoying yourself."

He gave her a long, slow grin. "I hope that's jealousy I hear in your voice."

"Don't be ridiculous."

"Well, I'll be damned." With a knowing smile he sank into a chair and watched as she carelessly tossed her handbag on the coffee table.

He didn't know why, but it gave him enormous pleasure to know that she was displaying signs of jealousy. Could it be that she'd missed him?

He leaned back, enjoying the sight of her. After so long, he'd been afraid that he'd magnified everything in his mind. But, if possible, Addy was even more beautiful than he'd remembered. The cocktail suit gave her a sophisticated polish that added to her allure. The sight of her hips swaying as she crossed the room gave him thoughts that would make her blush.

Crossing his legs he studied the toe of his new shoe for long minutes before saying, "Sorry I couldn't contact you. I've been in rehab."

As she swung around he saw the look of surprise on her face. "Rehab? You've quit . . .?"

He nodded. "No more booze. I'm on the wagon."

"Oh, Sam." She raced toward him, her face alight with pleasure. "I'm so glad. I thought . . ."

"I don't blame you. I guess that's what I'd think about a guy like me. Now, how about some coffee while I tell you the rest."

"The rest?"

He held up a hand. "Over coffee."

She hurried to the kitchen, with Sam trailing behind her. A few minutes later, they returned to the living room carrying mugs and a carafe filled with hot coffee.

"Now tell me everything," Addy said, filling their mugs.

"I'm going to start the search for your sisters." Sam drank, then looked up at her. "You know, I haven't really tasted coffee in years. This is good."

"How can you talk about coffee at a time like this? When are you going to start? And where?"

He drank again, causing her to squirm with impatience.

"I paid a visit to Fran Turner's widow, Betty, on my way here. We went through your file. The license number given to her husband by your old neighbour is missing. He apparently had it with him at the time of the accident. It was never returned with his belongings." Sam didn't add that Fran's car crash had the look and feel of a professional hit. "Tomorrow I'm heading over to Dry Creek. I'll pick up where Fran Turner left off."

"But with Cleo Bentson dead and the license plate number missing, what good will it do you?"

"You had other neighbours, Addy. Maybe they weren't as nosy as Cleo Bentson, but they might remember something. I'll piece together what I can. Just remember, the trail is cold. This is going to take time. But sooner or later we'll find your sisters."

She bit her lip and turned to stare at the lights of the city. "I wish I could be as certain as you seem to be."

"Relax." He set his cup down and crossed the room to stand behind her. He caught a strand of her hair between his thumb and finger and absently tugged it. "After what I've been through, finding two girls who've been missing for eight years should be a piece of cake."

He turned her to face him and his gaze fastened on her mouth. He'd been away so long. And now that he was back, everything seemed to feel so right. Being here with her, hearing the sound of her voice, breathing in the scent of her perfume, made him feel that he'd come home.

"It's funny." He took the cup from her hands and set it on a table beside them, then framed her face with his hands and traced the outline of her lips with his thumb. "It wasn't the whiskey I missed; it was you."

As his lips covered hers she tasted his hunger and answered with a hunger of her own. His arms came around her, drawing her into the circle of his embrace.

"Oh God," he muttered against her lips, "how I missed you."

He'd intended to be tender, but the moment his lips covered hers he forgot all his good intentions. His mind emptied as he filled himself with her.

For a moment he lifted his head as he struggled for air. His breath came hard and fast. His hands gripped her shoulders in a painful grasp, but she never cried out. Instead she lifted a hand to his cheek, as if to soothe.

That was his undoing. He dragged her against him and crushed her mouth with his.

She could feel the barely contained passion in him. Instead of being frightened of it, as she'd been in the past, she thrilled to it. It gave her a sense of power to know that she could take him to the very edge of his control. And beyond. Without the threat of the whiskey to act as a barrier between them, she opened to him, taking what he offered, giving what he demanded.

He felt the subtle change in her. Always before, she'd held back, afraid to let him get too close. But now it was as if a door had opened. She welcomed his touch. He took greedily.

A little moan escaped her lips. Her body ached for him. Just the thought of it made her shudder with pleasure.

It took a moment for either of them to realize that the phone was ringing. They tried to ignore it, but the insistent ringing finally caused them to step apart.

On trembling legs Addy crossed the room and snatched up the phone with a sigh of impatience.

"Yes?"

Over the pounding of her heart she heard Fingers' voice, high, insistent. "Addy, are you all right up there?"

"Yes. Why?" Her breath came out in short, painful gasps.

Across the room she saw Sam watching her. He turned away and paused in front of a huge vase of roses. He leaned close to inhale their fragrance.

"I don't like you being alone with that d'Angelo guy."

"Oh." She let out a little laugh. "Gianni left. Sam's here."

"Ah." She heard the note of relief in his voice. "That's okay, then. Sorry to bother you. I'll see you tomorrow."

"Goodnight, Fingers."

With a little laugh she replaced the receiver and said over her shoulder, "You've just received Fingers' seal of approval."

With a smile she turned. Her smile faded when she saw the scowl on Sam's face. Puzzled, she glanced at the plain white card that he held in his hand.

"I thought you said you didn't know d'Angelo would be at dinner."

"I didn't." She took a step toward him, then stopped as his frown deepened.

"The room looks like a goddamned hothouse. How many times has he been here anyway?" He knew he sounded like a jealous lover, but he didn't care. He couldn't stop the flow of angry words. "Dozens of white roses in perfect black vases. Looks like I stayed away a little too long. Or maybe, I just didn't stay away long enough."

"Sam . . ."

He tossed the card on the table and crossed the room, tearing the door open and slamming it behind him. As he crossed the hall and turned the key in his lock, he realized that his hand was shaking. Her taste was still on his lips. With a savage oath he slammed the door with such force it rattled all the windows.

* * *

Addy lay in her bed and struggled to hold back the tears. She would not cry over Sam Money. He wasn't worth it. So he had come back sober, and announced that he was ready to search for her sisters. Did that give him the right to question her every move?

He'd accused her of lying about Gianni d'Angelo. No man called Addy Starr a liar.

Still, he'd saved her neck tonight. What would have happened if Sam hadn't been here? Though it had all happened very quickly, she had to admit that she'd been frightened of Gianni. He had the calm, self-assured arrogance of a man who had no doubt that he'd get whatever he wanted.

She shivered and drew the blankets around her.

Was it respect she'd seen in the eyes of the other casino owners when they'd faced Gianni? Or was it fear?

Suddenly she thought about the strange conversation she'd had when the meeting was over. The other casino owners had almost mocked the ease with which Starr's had been opened. She struggled to recall the words. Cement workers' strike. Culinary workers' picket lines.

Addy sat up and peered into the darkness. Had it been merely good luck? Gianni's words taunted her. "Fixer. Under my protection. Why should a beautiful lady have to deal with such things? I let it be known that I would take it as a personal favour . . ."

But how could this be? She hadn't even met Gianni d'Angelo until the night of the grand opening. And even then, she'd certainly never asked for his help.

Still, the thought persisted. In the minds of the other owners, she was experiencing more than good luck. And now the seed had been planted in her own mind, as well.

Who was Gianni d'Angelo? And why had he singled her out?

She wished she could go to Sam with her fears. But he was already furious enough. If she were to tell him what Gianni had implied, he'd throw a fit. He'd certainly believe that there was more between them than a simple business dinner. Besides, he needed to concentrate all his efforts on finding her sisters. She wouldn't burden him with anything else.

Fingers. She'd seen his reaction to Gianni. Tomorrow she'd go to him and find out all she could about this mysterious man who made her feel so uncomfortable.

Chapter Twenty-eight

Addy sorted through the phone calls and messages stacked on her desk. Three calls, she noted, were from Gianni d'Angelo. She tossed the messages in the wastebasket.

Addy's conversation the previous day with Fingers had left her more shaken than she cared to admit.

"Johnny D works for The Man, Addy."

"The Man?"

"The big boss. Nobody knows who he is, 'cause he never does anything himself. But word on the street is that Johnny D is connected. Family. And whatever The Man wants done, Johnny D does it."

"What does he want with me?"

"You're a pretty girl, Addy. Johnny D always had an eye for pretty girls."

"And you think that's why he used his influence to see that our casino had no problems during construction?"

Fingers shook his head. "Naw. Johnny D's not powerful enough. That kind of order could only come from The Man."

"But why, Fingers? I don't even know The Man. Why would he send Gianni to protect me?" She had a sudden thought. "Jake. He once said his name would keep people from pestering me. Was Jake ever involved with The Man?"

"Jakie? Are you crazy? Addy, Jakie ran a clean business. He never had anything to do with those people. And because his place was so small, they never bothered with him."

"Then why, Fingers? Why me? Why now?"

He shrugged. "I don't know. I can't figure it out. But I'll

tell you what. I'll ask around, see if I can hear anything on the street."

Addy nodded. "Thanks, Fingers. I appreciate it."

Addy's musings were interrupted by her secretary.

"Call for you on three, Addy."

"Who is it, Paula?"

"Mr. d'Angelo."

"Tell him I'm down in the casino."

She strode from her office. Now, more than ever, Addy wished that Sam was here. But he'd left three days ago, and she hadn't heard a word from him since.

With a sigh she stepped into the elevator. The trick was to stay as busy as possible, so she couldn't find time to think at all.

*　　*　　*

Addy had been on the casino floor for over twelve hours. Before that she'd spent several hours in her office. But though she was exhausted, the thought of going up to her empty apartment held no appeal.

She thought of Jake's big old house, alone now except for Verna's occasional visits to clean. That was what she needed. A chance to escape the noise and confusion of this place. Time to think. Time to renew and refresh. And a chance to sleep in the big soft bed on the upper floor.

From her apartment she retrieved her purse and a change of clothes, and, of course, Chester. She knew the old cat missed his familiar surroundings. As an afterthought she snatched up a bouquet of white roses from her nightstand.

When she headed out the door Shorty tipped his hat and escorted her to her car, hastily brought around by the valet.

"You have a nice night, now, Mrs. Starr."

"Thanks, Shorty. You too." As she settled herself inside she called, "Tell me something. Do you ever sleep?"

He grinned. "I never go to sleep before dawn. But it's

been a good many years since I've seen the afternoon. I rise and shine around dinner time." He closed her car door and waved her off.

Chester settled himself onto her lap.

As she pulled into traffic, a car followed. After trailing at a distance for half a block, the headlights came on. Addy never even noticed.

Addy soon left the lights of the city far behind. She drove the familiar route without even turning on the radio. After the noise of the casino, the silence was a special gift.

When she pulled into the driveway, she sat a moment, trying to remember it as it had been when she'd first seen it. Shabby, neglected. Like Jake, she thought. Like Sam. Like the girl she'd been.

Racing up the steps she turned the key in the lock and pushed open the door. Chester ran off, as eager as a kitten. She walked through the rooms, snapping on lights as she did, until the house was ablaze with light.

She studied the polished wood, the freshly washed curtains. In Jake's old room she studied the hospital bed, and in the corner the electric scooter. She would have to find someone who could use them. Soon, she thought. But not quite yet. She wasn't ready to deal with that final parting just yet. She'd been a bride and a widow within weeks. Funny. She didn't feel like either.

In the kitchen she filled a vase with water for her roses. She snapped off the lights on the lower level and climbed the stairs, pausing outside the door of Sam's old room. Taking a deep breath she pushed open the door and threw on the lights.

One wall was dominated by a large fireplace, exactly like the one in her room a floor above. Pulled in front of the fireplace was an old rocker and footstool, and beside it, a table with an ashtray and several cigars. On a double dresser stood framed pictures of a beautiful blonde woman and a little boy with blonde hair and Sam's dark eyes. Addy stood for several minutes studying the pictures.

These were the people he'd loved and lost. The ones whose death had sent him over the edge. Looking at them, all blonde and beautiful, with perfect smiles, she could understand why.

She turned to look at the big double bed with rough scarred tables on either side. Each table held a lamp and stacks of well-read books. She glanced at the titles and was amazed at the wide range of Sam's interests. Mysteries, biographies, scholarly tomes. There was even a dog-eared volume of poems and sonnets.

Funny, she thought, that until this moment she'd never been in Sam's room. It told so much more about the man than she'd expected.

She turned off the lights and climbed another flight of stairs to her old room on the upper floor. Tossing her purse on the dresser she arranged the roses in the vase on the night table and sank down on the edge of the old bed.

She was glad she'd come back here tonight. Her exhaustion was suddenly overwhelming. She slipped off her business suit and carefully hung it in the closet. Wearing only a cream silk teddy, she pulled down the quilt and climbed between the covers. Within minutes she was asleep.

* * *

It wasn't really a sound that roused Addy from sleep; it was a feeling. A feeling that someone was watching her. Her eyes flickered open. She saw the figure of a man looming in the doorway.

With a gasp she sat up. But as a scream formed in her throat, she realized that the man was Sam.

"What are you doing here?" Her nerves had her pressing a hand to her throat.

He stayed where he was for several long moments. It had been the sweetest torture to see her lying there in her bed. He was aware of the sudden longing, of the need to belong to someone again. His solitary existence no longer held any appeal.

Forcing himself to move slowly, he strode to the side of the bed, being careful not to touch her. Not yet. The need was too strong.

"I went to the casino and Shorty told me you'd taken the car. I figured you were here." His voice was suddenly edged with steel as a new thought intruded. He leaned down. "Is anything wrong? Did d'Angelo . . .?"

"No. Nothing. I just needed to get away."

He let out a long, shaky breath.

In the moonlight he could see the spill of her dark hair across the white pillow. Her face and shoulders were luminous; her eyes wide and questioning. The outline of her breasts was clearly visible beneath the ivory silk.

He'd been worried about her. He'd spent far too much time thinking about her. And now that he was this close, he needed to touch her, to assure himself that she was really here and really all right.

"You shouldn't be alone out here."

"Sam, all my life I've been alone."

He heard the truth in that simple statement. "Is that the way you like it?"

His question caught her by surprise. "I don't know. Except for Jake, no one's ever wanted to be a part of my life."

She began to edge toward the far side of the bed, as if to escape the man whose words, and looks, were too probing.

"Jake isn't the only one." He sat on the edge of the bed and caught her by the wrist. Cupping her face with his hand he leaned close and kissed her, giving her no chance to escape.

Like the other times, the rush of heat was instantaneous. His arms came around her, drawing her firmly against him.

As before, his kisses weren't gentle. They were charged with anger and frustration, and a deep gnawing hunger. His mouth moved roughly over hers, assaulting her senses. He could feel her panic as she struggled against the onslaught. Now that she was here in his arms, he was determined to break down the last barriers of her fears.

When she tried to shimmy away he caught her by the hips, holding her firmly against him. The feel of silk was unbelievably arousing as he moved his hand upward along her spine.

Her flesh ran hot and cold at his touch, and she felt her breath hitch in her throat. At first she'd been drugged by sleep. Now she was jolted awake.

He could feel her lips opening to him and his tongue tangled with hers on a groan of pleasure.

Her fear was forgotten. Now there was only need. A need that pulsed and throbbed and drove her to forget everything except this man whose touch, whose kiss was filled with magic.

Her fingers tangled in his hair as she arched her neck and allowed him access to her throat. He ran hot, fevered kisses across her shoulder and along her collarbone.

She lay steeped in pleasure. Never before had she allowed a man, any man, such intimacy. But right now, at this moment, she couldn't imagine anything else. His kisses left her weak. She wanted nothing more than to follow wherever he led her.

When his hands left her she felt suddenly chilled.

"What are you doing?" She heard her own voice, a low, breathy murmur.

"Taking off my clothes."

"No, Sam. I'm barely awake. It's the middle of the night."

His hands left the buttons of his shirt to reach for her. He drew the thin strap of her teddy down over her shoulder and followed the movement with his lips. She trembled and gave a little sigh of pleasure.

He lifted his head. "Of course, if you'd rather, I could go down to my old room . . ."

She caught his arm as he started to get up. "Don't you dare."

"Why, Mrs. Starr." His laughter came out in an unsteady

breath. He'd gambled a lot on that statement. He suddenly felt like the biggest winner of all. He brushed his lips along her throat. "Does this mean you want me to stay?"

"Yes. Oh, yes." She drew him down until his lips covered hers.

He was unprepared for the swift rush of desire that left him trembling with need. He wanted her with a desperation that bordered on insanity.

He slipped the other strap of her teddy from her shoulder and watched as the bit of fabric clung for a moment to her breasts before pooling at her waist. Her skin was soft and smooth, and as creamy as alabaster. He was half mad to taste her. When his lips found her breast, he heard her moan of pleasure.

The current that shot between them electified them both.

When he lifted his head her mouth was eager, avid. It moved under his, seeking, taking. Each time they came up for air, their breathing was even more ragged.

She reached for his shirt, intent upon helping him shed his clothes. But her fingers were stiff and awkward as she tried to manage the buttons. His fingers closed over hers and he lifted her hand to his lips.

Their eyes met; hers, hot and bright, his, heavy-lidded with passion.

He knew, in that instant, that he'd taken her too far, too fast. For a woman unaccustomed to tenderness and love, this first time should be a long, slow journey of discovery. He pressed a kiss to her palm and closed her hand over the kiss, then pressed a kiss to her wrist, the inside of her elbow, her shoulder. He ran hot, languid kisses across her throat, then tugged at her earlobe with his teeth.

She sensed the sudden shift of moods and felt herself relax. The tension was gone, even while the need remained. Though she had never before trusted any man, she would trust him to lead the way.

He felt her surrender and gloried in it. He knew, in

that instant, that he could never do anything to betray her trust.

With his gaze holding hers he traced a finger across her brow, along the curve of her cheek, and around the outline of her lips, until she opened her mouth and nipped his finger.

With Sam she felt no fear, no restrictions. No man had ever touched her with such tenderness. Such gentleness. His loving touch unlocked all her inhibitions. She was suddenly free to taste, to touch, to explore.

With a little laugh she sat up and her hair spilled forward, tickling his flesh. She reached again for his shirt and this time her hands were steady as she slid it from his shoulders. Her mouth was greedy as she took it on a long, slow journey of discovery across his chest, along the flat planes of his stomach. For so long she'd denied herself this pleasure. Now she would have it all.

Power. She felt drunk with it as she realized that she had the power to make him desire her every bit as much as she desired him. She reveled in it as she brought her mouth lower and heard his quick intake of breath.

In one quick motion he rolled her over. His greedy mouth feasted on her breast, sending pleasure vibrating through her until she arched her body to strain against him.

She was beyond thought now. Lost in mindless pleasure, her body begged for release. Instead he took her higher, then higher still, until she could only clutch at him and murmur incoherent words.

The night air was sweet with the fragrance of the roses on her nightstand. An occasional moonbeam filtered through the folds in the drapes, gilding their flesh, turning the white sheets to gold.

It was quiet. So quiet that the only sound was their ragged breathing, and the sound of their heartbeats thundering. The ageing mattress sagged and whispered as they moved together.

He fought back his own needs and forced himself to go

slowly, to draw out the moment. He wanted her to taste, to touch, to savour every moment as she climbed slowly toward the final crest.

Her breath was coming faster now, and he tore the last remaining silk from her. He hadn't meant to tear it, but his hands were no longer steady. He knew he had only moments left before he slipped over the edge. He levered himself above her.

Her flesh was already damp with sheen as, with tongue and fingertips, he brought her to the first peak.

He heard her shallow breathing, saw the way she clutched the sheets beneath her. She seemed dazed by the tremors that rocked her.

Addy was stunned by the feelings that pulsed through her. For so long she had feared a man's touch, having known only pain and hurt. But Sam's touch healed her. And sent her hurtling to some new place where she'd never been before.

He could wait no longer. As he slid inside her, her lids lifted, her gaze met his. She gripped his shoulders and arched to meet him. And as they began to move in an ageless rhythm, he was unprepared for her strength. It matched his as they climbed, high, then higher still, until they seemed to reach the very edge of the universe. Together they tumbled through a shower of stars.

*   *   *

Still joined, they lay perfectly motionless. Sam's arms were around her, cradling her against his chest. His lips were pressed to a tangle of hair at her temple. The love he felt for this woman left him shaken.

Somehow, he had to convince her of that love. Considering what she'd been through, it was natural to withhold trust from all men. He'd been as guilty as the rest. After all, their initial introduction had been far from friendly. And his behavior since then filled him with remorse. But he'd find a way to make up for it.

He thought of his first reaction when he'd seen her step off the elevator with Gianni d'Angelo. Jealousy was too tame a word. His insides had knotted with raw emotions. He despised d'Angelo and everything he stood for. What's more, a woman like Addy wouldn't stand a chance against a man like that.

Addy sighed in her sleep and he drew the blankets around them. Studying her while she slept, he felt a surge of protectiveness. If anything or anyone threatened her harm, he'd kill for her. He'd die for her. There was nothing he wouldn't do to keep her safe and happy.

The phone rang, jarring her awake. He saw the surprised look in her eyes as they fluttered open. She wriggled in his arms and for a brief moment seemed puzzled that they were still tangled.

"Let it ring," he muttered as she tried to break free.

"But what if it's important?"

"Can anything be more important that this?" He kissed the tip of her nose.

"No, but . . ."

"Or this?" He pressed his lips to her throat and heard her little moan of pleasure.

"Sam, it might be . . ."

". . . my last offer." He ran slow, moist kisses along her collarbone to her shoulder.

A shaft of heat left her breathless. "Ummm. How can I refuse an offer like that?"

As the phone continued to ring, she wrapped herself around him and gave herself up to his clever hands and mouth. And then they were both lost in a world of intense pleasure.

*　　*　　*

Gianni d'Angelo sat in the back of the black limousine and listened as the phone continued to ring.

So this was why she hadn't returned his calls. His hunch had been right. While the world saw the prim, work-driven widow, living alone in her ivory tower, she was meeting secretly on the far side of town with her business partner. Very convenient.

He knew there was a reason why he'd hated Sam Money on sight. And not just because Money was an ex-cop. They were both sniffing around the same bitch.

His eyes narrowed. As far as he could see, there was no security. That meant that she felt safe here. He smiled in the darkness. All the better.

He still didn't understand why she'd been singled out for special treatment by The Man. Maybe he'd never know. But this much he knew. When the time was right, he was going to present his bill to the beautiful widow Starr for services rendered. And when he was through with her, he'd see to it that she kept her mouth shut.

Chapter Twenty-nine

"I wish I didn't have to go back to the casino." Addy lay in Sam's arms, her legs tangled with his.

"Who says you do?"

"My conscience."

"We're going to have to do something about that." He kissed the corner of her lips, then changed the angle and took the kiss deeper. Against her lips he murmured, "Why not take the whole day off? Maybe, if we're lucky, the phone won't ring, and we can pretend we're on a deserted island in the South Pacific."

"Does that mean I get to wear a grass skirt?"

"I like what you're wearing now." He ran a hand along her naked flesh and was rewarded with an easy laugh.

"Aren't you getting hungry?"

"Very." He nibbled at her earlobe.

She laughed again, low, easy. "I mean for food."

"Oh." He lifted his head. "Are you saying you can't live on love alone?"

"What did you have in mind?"

"This." He ran slow, hot kisses across her stomach. "And this." With his tongue he shot flames through her until her entire body was on fire.

"Sam." His name came out on a strangled gasp.

He left her no time to think as he drove her on a mad, desperate roller coaster that had her breathless and clinging. She hadn't expected this sudden explosion of feeling. As her eyes glazed with passion, he became even more ruthless, driving her to the peak again and again until at last he took her with a savageness that left them both shaken.

"How do you want your eggs?"

"Can you make them taste like steak?"

"Now you're beginning to sound like Jake."

Addy, barefoot, in faded shorts pulled over her silk teddy, stood peering into the refrigerator. Sam, wearing only a pair of jeans, was busy making coffee.

"See if Verna left any steaks in the freezer."

Addy opened the door and said, "We're in luck. Two steaks coming up."

A short time later they sat at the kitchen table and feasted on steak and eggs, fried potatoes and sourdough toast.

"This was what I needed." Sam sat back, relaxed, replete, sipping strong hot coffee. "After the night I've put in, I needed fortification."

"That tough, huh?"

"Lady, you just don't know how lucky you are. Usually I spread that kind of work over a week or more."

Addy collapsed into gales of laughter. This was a side of Sam she'd never seen. She found she loved him more with each new revelation.

Love. She went very still for a moment, savouring the thought. She loved him. Without question. Without reservation. She hugged the knowledge to her heart.

Casting a sideways glance at him she picked up her plate and said, "If it isn't too much trouble, do you think you can help with the dishes?"

"Are you sure you want me to waste this body on such mundane chores? I was hoping I might talk you into bed one more time."

"I think I can be persuaded." At the light that came into his eyes she added dryly, "As soon as we finish the dishes."

He picked up a dishtowel and nibbled the back of her neck.

                    *   *   *

Addy answered the phone on the second ring and shot a sharp glance at Sam when a woman's voice asked for him. She handed the phone over without a word.

"Hi, Carol. Yes, I'm glad you caught me, too." He saw the way Addy started to pull away and threw an arm over her, pinning her against him. "What've you got for me?"

He listened a moment in silence, then muttered, "I see. That's great. Thanks. I can be there in an hour."

When he replaced the receiver he leaned back casually, with his arm beneath his head, humming a little tune.

Addy sat up and glowered at him. "I suppose you're not going to explain."

He grinned. "Detective business."

"Or funny business."

His smile grew. "I think I like you when you get jealous."

"I am not jealous." Almost reluctantly she asked, "Who is this Carol and how did she know where to find you?"

"I thought you'd never ask. She's with Motor Vehicles, and I gave her all my numbers so she'd be able to reach me. When I wasn't in my office or my apartment . . ."

Addy didn't give him time to finish before clutching his shoulders. "Motor Vehicles? Why didn't you say that right away? What did she tell you? What has she found?"

"She said she has some information that might be useful. I'm heading down there now."

"I'm going with you."

"No." Sam caught her by the arm to keep her from scrambling off the bed. "Look Addy." He chose his words carefully. "I'm probably going to follow a lot of dead-ends before I get any real clues. This could turn out to be nothing. I don't want you getting your hopes up every time I get a new lead."

Seeing her look of disappointment he drew her close.

301

"Go back to the casino. Keep yourself busy. You know if I find out anything, I'll call you."

She nodded and watched as he hurriedly dressed. When he was finished he drew her close and brushed his lips over hers. "Looks like our vacation's over."

She watched as he strode quickly from the room.

* * *

Sam stood by the window of the dingy room and glanced out at the rain that had been falling steadily for hours. He'd certainly never expected to find himself in Argus, Oklahoma.

He'd phoned Addy from the airport to tell her he wouldn't be back for a couple of days. Now, glancing around the rat-hole they called a bedroom, he wondered why he'd bothered to come on this wild-goose chase.

The motel, as the owner had insisted upon calling it, had about a dozen rooms, each one dirtier than the other. Sam had refused three before he settled on this room.

The parking lot was full, but most of the drivers were across the street at the topless bar. Apparently this place made its money from the men who brought the dancers back to these rooms when the bar closed.

Restless, Sam spread the papers out on the bed and began to examine them again, one by one. He'd learned years ago that there was no such thing as an insignificant document. A doctor's bill, a school record, a change of address form, were all part of the paper chase. By piecing them together, he was beginning to get a much clearer picture.

Someone with money and power had gone to a lot of trouble to buy two little girls, only to separate them immediately. The youngest seemed to have vanished without a trace. Apparently the older one had no value to the buyer, so she'd been given to a middle-aged couple with no other children. Though their tracks had also been covered, there were too many people involved to keep the record completely clean. Through bits and pieces Sam had managed to learn all he needed to know.

The husband owned a prosperous grocery store, and worked twelve and fourteen hours a day. His lonely wife had explained the presence of the child to inquisitive neighbours by saying that it was a niece who had come to live with them. Within a year the wife was dead of cancer, and the grieving husband, unable or unwilling to care for the child, had given her to a cousin with two sons. When the cousin's marriage ended in divorce a scant six months later, both spouses fought over custody of the sons. Neither wanted the girl. A neighbour took the girl, then seven, and moved to California. A year later, when the little girl was forced to repeat the second grade, her current 'mother' went to live with a low-budget movie director, who decided a child would cramp his lifestyle. Rather than give up her chance at making it big in the movies, the woman sent the child to live with a sister in New Mexico. In less than six months another family took the girl to Idaho. Someone's grandmother had her for a year, and then a couple who ran a bar in Las Vegas. She'd been with them for almost two years before coming to live in Argus. No explanation had been given for the latest move, but Sam figured that the girl, now fifteen, would be a problem for anybody who took her in. The school records spoke of truancy and discipline problems. What else did they expect? There'd been not a shred of stability in the kid's life.

After re-examining the papers, he folded them carefully and returned them to the zippered pocket of his jacket. Then he unwrapped a cigar and bit off the end before holding a lighter to the tip. A wreath of smoke curled over his head as he began to pace the room.

He didn't like the looks of this. From the records he'd seen, most of these people were unfit to raise a dog, let alone a kid. And judging by her latest 'family', she was probably being groomed for a job across the street. Or worse, for a job right here at this sleazy motel.

At a knock, he stopped his pacing, crossed the room and opened the door.

A girl who could have been anywhere from eighteen to twenty-five stood holding a tray. "You the one who ordered soda and ice?"

"Yeah. How much?"

The girl pushed past him and placed the tray on a scarred table. Turning she eyed him with the coolness of a seasoned veteran. "Depends on what you want."

It wasn't what she said, it was the suggestive way she'd said it. Sam was reminded of his old days on the vice squad. The line was the same; only the town was different. He'd always hated it. The motels, the decoys, the tough-talking girls whose backs were to the wall and would do anything if the price was right.

She was wearing faded cut-offs and a skimpy bathing suit top. Sooty eyes were heavily made up. Her lips were painted deep wine and pursed into a pout. Badly dyed red hair had been teased and sprayed until it resembled a Halloween wig.

In the silence that followed Sam took a roll of money from his pocket. The girl's eyes widened as he began counting off the bills.

"What I'd like is some information."

"What about?" Her eyes suddenly narrowed with suspicion.

"I'm looking for a girl."

She put her hands on her hips. "What do I look like? Road kill?"

"This girl is called Emmy Lou."

She stiffened. "What're you? A cop?"

"No. A private detective."

"You from a department store?"

"Why? Did she shoplift something?" He saw the way she began to close up. "Can you help me find her?"

"Why should I?" She started toward the door.

"I'll make it worth your while."

She paused and stared at the money. "How much?"

"Fifty dollars."

"Fifty bucks." She turned and reached for the doorknob. "You lyin' sonofabitch. You are from that department store. Well I didn't steal any of that stuff. You don't have any evidence to hold me . . ."

Sam caught her roughly by the arm and flung her away from the door. Then, leaning against it, he crossed his arms over his chest and studied her carefully.

At her words he'd felt his blood turn to ice. Of course. Why hadn't he caught on sooner? Beneath the layers of makeup, and the world-weary attitude, was a scared little fifteen year old.

Though her name now was now Emmy Lou, he was looking at the girl who'd once been Erin O'Brien.

*   *   *

"Sit down." Sam decided to do his hard-nosed cop routine. It would probably work better with this kid than tea and sympathy.

She hesitated beside the bed. "You can't keep me here. My old man . . ."

"Would sell you off to the highest bidder. Now shut up and listen. I'm not from the department store."

"Then how did you . . .?"

"Don't ever play poker, kid. You'd telegraph your hand before the second card. Now pay attention."

She sat on the edge of the bed and boldly crossed her legs, swinging one foot in nervous circles.

"Do you remember anything about your early childhood?"

His question caught her by surprise. "Too much. What would you like to know?"

"Can you recall an older sister named Addy and a baby sister named Shannon?"

"What are you? Some kind of wierdo?"

"Just think about it."

She glowered at him. "There were a couple of step-brothers once. Bobby and Michael, I think." She shrugged. "Or maybe I just dreamed them. And a couple of step-sisters who were more like nightmares."

"Do you remember your real mother and father?"

She looked away, but not before he glimpsed the pain. "Not really."

"Can you remember anything about your early life? In a place called the Paradise Mobile Home Park."

He saw her head come up sharply. Then she looked away. "Maybe. For a moment it sounded kinda familiar. But I don't know anymore. I've had so many families, been so many places. When are you going to tell me what this is all about?"

"It's about a woman named Addy Starr, who wants to find the two sisters who were separated from her ten years ago. I have reason to believe you're one of them. Your real name is Erin. Erin O'Brien."

"Erin." She spoke the name almost reverently. In that moment, despite the layers of makeup, Sam could see Addy in her eyes, in her smile. "Erin O'Brien. It's not bad." She leaned back on her hands and gave a nervous laugh. "And it's a hell of a lot better'n Emmy Lou Chumly." She suddenly straightened and he saw the fear in her eyes. "Does this mean I've moving on to another family again?"

"Would that be so terrible?"

She looked up at Sam and he saw the way her lips trembled. "I don't mean it's so wonderful here or anything." She stared around the shabby room with dull eyes. "This place is the pits. But I always hate it when I have to start over with a new family. They won't like me. They never do. They'll just put up with me until somebody else comes along to take me off their hands."

"It's going to be different this time."

"Bullshit." She crossed her legs again and regarded him with anger. "That's what they all say."

Chapter Thirty

Addy watched as the burly men carried the hospital bed to the waiting truck. When they returned, one of them drove the electric scooter to the porch, where a hydraulic lift was used to get it into the back of the truck.

As she signed the receipt the driver said, "This was really generous of you, Mrs. Starr. The young man has just been released from the hospital, and was worried that he'd be confined to his bed."

"I'm just happy to find someone who needed this. It means a lot to me to know that it's being put to good use."

Within hours the new furniture was delivered and placed in Jake's old bedroom. Addy spent the rest of the day removing all her clothes from the upstairs closet. The master suite was completely renovated for her own use. And Sam's, she thought with a laugh. Although his things were still in his old room, she hoped he would want to spend time in hers.

By the time she left for work, the room on the top floor had been transformed into a teenager's dream, with frilly curtains and matching bedspread, new thick rugs covering the floor, and a TV and stereo installed in a new wall of cabinets.

She was grateful that her work at the casino would take up the rest of the night. She was far too excited to be able to sleep.

* * *

"Holy shit. Look at all the lights. It looks like Vegas."

Erin sat beside Sam as he drove through the streets of Reno. Extricating her from her latest 'family' had been even easier than he'd expected. Once confronted with the truth, the couple with whom she lived admitted that there had never been any legal documents signed. They'd been aware they were breaking the law, and were only too happy to let her go, as long as they wouldn't be prosecuted.

During most of the plane ride Erin had been sullen and silent. But since the plane touched down, the questions she'd been holding inside came tumbling out.

"What does Addy look like?"

"A lot like you. But her hair's darker."

"I wish I could remember her."

"Don't force it. Maybe in time some things will come back to you."

Sam knew she was scared. He wasn't feeling any too calm himself. He'd phoned Addy and tried to prepare her for what lay ahead, but how could anyone be prepared for this tough, troubled teen with a vocabulary like Jake's? Even now, with her face bare of makeup, at his insistence, and her hair pulled back in a simple ponytail, there was a certain street-wise sophistication that belied her tender years.

When he pulled into the driveway and parked beside the big old house, Erin's eyes widened.

"This is where she lives?"

"Where you live," Sam corrected.

Addy had insisted that he bring Erin to the house. An apartment atop a casino was not a proper place for an impressionable young girl, Addy had argued.

Sam grimly led Erin up the steps to the front porch. The door flew open and Addy stared hungrily at the girl who faced her.

"Erin."

Addy opened her arms to embrace her but the girl cringed and backed away, suddenly overwhelmed by all that had happened in the brief span of days. This beautiful, polished woman was now supposed to be her older sister. This magnificent old house was now her home. She knew the bubble would burst sooner or later and she'd find out it was all a dream. With her luck she'd be out on the street, with no place to go.

"I guess you're Addy."

"Yes." Addy hesitated in the doorway, blinking back tears. She'd promised herself she wouldn't make a scene. But now, seeing this stranger who, except for the red hair, looked exactly as she'd remembered her little sister, she was overcome with emotion.

Seeing their confusion, Sam said, "It's been a long trip, Addy. Erin's probably ready to drop."

"Oh. Yes. Of course." Stepping back, Addy watched as Erin moved past her and stared around the room.

"Are you hungry?"

Erin nodded. "There was food on the plane, but I was too scared. I've never flown before."

"Then come on in the kitchen." Addy took the shabby suitcase from Erin's hands and set it near the stairway. For a moment she felt a stab of pain, remembering her own second-hand suitcase when she'd arrived here. "Verna made lasagna."

"What's that?"

"It's layers of pasta with cheese and sauce," Sam explained.

Erin shrugged. "Sounds fancy. I think I'd rather have a hamburger. Or pizza."

"You can have anything you want."

Addy led the way. In the kitchen, the scent of garlic vied with the tang of tomatoes and Italian sausage.

"Smells like a restaurant where I ate once." Erin glanced around, amazed at the size of the room. "This house is bitchin'. None of the places I stayed were ever as big as this."

"Were they nice places?" At her question, Addy saw the look that came over Erin. But before she could stop herself she added, "I mean, did any of them feel like home? Were the people good to you?"

Erin's expression altered subtly. "Are we going to talk or eat?"

"We're going to eat," Sam said, holding a chair. When she was seated he dropped an arm around Addy and drew her close for a quick kiss. "And while we eat we're going to get acquainted."

Addy carried salad and steaming lasagna to the table. She'd sent Verna home early, so that Erin wouldn't feel overwhelmed by too many strangers. Now she found herself wishing she'd asked Verna to stay. It looked like they'd need all the help they could get to keep the conversation flowing.

"There's garlic bread," she said, lifting a pan from the oven. "Sam, maybe you'd get the milk from the fridge."

"None for me," Erin called. "Do you have any Pepsi?"

"Sorry." Addy placed the rolls in a basket. "I guess I just thought all girls drank milk."

"Shit. Got any kind of soda?"

Sam saw the way Addy's brow arched and he quickly intervened. "Yeah. There's some Diet Pepsi. I think I'll have some too."

Addy took her place at the table and watched as Erin took a tentative bite of the lasagna. "Hey. Not bad. It looks like something the dog threw up, but it tastes pretty good."

"Will you have some salad?"

Addy offered her the bowl but Erin shook her head.

"If I was meant to eat greens I'd have been born a damned rabbit."

Addy had a quick sense of Jake saying almost the same thing. When she glanced up she saw Sam smiling and knew that he'd just had the same thought.

Erin filled her plate with lasagna and began stuffing it into her mouth. She emptied the entire plate without once hesitating or looking up. In fact, Addy was certain she hadn't even paused to take a breath.

"More lasagna?" she asked.

"You mean I can eat as much as I want? That's great."

"I'll tell Verna you liked it."

"Who's this Verna? Another family member?"

"She cooks and cleans for us."

"Holy shit. You mean we got servants and everything?"

"Verna isn't a servant. She's . . ." Addy glanced toward Sam for help and found him grinning. At that moment she wanted to throw something at him that would wipe that foolish grin from his face. Instead she turned to Erin. "Verna was hired to help with the work because I spend so many hours at my own job."

"Yeah?" Erin tried to look interested, but it was obvious her attention was wandering. "So I suppose while you're off doing your thing, Verna is going to be my next mom."

Addy found herself close to tears again. But this time they weren't tears of joy. How in the world was she going to reach this lonely girl who'd been passed around so often she thought of herself as worthless?

"I can't be your mom, Erin. Our mother is dead. But I can be your big sister. It's what I've always wanted to be."

Erin looked past her to study a spot on the wall. Without emotion she said, "I had a big sister once. Actually she was a step-sister, but I guess it's the same thing. Anyway, her idea of fun was locking me in the closet until she heard her parents driving in from work. Then she'd unlock the door and watch me get all hysterical, so they'd take a stick to me and lock me in my bedroom." She gave a mirthless laugh. "I guess I was pretty thickheaded, 'cause it took me a long time to learn how to be locked up without going crazy. Now, shit, you could lock me up for a year and I'd just sit and stare at the walls without letting it get to me."

Addy shoved back her chair and walked around the

311

table. Placing a hand gently on Erin's shoulder she said, "Nobody's ever going to lock you up again. I promise. If I had it in my power, I'd take away all the pain you've had to endure. But the only thing I can do is promise to love you. Without condition."

Erin looked at the hand resting on her shoulder, then shrugged it off. "And I promise you, I'm not the lovable type." She yawned. "Where'm I sleeping?"

"I'll show you." Leading the way, Addy picked up the suitcase and led Erin to the top floor.

"I thought you might enjoy sleeping in my old bedroom. Up here you can see the stars and listen to the rain on the roof. The first night I was here, I thought it was the prettiest room I'd ever seen."

Erin glanced around without interest. "It's kind of old looking."

"It is old. But it's cozy, too. Would you like me to help you unpack?"

As Addy started toward her suitcase Erin moved to bar her way. "I'm kinda used to taking care of myself."

"Okay." Addy hesitated, then walked to the doorway. "If there's anything you need, anything at all, I'm just down two floors below you."

"Hey, I'm not a little kid. I've been on my own for a long time now. I think I can find my way to the bathroom."

Addy swallowed. More than anything she wanted to take her sister in her arms and hold her. It was what she'd been aching to do ever since Sam phoned to tell her that Erin had been found. But through the years of pain and disappointment, Erin had built a wall. A wall so thick, Addy knew she couldn't penetrate it.

"Goodnight, Erin."

"Yeah. 'Night."

As Addy started down the stairs she heard the door slam firmly behind her.

*   *   *

"Oh, Sam," Addy cried, throwing herself into his arms the minute she entered the kitchen. "What am I going to do? It's obvious she doesn't trust me. And she hates me for bringing her here."

"Hey." He gathered her close and pressed his lips to the top of her head. "Give the kid a break. These past couple of days have been pretty scary for her. She has to start over with another family, and try to fit into the way things are done here. And what's even more frightening, she now finds herself with someone who loves her and wants to get close."

She pushed away to look up at him in surprise. "Why should that frighten her?"

"Because," he said, wrapping a strand of her hair around his finger, "she thinks of herself as a tough little cookie who can take care of herself. But that's only because she'd had to, to survive. It isn't going to be easy for her to relax her guard and learn to trust."

Addy nodded. "You're right, of course. I'm going to have to give her a little room. But, oh, Sam, it's so hard. All I want to do is take her in my arms and tell her everything is going to be all right."

"It will be. Trust me."

She drew her arms around his waist. "How'd you get to know so much about my little sister?"

"By watching her big sister. In case you've forgotten, you had a pretty big chip on your shoulder when you arrived here."

"Me?" She started to push away but he grabbed her wrists and held her. "You were the one who had the problem, if you'll recall."

"Okay. We both had pretty big chips on our shoulders." At her knowing smile he added, "So give the kid a break and let her work it out in her own way."

She nodded and allowed him to draw her close again. This time he lowered his face to hers and brushed a kiss over her lips. They both felt the rush of heat.

"Come on, Mrs. Starr. I've been gone a long time and I'd like you to officially welcome me home."

She lay her head against his shoulder. "It would be my pleasure."

At the doorway to her bedroom he stopped and stared around in surprise. "What's this?"

"I wanted Erin to have my old room. Besides, I thought it was time I made this room mine."

He let out a long slow whistle. The floor had been covered in thick plush carpeting the colour of evergreen. A giant four-poster bed dominated the room. The coverlet and matching draperies were done in muted tones of sand and taupe. The fireplace and slate hearth had been cleaned of the years of soot and smoke until the stones gleamed.

"That's a mighty big bed for one little woman."

"I was hoping I wouldn't have to sleep alone."

"Then I'll just have to . . ."

They both turned at the sound of footsteps racing down the stairs. Erin, wearing an oversized football jersey, stood clutching a framed picture to her chest. Tears streamed down her cheeks. For the first time, she truly looked like a fifteen year old girl.

"I . . ." She sniffed and wiped her nose with her free hand. ". . . found this picture."

Addy automatically reached for it. "I shouldn't have left it upstairs, Erin. I'm sorry if it upset you."

"No!" Erin clutched it tighter. "You don't understand. I saw us. You and me and Shannon. And I remembered."

Addy was so stunned she couldn't move. When she could finally speak, her voice was little more than a whisper. "You remember?"

Erin began to cry harder. "I remember Mama snapping that picture. And then telling you that you looked just like her mama."

"That's right. Oh, Erin. You do remember." In her excitement Addy hugged her sister fiercely and began to weep. Once started, the tears flowed freely as Addy framed her sister's face with her hands and kissed her, again and again, then drew her close and began to sob as though her heart would break.

Sam stood back and watched the joyous reunion with a sense of wonder. Though he'd boldly counseled Addy that it would all work out, the truth was, until this very moment, he'd doubted the wisdom of her quest. Now all his doubts vanished. She'd been right all along. Further, she had a right to continue the search for her youngest sister, as well. Even if it meant intruding on someone else's happiness.

"I've got an old picture of Mama and Daddy," Addy said, leading Erin to the rocking chair. I know you'll be able to remember so much more when you see it."

Sam gave a last wistful glance at the bed before making his way upstairs to his own room. A trill of laughter followed him.

From the sound of things, Addy and Erin would sit up all night stirring up old memories.

With a contented smile he closed his door.

Chapter Thirty-one

"I remember walking with you to the laundromat," Erin said. "You always used to buy me a soda with the change." She looked up suddenly. "I guess I was about four or five. How old would that make you?"

"Eleven or twelve," Addy said.

"Twelve? Shit." Erin looked at her with new respect. "That's younger than I am now. And you used to lug that heavy basket all the way there, wash and dry everything, fold it, and then haul it back home."

"There wasn't anybody else who could help. Mama was sick a lot, and Daddy was always gone."

The two girls sat side by side on the sofa, snuggled under an afghan from Addy's room. Chester sprawled across their laps, lifting his head occasionally to be scratched.

For weeks Addy spent her time answering Erin's questions, and filling in the gaps in her memory. With each passing day the barriers between them crumbled a little more. They grew more comfortable with each other, indulging in the need to touch and kiss each other's cheeks affectionately. Addy felt her heart swell with love for this stranger who was her sister.

One day, Addy knew, Erin would talk about the years they'd been apart. And then, slowly, gradually, the wounds could begin to heal.

When at last Erin could no longer hold her eyes open, she fell into Addy's arms and hugged her, then climbed the stairs to bed, with Chester hot on her trail.

Addy made her way to her room. Slipping out of her clothes, she climbed into bed. Scant minutes later she scrambled from her bed and tiptoed up the stairs to Sam's room.

As she slid between the covers she heard his voice, rough with sleep. "Is it morning already?"

"Almost." She paused. "We have a few hours left. I just realized I've been neglecting you since Erin came to live with us."

He brought an arm around her and dragged her close. Against her lips he muttered, "I've learned to be patient, Mrs. Starr. Especially since the rewards are so great."

*   *   *

"What about Shannon?" Erin asked one morning at breakfast.

Addy and Sam had forsaken their penthouse apartments, at least for the moment, in favour of the big house, where they thought Erin would feel more at home.

With Addy's help, Erin had enrolled in school, shopped for a new wardrobe, and changed her hair back to its natural blonde. Each day she seemed to grow younger and more carefree.

She had absorbed the truth about their father's terrible secret as she'd absorbed everything else, with a maturity far beyond her years. Knowing she and Shannon had been sold for drug money made her past seem even more painful. One night, lying next to Addy, Erin dredged up the memories she'd locked away for so long. She tearfully revealed her own tale of terror when she'd learned that she was going to live with strangers. Her separation from her baby sister had been doubly painful, because Shannon was her last link to her past.

They cried together so often, Sam began calling them the Sob Sisters. Whenever he said it, they dissolved into gales of laughter.

"Well? What about Shannon? Are we going to search for her?" Fortified by the facts, Erin was now ready to write the final chapter on Addy's long odyssey.

317

At her repeated question, Addy glanced toward Sam.

He shrugged. "I've been searching. I have dozens of trails, all of them leading to dead ends."

"You think she's gone for good?"

He shook his head. "I still have a couple of leads." He didn't add that he intended to check one very strong lead today. There was no sense getting their hopes up until he had more facts.

As Erin pushed away from the table she said, "I'd like to get my hands on the sonofabitch that took her. I'd show him a few of the tricks I learned along the way."

"Maybe she's with loving parents." Addy had to believe that. Otherwise she'd go mad.

"Maybe. But I'd still like to meet the sonofabitch who cut the deal to buy us." Erin stormed out of the room, calling over her shoulder, "He'd be nothing but a pile of shit when I got through with him."

Addy rolled her eyes. "I swear Jake went to live in Erin's body."

Sam threw back his head and roared.

"What am I going to do about her swearing, Sam?"

"Relax. What did Jake once tell you? Some people swear because it's the only way they know how to express themselves. If she hangs around you long enough, maybe your vocabulary will rub off on her."

"Or maybe hers will rub off on me." At a knock on the door Addy looked up. "That must be Milt. I asked him to come here today to work on the books. That way I'll have more time to spend with Erin." She gave a little laugh as she started toward the door. "It's starting to feel like the old days, when Jake directed everything from this table."

Sam grinned. "I'd be willing to bet he still is."

*　　*　　*

"Addy." It was Paula's voice, low, troubled. "I think maybe you'd better get over to your office."

"What's wrong?"

"It's Mr. d'Angelo. When I told him you weren't coming in today, he said he was waiting in your office until you talked to him."

"You didn't let him into my office, did you?"

"I had no choice. He walked in and sat down behind your desk. If you want to come over here and ask him to leave, you can. As for me, I'm not going to face him again." Her tone deepened. "Addy, that man scares me."

"I'll be there in twenty minutes." Addy slammed down the phone.

A few minutes later Erin came bounding into Addy's room and found her changing her clothes. Her smile faded. "I thought we were going to spend the afternoon together."

"We are. Just as soon as I take care of a little business." Addy picked up her purse. "Want to see the casino?"

She knew the answer even before she saw the wide smile that split Erin's lips. Erin had talked of nothing but the casino since she'd learned that Addy and Sam were co-owners of the fabulous Starr's.

As they drove, Erin asked, "Think I could drop a few quarters in a slot machine?"

"If you do I'll have you banned for life. You could cost us our license."

"Hey. I was only kidding." She lifted her palms as if to ward off invisible blows.

"This is no joke, Erin. A minor caught gambling is a serious offense in this state."

"I'd never do anything to get you in trouble."

When they reached the casino, Addy introduced Erin to Fingers and left them together.

"I'm trusting you to see that she doesn't go near a slot machine," Addy said sternly.

"You can count on it." Fingers caught Erin by the hand and led her toward the coffee shop. "Rosetta makes a hot fudge sundae with whipped cream, chocolate sprinkles, nuts and a sugar wafer that'll knock your socks off."

"Bet you a buck I can eat two," Erin said with a laugh of pure delight.

Addy watched them with a smile. Her smile faded the moment she entered the elevator. When it stopped on the third floor she called greetings to the staff as she threaded her way to her office. Outside she was stopped by Paula, who placed a hand on her arm.

"I don't think you should go in there alone, Addy."

"Aren't you being a little dramatic?"

"Maybe. But he has fire in his eyes."

"I'm about to put out Mr. d'Angelo's fire."

Addy strode into her office.

Gianni was seated at her desk. Spread out on the desk top were the contents of her file.

"What do you think you're doing?"

At the sound of her voice he looked up and shot her a chilling smile.

"I'm examining your records, Mrs. Starr." He held up a hand as she opened her mouth. "Now, now. No need to thank me."

"Step away from my desk."

She watched as he leisurely stood and came around her desk. She was reminded of a sleek panther.

"The next time you want to see me you'll phone for an appointment like everyone else."

His voice was smooth, mocking. "That's very good, Mrs. Starr. I like the display of temper. It suits you. Puts a little colour in your cheeks." He took a step toward her. His hand moved so quickly she had no time to pull away.

He dragged her close and she felt the sting of his breath as he whispered, "Now say please."

"Go to hell."

"I'll do better than that. I'll take you to dinner tonight. And then I'll show you heaven."

"You pompous . . ."

As her hand swung in an arc toward his cheek he caught it and held it, running his thumb seductively over her wrist.

Though his face and voice remained unchanged, his eyes were hot with fury.

"I'm beginning to lose my patience, Mrs. Starr. And I assure you, you don't want to see that happen."

"I won't be threatened like . . ."

His voice purred. "I never make idle threats." He buried his hand in her hair and pulled her toward him.

The door to her office opened and he abruptly released her.

"Addy, I . . ." Erin glanced from her sister's flushed face to the man beside her. "Oh, sorry. I didn't know . . ."

In one fluid motion Gianni touched a hand to Addy's cheek. "And who is this lovely creature?"

"I'm Addy's sister, Erin."

"A sister. How – interesting." He crossed the room and offered Erin his most charming smile as he extended his hand. "I am Gianni d'Angelo, a very good friend of your sister's."

"It's nice to meet you Mr. d'Angelo."

"Please, don't be so formal. We're all friends here. It's Gianni."

"Gianni." Erin dimpled under his scrutiny. Turning to her sister she said, "Your secretary wasn't at her desk and I thought it would be all right for me to come in. Sorry if I disturbed something."

Addy's voice frosted over. "You disturbed nothing. Say goodbye to Mr. d'Angelo." She shot him a challenging look. "He was just leaving."

"Ah, but only for a little while." His smile was correct and courteous. "I will be calling tomorrow. You can count on it."

He bowed slightly before walking from the room.

When they were alone Erin sighed, "What a hunk. Did you see his suit? And that ring on his little finger. And from the way he was looking at you . . ."

"Don't be impressed by appearances."

"Yeah." Erin laughed. "I know what you mean. Look at Fingers. Who'd have believed he'd be so much fun?

I had a hot fudge sundae, and then I finished Fingers' sundae when he got too full. And then he showed me the video arcade. I'm going to need a pocket full of quarters to play all the games in there."

Addy dropped an arm around Erin's shoulders and felt the tension begin to fade at her sister's innocent chatter.

Had she only imagined it, or had Gianni threatened her with violence? She let out a long, slow breath. Maybe she was making more of this than was called for. After all, this was her office. She was surrounded by dozens of co-workers who could have walked in at any moment and come to her aid.

"Come on, Addy. You promised to show me everything."

With a laugh Addy followed Erin from the office. At Paula's arched brow she said, "I'm about to give my sister the guided tour. Hold all my calls."

"What about Mr. d'Angelo?"

"I'm no longer taking his calls. And, Paula, from now on, see that my office door is kept locked."

*   *   *

Sam bit down on his frustration. Another lead had gone sour. Now the only thing he had left was the license number that Cleo Bentson had given to Fran before his death. Fran's wife thought she could remember the numbers, but not necessarily in their proper sequence.

In desperation Sam had contacted an old friend in New York who was still on the force.

"I was able to access Motor Vehicles in Nevada," Vince Cooper said. "And I'm still running the various numbers through the computer. The problem is that with that many numbers and letters, the combinations are endless. It may take my computer a day or two."

"A day or two." Sam chuckled. "Vince, I was afraid you were talking about weeks."

"I'll fax this stuff to you the minute it's complete."

"I owe you a big one."

"Any time, Sam. I'm just glad to see you're not wasting your talents out there in hicksville."

"Don't kid yourself, Vince. Crime isn't just in New York." Sam's eyes narrowed as he caught sight of Gianni d'Angelo strolling past his office. "Some of the slime crawled out this way too."

*   *   *

"I'll have to be gone for a couple of days," Sam announced casually over breakfast.

Addy glanced up sharply. "You have a lead?"

He shrugged. "Could be." When he saw the expression on her face he added, "Don't go getting excited. There's no reason to believe this one will take us any closer than the others."

He waited until Verna shouted that Erin's school bus was at the curb. When they were alone he said, "I saw d'Angelo leaving your office yesterday. What did he want?"

"My company at dinner."

She watched his face and was rewarded with a scowl. "I believe you're jealous."

"You're damned right."

His words gave her a warm glow. "Well, you have no reason to be. I told him no. Emphatically. He wasn't pleased. And there's something else. He had my files spread out on my desk when I arrived."

"The arrogant bastard. Order your office locked."

"I already did."

Sam walked to the counter to fill his cup. Choosing his words carefully he said, "I'd like you and Erin to stay in your apartment at the casino until I get back."

"I don't think the casino is a proper place for a teen."

"For God's sake, Addy." He set down his cup so hard the coffee sloshed over the rim. "Stop worrying about a kid who's already been exposed to more things than you or I

323

could ever imagine and start using your head. d'Angelo is a snake."

"I agree. But he doesn't even know about this place."

"Who are you kidding? Half the town knew old Jake. Do you think they've suddenly forgotten about his house? If they know, Gianni d'Angelo's men know."

"His men?" Stung by his anger, her own temper heated. "You make it sound like a gang of criminals from the old West."

"This is the new West, Addy. But the crooks haven't changed much through the years. They're still bullies. And they still hang in packs." He crossed to her and took her in his arms. His voice warmed as he pressed his lips to her temple. "I have a right to be worried about you. I'd like to come back and find your usual warm welcome waiting for me."

"Then stop ordering me around."

"Promise to go to the apartment?"

She started to protest, but as his lips moved over her face she sighed and began to laugh. "You really know how to persuade a woman."

"You'll leave?"

She nodded. "As soon as Erin returns from school."

"I wish Verna wasn't here," he muttered against her lips.

"I could always send her to the store."

He looked up at the sound of the housekeeper's footsteps. "Quick. Make a shopping list."

Chapter Thirty-two

Gianni d'Angelo sat brooding behind his ornate desk. His golf clubs were forgotten for the moment.

In the other room he could hear his wife's voice raised in anger and his little daughter's tearful response. He'd hoped a child would make a difference, but his wife was already showing signs of discontent. It didn't matter. They would never divorce. She understood his business; had grown up in it. Their marriage had united two very powerful families. They knew what was expected of them. Away from public scrutiny, they led separate lives.

He picked up a fragile glass egg, a gift from a grateful senator, and swiveled his chair to stare out the window.

He had the polish and easy style of a man who knew he was handsome and charming. Women of all ages had always been drawn to him. It was a skill he'd honed since he was a boy of fourteen, and had, in a very clumsy fashion, seduced the seventeen year old daughter of one of his father's closest friends. All these years later she still blushed like a schoolgirl whenever she saw him.

There had always been women. But he had always known that they would never be a problem. They had nothing to do with his marriage. Or his business. But this casino owner, Addy Starr, was a problem. In fact, she'd become an obsession. Not only did she refuse to believe she needed his protection, but what was even more insulting, she refused to fall under his spell.

He clenched his hand. He would give her one more chance. And if she dared to refuse him again, he would show her his power. Then she would come crawling and beg him for his help.

He seemed surprised by the sudden pain and opened his hand, noting that he'd crushed the priceless egg. He was even more startled at the trickle of blood in his palm. Dropping the fragments into a wastebasket, he pulled a silk monogrammed handkerchief from his pocket and sponged the blood.

His eyes narrowed. The woman was a fever in his blood. No matter what it took, he would have Addy Starr.

* * *

"How would you like to spend a couple of days in the penthouse above the casino?"

Addy had to laugh at the expression on Erin's face.

"A penthouse? No shit. You mean it?"

"Think you can concentrate on your homework, and stay away from the video arcade?"

"If I get my homework done first, can I visit the arcade?"

"I don't see why not. Come on." Addy led the way up the stairs. "Let's get you packed."

An hour later, as they walked to the car, Addy heard the phone ringing. By the time she unlocked the door and raced to the phone, the ringing had stopped.

"Maybe it was Sam," Erin said as Addy returned to the car and admitted that she'd been too late.

"I hope so. If it was, he'll call my office." She started the engine. "I'll find out soon enough."

* * *

"Holy shit! I can't believe I'm really going to be living in a penthouse apartment. This looks like something out of a magazine." Erin ran from room to room checking out the sleek contemporary furnishing, the use of mirrors, the vases of real flowers. She let out a shriek when she saw the spare bedroom, with its view of the city spread out below, and an adjoining bathroom with a spa big enough to hold half of her classmates. "Wow! I've gotta be dreaming. This can't be real."

"I was hoping for a little more enthusiasm," Addy said with a laugh.

A little while later, when Erin had explored to her heart's content, Addy found her in the bedroom, trying out the dozen or so perfumes Addy had arranged on a dresser.

"I'm going down to my office for the next hour or two. That ought to give you time to get your homework finished before dinner, don't you think?"

Erin nodded and dabbed Halston behind her ear.

"There's soda in the kitchen, but not much else. If you get hungry, call room service. I'll be back before five o'clock. Then I'll take you to one of our best restaurants here in the hotel."

She kissed her sister on the cheek. "You smell like the perfume counter at Neiman Marcus." As an afterthought, Addy gave her a warm hug before hurrying from the apartment.

* * *

"Did Sam call?"

Addy's secretary shook her head and handed her the phone messages. "But Gianni d'Angelo called six times. He accused me of not giving you your messages."

Addy's head came up. "You didn't give him my home phone number, did you?"

"Of course not."

As her secretary left the office, Addy began to sort through the messages. She'd return the calls later, after she'd worked her way through a mountain of paperwork.

Minutes later Paula's voice on the intercom had her hand reaching for the telephone. "It's Sam on three, Addy."

"Thanks, Paula." Addy brought the receiver to her ear. "Sam. Where are you?"

"San Francisco."

"Another tough day, huh?"

His rich, warm laughter soothed her. "Somebody's got to do it."

She idly scanned a document requiring her signature and picked up a pen. "So I take it another lead fizzled out?"

"Not this time."

His words had her dropping her pen and scattering papers over her desk. "Have you found Shannon?"

"Not yet. But I've located some of her earlier medical records. And this time I'm on to something."

"Oh, Sam." She closed her eyes a moment, and pressed a hand to her quivering lips. "How soon?"

"I can't tell you that. All I can say is I'm close. The minute I know more, you'll hear."

"Sam." She felt her voice catch and paused a moment, swallowing hard. "I love you."

"That's good, lady. Because I love you, too. And I've already decided that the minute this is over, you're going to marry me, whether you like it or not."

"God, I love it when you talk tough."

"Then here's some more. Be extra careful. I don't want anything to happen to you."

She listened as the phone went dead. Then she pushed away from her desk. There was no sense trying to get any more work done today. Besides, she had to share this news with Erin. This called for a celebration.

* * *

Doctor Jess Thornton was middle-aged, soft spoken. He seemed grateful that Sam was willing to wait until all his patients had been dealt with.

Sam observed the patients who filled the doctor's waiting room. Thornton's was a family practice. Young women with sniffling toddlers and white-haired men and women with canes and walkers sat on well-worn chairs and couches that lined the walls. On a scarred old table in the center of the room there were dogeared magazines and children's stories of the Bible, along with broken crayons and much-used colouring books.

By the time the last patient said goodbye, the lights of the city had come on, and the lights in the other offices were extinguished.

"Now, Mr. Money. Why don't you step into my office. Sure you wouldn't like a physical while we talk?"

Sam shook his head. "I think you've worn out enough rubber gloves for one day."

"All right then." Thornton eased himself into a leather chair that was permanently tilted back. "What can I do for you?"

"I'd like to talk about a baby you examined."

"Sure thing. What's the name on the file?"

"That's the problem, Doctor Thornton. I don't know."

The doctor looked perplexed. "Then I don't see how I can help you."

"How far back do your records go?"

"All the way back to the beginning of my practice, I'm afraid." The doctor gave an embarrassed lift of his shoulders. "I don't have an office manager here. There's just me and my assistant. We never have time to clean out the files."

"And how long have you been practicing here?" Sam already knew the answer, but he was a patient man.

"Ten years."

"Then this baby would have been one of your first patients." The doctor suddenly became very absorbed in the task of yanking open a desk drawer and removing a pack of cigarettes. With an almost apologetic tone he said, "Don't use these much anymore. Been trying to quit."

Sam watched as he put a cigarette to his lips and snapped open a lighter. He inhaled deeply, then cleared his throat. "You expect me to remember a baby I treated ten years ago?"

"This was a special baby."

The doctor's expression altered slightly. He lifted the

cigarette to his lips and filled his lungs. "All babies are special."

"Yes, I'm sure they are. But I don't think you'd forget this baby, Doctor. She arrived here before your furniture, and long before you hired your assistant. She was, in fact, the reason why you were able to set up practice in this area all those years ago."

For a full minute Thornton looked like he had just taken a blow to the midsection. His mouth went slack, the colour drained from his face. He slumped back in his chair, his face devoid of expression.

"How did you find out?"

"That's my job."

"I thought . . . I thought I'd buried the past forever."

"You did a pretty good job of it."

Thornton stubbed out the cigarette and got heavily to his feet. "I have to leave now."

"You're not going anywhere until we talk."

"You don't understand." The doctor grabbed up his black bag and headed for the door. "He'll kill me if I talk to you."

Sam calmly removed the 38 Special from his pocket and placed it on the desk. Then he casually stretched out his legs, crossing them at the ankles, and pulled a cigar from his pocket. As he held a lighter to the tip he said softly, "And I'll kill you if you don't."

* * *

Addy phoned the maitre d' in the Goldrush Room, the hotel's gourmet restaurant, and reserved the finest table.

A few moments later the phone rang and Addy was surprised and pleased to hear Lil's voice.

"Chérie. It has been so long. How are you?"

"I'm wonderful, Lil." On an impulse, Addy asked, "What are you doing tonight?"

"Nothing. Giovanni has left for the club and I am alone."

"Then you must come to the hotel and join me for dinner."

"Chérie, I am delighted. Is this a special occasion?"

"I've found one of my sisters, Lil."

She heard the throaty laugh on the other end of the line. "Oh, Addy, this is indeed wonderful. I can be there in an hour."

"We'll be ready."

In her excitement, Erin tried on four different dresses before deciding on Addy's favorite, a simple silk tunic in hot pink over a very short pink skirt with tiers of ruffles.

While she fretted over her hair, Erin said, "I wish Sam was here to see me in this. Do you think he'd like it?"

"He'd love it." Addy turned to glance at her sister. "Got a crush on Sam?"

"Sort of. He's really handsome. I think he's the best looking guy I've ever seen. Except for maybe Gianni."

Addy shook her head. "I told you before, looks . . ."

". . . can be deceiving. I know. But Gianni d'Angelo's still a hunk."

They both looked up at the ringing of the phone. A moment later Addy said, "That was Bruno. My friend Lil is on her way up. You're going to love her."

With great affection Addy and Lil greeted each other before Addy said proudly, "Lil, this is my sister, Erin."

"How good to meet you, Erin." Lil hugged her and pressed a kiss to her cheek. "A long time ago Addy confided in me that she would one day be reunited with her sisters."

"Sam's in San Francisco right now following a lead on Shannon," Erin told her.

"That is wonderful news, chérie," Lil said, linking arms with Addy. "Tonight must be a special celebration."

Laughing and chatting, the three walked from the apartment and took the elevator to the main floor. Minutes later they were being seated in a private banquette in the beautifully appointed restaurant.

Lil insisted on ordering for the three of them in her

smooth French accent. Over Oysters Rockefeller, and a salad of hearts of palm, Addy and Lil toasted each other and Erin, who joined them with her glass of soda.

When the waiter brought the first course, Erin made a face. "Why can't we just have some real stuff, like a burger and fries?"

"If that's what you want," came a deep masculine voice behind them, "that's what you'll have."

Gianni strolled up, his lips parted in his friendliest smile.

"Wow! You look great." Erin openly stared at his tuxedo-clad figure.

"Why thank you, Erin. I only wish your older sister would show such enthusiasm."

At the first sight of him, Addy's smile disappeared. In a carefully controlled voice she asked, "What are you doing here, Gianni?"

"I hope you don't mind the intrusion. Actually it was Lil who suggested I join you for dinner."

Addy glanced in surprise at the woman beside her.

Lil placed a hand over Addy's. "My husband's nephew is such a charming man. I was certain you'd enjoy a little masculine attention."

While she was speaking Lil moved closer to Erin, and indicated the space beside Addy. "There is more than enough room, chérie. And Gianni is such good company."

Giovanni's nephew. Of course. It had been Lil who had first introduced them at the grand opening of Starr's. Addy felt trapped. This was going to complicate an already difficult situation. She wondered how she could extricate herself without causing a scene.

As soon as Gianni was seated a beaming waiter hurried over to take his order. "Yes, Mr. d'Angelo. What may I bring you?"

Gianni ordered without once glancing at the menu. It was clear that he was familiar with the restaurant and all that it offered.

When he was finished Erin said, "And could you change my order to a hamburger and fries?"

As the waiter opened his mouth to protest, Gianni pressed a hundred dollar bill into his hand and said pleasantly, "I'm sure one of your assistants can go and fetch the young lady's order from the coffee shop."

"At once, sir." The money disappeared into the waiter's pocket as he walked away.

A short time later, when their food was brought to their table, the waiter lifted a silver dome from Erin's plate to reveal exactly what she'd ordered.

"Thanks, Gianni." She shot him a grateful look as she popped a French fry into her mouth.

"It's nothing." He flashed his famous smile. "Though your sister refuses to believe it, I'm really a nice guy."

Lil gazed fondly at him, having fallen completely under his charm.

Beside him, Addy struggled with a growing sense of unease. The celebration had suddenly gone flat. Nothing about this evening was going as she'd planned.

*　　*　　*

Gianni was enjoying himself immensely. Addy's friendship with Lil had made it all so easy. He was glad he'd thought of using her. A simple phone call and he was home free. Of course, he hadn't expected it to fall into place so quickly. There was no denying that fate was on his side.

Now he was plying his charms on Erin, because he realized that she was the key to reaching Addy.

"You must try the special dessert, Erin." Gianni signalled to the waiter, who tripped over himself to reach this important customer's side. The generosity of Gianni d'Angelo was legend. As was his temper if he was displeased by the service.

"Bring the young lady your special dessert," Gianni said.

"At once, Mr. d'Angelo."

Minutes later, Addy sipped her coffee and watched as Erin and Gianni gleefully shared a bananas flambé. She had to admit to herself that it made her happy to see her sister having such a good time. Even if it was with a man like Gianni, who made her uncomfortable. It was impossible for Addy to forget that brief scene in her office. It was a side of Gianni that frightened and repulsed her.

"Didn't I say it was the best?" Gianni lifted a napkin to the corner of Erin's mouth.

"I've never tasted anything like this." Erin took a last bite and leaned back with a sigh. "What a great night. I wish it didn't have to end."

"Who says it's ending?" Gianni signalled to the waiter. "Send a bottle of your best champagne to Mrs. Starr's suite. And another order of your special dessert for her sister."

"No, Gianni . . ." Addy held up a hand.

"Oh, wow!" Erin interrupted. "What a terrific idea. Please, Addy. You said tonight was a celebration." Her eyes were alight with pleasure.

"Just what are we celebrating?" Gianni asked.

"Sam called Addy from San Francisco with news that he's located our youngest sister."

"Located her? Was she lost?" Gianni turned a puzzled expression on Addy.

Addy's lips pressed together into a disapproving frown. "It's – rather personal."

"We were separated years ago," Erin explained. "Sam found me living in Argus, Oklahoma. And now he's found Shannon, and we're all going to be a family again."

"Shannon?"

"That's our little sister."

Gianni's expression altered slightly. "So, where in San Francisco has Sam located this Shannon?"

"She isn't there. Just Sam." Erin clearly loved having so much information. "But when he gets home, he'll know where she is."

"Is that not exciting?" Lil squeezed Erin's hand and turned to Gianni.

"Very exciting." Gianni shot a glance at the gold watch that banded his wrist. "You'll excuse me for a moment. I almost forgot an important call."

Within minutes he returned. His features had relaxed into an easy smile.

"Chérie." Lil turned to Addy. "I think it would be fun to celebrate by drinking champagne and watching the lights of the city from your suite."

"I'm sorry. I wish the celebration could go on all night. But I'm afraid it's been an exhausting day." Addy forced a smile to her lips as she added, "And Erin has school in the morning."

"Where do you go to school?" Gianni asked.

"Middleton," Erin said proudly.

"That's across town, isn't it?"

She nodded, pleased that this man would be so interested. "Just a couple of blocks from our house. I'm trying out for the school play tomorrow."

"Ah. An actress. And a fine one, I'll bet. Then you'll need your beauty sleep." Gianni turned to Lil. "We'll celebrate another time."

As the maitre d' escorted them to the entrance of the restaurant, Lil kissed Erin's cheek, then embraced Addy warmly.

"Thank you for inviting me to dinner, chérie. You must call me again soon and tell me all your good news."

"Thanks, Lil. I will."

"I hate to think of that bottle of champagne going to waste," Gianni muttered as he took Addy's hand. "But there'll be other times."

Removing her hand from his grasp Addy dropped a protective arm around her sister's shoulders.

As they moved toward her private elevator, Gianni turned to watch them. Though the smile remained on his lips, his eyes were as hard as granite. It wasn't easy giving up a woman like Addy Starr. But business was business. And she had just become a liability. Still, she would be useful. And he would still show her how much power he wielded. Just before he killed her.

Chapter Thirty-three

Sam's face was a grim mask as he listened to Dr. Jess Thornton confirm his worst suspicions. The story was long and intricate. And sordid.

A phone on the desk jangled.

The doctor picked it up mechanically. "Dr. Thornton."

Sam watched as the doctor passed a hand over his sweating brow. "How did you . . .? Of course I . . . You know I wouldn't."

He paused, pinching a finger and thumb over the bridge of his nose. "Now wait a minute. This is insane. How could you . . .?" His eyes widened. "Christ. Is my office bugged?"

The line went dead. For a full minute Thornton sat, staring at the receiver in his hand. Then he replaced it and pushed away from the desk. Without saying a word he opened a cabinet, filled a syringe and plunged it into his arm. The entire thing was done in the blink of an eye.

Before Sam could get out of his chair the doctor had dropped to his knees. His skin lost its color. He pitched forward.

Frantically Sam felt for a pulse. Finding none, he stalked to the phone.

It was going to be a long night. At least he was familiar with the police routine.

*　　*　　*

It was six in the morning and Sam had been awake around the clock. As he boarded the plane to Reno, he thought about how good it would feel to shave, shower and change his clothes. His eyes were gritty. A growth of dark stubble covered his chin. His clothes stuck to him like a second skin.

Addy would be awake by now, getting Erin off to school. He'd have to hold her before he broke the news to her. Not just for her sake, but for his own. God, he needed to hold her.

With a vision of her in his arms he nodded off.

As the plane circled before landing, his head jerked upright. He sat a moment, trying to get his bearings. He had the prickly feeling that someone was watching him.

Sam knew that one of the reasons why he'd always been such a good cop was that he'd always followed his instincts. Every instinct now shouted danger.

Though he had no chance to check out the passengers, he bolted as soon as the plane door was opened. He was almost at the curb when he felt the jab of the needle and cursed the fact that his reflexes had been slowed by lack of sleep.

His legs buckled.

The men who took his arms and helped him into the back seat of a limousine were so smooth, nobody around them took any notice.

*   *   *

"What time will the tryouts end?"

"Four o'clock."

"Okay. See you at four. And Erin . . ." Addy drew her sister close and kissed her cheek. ". . . break a leg."

As she drove away, Addy punched on the radio and threaded the car through traffic.

At the office, she spent the morning going over the accounts with Milt, then met with Andrew Witherspoon.

"Where's Sam?" He placed a stack of documents in front of her.

"San Francisco. He'll be back later."

Her nerves were jumping. She'd heard nothing more

from Sam, and every few minutes she found herself watching the door, expecting him to walk in with a pretty little blonde-haired, blue-eyed angel, who'd hold out her arms and race across the room to hug her big sister. Instead she saw Milt Carver and Andrew Witherspoon and a parade of men and women whose only thought was the profit and loss sheet. And no trace of Sam.

Through the endless meetings she forced herself to concentrate. But her thoughts weren't on business. Where was Sam? Why hadn't he called?

The ringing of the phone had her jumping.

"Addy. Gianni d'Angelo on line three."

"No, Paula. Tell him I've stepped out of the office."

When her phone rang again she glanced apologetically at the promotor who'd been meeting with her about a proposed boxing event.

"Sorry, Moe. Let's continue this over coffee."

Ignoring Paula's frantic gestures, she led the promotor toward the coffee shop.

*   *   *

Erin was floating. She'd won the role of Maria in "The Sound of Music". She couldn't wait to tell Addy that she could sing as well as act.

It had always been a dream of Erin's. A dream, that until now, had seemed too far-fetched to even say out loud. But suddenly, after just fifteen minutes on stage, her whole life was changing.

Girls she didn't even know had come up to congratulate her. The teachers who'd attended the auditions were lavish in their praise. And the boy who would sing the part of Captain Von Trapp was one of the best looking boys in her class. She'd be working with him every day after school for the next two months.

Erin picked up her books and headed for the door. She was itching to share her news with Addy. It occurred to her that this was the greatest gift of all. Until Addy, she'd

339

never before had anyone with whom she could share her most intimate thoughts and dreams. With Addy it was so easy to talk, to laugh, to share.

As soon as she walked out the door the man approached.

"Erin?"

"Yes. Who're you?"

"Mr. d'Angelo sent me to pick you up. He said you'd meet your sister at his place."

She followed him to the curb, where a long, sleek limousine stood idling.

"Wow! You mean I'm riding in that?"

The man opened the door. As she slid in, she saw the stereo, TV, and a tall iced glass of lemonade.

"Mr. d'Angelo would like you to make yourself comfortable."

As the limousine glided into traffic, Erin flipped the channels on the television and picked up the glass.

A few minutes later the glass slipped from her nerveless fingers as she slumped to the floor.

*   *   *

Paula's voice sounded urgent. "Gianni d'Angelo said you must speak with him. He said to tell you it's regarding last night's celebration."

With a sigh of impatience Addy grasped the phone. "Yes, Gianni? What's this about?"

The voice on the line was smooth. "It's about your partner, the ex-cop. A funny thing happened to him on the way home from San Francisco." When she didn't say anything, he laughed. "Looks like he got himself a little too drunk to drive home. So one of my men brought him here to sleep it off. If you want him, you'll have to come and get him."

"Drunk?" Addy's blood suddenly turned to ice. "I don't believe you."

"Come over and see for yourself. If you'll look down

the hall, you'll see one of my men waiting to drive you here."

Addy glanced at the clock on the wall. "I'm afraid I haven't time for your little games. I have an appointment at four o'clock."

"If you intend to pick up your sister at school, you can forget it. It's no longer necessary. I've already seen to it."

Addy's heart stopped. She felt her breath catch in her throat. "What are you saying? Where is Erin? Is she all right?"

"She's safe . . . for the moment. But I can't promise you how long she'll be safe, unless you do I as say."

Addy's voice was little more than a whisper. Fear clogged her throat. "I don't understand."

"Oh, I think you do, Mrs. Starr. I think you understand completely."

"The police . . ."

"No police, Mrs. Starr, if you want to see your sister and your partner again. Unless you do exactly as I say, they will be only a memory."

"I don't believe you. I don't believe any of this. This is just some elaborate lie to . . ."

"Perhaps I'd better let you speak to your partner, just so you understand."

For a moment there was only silence on the other end of the line. Then she heard Sam's voice, low, slurred.

"Addy, are you all right?"

"I'm fine. But what about you, Sam?"

"Couldn't be better."

"Gianni said you were drunk."

"It doesn't matter about me. Listen carefully, Addy." He struggled to get the words out over a tongue that was too thick, and lips that refused to form the words. "My fingers are tied here. Whatever you do, don't get in that car, or . . ."

Addy heard the sound of a scuffle, and then Gianni's voice, low, menacing. "If you value your life and that of

341

your sister, I'd advise you to do as you're told. Let my man bring you here now, or Sam Money and the lovely Erin will disappear without a trace."

Addy gripped the edge of the desk. "Gianni, what is this all about?"

He gave a chilling laugh. "It's about you and me, Mrs. Starr. I always knew it was fate that brought us together."

Before she could ask more she heard the faint click, and then only silence.

Addy sat very still, listening to the pounding of her heartbeat.

There was no doubt in her mind that, despite Sam's warning, she would go with Gianni's man. She would do anything to save her sister. Gianni was banking on that. Slowly, methodically, she went over every word of Sam's conversation. He had sounded drunk. His usual staccato delivery had been slow, the words slurred. But he'd been lucid, even barking orders right to the end.

She went back over his conversation again. Why had he said his fingers were tied? The expression is 'hands' tied. Fingers. Fingers. She punched the intercom.

"Paula, page Fingers."

Within minutes she was rewarded with the ringing of her phone. She grabbed it up on the first ring.

"Fingers?"

"Yeah, Addy. What's up?"

Her voice was unusually calm as she laid the problem before him. When she was through she said, "I'm going to Gianni d'Angelo's."

"You can't go there. You know the kind of people you're dealing with. These guys have more power than the police force."

"I understand. But I have to go, Fingers. They have Erin and Sam."

There was a pause. "I get it." His voice was unusually gruff. "I guess I knew it was like that with you and Sam. That's probably why he wanted you to tell me. So I'd talk you out of it. But I know what Jakie would say."

She closed her eyes. "What would he say, Fingers?"

"Old Jakie would say, don't let anyone push you around, kid. You own as much of this world as they do. When they push, you got to push right back, no matter what it costs." He cleared his throat. He knew what he had to do. Now if only he and Bennie and Henry could get there in time. "Go ahead and give 'em hell, Addy."

"Thanks, Fingers. I'll do my best."

Addy hung up the phone and pushed away from her desk.

As she made her way along the hall toward the man who stood waiting to drive her to Gianni d'Angelo's, she swallowed back a knot of fear.

Last night, she'd been on top of the world. At this moment, she could feel her entire world crumbling beneath her feet.

*   *   *

The limousine passed by a guardhouse and through an electronic gate, moving slowly along a curving ribbon of driveway that seemed to go on forever. The house that came into view was a magnificent structure of Spanish design, with orange tile roofs and pale stucco walls.

Addy was ushered into a room with aged leather chairs and an exquisite Oriental rug set in front of an antique writing desk. In one corner was a complete putting green. Light poured through skylights in the vaulted ceilings. Addy had no doubt that the masterpieces on the walls were authentic.

A door opened and she turned to watch as Gianni walked toward her. Behind him, Sam was being helped in by two burly men. His gait was unsteady. They pushed him down into an overstuffed chair and took up positions on either side of him.

"Where is Erin?"

"She's sleeping peacefully in an adjoining office."

"I want to see her."

Storming across the room Addy glanced at the figure asleep on the sofa. When she turned back, Gianni was directly behind her.

"Addy. How good of you to accept my invitation."

She didn't flinch when he lifted her chin for his kiss.

"How could I refuse when you made it sound so intriguing?"

He chuckled, low and deep in his throat. "That's what I love about you. You're tough, like me. But smart enough to know when to admit defeat."

"I admit nothing." She nodded toward Sam. "What did you use on him?"

"You don't believe he's drunk?"

"Not for a minute. What was it?"

"I have . . . I had," Gianni corrected, ". . . a doctor, who used to provide me with whatever I needed for . . ." He shrugged. ". . . certain jobs. I never bothered to ask what it was. I only needed to know it would work. Whatever it is, your partner's high as a kite in a stiff wind. And just about as useful."

"Why did you drag Sam into this? And why hold my sister captive? If you want my casino, just name your price. You know I'll sell before I'll see anyone hurt."

"My dear Mrs. Starr, you're not making any sense. This has nothing to do with your casino."

"But . . ." Addy stopped, confused. "Why else would you drug my partner and sister?"

"Why, to get your attention, of course." He caught a strand of her hair and watched through narrow eyes as it sifted through his fingers. "I think it's time you realized the power I wield. With a simple wave of my hand I can have people kidnapped in plain view of hundreds of witnesses, and no one's the wiser." He tugged her hair, yanking her head back sharply. "And I can just as easily snuff out their lives." He pulled her close and smiled at the look of fear that came into her eyes. "That's better.

344

I want you to be afraid of me. Now you have some hard choices to make."

"There's no decision to be made. You know what my choice is. I'll do anything to save Erin and Sam."

"Anything?" He shot a smug look toward Sam as he ran his hand across her shoulder. "Even become my mistress?"

She struggled not to shiver. She was reminded of another man's hands grabbing her, soiling her, and the mute girl who'd come to her aid. She wasn't a helpless girl now, fighting for her honour. Now she was fighting for the lives of the people she loved. "If that's what it takes."

His smile was chilling. "If only I'd known it could be that easy . . ." His tone hardened abruptly. "Now it's no longer a simple matter of wanting you. Now you must be eliminated along with them."

"I don't understand. Why do you want to kill me?"

"You couldn't let it go, could you, Mrs. Starr?"

"Let what go?"

"Your search for your baby sister."

"Shannon? I don't understand. What has all this to do with my search for Shannon?"

"Don't you get it yet?" Sam's words had them both turning toward him.

"Get what? Sam, what is this all about?"

"It's about a man who paid your father all that money for a baby. It's about a man powerful enough to have all trace of her past erased. A man who saw to it that anyone who threatened to reveal his secret was eliminated, including your father, your neighbour, and the private investigator you hired."

Addy's eyes revealed her horror as the truth suddenly dawned. "Oh my God. It was you, Gianni." With her hand to her mouth she started to back away from him. "All those years ago . . ." She nearly choked on the words. "You're the monster who bought my sisters."

345

Chapter Thirty-four

"A monster." Gianni's eyes narrowed.

Addy shrank back from him. "All these years I've hated you. You had no name or face but I hated you."

Gianni's hands balled into fists by his sides. His voice was low with fury. "I did what I had to for the sake of my wife. She'd become obsessed with having a baby. To appease her, I subjected myself to the fertility clinics, the tests, the humiliating interviews with batteries of doctors. And all it brought was bitterness and accusations between us. We finally resorted to in vitro three different times, at the finest clinic. It cost ten thousand apiece. Each one ended in a miscarriage. And created more anger and exhaustion and misery, until, in the end, we hated each other."

"Why didn't you just adopt like other people? Why did you have to buy a helpless child?"

"Do you believe a man like Gianni d'Angelo, with his reputation, could adopt a baby legally?" Sam gave a harsh laugh.

"Precisely." Gianni's eyes narrowed, remembering. "But there was a doctor."

"Jess Thornton," Sam interjected.

Gianni nodded. "He was a weak man with a drug problem. I used him from time to time, when I needed someone treated privately, who couldn't afford to be seen in a hospital. Then one day Thornton did a foolish thing that cost him his medical license."

"What he did," Sam said, "was deliver a baby while under the influence of cocaine. You don't want to hear what happened to the mother and child."

Ignoring him, Gianni said, "This doctor knew a man, also a cocaine addict, who'd been complaining about having too many mouths to feed. When I heard, I told the doctor to make him an offer for the baby. I promised that if he was successful in obtaining a baby for me, I'd find a way for him to practice medicine again."

Addy stared at him in horrified fascination. After all these years of guilt and anger, she was face to face with the man who'd set into motion all the things that had changed her life forever.

"Why did you take Erin, too?"

"I had no choice. Thornton said they were a package deal. So I gave the older girl to a cousin who wanted her."

"You gave her . . ." The pain welled up, threatening to choke her. "Just like that."

"Yes. Just like that."

Addy wondered how much longer she could stand here before her legs would fail her. She didn't feel anger any longer, or bitterness. All she felt was a kind of numbness that was spreading to her limbs. "You bought my sisters and killed my father."

He turned on her with a look of fury. "I merely hastened his death. I knew that he would use the money to buy more coke. If one of my men hadn't steered his truck into the path of a train, he would have been found dead of an overdose anyway."

"And Fran, the private investigator I hired, and Cleo Bentson, my neighbour? Did they just drive into the path of something, too?"

"They had to be eliminated. It had been too many years. I'd covered every track. And then they popped up, making waves. They got in the way."

"And now I'm in the way. And Sam. And Erin." Addy sank down on the arm of Sam's chair and fought back a wave of helplessness. "If you kill all of us, someone else will come along, Gianni, and want to know why. And you'll have to kill again and again."

347

"Hey, you're making me cry." His tone hardened. "There will be a logical explanation for your deaths at the hand of Sam Money."

"Sam?"

At Addy's gasp of shock, Gianni smiled. "No one will question it. Sam Money is, after all, an ex-cop who can't hold his liquor. And he was the partner of a very wealthy woman. A large sum of money will be missing from your account, Mrs. Starr. And it will turn up in a private bank account in Sam's name."

"That's why you were going through my desk."

Without realizing it, Addy reached for Sam's hand. As he squeezed it he muttered under his breath, "Distract him so I can take out these two apes."

She glanced at him. Though his head bobbed at a crazy angle, his eyes were clear.

He wasn't drugged anymore. He was faking it.

Getting to her feet Addy walked toward Gianni. Despite the lump in her throat, she had to sound convincing.

"Before you kill me, tell me what you named Shannon, my baby sister."

If Gianni was startled by this sudden change of direction, he managed to cover it well. "Angela. After my wife's mother."

"Do you have a picture of her?"

He led Addy around his desk and handed her a framed picture of a little girl with long blonde hair and a dimple in her cheek.

Addy blinked back the tears that filled her eyes. "She's the image of my mother."

Sam bided his time, waiting until the exact moment when the two men became absorbed in the exchange between Addy and their boss. Then he moved so quickly they had no time to react. With a few well-chosen blows, both men dropped to the floor at his feet.

As he was reaching inside the breast pocket of one of the thugs, he heard Gianni's chilling voice.

"Don't bother with his gun, cop."

Sam straightened. Gianni had his arm around Addy's throat and was calmly holding a revolver to her head.

"You're such a pretty lady, Mrs. Starr." He slowly moved the gun through the tangles of her hair. "I had great plans for you and me." He nudged her ahead of him as he crossed the room to where Sam knelt over the two thugs.

Gianni was clearly enjoying himself. "You know, usually I let my boys handle these jobs. A legitimate businessman like me shouldn't get his hands dirty. So it's been a while since I held a gun. There's such power in a gun, don't you think, cop?"

"That's what every punk in the world says, just before he's blown away by somebody else's gun."

With a sneer Gianni lifted the hand holding the pistol and brought it down on the side of Sam's head, sending him sprawling.

"I wish I could shoot you here and now." Gianni tightened his grip on Addy's throat when she began to struggle. "But that would spoil all my plans. You have to be eliminated far from here, while my wife and I are attending the governor's cocktail party. And once you're dead," he boasted, his lips curling into an imitation of a smile, "there will be no one left to testify that Angela is not really my daughter."

Behind him there was a sound, like a child's cry. Gianni whirled. The door was ajar, but when he kicked it open there was no one there. A kitten arched its back and hissed as it looked up with frightened eyes before fleeing.

*   *   *

Erin struggled against the ropes that bound her. The drug had long ago worn off, and she'd been forced to lie helplessly on the sofa, listening to all the terrible words being spoken in the next room.

The gag in her mouth prevented her from swearing. But

in her mind she'd uttered every rich ripe oath she'd ever learned.

Hadn't Addy warned her against Gianni? So handsome. So damned smooth. She'd fallen into his trap like a stupid baby. Why now? When she'd finally found someone good and decent like Addy Starr to love her, why did it have to be stolen from her again?

Anger, at herself, at Gianni, at the world in general, made her twist and turn and struggle against the bindings until her wrists were torn and bloody.

When she heard the outer door open, she stopped and lay very still. Her breath was coming in short gasps as she squeezed her eyes tightly shut. She knew it had to be one of Gianni's thugs coming to kill her. She braced herself for the blow.

"Who are you?"

The voice was soft and high-pitched.

Erin's eyes opened. She turned her head and found herself looking into the pretty, troubled face of a little girl with pale blue eyes and soft blonde hair.

Seeing the cloth tied around Erin's mouth, the girl quickly untied it.

"I'm Erin O'Brien. Can you do my hands, too?"

The girl began working at the ropes. "Who are those people in my father's office? And what have they done to make him so angry?"

"Your father?" As soon as her hands were free, Erin bent to the ropes at her ankles. Without a glance at the girl, she flew to the door leading to Gianni's office. Over her shoulder she whispered fiercely, "If we don't stop him, your father's going to become a murderer."

*　　*　　*

Gianni thrust Addy away from him and nudged the thugs with the toe of his shoe. "Come on, you lazy bastards. Get up. I want these two, and the girl in the next room, taken to a car now."

350

While Gianni kept his gun pointed at Addy and Sam, the two struggled to sit up. When they were able to stand, one of the thugs reached into the pocket of his coat and pulled out a syringe.

"Who gets it first?"

"The cop," Gianna said. "I want him good and drugged before we leave this room. That way, he won't put up a fight once he's in the car."

As the two men grabbed Sam's arms, the door to the adjoining office opened and Erin raced across the room to throw herself at the thug holding the syringe. As she struggled to break his grip, he tossed her off like an annoying pest. She came at him again, this time sinking her teeth into his arm. He gave a scream of pain and the syringe fell from his grasp.

At that same instant three burly figures burst through the door. For the briefest of moments everyone glanced up in astonishment. Fingers, Bennie and Henry, wearing long black overcoats that made them look exactly like old-time mobsters, shouted, "Everybody freeze."

Fingers, who had set himself up as spokesman for the trio, glanced around until he was satisfied that Addy, Erin and Sam were alive. "Looks like we got here just in time." He nodded toward Gianni. "Back off."

Gianni's eyes narrowed, but he refused to toss aside his gun. As he studied the old men with their hands in their pockets, he suddenly gave a slow, dangerous smile. "I think you're bluffing. Let's see your weapons."

Henry shot a nervous glance at Bennie, and both men looked to Fingers, who reached inside his overcoat. But instead of withdrawing an automatic weapon, he withdrew a pool cue and brandished it like a sword.

Taking advantage of the moment's distraction, Sam pushed Addy and Erin out of harm's way just as Gianni fired.

In the confusion that followed, there was a tumble of bodies as everyone scrambled around the floor for the syringe. But as Sam's hand closed over it, Gianni leaped on him.

Holding the gun to Sam's head, Gianni shouted, "If anybody moves, the cop gets it."

Addy watched in horror as Gianni's hand fisted in Sam's hair, pulling his head back roughly. In that instant she thought about all the people she'd loved and lost. In the blink of an eye they would all be lost to her again.

"That's better," Gianni said with a smile as Addy and Erin drew together, as if for comfort. The two thugs shuffled to their feet, eager to redeem themselves in the eyes of their boss.

"Get the syringe," Gianni said softly. "We do the cop first, then the others."

The door to Gianni's private office was thrown open so hard it slammed against the wall, causing all of them to turn and look up in surprise.

"See, Grandpa?" called a childish voice.

"So this is what you do in my home? Under the very roof," the heavily accented voice thundered, "of my daughter and granddaughter?"

Addy gasped at the sight of old Horseshoe Joe, standing with his arm around a weeping little girl. When the girl looked up, Addy's heart nearly stopped. There was no doubt in her mind that this was her long-lost sister.

The old man blinked in surprise when he saw the casino owner in his home. "Mrs. Starr? My granddaughter has told me a very upsetting tale. I think you had better explain what this is about."

"Guido, this is private business that got out of hand." Brushing his hands over his clothes, Gianni strode forward, hoping to shield the others from view. "It doesn't concern you or Angela."

"Everything that happens in this house concerns me." The old man swept him aside, drawing the girl forward with him. "As for Angela, she overheard something that has her deeply disturbed. She overheard her father say she is not his daughter." His voice lowered to a chilling whisper. "And she says you are planning to murder these people."

The two thugs, who had come to attention, now looked from Gianni to the old man. When Horseshoe Joe waved a hand, they hastily moved to stand beside him as a gesture of solidarity.

"Now you will tell me everything." There was a hint of steel beneath the soft command.

Gianni lowered his head.

The old man turned to Addy. "Will you tell me, Mrs. Starr?"

As quickly as she could, Addy told him about her sisters. As she spoke, his arm tightened around the little girl at his side. When her story was concluded, the old man had tears in his eyes.

"Have you proof that Angela is truly your sister?"

"Early medical records," Sam said. "And a file kept by Dr. Jess Thornton."

"But the only proof I need is Shannon's face." Addy blinked away the tears that clouded her vision. "She's the image of my mother."

The little girl clung to the old man's hand, staring from Erin to Addy. The bond of affection between the old man and the little girl was obvious.

In a tremulous voice she asked, "You really are my sisters?"

Addy nodded. "Yes."

The girl began to weep silently. "Will I have to live with you?"

Erin interrupted. "That's what families do, isn't it?"

Surprised at the vehemence in the tone, Addy glanced toward Erin and knew that she understood what the little girl was going through. Maybe, with enough time and patience, they could find some of the love they'd been denied.

"I hope, when you get to know me, that it will be your choice, Shannon. It may take some time to clear all this up," Addy said, "but I'd very much like to have you live with Erin and me."

Horseshoe Joe turned to Gianni. "It is not enough that you bring disgrace upon our name. This news will break my daughter's heart."

"She knew. She knew from the beginning that the kid hadn't been legally adopted," Gianni said sullenly. "Maybe that's why she doesn't love the girl. Hell, she doesn't even like her. All she ever does is yell at her and pick her apart."

Hearing that, Addy felt a terrible sense of sadness for her two sisters. Their childhoods had been no better than hers.

Turning to Horseshoe Joe, Addy whispered, "I don't understand about you and Gianni."

"He is married to my daughter. I sent Gianni to smooth things out while you built your casino. I never thought such a simple request would bring such grief to my family and yours."

"But why? Why did you want to do me this favour?"

"Because you once did a favour for me. And I vowed to repay you."

Addy thought back to that night when she and Sam had helped the old man to bed. "But it was such a simple gesture. I wanted no payment."

He held up a hand. "You are a fine woman, Mrs. Starr. And I apologize for all the grief brought upon you by my son-in-law. But I would ask one final favour."

Addy waited.

"My daughter and Gianni . . ." He tried again. "My daughter was not the mother she should have been. But this child is my only grandchild. Even though all that has changed, I would like to visit her, to see that she grows to be as fine a woman as my dear wife was. As fine a woman as you, Mrs. Starr." He paused, searching for the proper words. "I am aware of my family's reputation. I give you my word, I will be discreet. I will bring no shame upon you or your sisters."

Addy held tightly to Sam's hand and said softly, "I can't promise you that. All I can think of right now is what Gianni threatened to do to my sister. And what he did to all of us."

"But she is all I have."

"And she and Erin were all I had, until they were taken from me."

The old man began to nod his head sadly. "I understand. The sins of the fathers . . ."

He drew the frightened child close and pressed a kiss to her head. "Angela . . ." He lifted her face for his inspection and wiped the tears that rolled down her cheeks. "Shannon, say goodbye now and give your sisters a welcoming kiss."

The girl threw her arms around the old man's neck and clung, crying as though her heart would break. But at a softly spoken word from him, she broke contact and slowly, hesitantly, walked to Addy's outstretched arms. Drawing her close, Addy gave a long, deep sigh of relief.

"Oh, you feel so good here," she whispered against the little girl's cheek. "I've waited so long to hold you like this." She turned to Erin and drew her into the circle, and the three drew awkwardly together.

The old man drew Sam aside. After a muted conversation, Fingers, Bennie and Henry left the room. Sam crossed to where Addy and her sisters still clung.

"Joey has ordered a driver to take us home."

"But we still have to call the police about Gianni and . . ."

He took her arm and began steering her toward the door. "The Man would like to handle this in his own way."

Addy turned to glance at Horseshoe Joe, wearing faded overalls, his white hair toussled from playing with his granddaughter. The Man.

Without another word she took hold of her sisters' hands and followed Sam out the door.

As they stepped into the brilliant sunshine, a car

rounded a corner and came to a screeching stop. The doors opened to reveal Fingers, Bennie and Henry, who had shed their overcoats.

"Get in," Fingers ordered. When the doors closed he peeled off, tires smoking.

"You risked your lives back there," Sam said grimly. "We owe you a big one."

"I wouldn't have missed it," Fingers said. With a grin he added, "Feels like the old days. I had to save old Jakie's hide a time or two."

He glanced at the taut expressions on the faces of Addy and the two girls, then at Sam, who sat in silence. He knew that he'd have to wait until much later to hear all the details. It didn't matter. Jake's widow was safe. Sam was safe. And from the looks of things, Addy's sisters were back where they belonged.

*   *   *

"Another hot fudge sundae?" Addy hurried toward the booth in the coffee shop where Shannon and Erin sat with the ever-present Fingers, Bennie and Henry.

"Hey, Addy, are you and Sam and Shannon really going to come to every performance of Sound of Music?"

"Absolutely. We've never had a star in the family before."

"You're a Starr," she said with a laugh.

Shannon giggled at Erin's joke. It was plain that she and Erin had begun to form a bond. But she was still shy with Addy, and they were all aware that the little girl missed her grandfather. Though all her belongings had been shipped to Addy's apartment, there had been no contact with her former family.

"Wait till you see the boy who plays Captain von Trapp. What a hunk. He's almost as cute as Sam."

Sam grinned as he took a seat at the table. "Thanks. I think."

"Now can Shannon and I go play the new pinball games?"

"Only if Henry, Bennie and Fingers go along until I can join you. I don't want you two out of their sight."

"Damn, Addy. I hope you're not going to keep on treating us like babies forever."

"No. I promise." Addy let out a shaky breath. "But just for a little while, I'd like you to humour me."

"Okay. Come on, Shannon. And you too, Fingers, Bennie and Henry."

As they shoved back their chairs they saw an old man in rumpled clothes standing in the doorway. With a little cry of delight Shannon raced across the room and threw herself into his outstretched arms. After a fond embrace, the old man pulled a squalling kitten from his pocket, to the delight of his granddaughter.

Glancing at Addy he said, "I hope you don't mind, Mrs. Starr. I will stay only a few minutes."

"Stay as long as you like, Joe. Would you like to go upstairs with the girls and have a visit in my apartment?"

His eyes seemed to fill with light. "I would like that very much."

Erin turned to her new little sister. "What do you call your kitten?"

"Nippers." The little girl looked doubtful. "I don't think Chester will be happy to see him."

"Don't worry. Chester will probably shit a brick when he finds out he's going to have to share his space with your cat. But he's a great old cat. He'll get used to Nippers in time. He doesn't take to too many people either, but he sure takes to you and me." Seeing the old man standing to one side, she added, "And I'll bet he'll take to your grandfather, too." Catching his other hand, she said, "You know, with all the families I had, I never had a grandfather."

The old man toussled her hair as he started toward the elevator. "I would be pleased to have two grand-daughters."

Fingers, Bennie and Henry followed along behind as

they exited the coffee shop. Fingers suddenly turned and made his way back to the table.

"You know," he muttered, "sometimes I swear I hear Jakie's voice coming out of that kid's mouth."

"I know what you mean," Sam said with a laugh. "Sometimes I feel the same way."

"Good. I thought maybe I was going nuts." He cleared his throat. "You think it's smart letting the old guy see the kid?"

"I know how it feels to lose the ones you love," Addy said. "I haven't the heart to stop him."

"Just stay with them," Sam said.

They watched as Fingers raced to catch up with the others. Addy was smiling when she turned to Sam. The look on his face had her heart stopping.

He reached across the table and caught her hands, lacing his fingers through hers.

"Now that we've taken care of the minor details like thugs and kidnappings, and a grandfather who commands an army of guns, it's time to get down to the really scary issues."

"You mean . . .?"

He nodded. "A lifetime committment. Marriage."

When she said nothing he felt a surge of panic. "I suppose I should have expected you to change your mind. Now that you have the responsibility of two sisters, you probably don't want to deal with another person in your life. The truth is, you can do a whole lot better than an ex-cop who's a reformed drunk."

When she remained silent he said, "I guess I should have had a contract drawn up first." He grinned. "That's what Jake suggested in his final note to me. He said you were a woman who was good at living up to the terms of a contract."

"So that's what Jake wrote. I suppose," she said, staring at their joined hands, "I could talk the decorator into transforming the convention room into a European cathedral, complete with pipe organ. The room will hold five hundred comfortably. We could have a reception similar to the one we had at the grand opening."

Sam groaned. She felt him tense. But when he looked down at her, he saw the teasing laughter in her eyes. "And how soon could the room be ready?"

"Umm. A month or two."

"I'm not sure I can wait a month, Mrs. Starr. I'd like to marry you now."

"You mean in a couple of days."

"No, I mean now. This minute."

"But . . ." Though she thought long and hard, she couldn't think of a single reason why they shouldn't.

"What about Erin and Shannon? We can't just run off and leave them."

"Why not? I'll phone Fingers and tell him to stay with them until we get back."

"When will we be back?"

He stood up and drew her up with him. "A couple of hours."

"Does it take that long to get married in Reno?"

"No. It can be done in minutes."

Neither of them was aware of the crowd of people in the coffee shop who watched as he framed her face with his hands and drew her close for a slow, leisurely kiss. "But I was hoping you'd take pity on me and agree to slip away to my apartment."

She pulled back to stare at him. "Now?"

"It's been a long time, Mrs. Starr. What with two new additions to the family and all." He kissed her again. "Too damned long."

He caught her hand and led her to the elevator. When the door closed they stood, hands linked. He knew he didn't dare kiss her, or he'd take her here, now. Instead he stared straight ahead, watching the numbers of the floors.

Beside him, Addy studied his strong profile and felt her heart fill with love. All she'd ever wanted was a chance to find her sisters. But she'd found so much more. At long last, she'd found her home. With Sam, she'd found the love of a lifetime.

Laughter bubbled in her throat. To think she'd wanted to invent a new life. This was better than anything she could have ever invented. This was real. Oh so real. And it would last forever.